Mu... I hope you this ride! I enjoyed writing it,

Janette Bach

Circe
Syndrome

By Janette Bach

#1

Rogue Divine Heart Stories

Janette Bach

Circe Syndrome

Rogue Divine Hearts Stories Book 1
Copyright©2018 by Janette Bach
ISBN: 9781792776373
All Rights Reserved

Printed in the United States of America

First Printing: 2019

Cover Design and Interior Illustration by Janette Bach:
www.springmore.net

Edited by: Avery Leinova, Eric Cousins, and Kelly
Sayre
(Any Errors still found are Janette Bach's Fault)

Table of Contents

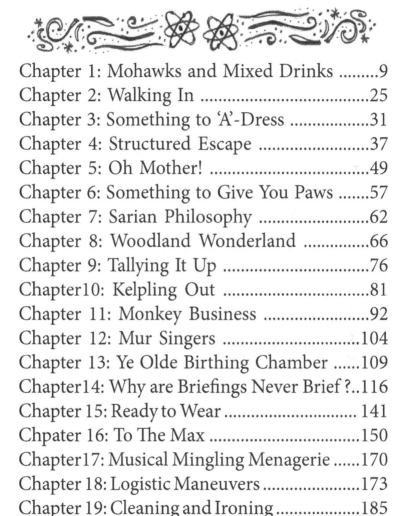

Janette Bach

Chapter 1

Mohawks And Mixed Drinks

The old rusted fans on a pulley system cycle on the ceiling, filling the air with the smell of rust and age, and a whisper of a current. The smell mixes with the stale sawdust, and peanut shells carpet the floor. I run my pencil across my sketchbook, I'm seated at a worn scratched up golden wooden table. It has a high polished sheen from years of cleaning.

I finish the ear on the drawing of a small rodent like creature with huge eyes. Next to the drawing, I start mapping out what its peptide strands in a DNA molecule would look like if it existed.

The hair on the back of my neck stands on end when a very male voice sounds, almost, in my ear. "Aww, how cute!" This condescending comment causes me to look up at the gaunt electric blue Mohawked man. His canines peep through his lips and I know I am looking at a newly changed vampire. My eyes wander down his sleeveless arms and I note the tattoos of vipers circling them, highlighting finely toned muscles. I look at his face and take in his mocking smile, shimmering with light from his various earrings that catch the flames of a flickering candle on the table.

I look past him. I meet the blue eyes of another man wearing an apron and bussing tables. He gives me a knowing smile. He is the head bartender of this establishment, of this little known bar called Sangria that caters to the undead community of Portland. It is located in the basement of the building south of Kell's Irish pub. I take a breath as the room shakes while a light rail MAX train zips by on SW 2nd Street. He rolls his eyes, fills the bin and walks away.

I take a sip of the sweet red Shirley Temple sitting in front of me. The tang of fake cherry makes me smile. My gaze lingers on the booth in front of mine, where a suave man with red curly hair gives me a toothy grin that reveals his long canines before he starts talking to the over inebriated blond sitting next to him. She giggles and starts to hiccup. I know him, too. He is Mothius, the closest thing to a vampire leader in the Portland area. We grudgingly tolerate each other. I try not to think about what he is doing as I watch him start to nuzzle the woman's neck.

I look back at the Mohawked man. I gesture to the seat across from me. "Thanks for the compliment; mister?"

He grabs my drink as he slides into the booth across from me. He takes a swig of my glass and starts to gag. "That's not blood!"

I'm amused, "Of course not, I don't drink blood." I say it like it is a matter of fact, like any other option would be ridiculous. I look back at my sketch. I'm not sure it's a viable animal for my current project.

He sits back and scowls, then puts a bored expression on his face. "What are you doing in a Vampire Bar, are you lost, little one?"

I want to laugh; he has just managed the right kind of intonation that I imagine a spider would say to a fly. I sit straighter; before I speak, I make sure I will include the command frequency in my voice that insures an answer. "Community service, what's your name?"

His eyes widen as he finds himself involuntarily responding to me. "Frederick Thomas Grout." I also hear him try to say Viper instead of what he says. Embarrassed, he tries to take back the conversation. "What kind of service could a tasty morsel like you do here?"

I set down my pencil. It rolls across the peptide sketch, and Viper reaches out and snags it. I pull out a black ballpoint pen and click it. I reach into my cargo pants and pull out a small, worn, red leather notebook. I write down his name and the alias he is planning to use. I fight the urge to shudder when the wireless camera hooked to my retina fires up, and I feel the presence of headquarters enter my mind.

It feels like a room full of clucking chickens has entered my mind. I fight the feelings of nausea and vertigo as they start scanning him using different filters on my retinal nerve. I see his skeleton, heat measurements, blood flow, imaging electric energy measurements and bacteria frequency patterns.

"OK, Mr. Grout how long have you been a vampire?" I look expectantly at him.

He frowns. His expression is sullen, "I guess it has been a week now. I don't see how this is your business?"

I watch him flex his muscles to stand up. I send a spell erasing the command from his cells. "And who was your mentor?"

He stares at his legs, puzzled, then shrugs. In a deadpan voice he asks, "Mentor?"

I gesture with my right hand, palm up, toward him as I hold the pencil in my index finger and thumb. The other fingers splay. "The vampire who made you?"

He begins to scratch his chin and look about the room calculating. "He called himself Claudius."

In the back of my head the chicken noise is calming down. A group of five minds start talking about my conversation. I bite my lower lip, pushing my thoughts of them back. "Do you live with him?"

A pained expression briefly crosses his features. It changes to one of indifference, and he starts to fidget with the chrome napkin dispenser. "No, he gave me a few pointers and disappeared."

A strand of my hair has fallen into my face. I blow it away and I stare into his chocolate eyes as I search for truths and lies. "Have you joined a conclave?"

He tries to shift his muscles. I feel a command come back down through his limbs. The five in my head start the usual debate about the ethics of me using mind manipulation at this point. His voice is derisive, "No, I have not!" He sits back and crosses his arms.

I haven't detected a lie yet. That was interesting, most beings start fighting back any way they can when immobilized. I realize that the vampirism bacteria strain he is affected with is an ancient and strong one. Its frequency playing repeat through my brain. The five in my brain debate which particular strain of bacteria it is. I'm not sure why they need to play it over and over to determine this? A supervisor walks into the discussion in my mind. He stops the repeating sound. I send him a relieved thought of thanks.

Brain conversations are weird. As people come into focus, others fade to the background. But, people don't ever look like people in thought form. They have these odd avatars that change with mood and thought. The administrator had just become a set of serious, grey eyes with bushy brown eyebrows feathered with silver. As he gives me directions his eyebrows move up and down while his eyes blink sporadically. "Recruit him."

I fight the amusement I know I can't hide as I send him back the thought, "Aye, aye captain." I change my posture. I sit back submissively, I change my thoughts to that of a person having casual conversation with a friend. The dictator interviewer vanishes from my body language. I cross my arms and lean in conspiratorially. "It's been about a week. How do you like the hunt?"

He gives me this cocky grin. "I love it!" He looks to the left and his aura turns a sickly green.

A lie, I think triumphantly. I worm my consciousness into his mind as I note his tanned skin. His mind is awash in the shock of his first kill, and there is a frazzledness that hasn't settled with his subsequent kills. The five in my mind start their distracting ethics debate again. I mentally sigh and send them a stern thought, "Quit it!" I tap my fingers against the smooth table top and begin to trace a scratch. I look forlornly up at him through eyelashes. "How about the sun?"

I feel his mind fill with anger. His aura flashes red. His nostrils flare and he stays still. "What about the sun?"

I look beyond him to Mothius. The woman next to him can barely hold her head up. "Do you miss it?"

"Every day." He sighs and deflates, his aura becomes a miasma of colors and emotions. He forces out a breath. It is weird to watch the undead breath. The air around them always smells off when they do it. His voice catches, "But, eternal life is worth the cost." Sounds like he is trying to convince himself, I think.

I prop my right arm on the table and rest my head on it. With my left hand I reach out and play with the straw in my drink. I give him a dreamy smile and softly ask, "Before you were a vampire did you believe in them?"

He snorts and pulls his arms sideways next to him. "Nope."

I watch him for a few heart beats. He is trying to remain calm, but the inability to stand and walk away is wearing on him. A slight tremor runs through his body. I moisten my lips and keep the softness in my voice. "If I told you now that the world had other strange creatures beyond vampires in it, would you believe me?"

There is nervousness to his gesture as he begins tapping his fingers on the table top. "Are you going to explain to me why a seemingly defenseless creature like yourself is sitting so relaxed here?" He gestures around. "In a bar of predators!"

I sit up and hold his eyes in my gaze as I pull back from his mind. "I'm not human, if that is what you're asking?"

His fingers stop tapping. "What are you?"

I look away from him and down at my notes. I flip the pen in my hand. Then I look back at him. "I'm a Heska." I can't help but involuntarily grin when I say the word.

He looks puzzled and throws up his hands. "A what? If you're not going to tell me and just waste my time. Please let me go."

I start to doodle in my notebook as the five in my mind start complaining about me doing it. The notebook sends everything I write to their database. The system doesn't know what to do with my doodles. "Reality is a more malleable thing then you realize. Those of us with the power to change it are called Heska. Popular media would call me a wizard."

He chuckles and throws up his hands. "Yeah, right!"

I sit back and cross my arms. "You have been wanting to leave this conversation for a while now. Why don't you stand up and walk away?"

"What do you mean?" he shifts. "I'm talking to you because I want to."

Circe Syndrome

I chuckle and cock my head to the left. He mirrors my expression. I lift my eyebrows and say, "Originally, yes." Then I look toward the bartender as I shake my head as if to imply no. I then lean forward and gesture toward his body. "Go ahead, try. Focus on it. Command your body to move."

He leans forward and presses his fingers against the table. He frowns. He doesn't stand. His pupils shrink and his aura is blood red. He makes an attempt to yell, I take the air from his vocal cords before they vibrate. He struggles for a good five minutes. Not a compliant being, "Good!" I think. Once he goes still and stops fighting the spells, I back off.

He licks his lips and straightens "What do you want with me?"

I stare at my drawing. I frown; I've made a mistake in one of the proteins I defined. I start to erase it. I blow on the paper and meet his eyes. He has calmed a little. His pupils are normal and his aura is a scattered mix of colors. "There is a secret war going on." I say quietly.

He gives me a sarcastic sneer. He takes a breath, "What kind of war?" He says this with a defeated sigh.

I stop messing with the drawing. I look at him and say, "There are different factions in the world who want to control reality. Here in America it is the Science Heska who control reality. They keep things following the rules of physics and prevent dragon, fairy, and troll infestations. They help everyone feel all is predictable and knowable in the world. Reality is as it is due to the American Collective."

He hits the table. "What are you talking about? Seeing a dragon would be cool!"

I give him a sarcastic smile. "On the movie screen sure. Barbecuing you, would not be cool in any sense of the word."

He lifts his index finger. "Funny, I hear what you did there, but fairies, what is so bad about fairies?"

I give him my best mysterious smile. "Look, I am at liberty to offer you an arrangement." I pull a ten milliliter syringe out of my bag.

All the background noise stops in the bar. The only noise is the squeaking fans. Mothius turns and meets my eye. With no ceremony I stick the syringe into my arm. I pull out iridescent red blood dotted with blue swirling vortexes. Everywhere beyond the booth there are eyes on me. I check the spells on the syringe that keep my blood from blowing a vampire to kingdom come.

Viper shifts uncomfortably. His pupils have dilated as he looks at my blood in the syringe. I can see he is puzzled, but memorized all the same.

As I tap out air bubbles, I speak. "My blood can let you walk in the sun for a day. It will let you be able to taste food again. You won't throw up. You will need no other blood. It lasts for twenty-four hours. I'm asking you to try it and if you would like more, all you have to do is join the American Collective. You will receive training and this type of blood every day. You won't need to hunt for blood again."

He sits forward. "What is the catch?"

I meet Mothius's eyes; I know he has been listening. Mothius adjusts the hair of the now sleeping blond on his shoulder and looks over at his usual companion, a beautiful woman vampire with freckled white skin and curly red hair, decked out in a bustier and tight jeans. She stands and walks to my table. She leans toward Viper. "Hello, Viper, may I be of assistance?"

He meets her eyes as he sneaks longing looks at my syringe. He bites his lip, swallows, then asks, "Samantha, is what she offering me true?"

The men in my head start an insistent whispering. If they were in the room with me I'd hit them, it is annoying. When they start the salacious comments in regards to Samantha's breasts, I send them a snarling mental "Enough!" They quiet down.

Samantha looks at the syringe, at me, then back at Viper. "She is offering you day walking, right?"

He nods emphatically. "Yes, is it possible?"

She cocks her head. "Ah yes, it comes with a great price, but it is true."

He turns his head between both of us. "Great price?"

Samantha looks at her fingers. "Loss of independence." She points at me. "Her type of blood is addictive and anyone who takes up the offer is not the same."

A fierceness appears in his face as he looks at her. "Have you tried it?"

She gives me a curious glance. "I've never been offered the bargain."

I shrug. Samantha wasn't interested, she loved her existence. It would be a complete waste of time to try to recruit her. I stare at the rodent drawing. Where in the eco system of the planet I'm populating would that work? Is it absolutely necessary? I start thinking about if I'm absolutely necessary. I push those thoughts away.

Mr. Grout leans conspiratorially towards Samantha as he starts the extreme fast speech of vampires. "Why don't we just jump her and drain her."

The men in my head start arguing. I push their comments to the back of my mind.

Samantha rolls her eyes and meets mine. "She can hear you." She says it just as fast as I nod in acknowledgement.

He looks puzzled. "What?"

I tap my finger on the table and speak at the speed they have been speaking. "I can hear you."

He stares back at me like a deer caught in headlights. I put my hand in my bag. I didn't think I misread him. I pull out a paintbrush wrap case. I recap the needle on the syringe. I put it in my paintbrush case. I start to fold it over. Grout's arm shoots across the table, he grabs my wrist.

He is puzzled. "Wait, I think."

I pause while the people in my head yelp. "You hooked him. Wait for an associate before you proceed."

I look towards the front door of the bar. The worn maroon door opens. A silhouette of a tall, muscular man with dark, straight hair buzzed on the sides and messy on top walks in.

Samantha crosses her arms and addresses the man. "As I live and don't breathe. Thomas, what are you doing here?"

He gives her a devastating smile. "Colorful phrase, Sam." He nods towards Mothius, "Moth." He turns his grey granite eyes to me. My heart betrays me and changes beat. His expression is impish as he winks and says my name. "Muriel."

Butterflies fill my stomach and I cringe. Thomas is my legendary recruit; he was a centuries old crony of Mothius I crossed over to the Collective. This accomplishment marked me as a valuable employee no longer a person performing community service. I blush against my will as I say with a forced casual smile, "Hey, Thomas."

He pauses. His eyes roam my body. I try not to shift, uncomfortable with the focus. He sighs, "You're working too many nights, Muriel. You need to get some sun."

As I give a forced laugh Grout gestures to Thomas. "Who is he?"

Samantha frowns and heads back to Mothius's table. Over her shoulder she calls out. "You look good, Tom."

Thomas watches her walk away. He turns his attention back to me. I try to think of ice water. I keep my expression neutral. He studies me then looks at Grout. He looks back at me. "So what do we have here?"

I nod with a hopeful smile towards Viper. "A possible new recruit for you, sir."

Thomas' smile is all predatory as he reaches for my brush case and pulls the syringe out. I roll the covered needle to him. He begins to screw the needle back onto the tip of the syringe. He leers at Viper. He points at him excitedly. "You Mr. Grout, what do you call yourself?"

Grout seems startled and cowed as he looks back at Thomas. "Viper."

Thomas looks at the syringe in his hand and back at Viper. "Nice name, so do you want to play or what?"

In a sober voice Viper asks, "Does it really work?"

Thomas laughs, his rich baritone filling the room. "Oh yes, I sunbath daily and other things." He begins to screw the needle back on the syringe slowly.

Viper trembles slightly as he stares at the syringe in Thomas's hand.

I feel uncomfortable for Viper, so I look down at the scratches on the table. I start to trace one. The voices in my head ask me to look up. I comply.

When my head snaps up, I see Thomas thump the syringe causing the vortexes in the blood to flash about. A reminiscent smile fills his face and he says, "Ah Heska blood, I still remember my first bit." He closes his eyes, "Smoother then silk and sweeter than honey on a winter's day. Plus, there is this little jolt of energy that hit's your pleasure center. Amazing stuff. If you don't want it, I'll take care of it."

Viper's hand involuntarily opens and closes. A look of hunger flashes through his eyes. "No, obligation just a free trial right?"

Thomas gives me a wink. Then he turns back to Viper. "I'm going to be your guide for twenty-four hours."

This reminds me of things in my own life. "Oh and I forgot to tell you. I won't be back for two nights." I had worked the past five nights and tomorrow was the beginning of my weekend, Friday night. I know the bar was more crowded during the weekends. But, I was less likely to find a recruit then. I wanted the desperate beings who were tired with this existence, not caught in the flow and pulse of it. Thursdays were always great recruitment nights. I run my hands through my bobbed hair. "So, you will have time to think about it and tie up any loose ends."

Viper splays his hands on the table and looks down at them. "And if I don't want to join, there will be no hard feelings."

I shake my head and meet Thomas's eyes. "As long as you don't join another army." Thomas reaches out a hand and starts to massage the back of my neck. It feels too good; I move away from his reach.

Viper watches us as he scratches his chin. His eyes moving between us are curious. "OK, I'll try it."

Thomas moves quickly and sits next to Viper in the booth. Viper looks puzzled. Thomas leans in conspiratorially. "You know the best place to get this is the base of your skull in the back."

I snort. "Asshole! I think, so manipulative. The voices in my head laugh. "Like you should talk." I pull the sketchbook back in front of me as I re-pocket the notebook. I address Viper with exasperation in my voice. "You'll be disoriented for ten minutes if you do it that way."

Thomas shakes his head in amusement. He points at me with mock disgust and says, "She doesn't get feeling everything for all it's worth! She doesn't understand the quest for sensation!"

I roll my eyes. I look at Viper. "Do what you want, but an injection in the arm is just as effective." My mind is wondering. I stare at my sketch and wonder about the other species on the planet I'm working on. I look down at the sketch again. The gaggle at headquarters asks me to look up. There are more than five people in my mind now, and I'm starting to feel crowded. I look up.

Viper is turned towards Thomas. Viper's head bowed to rest on Thomas's chest. It is a very intimate position. Thomas bends Viper's blue Mohawk away from himself as he positions the syringe at the base of Viper's skull. I hear several voices in my head start to get squeamish, as their random avatars start to pace.

With a confident stroke Thomas inserts the needle. The muscles on Viper's neck go tense. Thomas quickly presses the syringe. In my mind a few gasp and I hear some sounds of fainting. I'm not intrigued by what I just watched. I'm not horrified, I'm just indifferent. I've seen this before. The muscles in Viper's neck relax as my blood starts to travel through his body. Thomas gently sets Viper's head on the table almost like a father setting a toddler to bed. I check my watch, it's 10:43 PM. I tell the men still watching in my head that Viper will be out till 10:53 PM.

Thomas looks up and meets my eyes. I shift because he is using vampire compulsion pheromones, and they work quickly. I feel myself swoon. I keep my features placid. He leans forward with a confident smile. "So sweetness, I need some blood too." His intonation of desire causes my toes to curl. Headquarters confirms his daily dose. I fight the urge to look away first. I scratch the back of my head to make it look like I'm not responding physically to his charms at all. I start fishing out another syringe.

Without breaking eye contact, Thomas stands and walks to my side of the booth, he slides in next to me. He leans into my personnel space and with a playful grin says, "Nope, Muriel, let's neck."

I wince, pushing back the thoughts that say, "Oh yeah!" I force an amused, indifferent chuckle. I bite my lip. I reach out and push him back with my right hand. "What is your angle Thomas? Do you want everyone here to disrespect me? You're really poring on the pheromones."

He flinches and pulls back a little. I see a brief trail of anger travel through him. He leans forward. "Come on Muriel, you know you would like it if you would just try it."

I have no doubt about that. There is some kind of aphrodisiac in Vampire saliva that people get hooked on. I give him a sarcastic, unaffected laugh, to disarm him.

He sighs; he looks at his hands, "You really do know how to ruin a mood."

I hold up the syringe and wave it in front of him. "Syringe, OK?"

He pulls my sketchbook over and examines the drawing. "Sure," his voice is resigned.

I open the syringe and stick myself again. I pull out ten milliliters of blood. I run my fingers down the syringe casing making sure the spells there are in tact. Then I set the syringe on the table between us.

He picks it up and raises it to his jugular vein. As the syringe falls from his hand I catch it and let his head rest on my shoulder. I gather both syringes and put them in a plastic case I carry. I throw the case in my bag. I pick up my pencil. I pull my sketchbook in front of me. I start to doodle curly cue forms.

There is a moment when I feel Thomas wake up. I feel him staring at my chin. I act unaffected by, and unaware of, his consciousness. I count internally to ten then, glance at him. He gives me a glassy smile. "Still drawing weird, impossible animals and their improbable genetic maps?"

I move away from him and glance at my watch. "Yep."

He nods to the comatose vampire. "Do you think he'll join?"

I shrug. "I doubt it, but what do I know? I thought you wouldn't."

He scoots close to me and puts a lazy arm around my shoulders. "You look haggard."

I let him stay in my space, and I self-consciously move the strands of hair from my face. I think about what could be bothering me. I shrug. "Things with me are the same as usual. Except for whatever Sarina is up to."

He backs up and straightens. "Ah, your lovely sister. What's she up to?"

I tap my fingers on the table as I shake my head, I say, "She is doing some kind of sabotage with a drug cartel."

He frowns. "That's dangerous, I know she knows you and Yacob can bail her out, but doesn't she want to do something tamer?"

I sigh. Sarina is my older sister, and she has this wild streak. I rub my forehead. "Just me these days. Big brother is busy right now with his new bride."

"That is daunting. That is a great deal of responsibility to take on yourself. It is bizarre to think of your Casanova brother as a devoted husband." He turns and looks at the reposed form of Viper. A fondness briefly passes over him.

I chuckle, "I believe the word daunting was retired fifty years ago."

Thomas looks down at his fingers. "So, with this wedding, and 'devoted' husband does it mean there is another Anahat Heska on the way?"

I blink and move the hair out of my face. He shouldn't be asking me about children. In Heska culture this is a forbidden topic. Especially, since he is a vampire. With our great power comes certain vulnerabilities. As babies we are the most vulnerable.

In recent culture, we try to act more civilized about children, but in the old days, there was a culture of savagery, others enslaved the mind and love of a Heska child. Rival families would embed spells in babies that could trigger later in life, bringing a whole family down. Different supernatural creatures would kidnap babies and harvest power from them.

Vampires from time to time, who understand what our blood can do, have taken a baby or two, and used them as blood machines. The children taken would become inescapable bonded with a vampire, they would become a thrall. The will of the vampire dominates the person on whom they feed. Self-preservation and family is no more to the person being fed on. It is all about satisfying the bond.

Part of the education process of all operatives, including Thomas, is to know this history. His asking me this is inappropriate.

His mouth becomes a straight line. "You won't answer that question will you?"

I shake my head as my thumb outlines a scratch on the table. "Nope."

He gives me an imploring look. "I wish you could trust me as much as I trust you."

I laugh, "You deliver that passive predator line well."

He gives me a responsive chuckle. "If you would just fall for it that would be the actual compliment."

I lean on my arm as I take in his casual pose. "Are you saying, you don't appreciate my passive insult? I thought it was a fitting response."

He leans over, kisses my cheek and scoots back out of the booth. As I fight a shudder at the intimacy and promise in the touch, he stands at the end of the table.

I look back over at Viper's prone form. I change my vision to see his aura. He is awash of swirling emotions. The purple color of pleasure dominates the spectrum. As I stare at Viper I ask, "What do you think Thomas? Will he be usable?" I take this moment to check all my spells are off Viper. There are a few knotted strands here and there. I pick them apart and watch them dissolve into the aether.

He catches the eye of a buxom, pretty girl in a tight top a few booths away. As he preens he says, "I can get him to follow orders."

I think about Viper's conversation with Samantha when he suggested capturing me and draining me. "He already has some subversive ideas."

Thomas fidgets with his hands, then meets my eyes. "We all do at first." A serious expression crosses his face. "Wait till he comes up against the first dragon or worse, a fairy." He shudders, "He'll toe the line from that day forward."

I know a few fairies, hell I'm related to a few, they're some of the scariest creatures I've ever interacted with. They are ferocious and single minded to an obsessive level. They love to prey on Heska. They love using us as straws to draw in and process magic from the world instead of having to weave the wild eather themselves.

Viper starts to twitch; I close my sketchbook. Viper shudders; he wiggles his shoulders in a liquid motion, then backs up into a sitting position. He licks his lips and has his eyes open wide. He shakes his head. "That should not be legal. What a high, is it always like that?"

Thomas gives him a wicked smile. "Oh yeah, every time."

Viper gives me the look children give candy bars.

I focus on a stoic stance and emotions as I meet his eyes.

Thomas leans in, breaking our eye contact. "Quite a rush right?"

"Amazing!" Viper has begun to rub his chin, his gaze now thoughtful as he looks at me.

Thomas hits Viper's arm. "Let's go!" He gestures with his thumb to the door.

I watch him stand. I give him an encouraging smile, "I'll be back in two nights. The blood will only work for twenty-four hours. So the day after tomorrow don't go outside in the sunlight."

Thomas gives me a wink and usher's Viper out of the bar.

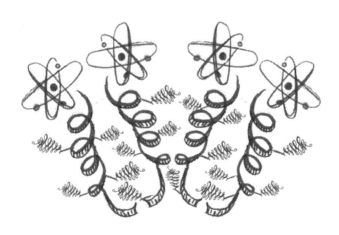

Chapter 2

Walking In

The rest of the night was quiet. I couldn't come up with any other creatures. The men in my head and their ethics debate had withdrawn hours ago. I absently think about Thomas's affectionate kiss on my cheek. I blush. This is a dangerous turn of thought. I wonder what he and Viper are doing. I check my watch. It was three in the morning. The bar is empty except for the bartender.

The quiet thudding and clinking of glassware going into his bus bin brings my attention to the bartender. Our eyes meet and he gives me a wave and a smile. I nod and pack up my stuff.

I exit the door to the bar and climb the stairs. At the threshold to the street I rest a moment to take a breath. As I do, I scan the vacant street, and as my breath releases, my sight shifts to energy vision. I stare out at the vast sky. I catch my breath because in this moment I catch a glimpse of the aether. The aether is the net of magic energy that coats the world.

25

Magic is a by product of life. The ebb and flow of mundane existence is an elegant dance that weaves energy of change through and around the world. The aether looks like a rushing river of multi-color corded energy. It constantly moves and changes. Some strands are transparent, highlighting different stars as they flash by.

I take another deep breath and change my sight back to the known world. I close the door and let the autumn wind push through me. My hair swirls creating a tingling sensation in my scalp. I start to walk in a measured, rapid pace north to Burnside. As I note the sleeping transients, I send a spell of warmth. A pack of dogs wanders by, they whimper and roam aimlessly. Only the wind and random leaves make any noise in the city of Portland. I do catch a whiff on the wind of hot fresh grease coming off the fryers when I hit SW Ankeny Street. Voodoo Donuts is up and running. There is an undercurrent of smoky coffee from the roasters at Stumptown.

These smells warm and comfort me as I replay the random comments from the five debaters who had occupied my brain. Now that I'm no longer in the moment, I can process all that happened a few hours ago. One particular comment stung. "Who authorized Mindworm Muriel to mess with minds? Aren't we playing with fire here?"

I wince and take a breath. The idea that I would purposely misuse my power hurts me. I am very aware what my species is capable of. My mother, during the Holocaust, had been held against her will by Nazi Mages during the Second World War. We are Jewish and Mind magic is actually forbidden to us. World War II changed that. Our tribe realized that forbidding the knowledge opened us up to a level of abuse we hope to prevent in the future. Mom learned how to wield it, to hold onto her sanity in the camps. There are several layers of rules she drilled into me that I adhere to before I practice it.

Circe Syndrome

In my youth I did violate one of the rules. Part of me being a member of The Collective right now was the result of a sentence of community service. It is humorous that the thing that brought me under The Collective's scrutiny is what they ask me to use the most.

I make a left on Burnside and head west. A strong wind almost knocks me down. I look about me. No one is around and I don't want to walk into that headwind. I change my sight again. I reach for the aether, a tendril lowers to me. As we touch I feel myself dissolve into light. This act is called dialyosefos. In milliseconds, I gather my matter and race through the aether cloud to the marker my family has left to mark our home. It is the Hebrew letter Chai, the symbol of life and the representation of the number of eighteen. It burns in the stream of light as a blank space.

I enter the letter and ride its legs down into my corporal body. I arrive in a wooden shed with worn wooden boards. I shudder and cough putting air back in my lungs and brace myself against the wall.

I walk out of the shed and stare up at the yellow Victorian house it is leans against. I walk towards the front on our cobblestone path that is peppered with moss. I notice the shield spells have been cranked up a notch or two. My steps hurry, this means one thing. Yacob and his wife Morgan are in residence. They have been away for four months.

As I walk up the porch steps I note that they creak. I pause at the screen door and look at the mezuzah adhered to the side of the door. It is made of glass with the chai embedded in it paralleling the mark in the aether. I unlock the door and step into the ante chamber. The lights go off and the interior door locks. Spell beams surround me. They are looking for rogue spells and the camera on my retina. A tendril reaches out and hovers in front of my eye where the camera is attached. I teleport the camera and listening device from my skull to the tendril that is waiting to take it. As I let it go a huge weight I hadn't realized I carry, leaves me.

Once it withdraws with the camera, the lights come back on and the interior door unlocks. I walk to the door and enter.

My mother, decked out in a Victorian dress and an apron from fifties, smiles at me. She has long, curly copper hair and dark blue eyes that sparkle. It cracks me up that when I see her I still get that feeling that everything is going to be OK. I reach out and give her a hug.

She chuckles as I scratch my chin where the lace of her dress has scratched me. She cocks her head." When will you be done with this community service, dear?"

I look expectantly about the great room. To the left in front of the window is a little parlor with a table and two wing back chairs. Behind a dividing wall is the dining table. Behind the dining table is the door to the kitchen. In front of me is a transitional space that leads to the stairwell. To the right is an expanse of couches, bookcases and a television.

No one else is about. I try to hide my disappointment at not getting to see my brother. I sigh, "It's a job these days Mom."

My mother rolls her eyes. "Sure, dear."

I look up at the stairwell. "Are Yacob and Morgan here?"

I start to walk to the stairwell. She walks with me as she looks me over. "Yes, you need to wash that vile vampire aura off you before you see them."

I smirk. She hates my job. She hates that The Collective owns me. "Yes, Mom, do you need any household help?"

My Mom nods. "Not yet, but when Merlin joins the world I will need help."

I process what she says. Merlin must be the name Yacob and Morgan had decided to give their baby. One of the reasons Thomas, asking about a baby had unnerved me a bit was that Morgan was expecting. Needing more help after he arrives is because family from all sides will flock to house for the first few months. We will all be on shifts to keep the predators, that want to exploit Heska children, away. I am distracted by one aspect of what she said. My eyebrows raise. "Merlin? Really?"

My mother suppresses an equally amused smile and her eyes sparkle as she says, "It's a family name for Morgan."

Wearily I say, "I think I'll go to bed, I'm a little tired. I'll wake up around noon."

She pats my shoulder, "Good dear, you need your rest. You do have the ball tonight."

"What?" I think. A vague conversation from six months ago starts to flow through my brain. "I do?"

Mom is looking up at the stairwell, her gaze not here, but in some memory. "It's the first one of the season Muriel! I can't wait to hear your take on it!"

I frantically start going through excuses in my head to get out of it. "Maybe I could...."

Her eyes narrow and she fixes me with the angry mother stare. It pins me. I freeze. "No, you promised, you are going to all social events this season. You need to associate with more than a paintbrush, DNA or a creature of the night. I want your circle widened! If you don't do this I'll start signing you up for blind dates!"

My mind begins to grumble. I know isolated Heska become psychotic, but I don't feel my life needs more. I sigh, "Yes, Mom." I hug her. I start toward the stairwell and call over my shoulder. "Good night." I pass hundreds of photos of me and my siblings growing up, smothering the walls, as I run up the three flights of stairs to my room.

I open the door, and lay my satchel on the corner of my unmade bed. I close the door and stare at the inviting window above my bed. It shows another world. Currently a moonless night with billions of stars. I head to my bathroom to take a shower and change into comfortable pajamas.

Janette Bach

I walk to my bed and pull the bag off the corner and hang it on a hook. A huge yawn takes my body and I climb into bed. I realize I forgot to turn off the light so I send a tendril of energy out and flip the switch to the light. I lay back, untangle my blankets, and cocoon myself in them. I set my alarm for twelve, set the dream influencer toward royal fantasy, and fall asleep.

Chapter 3

Something to 'A'-Dress

I swim out of my dreams; I find it startling to wake up still in the middle of my bed, staring up at the ceiling. I yawn and rub my eyes and stretch. I grope for my dreams, but can't remember them. The window above my head shines with the bright light of a midday sun. Purple dolphins jump in clear blue water and the bright yellow sand of the beach glows.

As I blink I look across at the door to my room, I notice something hanging there that hadn't been there before. On the door hangs a white ruffled dress dripping in lace. The full skirt wrinkles as it touches the floor.

I wince and close my eyes. I turn and look back out my window then back at the door. The dress is still there. I groan. I search the consciousnesses of the house. I smile when I realize my sister Sarina is there. Her mind is this faceted stone that shimmers with different emotions, that flash on and off like spotlights. I send a tendril of thought to her. "Hey, sis, would you come to my room? I need help with something."

Sarina sends me a perturbed amused thought. "Sure."

I sit up. I turn and stand and walk to the door. I take the dress down. I walk to my drafting table. The table has a button

31

on its side. I press it. The table flips up and becomes a mirror and the stand it is sitting on is a vanity. I position the dress in front of me and look in the mirror. The white makes me look pale and sickly. Nothing about it looks flattering on me. I wince and swallow. I hang the dress back on the door.

I return to the vanity and push the button again. It turns back into a drafting table. I stare at the drawing attached. It's a penguin with the mane of a lion. I touch the table next to the drawing. It becomes a video screen. A galaxy comes into focus.

There is a knock on the door. I touch the table and the screen disappears again. The door opens before I say anything. I look up and meet the magically altered lavender eyes of Sarina, my sister. Her long blond hair swings perfectly as she enters. She gives me a measured glance and crosses her arms. "Why am I here?"

I gesture to the door behind her as I change the curve of the beak on the drawing. She looks puzzled then closes the door. "Oh dear, Muriel, you didn't pick out your own dress did you?"

I lay my forehead on the drawing board. I sigh. "Well I forgot about the whole thing till Mom mentioned it this morning."

Sarina reaches out as if touching something rancid. "That is one of mother's hideous hand me downs. She came of age during the Victorian era after all!"

I sit back and play with my pencil. I give her a forlorn look. "Do you have any ideas for alteration, Sarina?"

She blinks. "You want my help?"

I throw up my hands "I'm so useless with this sort of thing."

Sarina takes in my pajamas. I'm wearing a plaid pair of pants and a licensed cartoon mouse shirt. She chuckles and shakes her head. "Apparently girl! How will you go on from being a hermit if you insist on dressing like a preteen?"

I laugh. "That is unfair to preteens everywhere. I believe most dress better than I do."

Sarina gives me a sober nod. She scratches her chin as she studies the dress. "First things first, that lace has to go." She snaps her fingers.

As she does this a tingle goes off in the back of my head. Sarina unfortunately was not able to be a conduit of magic. It doesn't pool in her, and she can't weave it into matter she can use. So my brother and I made her a power linking object. She can use it to syphon off power from either of us. When she uses magic, one of us always knows. She changes it into different objects. Right now it is a Star of David pendent made of platinum and gold on a necklace around her neck.

The lace spools off the dress into a roll at the foot of my bed. Sarina tilts her head in thought, her eyes looking beyond the dress. "Let's make it sleeveless." She snaps her fingers; the sleeves disappear. "I think a square neck is more flattering on you. Let's remove some bulk from the skirt."

She holds it up in front of me. "Try it on."

I take it from her. Instead of undressing and putting it on I just walk into it. My pajamas slide to my hands and I set them on the bed. As I look at the bed, I notice it's unmade so I send a current through the linens causing the blankets and sheets to hover, spread out, and lay back down.

Sarina gives me a sarcastic smile. She then spends time with her hand on her chin examining me in the dress. She makes me turn this way and that. "Let's put the details at an angle." She reaches forward and grabs a corner of fabric and extends it into a long two-inch swath and drapes it across my torso. Then does the same in the other direction. She frowns, "The square cut is not going to work with this." She hovers her hand over my chest and the fabric reknits across the neck to become a straight line. She pulls sleeves down at a 45° angle to my biceps. She shortens the skirt to my knees.

I reach down to my knees and say, "No, below the knee please. We will be dancing on air after all."

She gestures in the air with a wave of her hand. "That can be fixed with a spell. Plus, the required ruffles."

I meet her eyes and cross my arms. "Below the knees, please."

She chuckles provocatively, "You're such a prude, Muriel!"

"Someone has to be," I think as I uncross my arms. I hang them to my side and try to unclasp my fists. Why am I so tense? Oh yeah, I remember, I have to go to a dance tonight.

Sarina shakes her head. "You really should be using my 'breaking mother in time' and go wilder."

I sigh and run a hand through my bobbed hair. "I think I gave our parents enough of my wildness."

She snorts in disgust, "The world political meddling thing that should have landed you in prison?"

I feel the fire ignite in the back of my eyes as her disgust and dismissal downplay that crime that haunts me. I stare at her. I can't believe she would take that complicated issue and try to harness it into one sentence. "Yeah."

Sarina notices my look and shrugs. "That doesn't count. It was very noble of you, but you pissed off the whole magical community of the world with your meddling. They demanded your death. You really should try to live it up more!"

I sigh, "I'm going to the ball, aren't I?"

"Right," Sarina rolls her eyes, "I can tell you can't contain your excitement!"

Shrugging, I look longingly back at the drafting board.

Sarina gives me a thoughtful expression, looking me up and down, then gestures to my windows. "Where is that, little sister?"

Crap, I think. She is going to ask me a favor. I look at the brilliant beach scene and say softly but firmly, "No."

With a forlorn expression she stares at me. "What, I just need a break."

I look down at the dress. I make an attempt to distract her. "I like it. Do you like it? I think it needs to be a different color though."

Sarina reaches to the door and creates a full length mirror. "Why don't you keep a mirror in here?" She gestures to the mirror and me, then walks to the window. A sea breeze fills in the crack I keep open. Strands of her golden hair dance and her face fills with wonder.

I study myself in the mirror. As usual, Sarina knows how to bring the best out in someone's appearance with clothing. I pull the skirt an inch below my knee. The dress keeps its shape, but has the extra inch. I start changing its color.

The hair on my neck sticks up. I turn and see Sarina staring at me. "Muriel is it an illusion or is it real?"

I know she knows the answer. She just felt the breeze after all. I move to sit at the end of my bed. I'm trying to figure out how to stop this conversation. "Have you ever seen purple dolphins before?"

Her lavender eyes bore into me. "That is not an answer. I know who I am talking to. I remember Candyopolis."

I laugh. I made a planet of sweets when I was about five. That is when I found out what my dominate ability is. I'm a galaxy and world maker. It's rare. I can create and tweak creatures and species for planets. I give her a reminiscent smile. "Yeah, Candyopolis will spin by in the sky in a month there."

Her face fills with excitement. "So, it is real. What do you call it?"

I fidget in my lap. "Eco Spa," my voice is soft.

A puzzled expression passes across Sarina's face. "Why?" She leans on the sill and looks expectantly out the window."

I stand and move next to her. I point, "See that plant there."

She squints, "It looks like a chez lounge."

I nod, "That is how it grows. It needs regular reclining on it to bloom. It has a calming smell like lavender and will start to massage your body if you stay there long enough. The stone next to it has an umbrella drink, right?"

Sarina nods.

I trace a circle on the glass. "There are ants that create it every day. They break it down when not used and make another. If it is drunk from, they start producing more. It is part of their hive behavior."

Sarina looks cowed. "You didn't just create this planet? You tinkered with everything on it."

I nod. "Yes."

She cocks her head. "Is there more?"

I nod more emphatically. "Definitely, more, it would take hours to explain it all."

She looks at me excitedly. "I want to go there. Have you been there?"

I sigh and return to sit on my bed I stare at my drafting board. "What are you hiding from?" Something in the back of my mind says, "What could it hurt?"

Sarina looked at her fingers. I've seen this before; she is about to lie. "Nothing, I just need a break."

I look at her. "A week?"

She brightens. "Yeah!"

I decide not to inform her that an hour there was the equivalent of a minute here. "I will have to let you know a few things before I let you go there."

Sarina bats at the window ledge.

I sigh. "Not immediately, I'm sure Mom is expecting everyone to have lunch together."

She gives me a pleading look. "But, after lunch, right?"

I send the dress to the hanger while I magically don cargo pants and a t-shirt that says, "Atlas Mugged." There is a flattened god and bleeding planet pictured on it.

Sarina wrinkles her nose as if something smells bad. "Cute."

I smirk. "Whatever."

Chapter 4

Structured Escape

I gesture for Sarina to lead the way out of my room. I set a spell behind me preventing entry. I don't want her going to Eco-Spa without me knowing. She gives me a bemused look. I walk next to her and we walk down the hall to the stairwell in silence. The sound of heels hitting the stairs is the only noise echoing through the air. We reach the main floor and see our mother, brother and sister in-law gathering about the dining table.

Yacob darts across the room to give us both big hugs and then puts us each into headlocks. I yelp and twist my way out. He runs knuckles through my hair. "The sleeper has awakened!"

I frown at Yacob, then make my way to the very pregnant wife, Morgan, and hug her. "When did you guys arrive, last night?"

Morgan's skin is milk white, almost translucent. She adjusts her fiery mane of hair as we back away from each other. "I'm not a guy Muriel." A smile suddenly crosses her face and she pulls my hand to her stomach.

As I feel my unborn nephew kick, I feel myself light up with wonder. The idea of a person growing inside another is so surreal.

Morgan and Yacob return to the table. Plates start floating in from the kitchen. There are sandwiches with rye bread resting on them. The one that sets in front of Yacob has two pickles. The one that sets in front of Morgan has a salad next to it. Our mother's has a pickle and salad.

Yacob sits without ceremony and picks up his sandwich packed with meat and pauses to look at me. "We got in at around nine last night, little sis." He takes a huge bite. As mustard colors his cheek he closes his eyes and smiles as he chews.

I meet my mother's eye. "Those look amazing Mom. Do you have any extra?"

She raises an eyebrow. "Who do you think you're talking to Muriel? Of course, I have more."

I laugh and head to a seat opposite Yacob. Sarina takes the seat next to me. She looks at her mother. "I'll just take a salad, Mom."

Our mother narrows her eyes at her then shrugs. A plate of salad hovers in front of Sarina and then sets down. Another plate with rye bread and pot-roast comes through the door. It has spinach, with tomatoes on the side and a pickle. I smile when I note the sautéed onions on the sandwich also. I reach out and take a bite. The rich meat and onions combine with the bread, reminding me why living at home had a great deal of perks.

Circe Syndrome

My father appears in the kitchen door. He walks over and gives each of us a hug. "An improv family reunion, how wonderful!" He then walks to my mother and gives her a kiss on the cheek. She gives him a playful glance, then he moves to the end of the table across from our mother. A plate levitates to him.

I realize I don't have a drink. I start to back up my chair. My mother glares at me. I shrug, flick my fingers in a fan gesture toward the empty glass in front of me. It starts to split in two. A laser type cut appears in the middle of the glass. The top rolls to the table and starts to expand and morph into a teapot. The bottom edges roll out and a handle pokes out the side turning this portion into a tea cup. Once the teapot is stable, I grab a pitcher of water from the table and poor it into the teapot. I take my right hand and swivel at my wrist. With an open palm, I swirl air as I send a spell to excite the molecules to a heated temperature. I push the heated air into the teapot and it starts to boil.

Mom gasps as a ceramic plate morphs out of the tablecloth to support it. I go to ask her for some tea. I look up to see two packets of Stash Earl Grey tea flapping like a butterfly in front of me. I hold up my palm. The tea-fly lands. The animation stops and I am now holding two tea packets.

I rip open a package and start one brewing. Morgan gives me this look like, " and now you use your hand." I shrug. My father, who had taken a bite of his sandwich while I was doing this, finishes chewing and swallows. He makes a show of wiping his mouth. He leans toward me. "I hear you made it home this morning in one piece. What did you do last night?"

I look at my brewing pot. "Anyone else want some Earl Grey? There is plenty."

Yacob gives me a bemused smile over his sandwich.

My father continues to stare and I look to my mother. She shakes her head as if to say, " I'm not helping you out here."

Morgan's eyes meet mine and I smile. I find myself making shapes of new animals, inspired by her irises. "I worked last night Dad, you know that."

He grunts.

Yacob frowns. "Shouldn't you have worked off your public service sentence by now?"

I bring the sandwich to my face and pause before I bite in. "Yes, I did."

He frowns and crumples his napkin as he dabs at the mustard on his face. "You're still working? Because?"

I'm chewing on my rye, onion and pot-roast sandwich. I chew as the table full of people stare at me. When I swallow I look longingly at the teapot. I want to drink something to clear my mouth. I shrug, "It keeps me busy and I like it. So when is the big day?" I quickly try to change the subject and keep the attention off me. My family has too many opinions about my choices.

Morgan smiles and puts a hand on her belly. "Mom thinks in three days, Merlin told me in a week."

The tea looks ready, I pull the tea bag out of the pot and set it on the little dish my mother made out of the tablecloth. I nod. "Right, a week then."

My mother begins to tsk. "Your letting an unborn child choose his due date?"

The table erupts, everyone talking at once. I am riveted. I stay out the conversation and concentrate on eating and not getting burned by the tea. The last thing I heard Yacob say as I headed into the kitchen with my dishes was, "But Mom, it is OK to give a child choice; they get so little of that a growing up. How else is Merlin going to learn to make mistakes if we don't give him choices?"

I deposited my dishes in the sink which started washing them. I took a moment to look out the sink window at the blue wood siding on the neighbor's house. Other dishes start heading into the kitchen without people attached. I dodge out of the way as I make my way back out of the kitchen. Before I can talk to Yacob or Morgan, the doorbell rings.

Since everyone else is still engaged in the argument over the date of the birth, I head to the front door. When I open the door I am met with a very loud, "Harrumph!" My six-foot tall, aunt with red hair and a polka dotted dress leans in. She is followed by a large five foot, eight inches tall man with muttonchops and a mustache. He is stocky in build and has the same eyes as me, deep sea blue. He grabs me and hugs me fiercely and lets me go.

His wife follows suit, she takes my chin and examines my face. "Muriel, you are pale as a ghost. Are you getting any sun?"

I laugh. "You mean this year or normally, Aunt Shirley?"

My uncle gestures to the foyer. "Your mother's security measures are a bit obsessive Muriel."

"She is your sister, Uncle Mordechai. When one of your children works for The Collective, paranoia is necessary."

He gives me a measured glance. "Is that so? One of you works for The Collective, huh?"

I shake my head and give him a smirk. He was retired from The Collective and I'm pretty sure still in the loop with the mucky mucks. "It has been known to happen."

Aunt Shirley rolls her eyes. "You two, stop, I want to see Yacob and his bride."

I close the door and hear my father call out. "Oh, Mordechai, a fresh perspective! We are having the most interesting debate."

Janette Bach

Mordechai looks at me. He whispers under his breath. "You are not involved? I doubt it!"

I shrug. "No, it is! I'm just not in my depth in the debate. I leave that for the more experienced."

Aunt Shirley gives me a big smile. "That shows some growth on your part, I think."

I roll my eyes. "I was never that bad."

She laughs. "No, dear, you never were."

Her sarcasm makes me sigh. "Whatever. Do you two have luggage?"

Mordecai calls out to my father as he approaches, and hugs him. "Hey Daedalus, it is about time you joined the Zadie club."

My dad straightens and his eyes sparkle. "I'm not sure who is more excited, Maxima or me?"

Yacob yells out. "I am! It's my child after all!"

I meet Morgan's eyes as she gives me a wink.

Aunt Shirley pulls my mother into a hug. "Such a blessing, your first grandchild!"

My mother laughs. "Oh yes, I have tons of plans for Merlin and me!"

I give her a wink. "You are going to pay Yacob back for his childhood, hardcore, aren't you?"

She answers with a wicked giggle. "Oh the plans! You have no idea!"

Yacob manages to look like a deer in the headlights for a moment, and Morgan laughs. "You have to deal with what your mother does, dear. I'll deal with my mother's interference."

Sarina meets my eyes and points upstairs. My mother catches the exchange and glances at me. I give her a neutral expression. Sarina and I manage to stand back as Mom, Dad, Yacob, Morgan, Uncle Mordechai and Aunt Shirley follow each other to the living room lost in speculative conversation, pointing out Yacob's childhood hi-jinx. I head to the stairs with Sarina at my heels.

Our ascent of the stairs is quiet; I let her in my door and take a breath once inside my room. I gesture to the house beyond. "Are you sure you don't want to miss all this craziness while you're gone?" I try not to look her in the eyes. I'm kind of lying. It will feel like a week to her but only will be two and half hours here. "I mean the family stories are going to be the stuff to tell over and over at the Rosh Hashanah table."

Sarina sighs. "I'll hear about them then. Honestly, Muriel, why do you care so much about this family stuff. Yacob's having a brat, so what."

I turn from her. I don't want to watch her personal pain cross through her features again. Sarina had been engaged to the son of a prominent man in the Heska community. She had loved him deeply but when her disability was discovered the engagement was withdrawn, and an offer of mistress was put in its place. She had once been excited about family life, too. This pain had created what she had become. This bitter creature that did self-destructive things.

When I turn to look back at her, she is at the window leaning on the glass. She is tracing the stars.

I wait a beat to see if she notices the drastic time change and asks questions. She just seems enchanted by the starlight shimmering in the waves. I internally start calculating when I want to open the door between the worlds. We need to wait eleven minutes to give her a morning arrival. I sit on the edge of the head of my bed. I'm five feet from her. I look down at my feet and hit them together. "Sarina, what are you trying to escape from?" I look back up at her at the last word.

Weariness passes over her. "I just need a break, Muriel." Her voice is tired and resigned. There is her guarded edge but it is mostly exhaustion.

I chew on my lower lip, my mind trying to figure a way to get her to confide in me. I sigh. I know there is no way to that. I walk over behind her to a cupboard and grab some sunblock. Aunt Shirley's comment reminded me how photosensitive I am. I open the tube and start to apply some to my face. I hand it to Sarina.

She shuffles her feet and looks down at them. "I wanted to go alone."

I give her a smirk. "I understand that. I'm just going to show you around then leave you there for a week. Are you OK with that?"

She gives me an amused grin. "I can't imagine you would make a dangerous place."

I chuckle knowingly. There is another planet in this solar system. One with a hostile environment and savage, ruthless creatures. "You never know sis. Planet making requires balance."

She shakes her head, hugs her shoulders and looks longingly out the window. "Whatever, how do we enter? Mom has that teleport block on the house."

I walk around her to the window behind her. "She allowed me one portal, that isn't accessible to our world."

Sarina's lips press in irritation.

I know this grates on her. I'm her little sister, my power enrages her. Her lack of any and her dependence on me and our brother infuriates her. This just reminds her how much I possess. I turn away. I let her direct those emotions as I place my fingers under the ledge, and push the button hidden in the molding. The wall and window hinge into my room. A warm, salty wind blows in.

Circe Syndrome

Sarina hesitates. She examines the threshold. She straightens and strolls through. I follow. We walk out onto a worn, wooden porch with speckled sand sliding as the wind moves beneath our feet. The wood creaks with our steps. We walk to the steps of the porch and into the light yellow sand. It is warm and soft between my toes. I never put shoes on since I awoke.

Sarina starts cursing about her Faragamo Shoes. She pulls them off and sighs as her feet hit the sand. "Did you purposely pick the perfect complement of yellow to the purple sea?"

I give her a shrug and mischievous smile. I turn and point to where we just exited. It looks like a one story beach hut with two front doors and a wraparound porch. There is a swing by the other door. I point to the left. "The one on the left leads back to my room. The right leads to this house. This house is for your use. Come on inside, I'll show you around. I'll give you some area details then I'll let you be."

Sarina gives the building a sweeping gaze. I see her lean in and examine the walls close up. "Is this building alive?"

I meet her eyes and head in the door. I pause in the living room. Sitting there and looking at me is a startled feline creature. It has rainbow stripes and a spring shaped tail. I turn to look at Sarina when I hear the thwack of the screen door. "Ah, yes."

Sarina's eyes widened. The cat creature paces between my legs. I crouch and raise my palm toward the cat. I address the cat softly. "Hello, mistress?"

The cat meows and cocks its head. "Hestia, Lady Muriel."

I sit and nod toward Sarina to do the same.

Sarina sits next to me; her jaw has dropped. She sits there speechless for half a minute. "You're doing sapient creatures, too?"

I shrug. "Evolution does this. I can't." I look at the cat, "Muriel is just fine. This is my sister Sarina; she will be staying here a week."

Hestia's grey eyes dart about Sarina's form. "Welcome, Lady Sarina, I will be your butler while you're here."

I try to hide my annoyance at Sarina for not changing how the cat addresses her. I watch Sarina scan this main room.

There are several book shelves, driftwood furniture made with pillow husk blossoms as cushions. There is a Spartan kitchen hearth, water basin and a counter for prep. There are two doors. One leads to a sleeping chamber that has a swinging hammock made from the huge flower blossoms the hut grows. The other leads to a wash room. One of the house's sources of energy is made from the waste of creatures dwelling in the house. The toilet is formed from the roots of the house. A sink, shower and bath are formed from the leaves of the hut. When certain leaves are touched the house excretes potable water at different temperatures.

Hestia, the cat, starts walking about the room pointing out features. "You do not need to worry about making meals, but if the mood possesses you, there is space here for food prep. I must warn you that hunting is not allowed here on the island. All food comes from the garden."

Sarina's brow creases and she glares at me puzzled. She knows how much I enjoy meat. "So, this will be a vegetarian cleanse?"

I shake my head in a negative fashion. Then shrug. "Well kind of, but you won't feel deprived. I have plants that are gourds that are shaped and taste like meat. There is a chicken, beef, bison, fish, lamb, and, "I lean in and whisper, pork plant."

Sarina giggles and hits me playfully on the shoulder. "Does Mom know?"

I shrug. "I don't have to worry about what kind of feet it has, it's a plant."

Sarina crosses her arms and gives me a mock serious look. "How do you know what pork tastes like?"

I smile, "Hey, I went to college, too. I try not to be rude at people's houses."

Sarina gives me an incredulous look. "But the covenant with God?"

I shake my head. "Sarina, you are the last person to lecture me on Kosher living."

Sarina laughs, "I suppose there are shellfish plants too?"

I giggle, "Well, yeah! Hey, they all store better and there is no actual killing involved."

"How do you control populations?" She gives me a serious quizzical look.

I'm disarmed. This understanding of the science of environment from her throws me, but I answer as if talking to a colleague. "Conflict seems to be part of evolution, too. When you halt certain avenues, nature finds another way."

She gives me a sarcastic look. "OK, that sounds ominous."

I think about the cultural rituals of Sumans, the marine aquatic sapient beings that live in the ocean. A shudder runs through me. "Oh you have no idea. Just don't wander off this island." I try to quash a feeling of pride that runs through me. There are many sapient species on this planet. I seem to have figured out some keys to sparking that off in species. I'm just not sure what it was.

She points to the round dial at the top of a bookshelf. "What is that for?"

"You turn it to the genre you're interested in and all the books on the shelf turn into that genre." I stand and move to the shelf and turn the dial showing it in action.

She smirks. "Why don't you just use a kindle?"

"Very cute Sarina, I designed this before the kindle was about. There is no internet access available here. You can't make a phone call." I cock my head. "You OK, with that?"

She gives me a sarcastic look and shrugs.

I respond with an incredulous look. "I'm not that powerful."

She crosses her arms and snorts. "Sure."

I frown. I'm not lying. Hestia jumps on the end of the couch next to the bookcase between us. "Muriel, I can finish the tour and fill her in on all the rules."

I meet Hestia grey eyes. She winks at me. I gesture to the red silk pull from the ceiling. "OK, I'll let Hestia finish up, if things become unbearable, pull this sash."

Sarina stands and examines the pull. She runs her fingers through the silk. "How old world."

I nod and shrug. "You know me."

Sarina let's it go. "Why don't I just use the other door to get back to your room?"

My mind goes to the mechanics of the spells on that door. "Certain rotations of the planet block the access." I look at her expectantly; she might want a further explanation. She seems lost in thought as she wanders toward one of the doors. Hestia gives me a nod and follows Sarina. I've been dismissed. Being a little sister, I'm used to this.

I walk out the front door. I take a moment and let the breeze play with my hair. I look out at the horizon and think about what I've been trying to avoid. In the haze between the water and sky where illusions live I can still see him. Slim build with firm muscles, he had fins and emerald green skin. The fins on his head curled and made a spiking halo. His eyes were electric purple and could pin me with a glance. Seven months of my time I escaped earth and lived here. It was about a month at home almost five years here. I fell in love. He was a Suman; his name was Gregor.

My musings are interrupted by a formation of plaid seersucker birds flying near the horizon. I think I can hear their song, "So, so, so." I go to shake my head and wipe my eyes and feel the tears on them.

The memory of a long kiss that tasted of seawater fills my mind, and I head to the door to my room.

Chapter 5

Oh Mother!

The lack of sea breeze saddens me as the door to my room closes behind me. I stare back at the window. It's not like I don't know he's dead. I wonder if I could find him. I never felt as complete as when we were together. It didn't matter what we were doing.

There is a knock at my door. My mother's voice pierces the room. It's sweet, and there is an undertone of concern. "Muriel, dear, it's me."

I walk to the door and open it. "Hey, Mom." I say cheerfully and walk to my bed and sit at the edge.

Mom looks about the room and stares at the windows. She is the gatekeeper of the house. Anything entering or leaving is brought to her attention. She knows I opened the way. We have an agreement since the event seven months ago. She has an idea of all that happened to me there. I'm allowed to look, but not to spend a long time there. She threatened that she would move the galaxy to where I'd never find it.

I trace a pattern on my quilt. She looks at me expectantly. She doesn't say anything she just looks and waits. After a minute I sigh. "Sarina needed a break."

She pulls her gaze from me and nods. She starts examining the dress on the back of the door. "I was concerned you were going to avoid the ball."

I straighten and meet her eyes when she turns to look at me. "I promised."

She gives me the gentlest smile. "You are my daughter who keeps her promises." She walks next to me and reaches out and strokes my hair. "How long will she be in there?"

I pull away and stand and walk to the drafting table. "A week."

Her voice is amused. "And here?"

"Two and half hours." I turn and meet her smile.

"Does she know?"

I smile too. "Nope."

She shakes her head. "You're teasing your sister."

"She wouldn't tell me the problem she was escaping. She usually fesses up after she successfully avoids her problems." I sigh and start erasing a line on my sketch of a tortoise type creature.

She stands and walks to the dress. "Wise choice. Tell me what you find out."

I consider that. I know I'm the little sister, but I still try not to be a snitch.

Mom reaches out and rubs the fabric between her fingers. "Sarah?"

Sarina's actual name is Sarah; she personally changed it to Sarina to make it more mysterious and magical. She is always trying to get me to change my name too. I like the solidness of my name. Mother always calls her Sarah, she says she carried her and raised her, she gets to call her what she named her. I nod. "Yes, she altered it to fit me."

Circe Syndrome

There is a glint of excitement in Mom's eye. "How does it look on?"

I look back at the drawing board as I shrug.

I feel my mother walk behind me and tap my shoulder. "Go, try it on for me."

I take it from her and head to the bathroom. She doesn't approve of using magic to change clothes. I change and step out into my room.

My mother's face is full of excitement. "Oh Muriel! Twirl for me please."

I twirl and she says. "Sarah has such a great eye. I wish she would consider the fashion industry instead of..." She doesn't finish the sentence.

I look out the window. I straighten the dress. "I wish she realized we all love her and hate her taking the risks she does."

Mom frowns and looks at the window also. We can't look at each other right now. We would both cry. "The dangerous situations she puts herself in seem to give her something we don't. As long as we keep saving her-" She narrows her eyes and looks at me, "-she will go for riskier behavior. I'm afraid she won't learn her lesson till none of us can help her out."

I want to argue. I know my parents letting her go, was because they knew that Yacob and I have her back. There is a knock at the door.

I cock my head. I look at the door. "Come in."

There is a tentative opening and the red haired Morgan pauses in the threshold. "I'm sorry, did I interrupt something?"

My mother chuckles, "Not at all, just the same old argument."

Self-conscious about standing in the fancy dress, I cross my arms. "How are you feeling Morgan?"

Janette Bach

She gives me a sheepish look. "Pretty well. That dress looks lovely on you Muriel. Are you wearing it to the Gorge dance tonight?"

I give a sheepish smile, "Do you think I should?"

My mother and Morgan say in unison. "Yes."

Morgan shifts. "Do you have time to come check out the nursery we put together? I think it could use some artwork."

"Let me change." I nod, then look at my mother and gesture to the windows. "Should we give Sarah some privacy?"

As I walk to the bathroom to change I hear Morgan ask Mom. "Where is Sarina?"

My mother's voice is weary and resigned. The whole everyone using the other name thing. "Sarah is out there." I imagine she is gesturing to the windows.

The timber of Morgan's voice changes. "That is a real place?"

I come back out in the clothes I had on before the dress. Morgan gives me a disgusted look. "Nice shirt!"

I look back down at the Atlas Shrugged shirt and say, "Thanks, I got it online."

Morgan rolls her eyes. I laugh, "Lead on, my lady."

I look back at my mother. She lies back on my bed and looks at the ceiling. "This is comfy, I think I will nap here."

I giggle more, "Yeah, OK Mom." The doorbell rings, I can hear it because Mom is in the room. "Sounds like more family is arriving."

She sighs and sits up. "It's wonderful, but time consuming." She stands and darts out of the room.

Morgan shakes her head, "She is doing well. My mother would be beside herself by now with agitation."

"Mom loves this. Don't believe any other pretense she puts forward. She lives for spending time with family."

52

Morgan leads me up the stairs. "Right, let's go check out the nursery before I need to be paraded out again."

"Don't worry, in a few days you'll just be the stand holding Merlin, not the center of attention."

Morgan holds her stomach and nods. "Truthfully, that part is fine, I just want to sleep on my stomach, and not have to empty my bladder every five minutes."

I pause on the stairs and cock my head. "Mom letting you teleport that away or do you have to go every time."

She sighs, "Either I let her put a catheter spell on me." She pauses and rolls her eyes. "Or I do it the way most people do."

The intimacy involved in that type of spell tells me, that Morgan has to use the toilet like most mortals. "Ah, so let's get back to your room before you need to go again."

She shudders. "It makes me feel so primitive. You grew up with restrictions. How did the three of you manage?"

I shrug "I don't know differently. The ban on teleporting makes you really creative though."

We had walked down one flight of stairs and two doors down the hall. She opened the door that always led to Yacob's room. It included the no girls allowed sign with a scrawl of, "Except for Morgan!" written across it. Instead of being the room of Yacob's childhood, it was a spacious apartment. The first room looks like a living room out of the pages of a Crate and Barrel catalog. Two overstuffed couches with denim fabric. They framed a fireplace with a shaggy white rug on top of bamboo floors. Mirroring the fireplace was a flat screen TV bolted to the wall.

Morgan walked past them to an arching hallway to the right. It was a spacious room, painted light blue.

The crib looked mission inspired with a honey glaze to its wood. There was a glider chair emblazoned with iridescent stars and moons. There was a dresser with a change station on top.

Morgan gestures to the walls. "It looks functional but lacks something."

I recently went to an M.C. Escher show. There had been this piece called "Evolution". It started as a checkered pattern on one side then turned into animals tessellated into each other. The progression of animals was evolution inspired.

I thought about it and changed the colors to a rainbow stripe and expanded the animal groups. The first three rows would be different types of fish. The second three rows would be different types of amphibians. The third three rows were types of lizards. The fourth three rows were birds and the last five rows were mammals.

I stand next to the wall and the door frame, I place my splayed fingers on the wall. I focus my mind on the molecules in the paint. I start coding out the frequencies of color toward the molecules. It creates a wave matrix that coats the wall. The image from my mind starts to appear.

I stare at the ceiling. It is blank, and framed with a line of yellow fish at the ceiling. I excite the molecules beneath my feet and rise to the ceiling. I flatten my palm on the ceiling. My mind scrambles for another idea. I think of galaxies and space. I turn the color of the ceiling blue and spatter it with stars, galaxies, planets, and a few comets. I think about animating it but decide that should be Morgan and Yacob's decision.

Then I look back at the wood floor. I lower back down. I consider making a pattern of insects but realize that Morgan would probably hate that idea. I think of another type of species not represented and found on the ground. Plants, I think of a tessellate of plants, flowers, shrubs and trees. The wood pattern remains but forms these ideas in its grain.

Circe Syndrome

I look back at Morgan in the doorway to see if she approves. Her mouth is open and her eyes are wide. "Wow!"

I feel color come to my cheeks. "Do you really like it?"

She enters the room and spins in the center and spreads out her arms. "It is perfect. The contrasting colors and big pattern are perfect for a newborn's eyes. The patterns changing into animals will encourage questions as he progresses from toddler to child!"

I laugh, none of that had occurred to me. I just thought it would be fun. "I'm glad you like it."

We grin at each other a moment when a sound makes us both turn.

An authoritative female voice echoes through the apartment. "Morgan, darling, I'm here!"

Morgan's loose smile evaporates and her mouth becomes a straight line. She runs a hand over herself as if straightening her clothes and she calls back. "Coming Mother!" She pauses at the threshold and gestures for me to follow.

I really don't want to. My steps are slow and I shuffle as much as an adult can get away with.

Morgan's voice is tired as she addresses her mother. "Mother we have only been gone from your house for an hour. I don't understand the drama!" She crosses the room to the women with red hair gathered in a crown of braids spilling curls from its top. She hugs her.

The woman looks like a queen in a riding coat resemblant of the Tudor era, done with emerald green. Golden letters from different alphabets, including Hebrew, decorate it. She gives me a disapproving look when she spots me and pulls Morgan behind her.

"I didn't expect to find you with the criminal." She says with a sniff.

I nod and curtsy. "Nice to see you too, Aiofe."

Chapter 6

Something to Give You Paws

Aoife scanned the apartment and sniffed, "No teleporting in here? How are you going to give birth here?"

Morgan gives her mother a cautious look. "Maxima is a great Midwife and doctor. She has made a special room where teleportation within the room is possible."

Morgan then looks at me. "That reminds me. I want you in the delivery room too, Muriel. Your brother and mother insist that you are always helpful if a crisis arises."

I look down as I feel blood color my cheeks. I find this unexpected. "It would be an honor Morgan. Thank you."

Aoife sneers and snorts, "The criminal? You want the criminal in your delivery room. Where is the eldest girl, Sarina?"

Morgan gives me an apologetic glance.

I meet Aoife's eyes. I'm not going to act ashamed. I still stand by what I did. I don't have to explain myself to this pompous woman. "I was about to go get her."

Morgan turned to her mother with a scowl on her face. "Yes, go get Sarina. I'll show all of you the birth room when you come back."

I pause at the threshold of the room when I see Yacob standing there. He gives me a reassuring squeeze on my shoulder, then calls out to his mother-in-law. "Trying to terrorize my sister Aoife? You have only been here 5 minutes."

I am trying not to laugh as I watch Aoife puff up like a peacock.

I exit the room and take two flights of stairs back up to my room. I look at my watch; I'm five minutes late. I cross the room and pause at that window. I think of Gregor's arms around my waist. I sigh. I push the button and open the window to Eco-Spa again.

The bright, brilliant sun blinds me for a moment. I shield my eyes with my right hand and freeze. On the sand there is a finned muscled man with a bluer hue then Gregor sprawled over my sister. The movement is the marked rhythm of two lovers copulating. I call this species the Homo-Marinus and they named themselves Sumans.

I turn my head and head toward the cottage door. When the door slams I meet Hestia's hazel eyes. She stands from resting on the back of the couch. She rolls her eyes. "Is your sister in heat? That is her seventh partner."

I rub my eyes and sit on the couch near Hestia. "Perhaps, how did it go?"

The cat jumped to the seat next to me. "She seems very different then what legends say of you."

I startle, but try to hide it by examining the cushion. The fact that they have legends about me makes me cringe. I don't want a religion founded on me. Unfortunately, this location created a need for a caretaker and a secret order. As that which is inevitable in thinking creatures, a religion was developed. I trace a vague purplish form. "You know how siblings are. We are always trying to show our independence as individuals, so we polarize ourselves."

The cat paused. She sighs, "I do have siblings and you're right. I wonder what the reverend mother will do with this information?"

I meet her hazel eyes. "Do you really need to tell her about Sarina?"

I tried not laugh as the cat's eyebrows rise in unison and she gives me an imploring look. "I took vows, gracious lady."

I involuntarily frown. Religion with me at the center, not good. I say "I understand." I decide to distract myself, so I stand and move to the bookcase. I change the dial on the shelves from romance novels to fantasy, and grab a copy of Jasper Fforde's "Lost in a Good Book." I retreat to the couch and open the book.

I hear Hestia clear her throat. I turn and look down at my ankle. She looks up at me with a business like expression on her face. "As a dedicate, I have some questions!"

I close the book and shift uncomfortably. I pull a pillow across my lap. Philosophy questions are always dangerous. I run my fingers over the leaf patterns on the pillow. I hate that they revere me.

"You discourage multiple couplings, why? Your sister seems to have no issues with them. You seem to have no issues with her." The cat's tail springs and curls into a question mark at the end of each question.

I frown down at the pillow. I wish my opinion didn't matter here. I take a breath and begin. "I'm sure in the spur of the moment it seems like a good idea. More problems arise with the consequences. Disease, unknown parentage, hurt emotions are just the tip of the iceberg in terms of consequences. Mixing of bodily fluids can produce new pathogens. Offspring require a great deal of resources; help is needed to raise them. If parentage is unknown, the male of the species is unlikely to help, with the mind-set that it is not their problem. The social ramifications of being raised without a strong male model can be felt throughout the community."

Hestia jumps back on the couch and onto the pillow I'm mauling. She looks at me intently. "So it is not the act itself, it is the ripples it will cause."

I meet her eyes as I stutter. "Usually, yes."

She jumps to my side and stares at the floor with unfocused eyes. "I want to write a book about Sarina. I'm going to call it Sarianian Philosophy."

In an over spill of emotion, I flick out my fingers in a fan motion against the pillow. I try not to comment.

She nods with the conviction of a decision just being made. "I'm going to turn her into a cautionary tale. A harbinger of immoral acts."

I sigh and run a hand through my hair in frustration. "You really don't need to do that."

"I've taken copious notes and I'm well read on anything you have ever said. I think it will be well read and well received." She blinks at me repeatedly and fast as she speaks. As I process her words, I marvel at her hazel eyes and how parts of them glow, as if iridescent.

I think about religion on Earth. I sigh. I am certain this is going to mark a dark chapter in Eco-Spa's philosophical core. "Please, don't villainize her. Don't make it seem like she is responsible for all things wrong in the world."

Hestia pauses and stares at me. She looks up and back at me. "I didn't say I would do that."

I cross my arms and stare at her.

"It would make for more dynamic reading!" She poses straight and tall and looks at me over her shoulder.

My acerbic retort is unsaid at that moment. Sarina flushed and giggling enters the hut followed by the Suman. She pauses at the door and glares at me. "Is a week up already?"

Chapter 7

Sarian Philosophy

I pull the pillow off my lap. "Yes and a couple of extra hours."

Sarina walks to the counter. She pores two glasses of water, then walks to the Suman and hands him one. She makes a show of taking a drink. As she gives an exhale full of satisfaction, she looks at me and says, "How generous, a couple of hours." There was contempt in the last two words.

I was slouching in the couch; I sit up. I look at the Suman and meet his glass green eyes. "Shalom."

He smiles, walks across the room, and with an aura of friendliness and humility he holds out his hand. "Hello, gracious lady, I am Fargus."

I shake his hand and give him my most casual, friendly smile. "Is there something you wish to ask?"

He blushes; a crimson color fills his green gilled cheeks. He sits next to me. He looks down at his webbed hands and traces a pattern across his scales. "I've been married a few years."

62

Sarina gives a loud exhale. I look at her with a silencing look. She rolls her eyes and drinks her water and walks to the window and stares out. A frown on her face.

He watches her then looks expectantly at me. I gesture for him to continue. Their post coital glow is dimmed.

He rubs his forehead and starts again. "I've been married for four years now; we have not produced any children. Actually, my whole generation is having this problem."

I look at Sarina frowning and scowling to herself at the window. I speak to her. "Were all the gentlemen that you ", I pause and rub my forehead, trying not to sound judgmental "enjoyed." I wince at that word choice as I watch her slightly flinch - "Sumans?"

She turns with a cold stare and a hand on her hip. "No!"

I give Fargus an apologetic look and address Sarina again. "How many?" It's a whisper, with a tone that says I don't want an argument.

She sounds petulant as she says, "Four." Then she turns and looks back out the window. She raises an arm and rests her palm against the window frame as if using it to keep her standing.

I turn my gaze back to Fargus, who is looking apologetically at Sarina. "Is this the same request of your other three brethren or should I hear theirs too?"

He looks panicked a second. "Will you only help with one problem?"

I lean onto the arm rest and rub my head with my hand. "No, I agreed to the covenant of the legend. I will help all who answer the call to end the loneliness of the human occupant of this house."

He nods. "I'm not sure, but I can ask."

I nod in return. "Go ahead, find the other three; I will meet you at the big boulder out front in two hours."

He nods, stands, and crosses the room to Sarina. He shakes her hand as she stands there limply. He leans in and kisses her cheek. She runs a hand through her wind swept, long blond tresses and watches him leave.

I frown down at the book I didn't get to read. "Where did the other three gentlemen come from?" I put the book in the book shelf and look back at her.

She frowns at me. "How do you know I had seven partners?"

I keep my expression blank. I really have no opinion of her promiscuity, except that it wouldn't work for me. I know she is waiting for judgement so she can explode and rant at me. I watch her, blinking occasionally.

It takes two minutes of silence before she speaks. Her hands are in fists. Her voice is resigned and quiet. "Two from the forest and one from the sky."

I cover my face with both hands, trying to conceal my expression as I turn and stare, unfocused, at the bookcase. I take a ragged breath. The bookcase unfocuses before my eyes. Saplings, she had intercourse with two young trees. The local forest was infested with sapient trees. I had not created them and they were dangerous. They had even started evolving their own magic. A sign I needed to abandon this planet to its own devices. I couldn't develop species that had magic. When they reach mage level of power, I will be morally obliged to leave the planet to their care. They called themselves Arborthem. I'm going to have to go into the grove. This was getting complicated. I reminded myself that I was totally aware of what Sarina was capable of.

I calm myself to look serene when I turn to look at her. There was something else to talk about; the man from the sky. "Was it a bird man who you enjoyed?" I winced again.

Circe Syndrome

I was sure if her eyes were lasers I would be burned to a crisp. Her voice was steel edged "Watch it! Yes, he had wings and a bit of a beak."

I nod nonchalantly. I had an idea of the species and it was impatient on most days. It probably already received payment from her in some way. "Did he make a request of you?"

She cocked her head. "Are you asking about how we did it?"

I blush and rub my forehead between my eyes. "No, something that had nothing to do with sex or how you went about it."

She sighs. "I thought you were going to be fun for a moment there. There was something."

I look expectantly. "What?"

She chews on her lower lip, in thought. "Ah yeah, he asked me to color his feathers in a certain way. A way that would grow back in the same color pattern after he molted!"

I nodded. This made sense the vanity of the bird men was pretty much universal in the species. It was a genetic change he asked for, so I wondered if she could do it. I gesture to the necklace that was now the shape of an exotic flower. Curiously it was a flower I've never seen before. "Were you able to accommodate him?"

Sarina frowns "Yes, it took me awhile. Gene manipulation is not something I completely understand. I used wave vibration and protein manipulation."

I nod encouragingly "That should work." In my head I count down one down six more to go. I look at Hestia whose head has been bobbing between us the whole time, watching everything. I address her. "If an annoyed bird man shows up later pull the cord."

The cat bobs her head in affirmation. "Certainly, gracious lady."

I fight the urge to roll my eyes at this address. I look back at Sarina and nod toward the door. "You're coming with me!"

Chapter 8

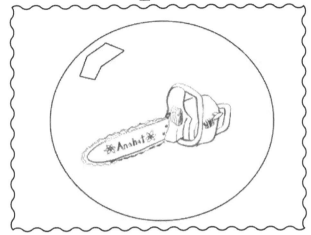

Woodland Wonderland

Sarina frowns at me "Where are we going?"

I gesture to the door. "Into the grove."

She says deadpan, "Cool."

I muse that she has no idea of the danger in what we are about to do. Once we pass the threshold outside, Sarina looks where she had been on the beach when I arrived. She gives me a casual glance "Did you see what we…"

I interrupt before she finished the sentence and blurt out, "Yes!"

She is quiet when she says, "Oh."

I take a moment to listen to the waves and feel the sun on my face.

Sarina kicks at the sand, "Nice spell, easing of loneliness."

I give her a half smile as I muse on how lonely I am normally. "It's a tricky one, illegal at home."

She chuckles and crosses her arms across her chest in a self-hug. "So little straight laced sister, do you have as much fun as I just did here?"

I chuckle and blush. "Not in the same way. I only end up with one unattached male being the whole time I'm here." I think about Gregor. After that affair, my mother had put her foot down. No more escaping the world. I needed to find a lover on Earth, preferably Heska or Human. One she could get grandchildren from.

Sarina unwound herself. "So the spell addresses temperament and intent too?"

I nod as I turn and stare at the grove. Light and shadows create a striped pattern across the horizon, crowned by a maze of branches. "Yes. I can't believe you engaged in relations with trees!"

"Trees?" Sarina asked puzzled.

I nod "The grove gentlemen."

She laughs "Those were trees? That gives a whole new meaning to hard wood."

I cover my mouth trying to hide my guffaw. Tears come to my eyes. "Saplings, they're young and can transform easily."

Her jaw drops. "Transform, you mean they have magic. I thought it wasn't possible to consciously make a magic being."

I nod in agreement. "It isn't; I didn't create them. They developed themselves and everything else on their own."

A tingling sensation travels up my leg and then my spine when I make this statement. I start to analyze this sensation when Sarina asks me a question, distracting me from the feeling.

"What are we walking into?" Her eyes are wide with apprehension.

I sigh in resignation. "Probably a trap for me."

She shakes her head at me. "You always so calm, little sis?"

Deadpan, I nod. "Right, on the outside. Inside, not so much." I pause take a breath and rub my fingertips together and stare into the grove. "Sarina, distract me a moment won't you? Why did you want to get out of town for a week?"

I watch the emotions war across her face. She wants to maintain she wasn't running from anything. She is also excited and proud that she avoided the fallout she created. Her smugness wins. "I've been having affairs with the two leaders of rival Meth cartels. Both are married, I am both of their mistresses. I've been leaving clues for their wives, to realize what is happening. I also make it appear that each man is blackmailing me, to sleep with me against my will. It should dissolve into a spectacular blood bath that will take two suppliers off the map."

I fight the urge to throttle her. "Isn't there a less violent way to do this?"

Sarina shrugs as her eyes shine with pride. "Not without major money and investment by the tax payers. Poof, it is destroyed with just a small police report and a couple funerals."

I sigh and stare at the grove. I think I see some movement then it all looks eerily still again. "Won't someone fill the void? How can you be intimate with these type of people?"

She gives me a throaty chuckle. "I'm not you, Muriel! Part of my thing is the sleaze factor. The more tainted and varied the person, the more turned on I get. The better the orgasm!"

I find myself speechless over her selfishness.

A pleading look comes across Sarina's face. "Did anyone come looking for me?"

I turn away so she can't read my expression and start walking toward the grove and gesture her to follow. "Not that I'm aware of." A true statement, I don't want to let her know she has only been gone from Earth for a couple of hours.

Circe Syndrome

She runs to catch up. "Oh, how did the dance go?"

I have reached the edge of the forest. I examine the trees. They are thick and soar to the sky, with a patchy white and tan birch bark. I step under the cover of the stretching branches; the birds stop chirping.

Sarina stops at the edge and reaches out into the air as if reaching for an invisible barrier. "Ummm, this feels different."

A breeze blows out through the grove and swirls around us. My hair blows back and it is filled with this seductively sweet scent charged with human pheromones. My body responds as if a lover has stroked me. I feel my vulva swell with liquid. My eyes widened. "They have learned some interesting things from you."

She has this blissful look on her face. "Mmm, that smells heavenly it reminds me of this time…"

I cover my ears. As we walk deeper into the grove the tree's bark changes from the smooth birch to a coarse, red wood bark. Blue green moss drips from limbs, some touching the ground and spanning across the path. The moss has buds that open and flower with tiny, rich purple, five petal flowers. They are clumped like grapes and speckled with yellow dots. The rainbow bushes full of pinecones scurry about the base of the trees like a litter of puppies.

I turn when I realize Sarina has stopped talking and isn't keeping up. She is about three yards back gaping and stopped. She stares up into the moss, then down at the moving bushes. She then looks at me. "What about you?"

I watch the shadows and bushes, and try to scan every tree as I respond. "What about me, what?"

She seems like she has a problem focusing and a bit of world weariness shadows her eyes. "What does the smell remind you of?"

Janette Bach

An intense moment with Gregor on a beach flashes through my mind and I push the lust from my mind, shake my head. "That the next time you want time away, I should just send you to Venice or Italy."

Sarina chuckles, walks up to me, and punches my shoulder. Then she sighs.

I shift because a breeze has caught my hardened nipples, sending a wave of pleasure and want through my body. I glare at the trees.

We start to walk further toward the center of the grove and come across a creek running perpendicular to our path. There is tree lying across it.

Sarina climbs onto the log before I can say anything and starts using it to cross. I go down to the creek bed, hoping if I don't say anything, nothing will happen. As I jump over the water dragging my right foot through the creek, the branches on the tree Sarina is walking on move like human limbs and catch her. The giant log sits up and then stands.

I look toward the grove center. It is five yards away. The tree leans in my direction, reaching to catch me. I dart out of its grasp. I notice other trees starting to animate around me. I notice that the tree is handling Sarina with care. There is a semi-circle of trees animating, and I feel like prey about to be herded.

Sarina had started screaming explicatives when the tree had first grabbed her and had become an amazing tangle of impossible obscene ideas spewing from her mouth.

I shrug; the tree's goal and mine seem to be the same. To get me to the center of the grove. I run to it. It's this quiet clearing; as I stand there, trees circle, creating no space between themselves, walling me in. The bark of the trees morphed into stern faces. I fought the urge to run in circles in the clearing. I look up when I hear the distinct sound of a chainsaw.

Circe Syndrome

I smell gasoline and immediately throw a web spell to catch Sarina she was falling with a branch and a chainsaw. I groan and shake my head doing fast calculations. I weave a force field around the chainsaw as it falls. I push it away from her trajectory. Sarina hits and bounces several times. As her inertia subsides, she scrambles to the edge of the web toward where the chainsaw landed. She picks it up and walks over to me and stands at my back. She revs its engine. I am sure she has a threatening expression on her face.

Meanwhile, the tree Sarina has just cut is screaming. It sounds like thousands of dried leaves turning and turning in a brass barrel. The orgasmic smell is interrupted by a sickening sweet sap smell.

I look at Sarina. "Stay here a second." She adjusts her grip on the chainsaw and revs it again. She nods.

I walk toward the tree she cut herself free of. Sap is pouring down its branch hand. I reach toward the hand with a gesture to let me see it.

The tree has sap tears on its face and gives me a mistrustful look. I stay where I am with a stern look of compassion. It scowls at me and lowers its hand as if it is about to hit me.

As the hand starts it's a quick movement toward me, it is interrupted. Another tree, slim and majestic, grows between me and swatting branch hand. The hand stops where it is, the air swirling with movement.

The slim tree has an aura of calm. It stares at the injured tree. It spreads out its hand branches in a welcoming manner. The injured tree looks like a corrected child, and presents its damaged limb to me.

I lean forward tentatively. I solidify the air around the sap and push it toward the sawed off tip. I sculpt it to reconstruct the finger. As I finished this, a tapping sensation travels up my leg. I look down to see the previous finger with roots poking me. I back away from the rooted finger. The majestic, slim tree picks up the finger tree and holds it out for its parent. The tree begins to croon. A soothing, rustling sound as it cradles it and moves back away behind other trees that crowd the space it left.

The majestic, slim tree transforms into a human form with white grained skin. Its voice is soft and soothing. "Greetings world maker, and?" She gestures to Sarina.

Sarina revs the chainsaw. I'm shocked that it works, most mechanical things work differently here. I meet the auburn eyes with bright green striations and oval pupils and say, "A friend." I wasn't volunteering anything more. I gesture to the trapping circle of trees. "Weird greeting."

The female form that had been a tree shrugged. "We wanted to make sure we got to talk to you, Oh Powerful One!"

I shifted; flattery is a very bad sign. I keep my voice matter of fact. "We have come to address the wishes of the two saplings." I pause a moment then sigh. "Who indulged my friend?"

The tree shaman's hand came out in an open gesture with the palm up. "She was quite helpful in our studies." Around her wrist budded and bloomed little pink flowers resembling a bracelet.

When the smell hits, it erupts through my senses, my nipples hardened and my vagina fills with fluid. I wince, I'm not comfortable. I steady Sarina as she involuntarily gasps. I take the chainsaw from her hand: it was precariously close to falling on her foot. I turn it off and set it down next to her.

I sigh and address the tree. "Obnoxious trick, you would make a killing in colleges in our world selling these date rape flowers."

Frowning, and with a look of confusion, the tree says, "What is rape? I don't want to kill you, I want to persuade you."

72

I wait and stare at the tree. It seemed lost in thought and purpose. "I'm sorry, what is your name?"

Startled the tree looks at me, "Glenprenode."

"Glenprenode, what do you want to persuade me to do?" I cock my head.

She nods. "Right, we want to be at your level of magic. Give us your abilities!"

Sarina laughs, "Yeah, like that is possible?"

Glenprenode scowls. "I demand respect!" A sound of hundreds of roots shifting and moving the earth fills the air. "You refuse to do this for me!" The trees around them began to rumble and pop out in flowers.

I grab at the air and create a force field to filter out the smell for Sarina and me.

Sarina sighs disappointedly. "That would have been fun."

I address Glenprenode's frustrations. "It's just not possible. Forces of the universe have certain laws. I can't give any species the ability to perform magic; that has to evolve naturally."

She narrows her eyes. "How about an individual?"

Sarina's hand subconsciously goes to her necklace.

That tingling sensation in my spine returns. I shake my head. "Your magic is alien to me. It doesn't work for me and mine won't work for you. Your ancestor Oakobert and I explored this idea. Nothing I enchanted he could use magically." I pause and scratch my chin. "Forgive me, Glenprenode, I'm not here to grant your wish. The two saplings who eased my, " I nod towards Sarina, "my friend's loneliness. Where are they?"

The ground rumbles, as if hundreds of roots were heading toward us. I lift the grassy field and root soil into the air and make the rest of the ground metal.

Sarina scowls, "Why don't you, just set them all on fire? Nothing like a forest fire to calm the citizenry!"

I give her a smile as I suppress a chuckle. "Thanks, for reminding me why I like to hang out with you, Sis. Nothing like demanding a hammer when the touch of a finger is all that is needed." I think about the tree I just helped heal and shudder.

She shakes her head at me. "Don't get all high and mighty on me, convict!"

I close my eyes. Her mentioning my transgression explodes the seeds of rage within me. I suppress this. I feel my nostrils flare, I start to measure my breaths, and everything becomes singularly focused. I try to loosen my stance and hide this anger, I calmly say, "Could we continue this charming conversation later when I don't have to pay attention to what is going on around us? Or should I just turn over this whole interaction to you?"

Sarina gives me a knowing smile, the one a sibling gives another when they know they have hit an emotional core. She picks up the chainsaw and turns it back on.

I hover so my face is level with Glenprenode, at this point visible electric cords are zig-zagging about my body. The condescending glint in her eyes has dissolved and she is fighting a look of panic. "Control your minions, please!"

Glenprenode tentatively steps back. "Ummmm."

I reach out and set Sarina's chainsaw blade on fire. "Now! Or I will let my friend have her way with you all!"

Sarina smirked and revved the engine. "This won't explode right, Muriel?"

I give her a mischievous smile and shrug. "I hope not."

Sarina nervously holds the saw further from her body.

Glenprenode raises her branch arm in a magic gesture.

I don't want to know what she is going to do. I set the arm on fire to distract the incantation.

She screams and the trees around her advance forward. I set them on fire also. I enhance my voice to drown their screams. "I will stop if you desist! I came in peace and you attacked me at least three times!" I rise up above the trees and look down at them.

Sap tears fill her eyes. She holds out her arms to me. "Will you heal me?"

I cross my arms and give her a stern look. "You're not truthfully bargaining in your current situation? Me, granting these wishes is a whim on my part. I will not be punished in any way for not doing this! Sure, if you want to ruin your denizen chances, keep it up!"

Sarina sighs. "I'd say it is ruined."

The shaman stiffens and opens her mouth to speak, but pauses when two wiry thin trees grow between her and Muriel.

In unison they speak. "We are the ones who amused your friend."

I look at Sarina for confirmation. "Are these the ones?"

Sarina shrugs "I'm not good at identifying trees."

I put on my politest smile "Can you manifest the shapes you used to seduce my friend?"

Sarina chimes in, "Hey!"

I give her an amused look with a raised eyebrow as I watch the saplings transform into young men that look like they stepped out of the pages of a GQ magazine.

Sighing, Sarina nods. "Yes, they appear so." She points to each one and asks them specific questions. Then she nods. "Yep, these are the ones."

I nod and address them, "OK, what do you desire?"

Chapter 9

Tally It Up

The saplings both stare at Sarina. Then they look at each other. There was a mutual nod and the one on the left said, "So that stuff we did with her that is how you humans pollinate and create saplings?"

I nod.

The one on the right says, "We want to experience pleasure also when we pollinate. Can you do that?"

I start analyzing their tissues. This odd combination of plant and animal cells is more of an in between shape. Kind of rounded hexagons. I try to figure out what the equivalent of their neuro net is. There is this sap strand that is almost looks like fiber optics. The ball of strands seem to move about the threads. It was fascinating. I narrowed in on the ball of strands and started recognizing similar structures to the human brain.

In about twenty minutes I figure out the gland control center and route it to the flowering branch of the cells.

I pause, "So both of you want this adaptation?"

They nod emphatically almost hitting me with their foliage.

I walk up to each one and lay my hands on them. I alter their cells. There is a look of wonder that crosses their faces. They kneel.

I sigh and pull them up. "Thank you again for helping out my friend."

Glenprenode sputters, "What have you done? Why didn't you wish for magic? Like we talked about!"

I look at Sarina, and toward the hut on the beach as all the trees start arguing, joining sides. Sarina stares slack jaw up at the bickering trees with an amused smile of wonder.

I sigh and grab her hand. "Come on, while they are distracted!" I drag her toward the hut.

She fights me, "It's not like you can't just levitate us out of here? This is entertaining!"

I frown, "Come on Sarina, they have magic, it changes daily. They might have a way to stop me they haven't thought of yet!"

She concedes and we run.   Sarina, out of breath, yells over at me. "Does checking out of this resort usually take this long?"

I chuckle, "Come now Sis, we must make sure all the help gets tipped appropriately."

"They got to sleep with a goddess and survived. That should be more than enough payment." She giggles.

I stop and bend in half trying to catch my breath, because I'm laughing so hard. I gasp for air.

She pauses and stands with her hands on her hips, observing me. "They weren't that great Murry!"

My eyebrows go up from the affectionate name she gave me as a toddler; I hadn't heard it in years.

Panting I laugh harder. I groan then catch my breath. "It is not about that specifically. This is about me keeping my word."

She shrugs.

We begin to run again. I look back and there seems to be nothing following us, so I return to a walk. Sarina follows suit.

As we approach the beach, four figures stand next to the biggest boulder on the beach. The two were talking heatedly to one another. One was down on his haunches looking at something in the sand. The fourth was leaning against the boulder looking out to the water.

Sarina giggles "Do you think they are all married?"

I shrug. "That is your preference. Some kind of desperate man that shouldn't be with you. I imagine so. The conception problem has put them in a desperate state to do anything to solve it. They would even cheat on the love of their lives. That's your other thing right, a normally incourruptible individual?"

"I didn't realize you knew me so well." Sarina smirks.

I laugh, "Not as well as the spell. I'm learning more than I really wanted to know."

She puts her arm around me, "You need to loosen up."

I feel my eyes roll. We were in hearing distance of the Sumans. "Hi." I wave at the four. The four individuals bow immediately. They murmur, "Your Graciousness."

I gesture for them to stand. "That is not necessary."

"Oh come on, Muriel! This is such a cushy setup you have here." Sarina kicks at some sand.

I glare at her. I look back at the men. "Thank you for spending time with my friend. Fargus tells me there is an infertility problem affecting your tribe?"

Circe Syndrome

The four Sumans nod at me in unison.

"You all want me to solve this problem?" I look at my hand.

The one staring at the sand stands and says. "Yes!" The other three nod empathically.

I nod and sigh. "Alright, let's go to your colony."

Fargus frowns, "How you breathe, air only? Correct?"

I nod, "Yeah, but I can change the composition of my lungs and breathe the oxygen out of the water."

Sarina turns and stares at me. "We can do what now?"

I start explaining the scientific process of turning the lungs into gills and harvesting oxygen through slicing breathing out of water. It feels like cutting through the water as the gills move in the water and the oxygen syphons into the gills. Her eyes get wider and wider. I know she is confused when I'm done.

I sigh, "OK, before your head goes under, hold your necklace. Take a strand of power and say 'Ay, ay shacka loot kay masm.'"

She groans and shoves me. "Why didn't you just start there? Say breathe underwater in Hebrew, honestly Muriel, a biology lesson really?"

I shrug as I adjust my stance from the shove. "Back home those are the rules."

She sighs, "We aren't home right now. We are in the world you..."

I raise my hand to stop her mid-sentence.

The Suman's shift uncomfortably.

I put on my best customer service smile. "Let's go."

I walk down toward the water. The water splashing at my ankles. My pants are binding and the hems are getting wet. I start transforming them into a wet-suit. I keep walking up to my neck. I pause and start the transformation. A sharp pain and burning sensation flows through my lungs they can't breathe at all at the moment.

Underwater I hear Sarina scream gasping for air. "Damn it, Muriel, you should warn a person about that amount of pain!"

I cough, "I know," shake my head and wince, "that burns."

Incredulous she says, "Haven't you done this before?"

I had forgotten about it, but I say, "Yes, but I'm a little distracted, sister dear. You have left me quite a lot to take care of."

"You knew I was a snake when you let me in." She snorts.

I nod to the Sumans quietly watching us with their arms crossed. "Lead on."

Chapter 10

Kelping Out

The Sumans gestured for us to follow them. Sarina meets my eyes and follows the Sumans. I take a second to mark where I am on the planet, and then follow them.

As we head out into the sea, we see a forest of blue green kelp with iridescent silver stars populates the floor of the breakwater. The leaves caress my skin as I swim through, barely making out the fins of the Sumans. Out of the corner of my eye, I catch the vague shapes of fins moving too fast. Their speed make; it difficult to determine the variations of the vibrant colors, or if they are menacing or not.

When I reach for the clear space beyond the kelp forest, I am pulled back. A tendril that resembled the kelp I swam through has wrapped around my ankle. It was actively pulling me back. I look ahead; no one has noticed. I make a high-pitched noise and they turn. I bend to the tendril. I now notice it is barbed and has injected my skin with a numbing agent. I feel a creeping, numbing sensation climbing my leg.

81

Janette Bach

I sigh, going through the database in my mind of creatures on this planet of which I'm aware of. I narrow it down to a cephalopod. It is a creature with hundreds of tendrils resembling kelp. They lurk in the kelp forest waiting to catch prey, blending in till they're ready to strike. I send a wave of burning heat through my leg toward my ankle. The tendril lets go. I kick away fast but I only have one leg to kick with, so I go at an awkward angle and my other leg is captured. Both of my legs are numb now. More tendrils start coming. I can't see light anymore. All there is, is a light stinging sensation and numbing feeling creeping through my body.

I feel the motion of being drawn down farther. I consider using an electric shock but realize, I would be electrocuted too, and will still be numb from the poison moving through my body. I look internally and start scanning my cellular structures. I see the poison clearly; I consider the tentacle around me. I realize the cells of the tentacles are pretty porous. I push the poison out one of the holes in my leg and send in onto the tentacles. The tentacle stops moving. I know what to do now.

I recruit some cells to hunt down the poison's composition and to expel it. I then let my skin cells know under no certain terms should they be letting that compound back in. Guard cells sent to patrol puncture wounds. Stuff for the lungs.

It's still dark so I can't see, but as I start to expel the poison the water around me develops this dusty, slimy texture.

Slowly, light penetrates as the tendrils fall away. I blink in the light and move my body freely, swimming away from the miasma of poison hovering in a cloud in the water. I swim to the Sumans who give me grave looks.

Fargus sighs. "We had no idea what to do Gracious One. The Kracious and you are both sacred to us. To hurt either of you would be sacrilegious."

I look at him with a blank face and shrug. "No worries." A carnivorous cephalopod is sacred? That was news to me. I push my unease about the direct reference to myself in that category.

Sarina sighs in disgust, and we all start swam deeper, to the open sea. A couple times the purple dolphins found us, jumped and swam circles about us. The Sumans and the dolphins exchanged jokes which the Sumans translated for us.

The fish were varied and strange, and some new ones I never designed followed us at different distances. We came to a fissure in the bottom of the ocean, filled with cliffs. The dwellings, the entire community was carved into the cliffs. The windows had boxes with sea- anemones, coral and kelp growing out of them. The milling population took a moment to pause and stare at us.

Sarina smiled at the attention, I tried to ignore it. The Sumans suddenly looked at each other, baffled at what to do. I sigh, "Can you introduce me to your wives?" They all look at Sarina. I nod and look at Sarina; "you are to act uninterested and bored."

She laughed, "That is easy, and I am."

I smile, and look back at the Suman's who each in their own way look a bit hurt. I look at Sarina to see if she notices, she is busy looking at the dwellings.

I find myself taking a moment to analyze the structure of the Suman's in front of me. I raise a hand. "First, show me a couple who have no trouble conceiving."

They shift nervously. I scratch my ear. "Is everyone having trouble conceiving?"

Fargus sighs, "Really private information Gracious One. Don't you have a way of knowing?"

I raise an eyebrow. "I'm not a god. I am not omnipotent."

He rolls his eyes. "Of course, Gracious One." He then proceeds to mumble about false modesty.

Sarina starts suppressing giggles.

I look around and try to note the number of children. I start to notice there are none under two years old. I look back at Fargus. I meet his green eyes and smile patiently. "How long has it been since a child was born in your community?"

He shifts uncomfortably.

I look beyond him relieving him of my direct eye contact. "Has it been a month?"

The three of them look away.

I sigh; this is going to be a very long conversation. After I list the months, then I start years at the two year mark, they all look at me.

I take a big breath. I look around the community. I am thinking what has changed in the environment here to affect so many creatures at once. "Is there another Suman community without this issue I can look at?"

I start scanning ten to twenty men and women. Noting similarities and differences between individuals.

Fargus starts a conversation with several other individuals and finally he gives me a concerned look. "There is one, Gracious One, but it's a week away."

I nod. "Do you have a map?"

A Suman with facial greying tufts approaches. "A map?"

I take a breath. "A visual drawing of the way there, and distance."

The Sumans look at each other.

I realize I need to take a different approach. "Has anyone here visited that community?"

A woman steps forward. "I'm from there, Gracious One."

Sarina scowls..."Gracious, seriously, these guys know nothing about you!"

I give Sarina an amused smile.

I step forward toward the female Suman "May I read your mind?"

Sarina snorts "You follow mind magic rules on your own planet with your own creations!"

I watch the Sumans around us pause.

I give her a scowl "It is important that I follow that rule, especially here." I turn back to the woman trying to look brave. "Forgive my companion's outburst. This decision is entirely yours."

She looks at Sarina and back at me. "Will it hurt?"

I nod with understanding. "No, you won't even know I'm there."

She scratches her chin. "Why do you even bother to ask then?"

I smile, "Ethics."

"Oh, will you find out personnel stuff?" She looks away.

"I will try not to. I will not tell anyone." I wait a few minutes then I say. "Well?"

The Suman sighed. "Why do you want to?"

"I want to figure out how to get to the other colony."

She sighs "But it takes a week to get there."

I look at Sarina who has a mysterious look in her eye. Then I smile kindly at the Suman woman again. "Please."

She shrugs. "OK."

I nod and look in. It takes a moment or two to find the memories I need her; alien brain uses a different organization system than most humans. I track the memories of the long trip here. I start making calculations on swim speed and distance and then geo positioning. I figure out where the other colony is.

I look at Sarina since I can only dialyosefos one other person with me I ask her. "Are you OK, hanging out here until I return? Probably be an hour?"

Sarina's eyes flickered nonchalant around the area. She shrugged. "Sure."

I feel my forehead wrinkle. "No nonsense."

She laughs, "I have no idea what you mean!"

I roll my eyes and look at Fargus, "Are you up to taking a quick trip with me?"

"I have to be home for dinner." he said startled.

"When's dinner?" I ask absently minded, then look up overhead to observe the sun, I realize that being fathoms underwater negates that type of time telling.

He sighs, "Five hours from now."

I nod. "Shouldn't be a problem." I gesture for him to stand closer to me. I don't need him that close, but it will help everyone around us understand something weird is about to happen. I look at Fargus, "So I'm going to take us to the other village, but we will not travel by swimming. We are going to travel in the life force of this planet."

He gives me a sarcastic look. "What?" Then he looks nervous. "Will it hurt?"

I take a breath, trying to be reassuring, but actually taken by the question. I had traveled with Gregor this way and he never complained of pain. "No, it shouldn't. It will be a little disorienting, though."

He nods.

I look around, "We should be back in thirty minutes, to an hour. We need to wait thirty minutes between dialyosefosing."

Sarina smirked. "OK."

Circe Syndrome

I look up or the aether then pause. I'm underwater. The aether is in the air. Fargus shifts uncomfortably and Sarina starts to laugh.

I sigh. "Sorry, we have to swim to the surface. Wait, I have an idea."

I send a call to the aether because I can still feel it fathoms above me. Its undulations mirror the ocean. I coax a thread down through the water. When it reaches me, I reach out and encompass Fargus with my mind. I find being underwater messes with my perceptions. Our particles are slightly in a different space. Then I see them, luckily they are moving slower due to the density of the water. As we blend into light, I hear the female Suman's gasp and I check the directions. We shoot into the aether. I note the location above water and we fall down into the water. The splash is huge and I misjudge the water landing, so I'm choking on air before I push the water through my lungs.

We swim downward to a huge coral reef filled with dwellings and swimming Sumans. They pause and look at us curiously. I start scanning them and comparing them to the other population. I analyze the water, and note they have offspring of all ages.

Fargus waves and starts to talk to an authoritative male, who has come to ask who we are and why we are here. Many gawk at me; they never have seen a human before. I listen to Fargus try to explain me, as I observe everything going on around us.

Finally I look at them. I ask, "Has anyone ever had problems having little ones here?"

They all look ruffled and look at Fargus in a way that says, "How could you bring such a rude creature here?"

I just looked at them expectantly.

None of them volunteers anything. A matronly Suman female gestures me over. She looks me over. "The maker?", she asks softly.

I frown, I nod. "Yeah, some call me that."

She sighs, "No troubles here, but in the cliff colony, horrible stagnation."

I nod, I point to Fargus. "Yes, he is from there, there hasn't been a new infant in their colony for two years."

She sniffs and gives him a pitying look. "So you're here?"

I shrug "To see what is different here."

"Different how?" She crossed her arms.

I shift and look about the community. "That's the question really."

She snorted. "I see."

I swirl the water around my fingers "Any ideas?"

She laughs, "Besides direct contact with the divine."

My eyebrows raise, "Hmmm, as you know sterility is not usually the goal of the divine with a thoughtful species."

"Usually?"

I shrug. "Sometimes, no intervention in self-destruction is a choice."

"I see." Sadness fills her face. "The Kowl."

I wince; I rub my scalp and pull my eyes from hers. This was painful. There was this engineering species that was amphibian and sapient. They went majorly industrial and poisoned themselves. I let them. I did warn them, but there are lines in the sand I will not cross. Plus, my mother had me trapped back on earth then. I stare at my right palm and massage it with my left thumb. I start to trace the lines on my hand, then I look back at her. "Any other ideas?"

Circe Syndrome

She shakes her head and I look back at Fargus. I gesture to the plants everywhere. "Can you tell me about these? We will be here for about thirty minutes."

For the next thirty minutes she showed me around. I noted so many things. I noted interactions, chemical compounds of plants, animals and in the water. My head was becoming a database of this community.

Fargus talked industry with the other males and I gestured to him swimming up when I was ready for us to dialyosefos again. He shook finned hands and I thanked the matron profusely.

When we arrived back at the cliff colony we noticed it was almost completely empty. Fargus' nares flair, and he gestures to the community center. We swam there to find three females growling and circling Sarina. The whole community cheering them on.

I sigh.

Fargus starts yelling and Sarina meets my eyes. I rub my hand across my face, I mumble, "Forty minutes, I only left her alone forty minutes."

I sigh, stand tall and take on a blue green glow of gene manipulations. The Sumans around me part as I walk to the center and past the circling females, who look at me fearfully as I stand next to Sarina. "You understand this was the nonsense I was talking about."

I watch a spark of anger flash through her. "You know I don't always start stuff, right?"

I look at the angry, confused women around me. "Yes, but I have spent a great deal of time with you. They figured out what their husbands had done."

"Apparently, the smell of their men permeates from the female they inseminate."

I nod. "OK, I see." I start realizing this is a good time to analyze the whole population. Since they are all here. I start a database of them and all the similar factors as the others. I start a comparison analysis.

Something becomes apparent. There is this protein strain everywhere here and not in the other community. I start marking its structure with my mind. The area is awash with it and the citizens filled with it.

The females had started moving forward, and one of their snarls brings my mind to the present. I send a command, sitting them down. They look about them, puzzled they try to get up as I banish the commands through their nervous systems. I look at Sarina, "Did you have a plan, have I stepped on your toes?"

She gives me an amused, sheepish grin. "Nah, but you didn't ask permission before you took over parts of their nervous systems."

I sigh, "You're right, bad Muriel. I think I know what the symptom is, but not sure on the cause yet."

"My promiscuousness?"

I tear up and laugh, "Yes, everything is about you, no, the fertility problem."

"Oh, that."

I look at her and take in the pheromones coming off her. I remove the Suman components.

The women stop snarling, they start looking puzzled at each other and Sarina.

Sarina pushes me "What did you do?"

I raise my eyebrow "Got rid of the evidence. It was a chemical reaction."

The women milled together and the crowd started to disperse. I looked about in a new vision that pointed out this foreign enzyme. It was permeating everything. I realized I needed to find its source; maybe back out of the community till I could see a trail.

I look back at Sarina. "I need to look at this community from a distance. Why don't you come with me?"

She smirked. "Why dear sister, would you ask that of me."

I kick at the sand and shake my head. "I'm not asking. I'm demanding in a polite way."

She looked about her and her color changed softly. "Yeah, OK."

After I explain to Fargus that I'm checking something out and we will be back, we swim toward the border of the community. We swim out about a mile. I start to see a current of the enzyme. I gesture her to follow and I swim farther. I start to determine where the current is coming from.

Sarina keeps asking me questions and I keep up a steady stream of what I'm doing and seeing in words. She just blinks and follows. About twenty miles of swimming into the current, we come across a land mass.

Chapter 11

Monkey Business

As we begin the climbing swim, up the slope of the island's crest, I begin to apologize. "I'm sorry, this is going to hurt again."

Sarina eyes the approaching water surface and asks in a tired voice. "Want to give me an idea on how to change back before it's critical?"

I laugh. "Yeah, OK."

I go through the mechanics of the spell and she stares at me. "Do I just say breath air in Hebrew again?"

I laugh "Yeah, you can do that."

She rolls her eyes. "Honestly, you make this difficult sometimes. Magic should be fun!"

Weary and still annoyed by this mess I need to clean up, I say, unguarded, "It shouldn't be this hard to check you out of a vacation."

She freezes and puts her hands on her hips. "What are you saying, Miss Perfect Muriel?"

I frown; this is not going to be helpful or productive. I'm trying to figure out how to shut this down. "Forgive me, Sarina. I love you."

She sighs. "It's OK we don't agree on stuff."

I nod. "I know; it's also OK the way you are."

She gives me a smile. "I know, just like I'm patient with how you are."

We are almost to the edge; our heads are going to start going above water. "OK, deep breath. You remember what to do?"

She nods. I start to focus on myself. The sharp pain shoots through my lungs. A piercing sharp pain that spreads like a dandelion outward. I cough and sputter water out and gag at the surface. I walk toward a dark brown cove. Sarina follows gasping, for air.

After I quit gasping for air my nose wrinkles. It's a strong smell, potent and herbivore, excrement. I realize the ground I'm standing on has a sticky, clay texture. An idea starts to form in my head and I wince and look at what I'm standing on. My toes are embedded and I sigh.

Sarina growls at my expression. "What is wrong, and God what is that smell?"

I scratch my neck and look down again at my feet. "You really don't want to know. But I have found the source of the enzyme messing up the Suman reproduction."

She squints her eyes, sniffs, and winces. She considers the mud we are standing on. "Oh man! Really?"

I shrug. "It seems so."

"Who leaves their dung like this?"

I walk further into land. "That's what I need to find out, then we need to have a few discussions about waste management." My eyes tear as we approach the dried mainland.

She frowns. "Yeah, alright." She follows me walking up the shore of what I now dubbed in my head, "Feces Beach."

I come across a creature standing upright with fur and a kerchief. Its head is angular, almost gazelle like. It bleats at me. I start a translation spell running. Its horns are straight up beyond its ears, but twist in a spiral curl. The ears are pointed, furry, and rotoscoping. Eyes huge and round, yellow with black stripes and a purple iris. Nose small and black like a cat. Its teeth are all wide for grinding vegetable matter, but I notice some pitting from eating something beyond leaves.

"Hi." I say

The creature backs away. "What? What? What? Are you?"

I frown. It's been awhile since I've had this conversation. I send peaceful intentions to the creature. "Nothing to worry about."

I hear Sarina start to snigger and I elbow her.

The creature looks at Sarina cautiously and back at me. We keep a good two-yard distance. I gesture to the piles on the beach, "Is there a community I may speak with? What do you call yourselves?"

She runs. It's a fast sprint, her legs slim and delicate. I note the direction she is going. I absently send a marker spell at her and watch the dot suspend in the air above her.

Sarina sighs. "Aren't we going to run after her?"

I sigh, "What, and engage in a predator behavior with a prey creature built to run? Nah, I just marked her in the aether. I can track her at a leisurely pace; hopefully she will run to the community."

Sarina cocks her head. "I can't see it."

Circe Syndrome

I start talking about visual frequency dilations.

She frowns and squints at the sky. "Just touch my eyes already."

I laugh and touch her forehead. She blinks up into the sky in wonder. "I never see the aether, I just hear you talk about it on occasion."

A sadness fills me, the one I try to hide from her. I wish power flowed for her too. I know she has other gifts, but sometimes just staring at the aether keeps me sane. Its wild impulsiveness grounds me like no other thing I witness. That life can spill beyond its host and animate the world is a miracle. And the fact a world I created generates its own, puts me in awe of the complex nature of the universe.

Her face is full of wonder. She stands there and stares up at the sky.

In the aether appeared a solid red gazelle, running and hopping. "That's it!" I say. It hopped about the power strings. We walk in the direction it runs. The ground changes to wide grass land with hoof worn paths. The grass is higher than our heads. I run my hands against the grass, brushing my fingertips with their segmented shafts. It tickles my palm, and I look at the brilliant waving aether in wonder again. My sister is still in a slight daze and seems to be humming, staring at the sky. The grass starts shortening. It's knee length when we see a clump of structures in the distance.

I pause and look at Sarina. "Time to focus on here. Do you want me to disable the sight?" I feel my eyebrow raise.

She clutches my arm. "No, how long will I keep it?"

I look away. I hadn't put a limit on it, but realize it would be a bad idea to leave it indefinitely; she was so distracted. I put a ten-minute countdown on it. "I think it has like eight minutes left."

She nods. "Can we wait, till I can't see it anymore?"

I change my stance to one of relaxation and nod and stare at the distance colony, watching the figures dart and become aware of us.

After ten minutes, Sarina blinks tears from her eyes and stares at me. "You can see that anytime you want, right?" I hear the anger, bitterness and jealousy creep through her undertones.

I reach out and touch her pendent in the shape of a Star of David again. "You can to."

She sobs and pulls away from me. "On borrowed power."

I sigh and turn away from her to let her collect herself. "If I could change that for you, I would. You know that."

"Shut up! You have no idea what this is like!"

I fight a chuckle at the absurdity of having this conversation right now before confronting some civilization on its waste management issues. "You're right!"

"Dammit, Muriel, quit it!"

"OK."

"Stop agreeing with me!"

I just sigh, and give her a look over my shoulder. I walk toward the group of beings who have noticed us and were milling in front of their buildings.

The buildings are made of bales of dried grass. The beings bleat softly to each other. The males have their chins down, showing me their horns. The smell of the dried grass tickles at my nose. I have the urge to sneeze. I sigh and take a breath. "Aah chooo....aah choo..." I start to sneeze. I go into a five-minute sneezing fit that brings tears to my eyes.

The biggest male stands in front of me with its upper appendages crossed. Two other males stand at his flanks with their heads lower aiming horns in my direction.

96

I stop. "Hi." I say casually, listening to the translation of bleats as I look down at the leader's chin, acknowledging authority and trying not to be perceived as a threat.

He takes a moment to look me up and down, then turns and assesses Sarina. He juts out his lower lip and frowns. "What are you? What do you want?"

I meet his eyes. "What I am doesn't really matter?" I bleat softly. "Why I am here, I would love to discuss."

He bristles "You will tell me who you are! I am alpha, you will follow my instructions!"

I sigh. "I'm a human; anyways I have come here to ..."

"Human? What's that?"

I sigh "A sapient creature evolved from apes."

He cocked his head. "Those silly tree things? No way!"

I shrug. "Where I came from. So the reason I'm here..."

He turns to the two at his side who look up at him and the three of them begin to laugh. Between guffaws he points to the one tree in the clearing. "Can you climb that?"

I consider the tree. And nod in affirmative. "I believe so."

He crosses his arms and gestures to the tree "Show me, then, maybe."

I take a breath and fight the urge to laugh at the absurdity of the question. I shake my head in negation. "You have to give me a promise that if I do, that you will discuss with me what I came to talk to you about."

He stares menacingly at me, and his two associates lower their heads as they bleat, "You dare to contradict the leader."

I widen my stance, I don't blink my eyes as I meet his. I shrug. "It will be amusing to watch me climb that tree, and then you have a conversation with me, what could hurt? Words usually create problems for you?"

He bristles, "All kinds."

I let my eyebrows raise in the expression of 'no kidding.' "It won't be that bad."

He lets out a snort through his black, wet nose. "I'll be the judge of that." He crosses his arms. After a minute of us staring at each other, he gestures to the tree. "Well?"

I move my head side to side. "I don't have your word yet, that we can have my discussion."

He snorts. "Fine, climb that tree and I'll let you have a conversation with me for, say, thirty minutes."

I look at the ground briefly and shake my head at the ridiculousness of the situation. I meet his eyes, and look back at the tree. "Sixty minutes."

He harrumphs, but I can see him fight a smile. "Twenty-five minutes."

I turn and look at Sarina. "I guess we should go."

Sarina nods, as if understanding everything. She instinctively knows the negotiation game. We turn in unison and start walking away.

He starts calling out.

Sarina says loudly. "At least you didn't have to look ridiculous climbing a tree."

I shrug, "Whatever, I was here to warn them about something that could kill them, but whatever, I tried."

The male voice of the leader brays out. "Hey!"

We keep walking exchanging conspiratory smiles.

"Hey! Monkey girl! Thirty-five minutes!"

I turn and wave. I notice he has moved from the pack and moved closer to me.

Sarina whispered. "You know an easier way Mindworm Muriel."

I jerk a look her way. "What did you call me?"

"Nothing." She looks away guiltily.

I am trying to stay focused on the task at hand. His gate is quickening. "Forty minutes!"

I glare at my sister. I keep walking away from the creature.

I hear his hooves stop.

I turn and look and note the area where he has stopped. About ten yards from the community; must be the limit of fast help from others. He moistens his lips. "Forty-five minutes."

I look at Sarina, she shrugs. "You could get him to go for hours."

I sigh and stop. "Nah, I think we are good." I turn, and walk toward him. "Yeah, alright. What tree now?"

He gives me a generous grin. "You were going to say, yes, the whole time, right?"

I shake my head, reach down and grab a stalk of grass, and twist it on my fingers as I stand up. He starts walking beside me and guiding me to the center of the colony.

The tree's base is about two yards wide, encrusted with a coarse bark that grows in fascinating hexagon tessellations. I know I didn't design this tree. The color is a reddish brown. Its broad branches, three feet thick, climb to the sky, they intertwine with vine type leaves that cascade down. They have a blue, silver cast and shimmer in the surroundings of brownish dwellings.

I pause; the air suddenly has a cloying smell. I look at the leader. "What's that smell?"

He grunts, "No talking till you climb."

I look at Sarina, "You smell it?" She nods and wrinkles her nose.

When we reach the base of the tree the colony surrounds us. I cringe when I realize it's the tree. It is coated with azure blue flowers that mirror the hexagon bark with a trumpet structure and bright orange accents. They smell of a mix of cotton candy, honey and candied apple. I feel nauseous from the smell. I turn down my olfactory senses.

As the smell dampens, I examine the bark. I reach out and touch it. I yelp "Oww." The bark was made of two millimeter barbs.

The creatures all laugh.

Sarina looks at me baffled.

I shrug, sigh, and make my skin thick and leathery. Pushing cells together. I start trying to figure out how to grab on, I'm bearly five foot and the closest branch is six feet up and so wide.

It takes a couple of jumps with me trying to grab onto the bottom of the branch, I fall down repeatedly. The creatures all continue to laugh.

Sarina sighs, "Muriel! Really is this necessary?"

I brush the clay from my pants and meet her eyes and wink. "Yes, I agreed to climb it."

She puts her hands on her hips. "You could just..."

I point my index finger at her, shutting her up. "My falling makes me more endearing."

She shakes her head in disgust. "No, just pitiful."

I shrug, "Toe mate toe...To maut o...." I examine the bark and work my fingers between the barbs. It manages to sting even with my hardened skin, but I figure I can endure it.

I jam my fingers in and start hugging the base of the tree. It stings everywhere. I take a moment to breath, and remind myself that the pain is temporary. I could numb things, but then my muscles wouldn't respond well and I would become sluggish. I start making my way up. I have a few slips and the audience chuckles.

I cling to the trunk as my heart pounds so my ears can hear nothing else. I take a breath, swallow the pain, and look for another crevice in the bark. I stretch out and lock my fingers in.

My foot slips. Tears escape my eyes as my face slides down the bark and I feel blood rush to it. I take a breath and let the sob escape.

I hear Sarina actually use a serious voice. "Muriel?"

I turn and look at her and let the other side of my face get stung and wink at her. I look back up at the tree. I forget about the watchers. I take in the tree's beauty, let the wonder of its life and evolution fill me. I stop thinking about me and my safety, I just look for the next finger hold. I use my knees to propel myself upward.

I'm sure I slipped some more; I'm sure I heard the crowd and Sarina gasp a few times. But the next thing I knew I was about two stories up in the tree, near branches that couldn't hold my weight.

The gazelle creatures bleated in wonder. The leader had a hold of Sarina's hand and was examining it.

I looked out at the sky. Clouds morphed and sailed by. Birds, lizard type creatures and other things I couldn't identify, flew across the sky. I take a breath and just drink in the moment. The height, the light sweet smell, the stinging sensation all over me. I look back down. They are all gesturing for me to come down frantically.

I sigh. These beings are so weird. First they want me to climb, then they want me down. So frantic all the time. That's when I notice a flying creature I couldn't identify coming at me. Its body is pure muscle, with sky blue variegated fur. Its wings are massive, each feather shaft at least an inch in diameter and feathering out about three feet. Its head was a combination of a lion and hippo. I frown at the dichotomy of the animal and the physics problems its flight at me presents. It has irregular, jagged teeth jutting in an under bite, and drool trails from its mouth. It's almost on me with outstretched forearms and huge clawed appendages.

I cry, "For heaven sakes!" I step off the branch when it goes to grab me. As I fall I manipulate the air as the creatures below scream. I fall in a controlled landing and the leader pauses.

Sarina snickers.

The creature in the air shrieks and heads toward the colony. I sigh. I throw a spell at the creature, freezing it in air inches from the citizens. As they scatter I walk to it. I stand before the creature with a frozen body in air is snarling at me. I look it over. I start biological scans; I'm interested in its evolution; another creature I didn't design. "What is this?" I gesture to it casually with my thumb.

I watch the leader swallow hard. He gives me a look of fear. "A Lockjaw." He is starting to tremble as the creature writhes in the air.

My mind is wondering on the hows and whys of it. My hand is on my chin and I tap a rhythm on my cheek with my index finger. Fur creates such a drag during flight. So, impractical, where did the creature evolve? The blue I get; the wing span and wings definitely. But the size and fur are baffling.

The head Gazelle man starts backing away. I stare into the Gazelle man's eyes. I find myself wondering what these beings call themselves. "What are you? What do you call yourselves?"

He cocks his head. "I'm Gris."

I sigh "No, I mean, like, I'm a human, you are a…"

He stares at the Lockjaw inches from my face, and me not flinching. There is a speculative glare in his eye. "Gazis."

Circe Syndrome

"What would happen if I let this go?" I gesture with my thumb.

He shuffles nervously. "We have been in an uneasy truce with it for a while. We give it offerings daily. If we don't it will raze our village and kill scores of us."

I start chewing on my bottom lip, in thought. This gives me an idea. "Alright, give me a second." I probe its brain, a mash of instinct and territory stuff. "I can make it think its territory is elsewhere. But I'm gonna want a favor in return." I meet his eyes, release the barrier more in his direction the Lockjaw charges a foot from him snarling. Saliva hits his face and drips down his chin.

The leader is trying to hide it but he begins to tremble. The Lockjaw, sensing his fear, snarls and snaps its teeth.

I take a breath and let this tableau remain.

A sharp, strong smell of herbivore sweat hits the air, the beads of liquid spilling off him are no longer just saliva, but his sweat. Sabrina uses a sharp tone with me. "Muriel!"

I stop analyzing the creature's structure. I look at her. She waves at the leader. "I think he is ready to negotiate. Let him relax a moment...seriously, if I am uncomfortable then you are pushing it too far."

I nod as I pull the Lockjaw back and perch it on the tree.

The leader's jaw is hanging as he looks at me. "How, what, you acted so harmless when you came?"

"We have several issues to discuss."

Chapter 12

Mur Singers

The negotiation with Gris was exhausting and unproductive. His primitive mind couldn't grasp what I was saying. I was standing on the beach I had been at it for hours. A few of the Sumans had come to help with the discussion. As I am trying to explain it to them, all I want is to find a wall and just beat my head against it. The species start talking together adamantly.

Sarina was whispering, "Just compel them all."

I glare at her. Then stare down in the water at a mollusk. I have this memory of the Hudson Bay being cleaned by mollusks. I bend down as the Sumans and Gazis joke about my odd conversations. They are buddies now in their mutual amusement of me.

I reach and pull out the mollusk. I analyze it and notice it likes the enzyme, the dung is producing. I can modify it more, make it harvest larger quantities of the enzyme. Expand its size, make it very absorbent. Make tons of them. I start to tinker with the one in my hand and set it back in the water and check the water running from it. It is starting to clean the water. There needs to be a copious amount of them.

I find a few and start changing them. I start varying the gene pool. I encourage some mating chemicals. I create the zygotes and mess with them. I start a geometric growth process and start spreading them out in the lagoon. This is all illegal on earth. I feel a pang of guilt but continue. The creatures are scratching their heads watching me. I go under and continue the process. I distribute a five-mile carpet of them around the beach.

I return to the lagoon to fetch Sarina. She gives me a glare. "I thought you forgot me."

I shrug.

"What have you done?" She gestures to the bloated mollusks.

"Think of them as water filters."

Sarina gives me a sly look. "Filters?"

I shrug. "Yeah."

" OK, can we leave now?" She nods toward the talking creatures and to the ocean.

I sigh. "I don't know. I need to check out the water beyond the seeding and then arrange a schedule to come back and check stuff out. Hmmm, I wonder if the Suman females can eat the mollusks and use them for birth control?"

"Whatever, let's go!" She throws up her hands.

I nod and look over at the Sumans and Gazis, "Thank you for your time. I figured something else out. Sarina and I are heading back to the Suman colony. I need to investigate this matter further."

Fargus, who is one of the Sumans with the group, nods. "We will come with you."

I nod. "Of course." I turn and look out across the horizon of ocean. The blue green water crashes in waves and birds two feet long, with bluish green plumage and giant beaks, dive through the waves. This is a familiar species, one I developed from pelicans on earth.

A smaller bird calls out with a swallow wing pattern. It has white and light blue hourglass patterned wings. The beak is bright orange in contrast.

Fargus watches me a moment. "The singers are a mark of a blessing. Have you blessed us?"

Sarina looks at the birds thoughtfully. "What do you call them?"

Fargus' cheeks color. "Mur's Singers."

Sarina meets my eyes. "Did you make them?"

I take a breath and observe them and listen. "Yeah," I note my signatures in the protein strands. I blink into Aether view and note the way the aether flows through their cerebral cortex. "They are Aether prisms."

Sarina shudders. "What?"

"They separate Aether into different waves and reweave them. They have access to the movement of life here."

"They can predict the future?"

I shrug. "I'm not sure, but they definitely have a spirit connection with this planet."

Sarina crosses her arms "And you."

I laugh. "Possibly."

Fargus moves uncomfortably close to me. He fixes me with a stare of wonder. Absently, I stroke his cheek in memory of Gregory. A look of tenderness fills him, mirroring my own, as my mind slips to another time. I pull back returning to myself. He whispers, "You've loved a Suman before, Gracious One?" He looks startled.

106

I subconsciously play with my hair and nod. Then look back out at the crashing waves. Letting their patterns soothe me and root me to the now.

Sarina sighs, "Are we going to go or what?"

I turn and look at her. I nod. "You remember what to do?"

She rolls her eyes. "Yes, Muriel."

Sarina, the Sumans and I wade into the lagoon. I take a tortured breath as the transformation happens. I blink my eyes at the submerged world now filling my vision, and admire the mollusks working.

We quietly swim in an unformed group toward the colony. It takes me twenty minutes to piece out a detection system that can send me updates on its progress.

I nod toward the Sumans and tell Fargus about how long I predict it will be before some of the females might start having children again.

It takes twenty minutes to disentangle ourselves and I pull Sarina to the surface with me. I dialyosefos us to the cabin. We say good bye to Hestia and head back to my room.

As we enter my room I feel my whole body relax, I had no idea I was so tense. Sarina laughs, "Whew, I think I need another vacation!"

I glare at her and shake my head. "No, way!"

She laughs harder, then looks longingly out the window. "That is quite a planet you made, Muriel."

I absently finger a lock under the lip of the window. "Did you have a nice time?"

Sarina's smirk was full of lustful intentions, "Nice, doesn't even begin to describe it."

My eyebrows raise, "Enjoyable?"

Her laugh is throaty, "Nope, fucking fantastic."

I snort, "Definitely an emphasis on the fucking."

Sarina raises her hand at me, tilting her head toward my door. "What is all that noise? The family is still descending? Isn't the little bundle of joy already here?"

I nod and look past her, "Time works differently on that planet."

"What?"

I give her a cat eating a mouse sibling grin, "Your body got a weeks vacation, but you only missed a few hours here."

Sarina darts to the window and bats at the latch. Since I locked it, it doesn't open.

"You are going to have to find some other way to avoid what you have done. Meanwhile, Aoife is here and wants to see you." I gesture to my room door.

She glares at me, "Are you sure, you came to pick me up over eight hours ago."

I nod, "It was only eight minutes here. Do you have any sand in your hair?"

Sarina reaches her right hand to her necklace and runs her left hand through her hair. She went to my mirror behind the door and stretched it full length. She runs her left hand over her clothes changing them into a trendy tunic with well fitted dark jeans. "I'm going to get you back for this, Muriel! Where are they?"

"You tortured me as a little girl. We aren't even close to even." I laugh, "They are in Yacob's room."

Chapter 13

Ye Olde Birthing Chamber

Aoife in her crinkling crinoline dress was across the room hugging and exchanging air kisses with Sarina as she walked in. Aoife put an arm around Sarina and started motioning her to walk with her. "Morgan is about to show us the birth room your mother designed for her." She paused for dramatic effect and narrowed her eyes at me. She pulls Sarina conspiratorially close, "I'm sure Yacob and Morgan would appreciate your help in the delivery room."

I try not to guffaw. The last place anyone wants Sarina is in an emergency, especially a medical situation. I watch Sarina blanch; I look away and meet Morgan's terrified eyes.

Sarina pauses in the motion. She swallows, "Um, Lady Aoife, I'm not great at medical situations. I tend to freeze and get in the way."

Aoife face changes to a look of compassionate disbelief. "Really?"

Sarina flashed Morgan an apologetic look. Morgan looked away to hide her smile of relief. I know Morgan has witnessed, on one or two occasions, Sarina's voyeur fascination with others' pain.

Aiofe straightens and nods sagely as she pats Sarina's shoulder. "It takes a strong person to admit when they are not up for something."

Sarina looks away but catches my eye with a smirk.

Aoife gestures at me with her hand. "Morgan, you don't need the convict either!"

Morgan gives me an apologetic look. "Mother!"

My brother yells out at the same moment. "Aoife!" His baritone rocking the room. I puzzle over when he acquired that skill.

I realize this is about to digress into something unpleasant. I shrug, and address Aiofe as if no one else in the room. "Do you really want to know what I was arrested for?"

Yacob fumes, "You don't have to."

I nod, "I know."

Aoife sneers, "Just violation of treaty 365 with the Middle Eastern Consortium. Your recklessness caused the pock market breakout. I still can't believe you are alive!"

The pock market breakout was a genetically engineered virus that affected all people who worked the stock market or finances. Thousands of people in American financial sectors died from it. It had been engineered by the clerics of the Middle East in retaliation for a mind worm I had set loose in their culture.

"Reckless, perhaps?" I look off in the distance recounting my memories. "When I was in college I took a class in Women's Studies. It talked about things not discussed in the news. One thing that struck me in all the studies of unequal

110

cultures, the idea that women are only good for sexual and reproductive uses, was repulsive. Saying that the only ways to decently dress a woman is in completely veiled and covered clothing doesn't really show respect, it shows an overly sexual view of women. This baffled me; plus there was this whole idea how they themselves were in charge of raising the kids, and this idea was still being passed on to each subsequent generation. I was young and impulsive. I sent a mind worm to discourage the reinforcing of those ideas in parenting. It was undetected for five years."

Aoife's snarl dissolved to a look of shock, and wonder filled her face. "Five years, that is impressive."

I shrugged, "Truthfully, I'd forgotten about it. The new cleric of Al-Queda found the worm in his harem. It had changed. It had changed into a human rights worm."

Aoife frowned, "I know some people in Spec Ops who might want to recruit you."

I found this change in her feelings toward me amusing, "Yeah, right!"

Morgan cleared her throat. "Mum, Muriel is still doing community service for the ASC!"

"American Science Collective?" Aoife snorted. "A bunch of amateurs! Their organization has only been around for 234 years!" She paused, "You are not plugged in right now, are you?" She looked about the room as if being watched.

I shrug and watch the way her dress moved with her breathing. "I am under Mom and Dad's custody."

Sarina draped her arm around my shoulders and purred. "Sure, good excuse for still living at home."

I fought the urge to ask Sarina about her own home being ripped apart by drug factions.

Aiofe looks thoughtfully in the distance. "Your mother's precautions make more sense now. You are not allowed to be wired in the house. Your family is as ancient as mine, with secrets The Collective doesn't need to know about."

I think about some of the projects of my parents, my brother and even some of my hobbies. Things that could open a bunch of demands and requests from the American Collective. I find myself suddenly wondering about Morgan's family. "No, I'm not currently wired. Mother would not be happy."

Aiofe gives a forced smile, "She is such a gentle woman, but when you guys make statements like that, you make her sound ominous." She makes a show of examining her nails then looking at me with a pointed gaze.

My brother and I laugh, as I gasp out, "You don't want to know."

Aoife gives me a frown and looks at one of Morgan and Yacob's bookcases.

Morgan clears her throat; she gestures toward her mother "Come see the suite." She winks at me and gives me a nod.

We all follow her to a circular room with windows all the way around. We all line up around the room looking in. It had medical equipment, a bed with pristine linen, and vibrant art. The air inside looked still. Every surface gleamed; I could not see a speck of dust anywhere. It gave me the chills to stare at something so sterile and devoid of life. I know it is necessary for protecting a newborn; I still find it unsettling.

Aoife's gaze was critical, trying to find a fault, or something else that was needed.

Morgan traced a circle on the window. Her voice was bored as she said, "No one is allowed inside till the event."

"Hello, where is everyone?" I hear my mother's voice call out from the front room.

Aoife was the first to the room and I could hear her voice take on the tones of someone forcing themselves to sound pleasant, "Hello again Maxima, we were just admiring the birth room you designed. Why is there parallel universe radar in there?"

My mother shrugs, "Sometimes, newborn wizards get a little anxious and over shoot their consciousness outside of their bodies to another dimension. It's just easier to tag them beforehand. Then the hunt becomes easier than aura tracing."

Aiofe looks confused, "I never seen that happen."

Mom comes over next to me, "Unfortunately, it is a common occurrence in our family." She nudges me, "It took me two months to find Muriel!"

Aoife's eyebrow rises.

Yacob starts to laugh, "Where were you, little sis?"

I shrugged; I couldn't believe Mom was bringing this up.

Mom gives me a wink, "A bouncy castle dimension."

Morgan's jaw dropped, "What? That is harsh for a newborn. Isn't it?"

My mother was joking, but I decided to play along. "It was just my consciousness. Nothing physical."

Sarina sighs, "This explains why your brain and priorities are such a mess!"

I break my straight face and chuckle, "Mom is joking. It was a Shakespeare dimension. The plays were being acted out all the time in different contexts."

Yacob laughs and points at me, "That explains why your first verbal word was thou!"

My mother hugs me as I say with a smirk, "Thou are correct."

Everyone chuckles and Aoife gives me a smirk. "Acted out in all the contexts, around you? The bard's words? How are you sure you have made it back to the right dimension?"

"True, who really knows?" I shrug, "At this point what does it matter anyway?"

My mother suddenly puts a hand on me, "There is a phone call for you." Her gatekeeper relationship with the house does this to her.

I nod and look at Morgan, "I'll be there. Great room you and Mom put together." I say to reassure Morgan I would be there for the birth. As I walk out of the room to get the phone, I hear my sister call out to our mother.

Sarina's voice is full of excitement, "Hey Mom, can I stay here while we are waiting for the big day?"

I have closed the door. Walking on to the landing, I hear my Mom 's thoughts reach out to mine and ask, "She has a mess she is avoiding?"

I laugh, "Oh yeah!" I send back to her. I'm scurrying down the stairs.

Her mind is amused and quiet with an undertone of trepidation, "Will you tell me later?"

I send her a nonchalant, "Sure, I am almost to the phone."

Mom's voice in my head is soft and kind of excited about having all of her children under one roof. " OK, I'm going to say yes!"

I send her a chuckle and an image of me smiling, "I know."

I shake my head a second to release the connection with Mom. The vibrant string from years of use deflates, and I pick up the bulky headset from the black rotary phone in the alcove by the bottom of the stairs. "Hello." I say pleasantly.

The voice is tentative and sounds like a young man. "Agent Anahat?"

I scratch my head, confused for a moment, "I'm not really an agent, but this is Muriel Anahat. Who is this?"

"I'm Private Redshirt. Ms. Anahat, there's an emergency meeting at headquarters in twenty minutes. Your attendance is required." His voice is that of one reading a script.

I find myself frowning at the cherubs decorating the rim of the alcove. This was highly irregular. I'm not required for anything. "What happened to Gladus? It's my day off. Are you sure you need me to come in?"

His voice is stern with no explanation, "It is an emergency Anahat. Head in immediately!"

I sigh, "Sure."

He hangs up.

I stare at the phone before I set it back on the cradle.

Chapter 14

Why are Briefings Never Brief

"What could they possibly need me for? Some emergency recruitment of a vampire?" I think. I try to quash my hope that it will make me too busy for tonight's festivities. I send a thought tendril toward my mother, "I have to go out to headquarters."

While I had been standing there, my Uncle Mordecai had walked over. He reaches out and gives me a hug as I turn from the alcove. He starts talking. I hear none of it as I nod like I'm listening.

Mom's reply is indignant in my head, "It's your day off, and you have an important engagement tonight!"

I send her a reassuring thought, "I'll see you soon." I rub my forehead to clear the connection and look at my Uncle and speak to him, "This is quite diverting, but I have to go to work, real quick."

"Work? You have a job, child? Oh yeah, I think I remember Maxima mentioning you work for The Collective now. Why ever did you decide to do that for?" He is frowning.

I'm trying not to laugh; he worked for The Collective for decades. I sigh at this old game. Deadpan, I say, "Community Service."

He smirks and uses air quotes, hilarious on an old, balding, pouched man, "Oh, I remember the international incident you created." He ruffles my hair.

Normally his quick affection pleases me, but I frown. Ten thousand dead was not an incident to me. It was a catastrophe. I think I begged them to destroy me at one point. I start heading to the door.

"Wait!" Aunt Shirley's gravelly voice calls out as she frowns. "You are not going out dressed like that?"

I look down at my tan cargo pants and Atlas Mugged t-shirt, "Oh yeah, I need my wallet, phone and keys."

She clears her throat indignant, "You said you were going to work. What about makeup, hair and a dressier shirt?"

I had sent out a telepathic string to transport those items to me since dialyosefosing wasn't allowed in the house. I laughed as I raised my hand to intercept my phone, wallet, and keys flying through the air. "It's my day off, Aunt Shirley, maybe I'll scare them enough to where they won't ask me in again when I'm not on duty." I'm struck again by how odd this request is.

Just before I head out the door, I hear my mother calling down the stairs. "Dinner will be at 5 o'clock, I'm making a brisket! You need to catch the MAX for the Gorge Dance at 7:30."

I nod and head out the door. The robotic arm grabs me in the breezeway. A mechanical voice says, "Stand still for video installation." I stare at its copper mechanisms a second. I am not in the mood. I scratch my head. "Belay that, weekend stance!"

The arm retracts and I head out of the front door. I take a breath of free air, unwired. The lawn gnome stands in front of me tapping his foot and frowning. He is puffing on a pipe that is leaking bubbles. "Muriel, be wary, there are trolls about!"

I nod, "Sure, Gnasher, I can't chat right now." He begins every exchange with this statement. I usually enjoy the exchange, but right now I need to go.

He harrumphs and moves out of my way.

I head to the right side of the house where there is a wood structure that looks like a firewood shed. It was our safe, secluded place for dialyosefosing. I stare at the wood grain of the board in front of me. It is actually a map of the supernatural power rivers that coursed through the Portland area. With my mind's eye, I can picture the currents around me. I try not to slip into energy sight, that can be confusing.

I'm an amplifying conduit and the power molecules that run through me multiply in force. So I see all that when I go into power sight. I won't see the rivers I will see a whirlpool of energy channeling through my heart and blood vessels. That wall of energy is blinding.

So I picture this map in my mind and focus on latching onto the river that runs toward Pioneer Square. I feel myself dissolve. I hold my matter together and blink. As I let go of the river I feel myself solidify and I slam into a wall, causing myself to see stars. I fall to the linoleum floor as I groan and rub my head. It's a poorly lit hallway which truthfully helps with what I just did to my head. This hallway is behind the customer service desk of the Trimet office.

I take a breath, push myself off the floor and lean against the wall. I trail my fingers down the wall as I look for the hallway hidden in plain sight by illusions and paint. My fingers catch on the corner and I head into the hidden parallel hallway. I walk until I almost run into a steel fuse box.

I wince, I hate this part. All Heska have some steel sensitivity, but I have a full blown allergy. Rumors explain that there is too much fey blood in my family line. It made for powerful ancient magic but was a down right disability in the modern world.

I'm pretty sure this was one of the reasons why Aoife approved of Morgan's marriage to Yacob though our religions are so different. She knew she could still relate to the grand kids.

I took part of my shirt and opened the panel and winced as a part of my skin touched the metal. A red mark appeared immediately, while a sensation of nausea traveled through me. I started flipping the plastic switches to the combination that caused the panel to slide away, and reveal a plastic slide. It was the only way for me to get into the 4-foot steel walls encasing headquarters. Steel blocks the flow of magic, going in or out.

I climb into the slide. I dry heave a few times when my hand makes full contact with the steel. I take a breath and let go. As I go deeper into the steel structure, pressure builds in my brain and my stomach turns into a churning mess. I land with a headache and a bleeding nose. I taste metal and someone hands me a bucket, I have no time to look as I lose the contents of my stomach. Hands pull me from the landing pad and set me in a chair. My eyes go blurry from the pain suddenly coursing through me I am mumbling thanks to the blob I can't make out, helping me.

There is a buffer layer of ten feet of wood inside Headquarters walls between the office space and the steel shield. The blob pries open my hands and places some raw elm wood in them. I gasp in relief and take in its scent cutting through the metallic smells still permeating everything. The pressure of the steel encasing the room is stifling. I am able to relax as my heartbeat slows down and my eyes clear. The nausea goes to a slight sickening, and the headache becomes a lite pressure.

I take in the blob. The charming smile of Thomas looks at me with amusement, "Welcome, to the party, Muriel!"

I wince.

He laughs, "This explains why your desk is empty."

I give him a puzzled look, "I have a desk? Why would I need a desk?"

A slim built man with a short cut on sides and greying hair long on top walks by. "You will be an agent someday, girl!" He is the head of this division, Mr. Jack Oppenheimer.

I fight the urge to frown, "Not if I can help it." I think to myself. I laugh out loud and say, "Yeah right, my mother would have a fit!"

Mr. Oppenheimer winks at me, "Cassandra has confirmed it."

I shrug, "Are you sure it is this universe, Jack?"

He snorts and gestures toward the briefing room, "Let's go start the meeting! Someone's mother called and wants them home in time for dinner and the Gorge Dance!"

I feel myself blush. I slap my face; I can't believe my mother did that. It is so fun being an adult under the custody of one's parents. "How embarrassing!" I sigh.

Thomas chuckles, "The Society Ball. Muriel, do you need an escort?"

Both men were grinning like Jack'O lanterns. I rub my head so I don't have to look at them as I gasp out, "It's a singles dance."

Thomas starts to laugh uncontrollably. First time I've ever seen him do something without any self-censure.

Jack puts the folder in his hand in front of his mouth. I can see the laugh lines around his eyes.

I look at the floor and shake my head. I'm mortified, but want to laugh, also. I don't know how I manage this, but I keep my voice steady and level, "I don't understand why you guys called me in." I look back at them and raise both hands in surrender, "The social functions are part of my sentence, too."

Thomas stares at his right hand, collecting himself. I watch his normal mask take back over. "I have a crucial black ops coming up and I requested to have your blood specifically."

I stare at him blankly. This is so wrong; he knowing what my blood can do is a problem. I want him to say it out loud. Especially with our superior here.

He looks at Jack. Then back at me and shrugs, "I obtain different abilities with each person's blood. I know what I can do with yours!"

All I can think is, "I bet." I stare at Jack. This troubles me, I could totally see The Collective start to map out family abilities using blood and a vampire. I shudder at the thought that big brother is so here. I address Jack, "The mucky mucks? Are they OK with this?" I doubt I'm hiding my disgust or alarm.

Jack smiles condescendingly, "Yes, come on you two." He heads toward the briefing room.

The briefing room was filled with an array of chairs in a semi-circle, around a dry erase board at the center of the bowl shaped room. Jack made his way down to the center of the room and stood at the dry erase board. The chemical smell filled the room as he uncapped a red marker with a snapping sound and started staring at the board.

I found a seat to the side as I watched Jack contemplate the board. Thomas sat next to me. I wasn't sure how I felt about this caretaker role he was assuming but it wasn't annoying me at the moment. I lean in conspiratorially towards him and whisper. "So do you get as ill in here as I do when you are only on my blood?"

His smile is friendly, and full of compassion. Weird to see on a vampire. He says, "Completely."

Jack clears his throat and the whole room stops making rustling and whispering noises. He stands to the side of the board. Two words written in large letters three inches high read, "Circe Syndrome."

There are few witches in the room. They begin to chuckle and some men let out a low whispered convicted word of, "Damn!"

The chairs have those flip over desks to the side like you'd find in some college classrooms. I flip mine over and lean my elbow on it to prop up my head. I am still trying to feel normal, I just feel completely spent, and have a hard time focusing.

Jack underlines the word Circe, his voice is clear and booming, "We have a Circe situation in town!"

Thomas frowns as I tap my cheek. Thinking about this development, I wonder how often this happens.

Jack's voice is resigned as he looks about the crowd, he must see confused faces because he starts to explain further. "For those of you not up on your Greek Mythology, a Circe is a woman who has just been granted a magical ability, but due to the trauma activating it, she is involuntarily transforming people. Most likely unaware she is doing it.'

Out of habit my brain reviews this in more detail. Who grants a family a magical ability is an unknown, some quirk of the universe. Great trauma is usually the reason and in the case of a Circe it is usually in genuine men. Their hearts are broken over and over. Their frustration and anger break the mortal barriers and release their Chi to access power manipulation. They are named after the witch from the story of the Odyssey, who transformed men into pigs.

"We need to identify this person. We need to contain her and help her through transition!"

Madame Kay, a woman with glowing ebony skin and hundreds of braids, raises a bejeweled hand.

Jack nods toward her.

"Are they finding pigs all over town?" Her Louisiana accent punctuating the vowels as she speaks.

Jack smirks and pulls down a map. "As you know not all Circe's make pigs. We have been finding dogs. The main cluster of transformed dogs has been found in the area of 3rd and Yamhill."

A man with a muscular build and copper eyes raises his hand.

Jack looks at him, "You have a question, Anthony?"

He nods "How do you know the dogs are transformed humans?"

Jack smiles, "They try to order lattes at Starbucks."

The witches titter, and I frown, trying to figure out if he is joking.

Anthony sighs, "Really?"

Jack nods, "Yeah, they go into the Starbucks and go on their hind legs and make random soft dog noises. Then seem shocked no one understands them."

Madame Kay blurts out, "Don't forget to warn all these young ones here to just identify, if the Circe is discovered. There will need to be a Circe extraction team. No one should try to contain a Circe by themselves, you all."

"Precisely, thank you for the reminder Madame Kay. Please do not attempt to subdue a Circe on your own."

Anthony flicks his blond hair from his eyes, "What if you're a Heska?"

I roll my eyes at his audacity, as the witches hiss.

Jack shakes his head and gives him a no nonsense look. "Call for back up."

I remember Anthony from school, his whole family exuded arrogance. Sarina had been engaged to his brother. I was hoping that Jack's statement would keep him from saying something stupid like...

"I mean any Heska should be able to handle a fledgling witch," Anthony says with a sigh.

Jack's forehead creases as the room fills with mumbling. An undercurrent of "they think they are better than us fills the room."

I lean into Thomas, "You would think the queasiness would curb his obnoxiousness."

Thomas gives me an encouraging smile and whispers back, "He's an Elemental mage, the steel doesn't make him sick."

I was trying to not let the color drain from my face. This was becoming very big brother; The Collective knew Anthony's family magic. This was so dangerous. When someone knew your dominant ability, they could contain and destroy you. In our society, we never let anyone know our dominant ability.

Jack sighed and looked at Anthony, "Let's talk after the meeting in my office. Any other questions?"

Nobody said anything, "OK, you're all excused!" He walks over to me, "After you help Thomas, with his matter, you can go back to your day. Good luck tonight." He nodded at Anthony who stood to follow him.

As he headed toward the office, Madame Kay approached me. She looked at me appraisingly, "I just wanted to let you all know that I have a son around your age."

This caught me off guard and I let out a nervous chuckle, "Oh, you do now?"

Thomas gives me a huge grin and a wink. He crosses his arms.

I look back at Madame Kay, and regain my manners. "I don't believe we have been introduced I'm..." I reach out my hand to shake hers.

She gives me an amused smile, "Shush child, I know who you are. Those blue bloods have no idea what a treasure you all are, for sure."

I feel myself blush, "I'm flattered, surely. But what do you really know of me except my spotty reputation?"

Madame Kay cocked her head; the braids swayed knocking beads together, creating clicking sounds. "Well, for one thing, you don't magic yourself into looking like a super-model like the rest of your kind."

Thomas laughs and messes my hair like a sibling, "You like the bump on her snub nose that shows it has been broken once or twice."

I give him a bemused smile, flattered that they noticed, "Only once, I was a rambunctious child. I wanted to climb everything."

"Most of your kind would make that disappear." Madame Kay's smile was generous.

Self-conscious; I am not use to flattery. I look at my fingers and fidget with them, "Maybe I'm just not that powerful?" I look back up her under guarded lowered lids.

Madam's K laugh was warm and reassuring, "I'm not blind y'all. So guarded, you wiz..." she pauses and shakes her head to correct herself. I watch those braids and listen to the clinking beads and a whisper of spells echo off them. "I mean Heska must have horrid personnel lives."

I find this woman charming. My mind goes over what I know about her. Madame Kay was a Voodoo queen descendent of Marie Laveau. She lived in New Orleans till Katrina drove her out. I wonder if the gift of power sight runs through her family. The statement of not being blind hinted that she could see the power vortex that normally surrounds me. I find myself wondering why she remained in Portland since the rebuilding of New Orleans was underway. I always thought voodoo was a location, ancestor remains particular. I look at Thomas; I think about his advances that get harder to resist the more time we spend together. I think a relationship with a vampire would be horrible. "Sometimes we do." I think about my sister's past relationships, some of Yacob's and then my own with a creature from another world. "Usually, actually."

Thomas shifts and surprises me; he actually sends a mental thought to me. "I want to be part of your life, won't you let me in?" Out loud he says, "Doesn't everyone."

Madame Kay uses a critical eye looking over Thomas. I find myself wondering about some vague memory of a history of vampires and the voodoo religion. It tickles the back of my brain but I can't access it. I figure it is some horror movie reference.

I watch Thomas straighten under her scrutiny. He bows, "This is quite a diverting conversation Madame." He nods toward me, "I need to debrief Muriel then help her out."

Madame Kay nods with a thoughtful expression and walks away.

Thomas offers me his arm in an old world way. I find it charming and take it. He leads me to a vacant desk. It has an institutional feel. He pulls out the chair. "Have a seat."

I let go and plop down on the very firm chair. A wave of nausea flows through me and then a burning sensation. I wince and jerk up as the taste of metal flows through my mouth. "Steel!"

He catches me and looks confused. I watch his features go from confusion, to anger, then disgust. He gives me a pained expression, "Sorry, no one uses your desk so the chair no one ever uses ended up here." He grabs a wooden chair. I sit in it as he seats himself in the metal chair. He leans in and opens the top drawer, where he pulls out a blood kit and seven 10 ml vials.

Circe Syndrome

I am confused about a couple points, so I frown. Why do I have a desk at headquarters, I never come there, this I keep to myself. The other query I voice, "I thought you only need enough for three days? Does this count as my bi-weekly donation?"

He wraps a tourniquet around my arm, "You never know what will happen on a black op. No, you are still scheduled for your bi-weekly Tuesday to add to the mix."

The mix is the concoction of all the Heska members of The Collective's blood that is kept in storage to feed to the vampires of the Collective. What they normally feed on is mixed to prevent what Thomas has just done with me and possibly Anthony. He is using and mapping out a specific person's abilities like donning clothing with our blood. I have put on a mask of indifference. I don't want him to know how alarmed I am about this. I look across the rows of desks, and watch the people as they look busy, and try not to look in our direction. I decide to distract myself and ask him a question. "How is Mr. Grout?"

Thomas is tapping my arm and positioning a needle. "Who? Oh Viper. He will make a good soldier." He pokes me and starts filling a vile. "Good work with that one. I watched him try not to cry when the sun first hit him in the morning and he didn't dissolve." He changes the vials in quick succession using vampiric speed. "He'll never go back."

He is half way through his vials when the needle clogs. He sighs and shakes the one's he has harvested from me. He pulls out the drawer again and finds an agitator and sets them in it.

He pulls another needle and pokes me again. No blood comes out. He frowns. I sigh and take the needle and put it in my other arm and fill the rest of the syringes, as I watch him stunned, trying not to salivate. I am trying to figure out my culpability in this whole crime. All these witnesses and permission. I drop the vials with the others. They make a light clinking sound, which makes him wince.

He grabs a bandage. I move my hand down to heal the spots instead, and then freeze. I was reaching to the aether, there is none. The steel has sealed me from it. I feel a sense of claustrophobia. There is just my life force to use I am not going to touch that right now.

He sets some orange juice in front of me.

I give him a smirk, "You didn't take that much."

He cocks his head and shrugs, "I know, but you look peaked, maybe it will help with the steel illness."

The clean smell of orange was a welcome smell cutting through the metal tang still circling in my mouth. I want to drink it. The problem is I don't trust Thomas. Especially with what just went down. I speculate on how I could check this liquid for foreign elements like drugs or spells, but that would reveal that I could still do magic cut off from the aether. I don't want to reveal that. I am already uncomfortable with what Thomas has found out. Luckily, I'm very different from the rest of my family. I know orange juice can hide all manner of things so I pretend to retch, "No, I don't think it is a good idea."

He shrugs and drinks it.

I fight the urge to shudder; I can't get past the undead consuming human food.

He stands and gestures to me with a nurturing gaze, "Come on, let's get you back to your day." He starts to escort me to the exit.

We are stopped by a young man. He has freckles and bright red hair. "Um, Miss Anahat?"

I look at Thomas curiously, who shrugs then look back at the young man, "Guilty. That's me."

He reaches out his hand for an awkward shake. "Hi, I'm Private Redshirt. The new communication officer for headquarters. We talked on the phone earlier." He emphasizes the word phone.

I nod, "Yes, hi, nice to meet you." I shake his hand and pull back.

Color drains from his face as if he is embarrassed to ask the question he wants to ask, "Why can't I just mentally call you like everyone else?"

I shrug, "I don't like being wired twenty-four hours a day. When I'm home and off duty I avoid being that accessible."

Redshirt frowns, "You are property of the Collective. You should be accessible at all times."

I pause. Technically, this was true, them sparing my life and putting me in this community service was my sentence. No one had been this blunt before. I feel Thomas start to fume next to me, that this fledgling would talk to me this way. I squeeze Thomas' arm reassuringly, to let him know I got this. "I believe I own me. My understanding is this is a free country, Private, what we are all trying to preserve."

"Yes, technically, but using the phone is so last century! Quite inconvenient!"

"I'm a recruiter, Private; I shouldn't be called for emergencies." Internally I think I don't give a damn about what Cassandra says. I cock my head, "I am actually in the custody of my parents, Private, and my mother has rules about what happens in her house. There is no mind magic through her protection barriers."

He frowns and puts his hands up in frustration, "Why?"

I sigh, look about the room and watch people take us in. I finally just lean in and whisper, "Your family is new to the world of the supernatural, isn't it?"

He gives me an indignant look, "I'll have you know magic in my family can be traced back one hundred years!"

I am fighting the urge to roll my eyes; I'm not going to bring up my family's 3000-year history steeped in it.   I am not trying to brag; I'm just trying to get him to understand

129

that making things convenient for him is not worth the danger it would put my family in. I lean in again, "Your family is lucky to never have been attacked by malignant mental magic in its hundred years."

Color drains from his face as he is trying to find a retort, I'm not following his rules of engagement. He had expected something else.

Thomas steps between us. "Fred, sorry to interrupt this fascinating conversation, but this little lady has other plans today. I'm escorting her out."

The Private stares at him blankly, "What she just hinted at, is real? How old is her family?"

I sigh; I don't think I hinted, I think I just stated a threat that existed. I nod at Fred, "Nice to meet you, Fred. I hope this does not become a normal occurrence."

Thomas gives me a teasing smile as we walk away, "My darling, you're so popular."

I laugh, "Not really, you are interested in my blood, Madame Kay wants her family to evolve and the Private thinks I'm a Luddite. He finds that obnoxious and anti-science."

Thomas's raises his eyebrows, "Anti-science, that is a big insult! If he only knew you beyond this one moment."

I laugh, "Yeah right! Why learn the patterns of electron rings if I'm not going to use it anyways?"

He pauses and shakes his head, "You're such a nerd. Yeah, the blood is why we pulled you in for this. Sorry for the inconvenience."

I nod, "Maybe, Jack and you can work out some other system instead of dragging me to puking central."

"I also do enjoy your conversation, Miss Muriel." He says this quietly.

This sparks my pleasure center in my mind. I feel endorphins course through me, then I feel chills. I focus on keeping my voice even, "Your attention is flattering, Thomas."

He gives me a bemused smile and a slight shake of his head, "Oh, a compliment, how marvelous."

We had approached a door that was metal and two yards wide. It was surrounded by a curtain of spell webs. Spell webs were made with woven rope and imbibed with ley lines woven into them. These webs could cause spells flying through the air to merge and dissolve into them. Thomas held back a curtain for me and then we both stepped through. There were people in uniforms who held up fingerprint readers to check our clearance, and determine if we are OK to leave the premises. Five other individuals joined us in the curtained area. Alarms sounded out. As we stood there, two uniformed people pulled steel screens in back of the webs. This created triangular space of metal with the door wall. The hair on my arms stood on end as electricity filled the air and the door's handle twisted open, revealing a four-foot-thick steel tunnel.

When this process had started, I had taken and held a breath. I had to breathe again. I whimper a little when the metal stained air enters my lungs, and fills my perception. My lungs burned and it felt like shards of metal were jamming into my pores. All I can smell now is cold steel. I feel Thomas gently but firmly push me toward the open door. I stagger. Every part of my body is screaming at me to stop. I'm forcing myself forward.

His voice is insistent, "You can do this Muriel, right foot, good, left foot, good, right foot."

The world dissolved into Thomas' voice and his commands; thinking about anything else brought pain and a metal taste in my mouth. I know this tunnel is only four feet in depth, but it feels like miles, and these moments feel like hours. I shuffle forward, exerting great will and feel myself sweat.

When we reached the end, Thomas was boosting me forward. Every limb had become sluggish and unresponsive. When we exited the tunnel energy returned, and I felt the hum and cords of aether strike through me. I stood straight and disengaged myself from Thomas. He gives me a pained expression. I was mumbling thanks as I started to take in the surroundings.

It was a room filled with tranquil music and the scent of olive oil. There was a massage table. The other people we had travelled through the tunnel with took turns queuing up to the light switch. They would flip the switch and an attendant dressed as a masseuse would come in and escort the individual out. A couple people just teleported.

I swayed a little in the currents of the aether, enjoying their sensation running through me. Thomas reached out, alarmed, to steady me. I gently push him away. A fast frown passed across his face. Even though I know I shouldn't, I reach out to read his mind to understand why he frowned. I am blocked, I pause. This was unexpected.

He laughs and gives me a mock jaw drop as if shocked, "You just tried to read my mind!"

I give him a smirk, "You noticed."

His chuckle takes an edge, "Yes, nothing much slips by me these days."

I look away from him a bit embarrassed over what I just did, "Do you have any signal ideas for the future?" Trying to take the conversation back to the when he needs blood conversation.

"Such as you changing the subject?" He leans against the wall by the switch.

I shrug, "I believe that would be confusing, we do that a great deal."

He puts his hand over his mouth and shakes his head. His look just says, come on?

I sigh. He wants an explanation, and will take no distraction, "I was curious as to why you frowned when I pulled away."

He sighs back, "Gee, Muriel, were you raised with a vow of silence? You could have just asked."

I look at my feet as I feel the color come to my cheeks, "But, that is so direct."

"I was disappointed you pulled away so quickly." He is non plussed and there is no inflection when he speaks.

I roll my eyes, "Yeah, right, it's none of my business anyway. Please forgive me!"

He shakes his head as if trying to figure out something, "No indignation, you own up to what you do. You just apologized. Why can't we have a romantic relationship? Please explain this to me."

I run my hands through my hair, trying to process what he is saying, "You and your flattery! You just want an unlimited supply of my blood. It seems you have already worked that out with Jack and the council. You don't have to keep playing the I'm attractive gambit!"

A pained expression flows across his face, "You look timid, but you are heartless with your insults."

I snort and cock my head, "Let me know when you work on that signal." I make to walk to the door. It opens unexpectedly.

A tall, red haired, wire thin women dressed as a masseuse walks in. She smiles at me like a cat staring at cream. "Would you like a massage?" She clasps my arm, as she says, "Something to relax you." I feel this sponging feeling as her touch starts siphoning magic off me. I note her pointed ears and teeth. The ruthless glint in her eye. She was a Fairy.

Fairies loved harvesting magic off Heska. We were like filtered straws in which to drink in the refined wild energy of the aether for them. My particular relationship with the aether made me look like a chocolate malt with whipped cream to her.

I make slight calm moves and remove her hand gently. As I clear my mind of the adrenaline panic that had moved in when I realized what she was, I said, "Not today, for me, but this gentleman would love one." I gesture to Thomas.

He understands the game well and gives the masseuse a toothy smile revealing his canines extended. Vampire energy is like a gnat caught in their ear to them, she backed up forcefully.

Then she laughed, "Sir's muscles would be too stiff to loosen."

His look becomes apologetic, "It would be heavenly for me, but I'm sure you would rather jam bamboo under your fingernails." He looks at me and touches my arm where her hand had been. As I am processing this gesture he says, "Besides, Muriel, I'm going to make sure you make it home safe. There is a Circe on the loose after all."

The Fairy looks me over and hands me a card, I still see the look of a child staring at a decadent dessert on her face. "If you ever decide you need a massage, keep me in mind."

"Certainly," I actually have a masseur who is fey that I see regularly. Some of us need to be careful; these relationships become addictive and abusive quickly. The masseur I see controls his hunger. I'm not so sure about this woman. "Certainly, Lady Ambra."

As Thomas followed Lady Ambra, I stared daggers at the back of his neck. I was slightly annoyed. When we're clear of the spa, I address him. "I don't need an escort home."

He gives me an amused glance. "It's not up to you. I have orders."

I take a breath and try to clear my head of negative thoughts. Resigned, I say, "Fine, walking and streetcar; OK, with you? Or would you prefer we dislyosefos?"

Circe Syndrome

We are under an awning looking out at the street. He holds a hand out. I see the sprinkles dot his hand. "I don't think I can keep up with you in the Aether."

I nod, "Walking and streetcar it is then." As I walk out to the uncovered sidewalk, I feel the rhythm of the misting rain. It cleans the air I'm inhaling, and the expansive air helps spread out the pheromones Thomas is pumping out. Even though I find myself wondering what it would be like to be embraced by him. I shake my head to clear it.

We walk in silence for a few minutes. We start to head west.

He cocks his head at me. "Would you like an escort to the dance tonight?"

I spell a dollar with a charm for good luck and hand it to a stoned transient on the corner. Paper thin young man with an aurora of pain coating him. I look at Thomas. "Are you offering your services?"

I almost swoon as his hormone saturated air increases, and I find myself wanting to touch him. His voice is earnest, "Yes, I would love to escort you." He takes my hand.

I can't believe how amazing this feels. I try to hide my attraction. I only let my polite smile drape my features. "It's not that kind of dance."

He frowns, "I have to be a wizard to attend?"

I squeeze his hand reassuringly, "That and no one comes with a date. It's a singles dance. Everyone comes alone."

His eyes widen in surprise and he cups my hand in both of his a second and stares in my eyes, "Oh?"

As we walk we swing our hands and I say with a shrug, "Yes, it is a singles mixer for lonely wizards disguised as a debutante ball."

He stops and looks at me and strokes my hand with his thumb, "But, you're not lonely Muriel? Are you?"

As I think, "Yep." I look past him, refusing to answer that question, or let him see how completely lonely I feel, I say, "It is my mother's demand of me. I'm under my parent's custody and part of their stipulations for me staying with them is attending these functions."

He rolls his eyes and starts walking again. He exaggerates his words. "Oh yes, I forget you're a convicted criminal!"

I laugh at his sarcasm. I swing our hands out, "Yes, are you sure you want to be holding my hand? I could do something unspeakable, like agree to go on a date with you."

His grip tightened and there was a slight growl in his response, "If only you would."

I shake my head and laugh harder, "You are expert at this."

He raises an eyebrow, "At holding hands? You should try my hugs sometimes."

I didn't mention I meant his seductive ways. I shift my focus to the pat, pat sound of the raindrops on my hair. The ends were saturating and starting to curl and tickle my ears. My fingers start to tingle with his cold grip. I wiggle them and send a spark of heat down my arm to wake the fingers. He winces and drops my hand.

I fidget with my hand, "I'm sorry, my hand was falling asleep. I didn't think extremes bothered you."

He pauses, looks like he is startled too. "They don't, usually."

As I look at my fingers and flick them in a fan pattern, I give him a sly glance as I ask, "How long have you been using isolated blood?"

He is frowning down at his hand in thought. In a distracted voice he says, "Four months."

I see this as an opportunity to get more information while he is distracted, "How does it affect you?"

He gives me a guarded glance, "It depends on the donor."

I figure it is a good time to ask the big, loaded question in my mind, "Do you get magical abilities?"

He looks away from me and around us, "Sometimes."

I hug myself, "What does mine do for you?"

He looks thoughtful, "You're versatile. Science, elemental, string concepts and phantasmic magics work through your blood." A gleam comes to his eyes and he rubs his hands together, "I especially enjoy the phantasmic aspects. The steel allergy is horrible though."

I am completely horrified. I am using every piece of self-control I have to act as if this conversation hasn't terrified me. It is dangerous, what he knows about my power. We all dabbled in more than one type of magic so no one knew our dominant or natural alignment. The quickest way to kill me is to cut me off from my natural casting style.

His voice betrays no notice of my panic. Lost in thought he says, "Hey, the phantasmic magic and the steel allergy are confirmation that there are fey in your ancestry, right? That's bizarre given you're Jewish, right?"

I look away and give him an amused smile, "We as a society sometimes like to believe mixed marriage is a new thing. Nothing really new under the sun, right?"

He chuckles, "No! I have been around long enough to know that!"

I want to ask him how old he is. I've tried to before; he always evades the question. So I ask him something else. "Do you talk to others about what you have learned about Heska blood?"

He snorts, "No! Of course not, I would be locked up and they would throw away the key. I know you Muriel, you don't sweat the small stuff. It's fun to talk to someone about it."

My hair has flown across my eyes in a gust of wind. I pull it away and give him a casual gaze appraising his demeanor. "Jack knows all this, right?"

Thomas looks at flyer on a light pole. "Yeah, me being able to reliably perform certain spells during ops has helped our excursions immensely."

"That doesn't happen with the normal compound?" The flyer is about a missing man.

He looks at me with a smirk, "You're digging."

I blush, "I can't probe your mind anymore."

His smile is sheepish, "Maybe you will have to sleep with me to get the information you want."

I shake my head in amusement, "One of these days I'm going to say yes, then what will you do?"

He nudges my shoulder with his and his features take on a predatory smile, "Hurry you to a private spot, before you change your mind."

I sigh, "Yeah, then ignore me the rest of my life. I do know a heart breaker when I see one."

He shakes his head, "You are not right about everything you know."

The rain which was drizzling makes a more intent patter, we quicken our steps.

"Are you Circe hunting tonight?" I ask over my shoulder as I start walking across a street.

He gives me a conspiratorial glance, "I hadn't planned on it. It could be fun, right? Why don't you ditch the dance and partner up with me tonight?"

I give him a wistful look, "Sounds intriguing. No one crosses my mother, though."

He catches up to me, "You mother is a force, then?"

I shake my head; no one gets this, "Fierce."

He makes to adjust cuffs he doesn't have. I'm trying to speculate what century was he from? "Whenever I've met her, she has been charming."

I nod, "Oh she is, fiercely charming! Just don't cross her!"

He uses a pedantic voice, "So, if Mommy says go to the dance..."

I smirk, "Nice!" I comment on his tone, then say, "I go to the dance." I sigh and stare at the trees we are walking under and watch the leaves fall. "Besides, she is right, I've been too isolated. It will be good for me to get outside my comfort zone."

He takes on a thoughtful expression, "I guess I could call you and ask to meet you somewhere."

I blink, realizing he was going back to the meeting for blood issue. I nod, "That could work."

We have arrived on my city block. I give him a nod, "Thank you for the escort. As you can see, I'm fine again."

He stays by my side.

I look at his strong, chiseled chin and grey eyes full of amazing shapes. I blink as a rush of interest runs through me. I remind myself he is pouring out pheromones. "You have my number, right?"

He leans in with a smile looking at my mouth, "Yes, I do."

I dodge, "For setting up the meetings." I reach out my hand for a handshake.

We were at the bottom steps of my parents' house. He gives me a hurt expression.

I take a step on the first step. "Well, I'll talk to you later?"

His eyes roam my body, "Aren't you going to invite me in?"

As I try not to shudder, I nervously speak, "I've got to get ready, and I don't have time to socialize. Perhaps another time?"

He leans close and in my ear whispers, "Please."

"Muriel!" My mother's voice makes me look at the top of the stairs, "Come in and get ready!" Her arms are crossed, and there is this dangerous look that she is giving Thomas.

I give her a relieved smile, "Yes mother, see you later, Thomas!" I scurry up the stairs.

I hear them exchange words behind me.

Thomas voice is cool, "Lady Maxima, so nice to see you."

My mother's voice is too polite and bright, "Hi, Thomas. Enjoying the day?"

Thomas voice is smug, "Always!"

I am through the door and can't hear anymore.

Chapter 15

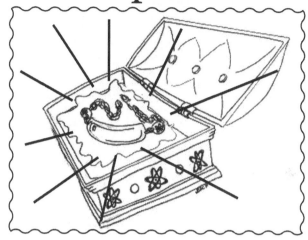

Ready to Wear

    I let the door slam behind me.   A huge moving homunculus of red clay moved close to me.   His great hand reaches out to shake mine.   His voice is a deep baritone with a resonant reassuring tinder.   I smell the slight, spicy, comforting earth smell emitting from him.   "Muriel! What is up?"   He pauses and cocks his head, his features always in a big innocent grin, "Did I use that correctly?"

    He is Clay, Uncle Mordechai's and Aunt Shirley's Golem. His blue literal sapphire eyes twinkle in the light of the room. That feeling you get when you talk to a puppy or a baby fills me.   We have a history; a Golem is traditionally a slave to their owners.   I made Uncle Mordechai aware that Clay had wants and desires of his own.   They make sure now that he is treated like family and has free time.   He has spending money and independence.   One of the things we bond over is music.   He spends all his free time listening to music.

His smile is contagious and I smile back, "Yeah, you used that correctly. I'm required to attend a dance. How about you? What is up with you?" I pull our handshake into a hug.

My mother comes into the house with a chuckle, "That corpse has some nerve."

I pull back from Clay and look at her. "He is charming."

She puts an arm around me and pulls me into a hug. "Time, Muriel, you just need time. You need to spend time with your own species. There is no future with a corpse."

"Yeah, I get it Mom." I think about Gregor.

Clay looks at us both and blinks, "I'm not being required to attend a dance. I am familiar with doing things I do not enjoy, though."

I give him a concerned smile, "You are getting a chance to do things you prefer, too? Right?"

He chuckles and looks at my mother affectionately. "Yes, of course, you and Yacob's intervention on my behalf has stuck. Your Uncle and Aunt are amazing people; we are all family."

I smile, "Good."

My mother ruffles my hair, "Muriel! Quit jabbering with Clay and get ready. Don't forget to cleanse your aura, it is shot through with vampire funk again!"

I sigh and nod and start walking toward the stairs, "Yes, mother. Excuse me, Clay."

He gives me a wave. As I start up the stairs I have to duck to the side. A wave of family that has arrived in my absence descends. We all do quick greetings and I continue to head up. It seems every few steps I have to talk to an uncle, an aunt or a cousin.

When I get to my door, my sister is standing there leaning against it. She gives me a predatory glance and smirk. She is chatting and twirling her hair, talking to a muscular cousin of

142

Morgan's. She nods at me, "Hey sissy, what are you going to do with your hair?"

I laugh, this is the last thing on my mind. "What? No idea, " I shake my head in disgust, "You?"

She caresses the man's bicep as she looks at him and gives me a side long gaze. "I have some ideas."

I just want in my room. Watching her flirt is not something I enjoy. I gesture for them to move out of my way. "You want to help me get ready?"

She pushes the young man back and nods at him to leave. He gives her a wistful smile and me a wink and walks off. Sarina gives me a business-like expression as I open my door. "Like you had any other choice, Muriel?"

I raise my palms as I enter and let her follow and close the door behind us. "I can dream."

Sarina laughs.

A cool breeze catches my attention. I look across the room and the curtains are streaming inside. A strong gust of wind bringing sand and salty seawater spray blows through the room.

Sarina pauses. "Oh my!"

I walk to the windows. I begin to shut them. I puzzle over how they all got open. The room now smells of the ocean, and I pause at the last window to take in more breaths. I want to go back there; I don't want to go dance. Taking some time to lounge on a beach suddenly feels so appealing. I look at the puddles, and sand on the floor. I wonder if there are footprints. But shake my head, accusing myself of finding patterns in chaos. It's just water and sand.

The eddies of wind, swirling sand and water through the room, stop.

I turn around and find Sarina holding my dress, frowning. "It's soaked, Muriel!"

I nod at the obvious statement. "You're right it is!"

Sarina scowls at me, "Aren't you upset?"

I tap my foot in a puddle on the floor and create a small splash, "Should I be?"

She holds the dress in front of herself and points to its condition. "It's ruined!"

I reach out and touch the saturated lace fabric. It wrinkles. I meet her eyes, and give her a grin, "It's not."

She frowns at it and me, "Are you sure?"

Her outrage and disgust spurs me to showmanship. Something I rarely stoop too. I snap my fingers as I focus on all the fibers of the dress and have them all twist themselves, wringing the water to the floor.

Sarina shudders, blinks her eyes and looks away. "Gah, Muriel! What did you just do? That was disturbing to watch! It looks like the dress became a bunch of moving bugs!"

I look away at the puddle on the floor. My voice is just informative, "I just rung out the dress by each fiber, then by weave."

A sound of wonder and understanding comes out of Sarina's mouth, "Oh?" She reaches forward to check the dress, her expression and voice full of surprise, "Seems to work. It feels dry now. What are you going to do with the puddles?"

I smirk and walk into the bathroom and pull a couple towels. I walk back to my room and start mopping up the floor with them. It takes a couple trips. I ring the towels out like I did the dress over the sink.

When I finish, Sarina starts shaking her head at me with a pained expression, "Why did you do that manually?"

I snort and chuckle at the disgust in her voice and the incredulous expression on her face, "I got to keep my girlish figure some way. Besides, how can I relate to other people if all I use is magic?"

Sarina raises an eyebrow, "With you burning body mass performing magic and me also draining you, there is no need for you to do extra to improve your figure."

I sit at the edge of my unmade wet bed, and look at her, "So? You have ideas for my hair?"

Sarina was looking out the windows. Naked rage coated her features. She had just admitted her weaknesses and dependence on me. This is familiar to me; I don't move. When she was a child, she would do cruel things; now it just reminded me of those incidents. She hadn't done anything purposely cruel to me in a while. She turns and looks at me.

I have a mask of indifference; I can't show fear.

Sarina's malice is gone. She unconsciously moves a blonde strand from her face carefully behind her ear. "Yes, I have some thoughts. Seeing Aoife's hair gave me some ideas."

I give her a weary expression, "You are going to make my hair red?"

Sarina laughed, "No! I liked the braided crown with the curled tendrils."

"OK," I set down on a chair by my vanity. It was covered in art supplies, and the middle stretched out as an easel table. There was a picture of a half-painted dragon taped to it.

Sarina made a tsking noise as she picked through the paint tubes, pastels and pencils. "Is there even a comb here?"

I push back Sarina's hands gently. "Wait a second."

I lean down and push on the second set of drawers. The easel flips up revealing a mirror. The top, covered in supplies slipped away and traveled in an elevator motion down the side of the table. The legs stretched and the top was absorbed into the bottom. The second drawer contents become the top. There is a comb, a brush, about five bobby pins and two elastic bands.

Sarina rolls her eyes and holds a necklace in her right hand and passes her left hand over the tabletop. Jeweled pins, a make-up kit, tiaras, curling steels and hair products appear. "That's better, sit up straight Muriel."

I sit up and look in the mirror at Sarina, who has grabbed a brush and is absently stroking my brown hair. "You could use some highlights here and here." With each word and touch they appear, snaking down through the strands of my hair.

I want to protest, but she is right. My hair suddenly looks more lustrous.

A grin lights her features, "For tonight, let's let them sparkle." Suddenly my hair highlights shimmer, like they were made of glitter.

I'm shocked and say, "Sarina!" in amazement.

"Shhhh, I'm thinking." she says softly, as she runs her fingers in my hair, leaving streaks of purple that match the dress color.

I find myself smiling at the edginess it gives to my appearance.

She ties my hair into a high pony tail and fits a tiara around it.

I shift, uncomfortable with the physical weight of it. "I think this is too elegant for me."

Sarina sighs, she takes down the pony tail. She plugged in the curling iron and started running the comb through my hair again. "How about ribbon decorations instead of jewels."

I wince, "That depends! How many ribbons?"

Sarina laughs, "You know two pig tails and ribbons around the stems."

I give her a pained expression.

"I'm only kidding Muriel. I was thinking of a headband decorated with ribbon pushing back curly hair."

146

Circe Syndrome

An hour later, I'm in the dining room completely done up. Aunt Shirley, Aunt Hannah, Clay and my mother are playing Mah-Jong. They all coo at me and exclaim in excitement. I feel over exposed and afraid to move. Sarina even tried to modify my eye color. That had been an argument. My nails were polished and the weight of the polish makes me feel like I should be dragging my hands.

My mother stands with a sigh, "Excuse me, wait a second, Muriel!"

I fidget as my mother goes to a bureau and pulls open a drawer, I look at the game tiles. "Who's winning? Aunt Shirley?"

Aunt Shirley raises her eyes with a knowing smile and gives me a wink. "Me, of course."

There is an exasperated sigh, "She is not cheating! I've checked a dozen times!" Aunt Hannah pipes up.

My Mom had wondered off to the kitchen and returned with a box of kosher salt. "You look great darling, but you forgot to cleanse your aura." She starts to mumble the Shemah and throws the salt in the air.

Sarina snorts as she walks in the room, "Mom, it took me forever to clean her up! Don't go coating her with more gunk!"

I blink and a large salt granule falls off my left eyelash. Mom then hands me a square paper box with metallic gold paper embedded with The Collective emblem. An atom particle. A sphere with oval paths circling it. It is the size jewelry is usually given in.

I step back shocked, "Mom, what did you do?"

My mother gives me a pleasant smile, "It's nothing dear, it's not even from me, it's your dance card."

I am puzzled, "My what?"

Sarina laughs, "It won't bite Muriel. Honestly, it's as if you've never been to a dance before."

I give her a nonplussed look; Sarina raises her hand to her forehead, "You've never been to a dance before: Mom! How could you allow this? How old is she?"

Our mother chuckles, "Yes, Sarina, give me a lecture on controlling my daughters. I've done so well with you."

Sarina blushes. I'm amused. This is rare.

I look at the box and take it tentatively. I take a breath and open it cautiously. Inside, nestled in iridescent tissue paper, was a gold bracelet. Every other link was a disc with The Collective insignia logo with sapphire occupying the nucleuses. There was a blank metal plate like on an ID bracelet.

I give my mother a puzzled look as I hold it up in my hands. I swallow, "How is this a dance card?"

My mother smiled and nodded at my wrist, "Put that on your left wrist. The gentlemen will have gold wands. Don't get defensive if they point them at you. The bracelet will keep track of the dance. Your partners, at the end of each dance, look at the metal plate. It will show you your next partner's name and a little picture graph of them. It is a charming spell, it won't look digital, it will look as if it has been engraved there for ages."

I nodded with understanding, but I had a question, "How do I choose a partner?"

My mother blinked and gave me a blank stare.

I sigh, "Come on; Mom, this is the twenty first century!"

Mom looks at her sister Hannah, who rolls her eyes and clears her throat, "Through the age-old habit of womanly wiles dear. You just smile or wink at a guy, he'll take care of the rest."

I frown, "What if he's clueless?"

Aunt Hannah examines her tiles, "His loss, my dear, his loss." She waves her hand in the air.

Circe Syndrome

My mother smiles and returns to her place at the table. "Have fun, Muriel! Four bam!" She places a tile with four pieces of bamboo on the table into the center of the Mah-Jong playing area.

Aunt Shirley grabbed it, "Mah-jong!"

The other three groaned.

Chapter 16

To the Max

I gave Sarina an awkward hug and thanked her. Then I headed for the door. As soon as I stepped outside, the wind churned my skirt. I shivered as I headed through the yard, past the huge oak tree and to the sidewalk. The orange and red leaves of the nearby maple fall in spiral patterns as I walk to the street car. I'm lucky it arrives at the stop at the same moment I do. I get on and note the tired looking people staring at their phones as they move to make way for me. I grab the overhead bar just before the street car takes off again.

I look out the windows and watch the huge orange moon fill the sky. I get off near the Goose Hallow MAX light rail station.

I wait five minutes at the stop for a MAX and take it West into the tunnel. Beneath Washington City Park that sits on a foothill, the MAX has a tunnel heading to the suburbs of Beaverton and Hillsboro. There is a stop beneath it called Washington Park Station. It is one of the deepest train stations west of the Rockies. It is a stop with an elevator that takes people to the main attractions of Washington Park: the Zoo, Children's Museum, and the Forestry Center.

This is where I get off. I consciously push away my thoughts about how much earth is piled on top of me. I walk off the platform and to the elevator. The doors open and out pour families with toddlers exhausted from the zoo. A balloon hits my head as they walk in zombie motions toward the platforms. I go into the elevator. No one else has entered with me. I find the hidden down button that can only be seen with power sight. I push it.

The doors open to the hidden station below the Washington Station. Other Heska dressed opulently mill about the platform.

A woman with an hourglass figure, long ebony hair and caramel skin approaches me. Her tight dress is fire-engine red. "Hey, Muriel, is that you?"

I give her a warm smile and take her quick hug. "Isabelle? How long has it been?"

She shrugs, "I don't know, five years."

I marvel on how time moves, "How have you been? What have you been up too?"

She gives me a mischievous smile, "Oh a little of this and that. Your parents making you come too?"

I nod, "Yes."

A male chuckle from behind me makes me spin. His cultured voice says, "Me, too."

I turn and look at a tall, gaunt man with sandy curly hair, lavender eyes and a pointy chin. I feel my smile course through all of me. I know him, too. "Oh hey, Jasper. This might not be so bad."

Isabelle squeezed my arm, "Yes, darling, we can sit in the corner and make fun of the trendies, like back in the day at school."

I smile at the memories. The three of us never really fit in. Isabelle was half Enchantress from a siren branch and Jasper's spells only worked half of the time.

I give them a sad smile, "I promised my mother I would participate."

Jasper winks at me, "Cool, I'll sign your dance card."

I shake my head, "Thanks for the charity, Jasper."

Isabelle tapped his arm with her elbow, "What about me?"

He reaches his arm around her familiarly, "None of us are allowed to dance with one person all night darling. But, I will take every dance I get with you. Let's face it, if there are going to be brawls, it will be over you."

She puts her hands on her hips and smiles predatorily. "You're damn right there will be." She pulled out her phone. "Muriel, what is your number? Since you're back in town, we should get together."

Jasper nods also and pulls out his phone.

I laugh, "It's the same as before, I'm living with my parents."

Jasper shakes his head and gives me a mock sad face, "You poor thing."

Isabelle shakes her head, "You have a cellphone, right?"

I exchanged numbers with them. Suddenly the air pressure on the platform changes. The giant tunnel to our right expels a huge amount of stale air. My hair swirls in my face and I push down to keep my dress from flipping up.

Out of the tunnel comes a MAX train. It barrels through the tunnel with a sign in purple that reads Multnomah Falls on its destination plaque. Everyone who had been milling about turns to watch it arrive and stop. Everyone hustles to get on board.

Circe Syndrome

I am apprehensive that I might trip and cause myself trauma in some way. I make my way in the doors with no injury and grab a bar from overhead. A young blond woman next to me complains to a person next to her. "I wish they wouldn't put a block on dialyosefosing around the Falls for the dance. It's so common traveling this way."

I try not to snort out laughter as I take in her posture, and condescending attitude. So I start to look at the advertisements on the MAX Car. One has a picture of an alluring female elf and a handsome male elf. Both were looking over their shoulders and using beckoning hands. The bold print said, "Fairy Escort Service." The fine print read: Your offspring too big headed to settle down? Hire one of our escorts to knock their ego down a notch or two."

I suddenly wonder about Yacob and my parents. I have this nagging memory of him dating a fey for a bit before meeting Morgan.

Another ad was for Match.com. Strobe lights for the levitation bar, called Feather Weights made my eyes tear.

A curly red haired boy next to me raises and eyebrow, following my gaze. "No pressure, right?"

I give him a smile as I think, "Yeah, right."

He reaches out his hand, "I'm Andy, and you are?"

I switch my grip and reach out to shake his. "Muriel."

He pauses. His gaze sweeps me completely. He cocks his head and his eyes narrow. "That's an infamous name."

I look away trying to figure out how to answer.

The woman next to Andy nudges him, she whispers loudly, "It's her!"

Andy looks incredulous, "You're Mindworm Muriel?"

I feel my eyes widen, I really hadn't heard this before. I have heard it explained to me how I was referred, but this was my first time hearing the way it was tossed around when I wasn't there. "Wow! That is what I'm called behind my back?"

The woman nudges him again and gestures to another part of the train in an urgent tone. "I think there is room that way, let's go over there!"

He pulls away from her and leans close to me. Inches from my face he grins and says, "Maybe I like bad girls."

I snort and start to laugh. I gesture at myself. I'm petite, with a round face and light brown hair mixed with wandering blond highlights. "Do I really look like a nefarious person?"

He stares in my eyes and reaches for power. He reaches for my mind and tries a mental suggestion, "You want me!" Out loud he says, "No, you don't, but your reputation suggests so."

I am suddenly angry. I want to take that mental probe and follow it back to his mind and dart it back into his brain with an ego crushing command. I had been trained my whole life to not use mercy when attacked mentally. The history of magic and my Jewish family and mind magic was twisted. It was not a natural part of our faith. It was very contrary to our views. Individual thought is encouraged. But, because of lack of training, hundreds of Jewish families had been held during World War II, by Nazi mind wizards. There was a secret order wizards called the Non-Secular Humanistic Knights. They rescued my mother and taught her to guard her mind. My father had been one of the Knights. Both parents were adamant about all of us all learning to protect our minds and defend ourselves.

It was good to be prepared, but at the same time mind magic is seductive. I had just used it yesterday on Viper. I of course had legal permission then. I was not currently on duty. I do an obvious duck because I know everyone around us is watching and witnessing, looking to accuse me of inappropriate behavior. I pushed his spell toward the aether as The Collective witnesses stopped holding their breaths.

I give him a smirk and gesture to the remnants of the spell, "You know what happens to the criminals who do something thought impossible, right? They become part of the establishment. Do that again and I will arrest you."

He threw up a hand, "Come on, it was a joke. I wouldn't have tried if I'd known it would have succeeded."

I give him a deadpan sigh, "I guess I have no sense of humor."

He pulled out his dance wand, "Oh, I'm adding myself to your dance card." He pointed it at me.

As I fought the urge to be on guard, I felt my bracelet tingle. It was followed by a few more as other men did the same thing. I laughed, shook my head at the absurdity of what can attract men, and looked out the window.

Andy leaned in, his breath on my ear startled me. "So, you are part of The Collective now? "

I moved back an inch and nodded as I adjusted my grip on the bar that felt over warm from my grasp and undisplayed emotions.

He tapped his chin and cocked his head, "What do you do for them?"

I give him a warm smile and lean in familiarly, "A recruiter, you interested?"

He backs up and looks like he smelled something bad, "Hell, no!"

We were running parallel to I-84 freeway now, beyond Portland and heading East. I was staring at the Columbia River reflecting the stars. I watched a shooting star in the reflection. This reminded me of Paddleboarding in the Meteor Belt. How long has it been since I did that? I remind myself to breath, not to get anxious around all these judging strangers. I just need to keep breathing and be gracious tonight, then I'm free of it.

Andy started a conversation with other people and gives me back my personal space. I felt myself relax, and in my sweeping gaze of the compartment caught a sympathetic look from Isabelle.

A familiar whisper froze me in my spot. "I know what you're thinking about." I looked up into Jasper's lavender eyes.

I move my hair from my face, "Oh hey, Jasper, where did you come from? We all got separated in the crush in."

He nods up at some black domes distributed around the car ceilings. They look like video cameras, "You mean by the dispersion charm that encouraged us all to disperse. They want us all to mingle with a capital M."

I blush, realizing I had been clueless, "Oh?"

"Asteroid paddleboarding." His voice was a soft purr of want.

A longing that I can't contain fills me and I look back out at the river. "It is fun."

He leans close, "How long has it been for you?"

I smirk and shake the cobwebs in my head trying to remember. "I can't recall, you?"

He gives me a nudge, and looks down his nose at me, "You know I can't without a reliable spell caster with me."

I nod, "We should go again."

He smiles, "That would be diverting. How about after the dance? Or do you have a curfew since you're living at home with your parents?"

I consider his request. My longing is palpable at this point. To feel the universe coast by and watch the stars burn. To swirl my fingers in the dust and watch the prisms of star fire reflect through the asteroid ice. "Yeah, that will be a enjoyable stress reliever after the dance."

I grab tightly to the bar above as I feel the drag force affect the MAX as it slows. My body wants to pull back, I tighten my muscles in my arm and it burns trails through me. We have stopped on the freight tracks just below the falls.

Jasper gives me a big grin and his voice is light, "I'll let Isabelle know."

I find myself nodding.

Suddenly, I hear the whistle of a train. A specific whistle the harsh blaring horn of a freight train. I turn and look out the front window. There is a huge magenta engine steaming at us. Adrenaline spikes through my body. My blood runs fast and I feel like bolting. I reach for the aether but the force is diverted from my grasp. Sweat coats me and the others cry out. The whole MAX shutters. There is this sound of metal and steam releasing and I feel a sinking feeling. The train is lowering. As we descend I start to see a mechanism that is moving another track to go on top of us.

Everyone is quiet as the train goes down to the level of the walkway and the other track locks in place just in time for the screaming freight train to power over us. The MAX shakes with the vibration.

When the doors open there are tunnels made out of the stone that support the track bridges. They lead to these ramps made of woven branches that had grown out from the trees. They join our path to the cement path that leads from the parking lot, by the stream that flows from the waterfall. As we walk away and the car empties, the tunnels disappear and the branches retract to the trees. I pause when I look up at the falls. It is festooned with balls of glowing yellow spheres floating at different elevations. Couples in formal wear are already dancing in the air around the spray.

Another attendant pushes me forward. I start the walk. I find myself musing at the rainbows created in the spray by the lights, and by how surprisingly balmy the air suddenly feels on this autumn night. The people around me have this air of excitement.

Isabelle finds me and grabs my hand like we are little girls again and tugs. "Come on, Muriel!"

I blink, it's so beautiful. Everyone looks so highly polished and I look down at myself self-consciously.

She chuckles, "You look fine. Let's go check in."

I shake the bracelet on my wrist at her. "Don't these take care of that?"

She nods, "Yes, but we all need a chance to mingle and have a drink or two."

I smirk as Isabelle drags me up the hill toward the short order grill stand. It has been converted into a bar and all the tables now have tablecloths. There are waiters and waitresses in smart costumes carrying full trays of glasses with bubbling lavender liquid.

A blue demon waiter walks up to us. He speaks in a cockney accent, "Hello, hello. Would you care for a refreshment?" He winks at me and gives Isabelle a salacious leer.

I find myself wondering how this bracelet wand thing works for homosexuals. Isabelle grabs a glass and downs it in one swig. She sets it at a table, stands with a very straight posture and wipes off imaginary dust, "Well, here I go once more into the breach, my friend. I'll meet you and Jasper down at the tracks afterwards, for some paddleboarding."

I give her my warmest smile and a salute with my glass. As I take a sip of the sweet liquid with a tart aftertaste, I watch Isabelle swallowed up by the crowd of elegantly dressed people. I wish I had a sketchbook. There was so much to look at and see. So much to try and draw.

I ponder at the amount of inebriated wizards there were about to be. This could get terrifyingly entertaining fast. I look at the lavender color of my drink and reconsider its taste and realize it is Firtfile not wine. It's an elven concoction made from sap, elderberries, and if one is to believe elves fermented with poetry. It loosens inhibitions, but keeps one in control of their faculties.

I take a breath, steeling my resolve. I remind myself I can do this; everyone here is here for the same reason. No reason for fear. I stand and turn in time to see the blonde, arrogant wizard from headquarters. He is wearing a pinstriped black tails tuxedo and has on blonde mutton chops. His hair is perfectly styled. The mutton chops go with the tux but hadn't been there earlier today.

I thought about his older brother and how he had broken Sarina's heart. The Phoenix family would not allow someone without power to marry their son. She had been offered the role of a mistress. I know I shouldn't judge him on their actions. I'm completely aware of how overcritical of him I am.

He reaches his hand out to me. "Hey, Muriel, right?"

I take his hand and shake it. "Hi, Anthony." I say softly.

He crosses his arms and blinks his eyes. "I must say, I'm shocked to see you here."

I grin and nod at him, "Same here, I thought you were going to single-handedly hunt down the Cir.."

He shushes me. "That is Classified."

I shrug, " OK", I look at him expectantly. I figure he will explain why he originally approached me.

He raises a golden wand and points it at my wrist. He gives me a big grin. "See you later." He walks away.

I am puzzled, I close my eyes to ground myself again. When I open them, there is a heavy set man in a black Armani suit standing in front of me. His black hair curls about his round face. He is looking about nervously, and sweating.

Wow, a newborn Heska I think. I give him a reassuring smile, "Hi, are you new to our world?"

He gives me a grateful smile, "Yes, how could you tell?"

I look at the ground to hide my grin; he has no idea, but he is about to be assaulted by some of the most attractive women at this party. Heska families were always looking to diversify the blood lines in magic lines. People just new to their power always yielded powerful offspring. I move a strand of hair from my face when I look back at him. "I'm Muriel. How did you find out you had magic?"

His eyes take on a glassy sheen "I'm Irving, It was two months ago. My family runs a jewelry shop and two thugs came to rob us. I transformed them into roaches and stepped on them."

I nodded in understanding. High stress situations were often triggers. I gestured for him to continue. The Collective could not have found him from that.

He gives me an embarrassed smile, "I went to the stock market and tried to manipulate the numbers. That is when The Collective found me and taught me the way of the world. I'm in night school for Magic and Ethics now. It's nothing like Hogwarts. It's a little dry."

I give him a lite encouraging chuckle, and pat his arm, "It will get better and more interesting. Do you get along with your classmates?"

Before he could answer a Cindy Crawford look alike sauntered over. She gave him a long smoldering look, "Hi, I'm Cleo, I could not help but notice you."

He started to stutter and a few other equally gorgeous women surrounded him. As they began talking to him they modifying his appearance.

This was illegal, modifying him without his permission. I debate my options here. I decide to just reveal to him what is going on but let him decide what he wants done. I gather the air molecules near him into a dense reflective cloud. A mirror appears next to him. He turns his head and pauses and realizes the reflection is him.

"How is that me?" The women around him giggle. He looks at me puzzled, "Isn't that illegal?"

I nod slowly as I meet his eyes and give him a speculative glance. I then glance at the women, "Direct them, give them permission or don't. Decide now."

He cocks his head. "Would you thin my face more?"

Cleo gives me a wink. I take that as I have been dismissed, so I turn to walk away as I hear Cleo's low pitched voice say, "Certainly, Irving."

I wince as one of the women admires the size of his wand, and jiggles her bracelet in front of him. I make a break for it. I can't get away fast enough.

As I flee, I run into Jasper. He points his wand at my bracelet as he says. "Would you check my shoe enchantment. I'm pretty sure I didn't spell them to levitate correctly."

I involuntarily smirk, and look down at his shoes. I call on power sight and note how the strands of energy are woven about the shoe and the frequencies captured in the weaving. I absently say. "Hover a bit."

His gaze is distant and his body jerks into the air. He shoots up wobbling beyond my head in seconds. I reach up and grab his ankle. I pull at the spell and pull him down. I involuntarily nod. "Stabilizers, you need some. It helps prevent jerky ascents and descents."

He sighs and cocks his head at me. "Oh yeah? How are you going to do this? Did you enchant your shoes?"

I laugh, I hadn't thought that far yet. I shrug, "Nope, I just mess with physics equations and use helium instead of Oxygen." I make my voice go higher, I get a squeaky voice. "Should be appealing to suitors right?"

He chuckles back at me. "Fine, don't tell me how."

I look beyond him to the stairway that leads to the walkway to the falls. I watch the people moving about me and dancing in the air. Shapes blur together, making a moving abstract composition. I listen to the music and feel the moisture in the air. I take a breath. I'm about to walk toward the dancing people.

Jasper's voice makes me focus back on him. His eyes are filled with a weary sadness. "I heard Aunt Aiofe arrived today."

I ponder what the sadness is about, not sure. I don't think it's about his aunt. "Yeah, she did." I try to say as brightly as possible.

He gives me a fond smile. "How is Morgan doing?"

I nod, mirror the smile, everyone who knows Morgan is fond of her. "She seems content, are you coming to visit soon?"

He grins and runs a hand nervously through his hair. "Yes, mother didn't want everyone inundating your mother quite yet."

"Our own family is doing a spectacular job. But not enough to distract her from what she wants me to do." I sigh.

He shakes his head and looks at the ground, "I still would like to be a fly on the wall when Maxima and Aiofe go at it. Your mother getting," he pauses and looks about the crowd, "the event to happen at her house is quite a coup."

I look about nervously, "We really should talk about something else."

At that moment a blue demon walks up to me. "More wine, my lady?"

I go to run my hand through my hair at the awkward embarrassment I feel at being called lady. A leftover piece of salt from my mother's ministrations flies out of my hair and lands on the demon. He starts to scream and jump as the granule of salt is burning a hole into his arm.

I sigh, disgusted with myself for causing this discomfort in another being. I reach to take his arm.

He shrieks at me. "Don't touch me!" Everyone in the vicinity has turned to stare at me and the demon.

I murmur, "I'm sorry, I can heal you. Just give me your arm."

The demon screams at me, "Who goes to a social event covered in salt?"

I keep the concerned look on my face as I watch the salt burn a centimeter down into his flesh. "My mother caught me as I was heading out the door. It won't hurt, please at least let me take the granular off you before it burns completely through."

A male fairy in tails and a waistcoat, with a serious, disapproving look, approaches us. "What is going on here?"

I meet his lavender eyes, "I accidentally flicked salt on this gentleman."

He puts his hands on his hips and glares back at me. "Accident, sure! Demons have rights too, Missy!"

I take a breath and just grab the demon's arm. "Let me heal this before you start bleeding monsters. I am truly sorry."

The demon is staring at my hand on his arm and blood sweat starts to pore out of his face. He seems shocked that my touch wasn't burning him. I levitated the salt out of the wound. I willed the blood to fill the wound and heal.

He pulls his arm away quickly as I let go. He has started mumbling to himself.

I really wanted to apologize further, but realized that complaining was something he seemed to be enjoying. I turned to find Jasper in tears of laughter.

I look at him deadpan, "What?"

He is shaking his head, "Only you Muriel, only you!" He is gasping for air between words.

I scratch my ear and move a strand of hair behind it. "What?"

He squints at me. He starts picking more salt off me. "I know Maxima isn't some shrinking violet, afraid her children can't handle things. Why would she sprinkle you with salt? What were you doing before this dance? As I process his questions, one of his random thoughts escapes his mind and I involuntarily hear it. "How does she use magic on salt? Salt usually dissolves spells!"

I blink trying to concentrate on what I am supposed to answer. "Oh, I was hanging out with a vampire. Mother thought that the aura would be off putting to certain dance partners."

He raises one eyebrow. "A vampire? I can't see the influence in your aura. Oh the salt, I see."

I stare back at the stairs to the waterfall. "How do I know it is time to start dancing?"

He nods at my bracelets, "When you actually decide you are ready the name of your first partner will appear."

"So men control who they dance with and women control when?" I look down at my bracelet and Jasper's name looks engraved on it. "When did you add me?" I teased him.

He gives me an amused, secretive look, fully aware I watched him do it earlier. "We aren't all showboats in our actions."

"Will the order be who targeted me first?"

Jasper looked thoughtful, "Not necessarily, there is some sort of database managing who and when since there are multiple partners and variables. The goal is you will dance with all who targeted you at least once."

I frown trying to understand, "So, I could dance with someone more than once?"

"Yes, the bracelet monitors mood and body signs for stress and pleasure."

164

I blinked, alarmed and a bit miffed at the intrusion. I then shrug, "Are you ready to dance?" I am happy it went with someone I know and am comfortable with first.

He smiles, bows and offers his arm. In tandem, we saunter up the steps toward the bridge. At the bridge we step like we are walking on stairs and climb into the swirling pattern of dancers. The pattern is a spiral up and another down. The dance itself is a waltz and the music playing is Mozart. The dresses sway in the breeze, different birds swirl and sing in tune with the music. The movements transfix me. I'm swept into my senses unable to think, I am just a being lost in the swirl and a part of the beauty around me.

Two minutes into this trance, I hear Jasper laugh, "You seem overwhelmed? Are you going to be able to keep this up the rest of the night?"

Incredulous, I feel my eyes widen as, surprised, I say, "It is fun, huh?"

He gives me a nurturing grin, "You seem shocked."

"I never really thought about what this would feel like. I think I was overly focused on forced conversations." I watch a bubble light bobble in a current of air.

"Talking is not necessary in this setting. But it would be a good idea for the...", he sighs, "the purpose of the dance."

We danced for a while till I paused, and with a vibration on my arm, radiating from my wrist. It was the bracelet.

Jasper noticed where I was looking and reached out and placed an index finger on the bracelet, stilling it. He gestured toward the bridge. "Time to mingle. So I'll meet you under the railway bridge, after, for paddleboarding?"

I nod and stare at the name on my bracelet. I have no idea who Admantis is. I find myself wondering how we are supposed to connect. I look up to see the red haired man from the MAX leering at me. He bows and offers me his arm as he says, "Andy, is just easier than Admantis."

I was on guard, I stiffened my back and gave him my politest smile, "I see.", I took his arm.

As we started the climb in the air to join the dancers, he mumbled apologies about his vibrato on the MAX. "Sorry, I outed you there. You are really brave to come to an event like this."

I give him a shrug to mark my acceptance of his apology. "It wasn't ideal, but thanks for your apology."

His jaw was tight as he watched the dancers, then relaxed. He pulled us into the swirl of dancers. I was busy counting his steps and watching his feet. I felt so much like an albatross in this setting. My emotions are still guarded and I find myself waiting for him to say something harsh or demeaning to me.

He gave me a reassuring smile and a squeeze on my hand. As we swirled about the waterfall and he stared into my eyes, there were no stray spells. In this pregnant pause he cleared his throat, "How are you liking the dance?"

I cock my head give him a guarded look and then just decide to relax and let what will happen, happen. I decide to try not to anticipate everything. "It's fun! How about you?"

He shrugs, "I don't know, I just started, a bit puzzled though, I thought we would have more to talk about."

I nod encouragingly, "Such as?"

He sighed, "I don't know, how horrible I was to you on the MAX."

I look past him and frown a little then look back at him, "It wasn't particularly pleasant for me. Was that fun for you?" I am curious if he is one of those people who enjoy making others uncomfortable.

He looks puzzled, as if he didn't think about it in that way, "I don't know. I was just startled I guess."

There was a long pause and I thought the conversation was over. Until he swirled me and then asked, "So that salt trick, how did you do that? Most salt deactivates magic."

I was surprised, I know a lot of people witnessed that, but I was too busy in the moment to note who. "You saw that huh?"

He shakes his head and with a voice of wonder says, "Only people dancing high up didn't see that!"

I feel the blood rushing to my head. I know I'm blushing.

"Its fine, you handled yourself well." He pulls me playfully in a fiercely close manner, "I'm racking my brain and baffled, please tell me how you did that?"

I find myself liking this straightforward question. "Physics." I say nonchalantly.

He snorts, " OK, I'm listening."

I pull my hand from his shoulder and scratch my chin nervously and move a stray strand of hair from my face as I assemble my answer. "Basically, I send a breeze across its surfaces to diffuse the atmospheric pressure keeping the salt where it is. The air around it pushes it up." I had been staring into his silver eyes and finding myself wanting to dive in so I stare past him at another dancing pair. "I had to make some allowances for the limited air in the pit it was digging, of course."

He chuckled, "Of course!"

We dance together for a bit and then he meets my eyes again and gestures to the air around us, "Air and the unseen forces around us, we all take for granted so much. You know when I was a kid I used to like to skip stones. Have you ever done that?"

I nod and adjust my hand in his. "Um, toss a rock across the surface of water and get it to jump?"

He nods and tightens his hold on my hand. He gives me a smug grin and moves further into my space. "Yes, anyways, there was this pond I loved to go to daily. I'd stand on the edge and find the perfect stones, and try to get them to skip twenty times."

I know my eyebrows rose.

He sighed, "It can be done, I've done it. Anyways, every day I would go there and skip stones. One day when I was skipping stones, I was lobbing this huge one. It had the perfect spin and balance when I released the stone and it started to skip. The first five were quick, small jumps, webbing out rings of water drops. I thought it would drop but it continued. So it stretched out and hit a boulder. This changed its angle and hit a frog... it let out this croak that sounded like a yell of, Hey!"

"What? No way!" I shook my head and he spun me. A dark expression briefly went across his features and the smile returned.

"I kid you not. The frog screamed, 'Hey,' in a bit of a New Jersey accent!" He gripped me tighter and climbed us higher in the air. The spray misting about us created rainbows in the light. "It's not a joke."

I cock my head in acquiescence, " OK, so what happened next?"

"The frog swam under the water and came and splashed me."

"That's a brave frog." I say incredulously.

He shakes his head. "It wasn't a frog."

"It wasn't?"

He gives me a knowing smile, "Come on, you are not that naive."

I sigh, "A water spirit, huh?"

He spins me, "Yeah! A water spirit, the 'f'ing guardian of the pond!"

"Oh!" I say worriedly, "That can get dangerous."

He shrugs, "It did become a thing, every day I would go to skip stones, and now because I was young and strong headed, and in my mind had lost face when the spirit splashed me. I would hunt it out and specifically aim for it."

I find myself wondering what the avatar of Multnomah Falls would look like. I watch the spray. "That sounds unwise."

He sighs, "Yes, every retaliation got more and more violent.... the second time it tripped me, the third time it sent waves to soak me and one day someone else went to the pond and accidently hit the frog and it drowned them."

I feel a wave of sadness swarm around him in a miasma of spectral bees swarming and humming a sad song. The emotion travels through me and a tear comes to my eye. "How horrible." I whisper.

He gives me a serious nod, "Sorry, I didn't mean to go all dark."

"So, you were a rambunctious child." I give him a smile, "Sounds very much like something most boys and many girls would do. Unfortunately, nature spirits rarely have the sense of humor to appreciate it."

He frowns down at my hand then looks back in my eyes. He takes a breath and spins me again. I feel dizzy and the bracelet vibrates. He gives me a weary nod. He guides us toward the bridge to change me off to another partner.

Chapter 17

Musical Mingling Menagerie

I ended up dancing with ten other men, then I came face to face with Anthony. His expression is blank and bordering on stern. "Miss Muriel?"

"Mr. Phoenix." I look up at the other dancers. I am still puzzled by him wanting to dance with me.

He steps into my space and holds out his hands. I hesitate then raise my hands to meet his. He starts our climbing immediately.

"How is your sister doing?"

I blink as comprehension takes hold. "My sister? You know her?"

"Sarina, yes. My brother was quite dumbstruck by her." He manages to shrug while keeping his arms in position. "I am his little brother, so of course I think she is the pinnacle of female perfection."

Circe Syndrome

I smirk imagining him as a young man, catching glimpses of his brother's ostentatious fiancé. Sarina had been wild those days with an infectious aura of joy. She had loved his brother so much. She was always the perfect picture of grace and heightened beauty. "She is doing well." I look away and think about all the polite lies everyone tells each other. And the one I just said was a whopper.

We dance a few more beats and he smirks. "Is Sarina seeing anyone?"

I laugh shake my head. This is not a new question for me, "Seriously?"

"Yes, seriously or casually?" He blushes.

I realize I said seriously because I was a bit exasperated; he is here to meet people, and he is asking me about my sister. I look past him with my practiced, "everything is fine" expression, but I do wonder if I am that unappealing. Not that I'm interested in him, but once in a while I wouldn't mind being one the person who am talking to, is interested in. Instead of always being the intermediary. "Not anyone serious, that I'm aware of."

His face fills with hope, "Can you let her know I was asking after her?"

I frown, thinking about his family's history with her. "That depends, are you looking for the type of relationship Simon was looking for?"

He frowns and annoyance passes across his face. "No! Of course not."

I give him a reassuring smile, "I'll let her know."

He gives me back a big grin, "Thanks, say I heard something about some asteroid paddleboarding after the dance. Are you up for others tagging along?"

I pause, I hadn't expected this question, "Have you paddleboarded in the asteroid trails before?"

He nods, "Yeah, Simon hung out with Yacob sometimes and went. Do you remember?"

I spin my ankle in thought, "I remember him going, I don't remember seeing you."

He gives me a brilliant smile, "You were a good teacher, Simon felt confident going himself and with me, once you taught him how to predict currents."

I look him over and realize the arrogant guy from headquarters wasn't here at the moment, "I'm OK with you coming, don't invite too many, alright?"

He nods, "Where are you meeting?"

I nod toward the train tracks, "Under the railway bridge."

"I'll see you there." He looks around a second, noting the dancers and the spray. He shakes his head, "This is bizarre. Right?"

I give him an amused smile, "What? Dancing on air around a waterfall or people our age reduced to this awkward social convention for meeting people?"

He swirls me and smiles broadly, "Yeah!"

I smile and look beyond him to the Columbia River, with its reflective stars. The cool approaching autumn air caresses my cheek and swirls through the dancers, moving the fairy light globes. I mentally make a memory of the feeling of weightlessness, the pine smell and the moist air. I note the song and muffled conversations. It all feels like a perfect moment to cherish.

Chapter 18

Logistic Maneuvers

Four hours later, I stare at my shoes as I listen to Isabelle and Jasper flirt with one another. They were in a relationship their parents never approved. They were in this debate about who would win in a fight between He-Man and Conan the Barbarian.

Anthony approached us with four other young men in tow. Irving also showed up followed by five other women. They included Cleo. It took me a moment to realize it was Irving, he had been majorly altered.

Anthony stood in front of me with a bit of that arrogance I've seen at headquarters. He crossed his arms and nodded towards the people with him. "This OK?"

I look them all over, again. I have paddleboarded with these men and my brother occasionally. Only one of the women before. I nod towards Irving. "Who is going to be responsible for him?"

Cleo steps forward. "I will."

I look at Anthony and then back at her, " OK, have you asteroid paddleboarded before?"

She gives me an amused smile, "Who hasn't?"

Irving catches my eye, "Um, I would like to be responsible for myself. What do I need to know?"

Everyone around us starts talking amongst themselves in an obvious fashion.

I rub my chin and consider him. "Technically, in space, you are out of any country's jurisdiction. All magic types are allowed, and don't need a scientific explanation to back up whatever you're doing."

He bows his head in acknowledgement.

I scratch my head; I want to give him some hints, but there are vast amounts of different tracks for doing the same thing. "I don't know what your spell set is?"

He starts to talk "It's..." Everyone's head around us snaps up, paying attention.

I hold up my hand stopping him, "You know, right? You don't want anyone to know that!"

He looks puzzled, "Ummm, no. I didn't know that."

I shake my head, "You haven't announced your primary ability to anyone, have you?"

He pales, "Why? I mean it explains why most people interrupt me before I say it."

I sigh, "If other Heska know your spell set then they know what your weaknesses are and can destroy or control you."

His face becomes sober.

I tap his arm gently, "No use crying over spilled secrets. Going forward don't tell people. Besides, you're new to this world, you might not actually know yet, your strongest form."

Circe Syndrome

He swallows his eyes moving back and forth in thought.

I struggle for a moment about where to begin explaining different options for how a Heska uses a paddleboard in space and survives. I decide to focus on equipment. "I manufacture boards made out of living wood. Living in these boards are a moss that have a symbiotic relationship with it, that generates nutrients that from molecules floating in space. The wood, the moss and a person create a little oxygen bubble with pressure in space. The moss tethers you to the board. The thing is, part of the moss will stay with you the rest of your life."

He squints and strokes his chin, "Does it hurt?"

I nod, "Just a pinch, when you connect."

His eye widened in wonder and a bit of fear. " OK."

I shrug, "You don't have to go."

"No, I want to come. It's just a lot to process."

I splay my hand, " OK, before we cover the paddleboard part you need to toughen your skin. Asteroids are pretty jagged."

He looks at his feet.

I wait.

He swallows, "How do I do that?"

"A couple ways. Take a Kevlar suit and incorporate it into your cells. Go into your DNA, encourage the cells to be smaller and group themselves together. Take on some armadillo DNA and splice it on to yours. Or do what Metal Mages can do: plate their skin cells with metal but that limits how you move on the board. I believe one of the incantation words is, 'Firmalite.'"

He gives me a puzzled look.

I look up at the sky. "Think about it a moment. Just relax." I point at the women, "Forget about them and me." I look beyond him over the tracks and consider the stars. "Let your mind float, think about what you love to do with magic.

175

Forget about what I'm asking you to do." I stop and listen to his heartbeat and I see a pulsar of a star mirror it to the beat.

It took about five minutes. I could tell his skin was toughened, "OK, none of us can dialyosefos here. I'll explain more as we walk away from the waterfall and toward the river."

They all give gestures of affirmation. As a group, we move beneath the walkway under the train tracks, to the parking lot, off the 84. As we walk I start discussing the mechanics of moving in space.

Irving and the women give random gestures of comprehension of what I am explaining.

We walk till we get to the river. I survey the group and ask, " OK, how many people need boards?"

About five people raise their hands. I bounce my head, "Alright, let's meet at the big curve on the Ceres Asteroid in thirty minutes." I look over at Jasper and Isabelle, "Isabelle? Jasper? Are you with me?"

They both give me smiles of affirmation. We were beyond the dialyosefosive barrier. I reach out to the green oxygen producing lines of magic flowing from the trees. I wrap it around Jasper's and Isabelle's waists. I reach out to the aether and pull them with me to Europa, one of Jupiter's moons. I keep my workshop for paddleboards in an ice cave there. I had started these experiments in Paddleboarding in space between Ganymede and Europa moons. My workshop blended into the landscape as it was in one of the ice caves. I also had a garden of trees in there since the ice was translucent and let the light through.

We appeared at a space at the edge of the trees, Isabelle and Jasper's eyes grew wide. They looked around hungrily taking in details. Jasper laughed, "It's twice the size it used to be - and is that a forest growing in here?"

We can't dialyosefos for another thirty minutes, so we chat about the forest and our old antics.

Circe Syndrome

Eventually, I giggle at something, I acknowledge the time. I hand them each two boards and paddles. Then I grabbed my board decorated in dragons and extra one. I place two paddles under my arm. I wrap the tendrils of magic around them again and transport us all to the curve on Ceres, one of the largest asteroids on the asteroid belt.

I stood on my board and removed my shoes. The moss that I developed to work with the wood and live symbiotically in me also reached down through my heal into the board. As a stinging, tingling feeling moves from my heel and up my leg, a pressurized bubble of air appeared around me. I picked up my shoes and clipped them to a carabiner I keep attached to a string at the front of my board.

Jasper and Isabelle set down their respective boards. They stood on them as the three other people without boards came to take the extra ones we each brought. I nod at each of them. Out of the corner of my eye I see Jasper and Isabelle remove their shoes. I watch Jasper and Isabelle both wince as the moss takes root in them. They look at each other, shudder, then look at me.

Jasper moistens his lips, "That is so unsettling."

Isabelle nods, "Like a creature moving in, slithering through me."

I shrug, "Well, it is."

Jasper covers his face, "Don't remind us, Muriel, please."

I look away from them and watch the others mount up. I'm trying to gauge all their capabilities. I feel responsible for all of them. I just sigh and send magical tethers out and attach to all of them. For Jasper and Isabelle, I use more protective spells. Jasper requires a great deal, he has this talent to mess stuff up - something in his aura - Murphy's curse on the family. With these two, I have a link to their vitals. I look at Irving and just send one of those links to him, too.

I ask them, "You all ready?" As they mill about talking, I look at Jasper and Isabelle and I look toward the edge. "I'm heading off. You staying here?"

They both cock their heads and wave at me.

I examined my paddle. It had a magnet on each side, one polarized negative the other positive. There was a battery attached and some wire coils. I was going to try it without a current at the moment. I find the side that has the opposite charge of the paddle I'm using and use that near the meteor to push myself to a jagged edge on Ceres. As I crest my board on the precipice I pause, and feel the currents of debris in this orbit of our solar system.

I lean forward on the board. It is a slow start; the gravity here is much less then Earth's. I start the board sliding down this huge crater the size of a blue whale. I pushed with the opposite magnetized side of the paddle creating friction and causing speed. My momentum increases, and my hair flies about my face a bit. I ride up to the other side of the lip of the crevice, and, once I hit that point, I lean the board out to a 360° turn, to open air and coast away from Ceres.

I am now traveling in the orbit of the asteroid cloud. I have to bank and turn using the paddle to find the opposite charges. The silence of space is deafening. All I can hear is my heart beating and my blood churning. My mind clears of my worries: Sarina's safety, Yacob's fatherhood, and the blood knowledge of Thomas. I feel I am just another piece of debris floating in space.

After about thirty minutes the moss inside me shudders. I pause and look about me. Ceres is pretty far behind me and the tethers are pretty thin and taunt. I reach my mind down the strings toward the other paddleboarders. Most of them were still on Ceres. I start mapping out a way back. I'm going to be going the opposite orbit of most of the asteroids on the belt.

I will probably need to turn on the current to boost the magnets to help pull me towards Ceres.

It takes me about half an hour to return there. I arrive in time to watch Anthony do a triple flip with the paddleboard. I was impressed. I never tried to do something like that. I note his metal sheen. He was having problems stopping. When he does, he loses the contents of his stomach, which started to float toward Cleo.

Cleo shrieked and created a Tupperware bowl and caught the vomit in it. She lidded it and handed it to Anthony, "Remember, leave no trace," she said, disgusted.

Anthony, looking green, took it from her.

Jasper paddles up to me. "How far did you get?"

I wobble my head, "It's hard to gauge."

He gives me a knowing smile that I don't think he knows me well enough to give me. I look away and survey the rest of the paddleboarders. I watch Anthony's face slowly regain color. I feel tension drain from my body that I had no idea was there.

Anthony and Cleo meet eyes and start to joke and flirt, and Irving comes close to me and clears his throat.

I turn to him. "Hey Irving, how are you liking the paddleboarding?"

He gives me a forced smile, "It's definitely a different experience." He looks back out at Cleo and a wrinkle crosses his brow. "She is not really interested in me as a person, is she?"

I shrug, "I really don't know her." I watch Anthony and Cleo interact. There is a comfortable ease but not anything really sparking. "You and Cleo have just met and she just met Anthony. That is kind of what this night is about, meeting new people."

He stares into my eyes and raises his eyebrows, "That is true and I just met you."

I stifle the urge to laugh, and gesture at Isabelle who chose that moment to slide up near us. "Have you met Isabelle?" I pull my hand in a sweeping motion toward Irving, and Isabelle gives me an amused glance before giving him a flirty smile.

He takes in her generous hour-glass figure and one can tell he skips a beat where his mind goes to a bedroom somewhere. "No, I do not believe we have met."

I start them talking about expensive jewels and then back out of the conversation.

Jasper shakes his head at me and gives me a mock frown. "What have you done?"

I give him a small smile and cock my head, "It's a conversation, not a marriage proposal."

He crosses his arms and rolls his eyes, "So that flip off the asteroid you did? How did you do that?"

I start to explain.

Anthony wanders over to listen to the explanation, then charges off. He yells out "Like this?"

He 360's out into the space and stumbles on the board a bit. But he gets his bearing well, though there is a battle with his paddle being attracted to his skin since he made it tough with metal plating. He eventually starts a rhythm and begins to navigate the asteroid belt. I watch with admiration and then something starts to nag at my brain. Something I forgot to say, something that is menacingly coming close to happening. He's edging toward a grouping of asteroids that are crowding together and hitting one another hard enough to break off parts of stone.

I take a breath and frown. "I need to go fetch him. I need you all to make a tow line."

The people immediately around me give me puzzled looks. I catch the eye of two young men with whom I have paddleboarded before with Yacob. One follows me as I start heading to the edge of the asteroid, and the other starts gathering everyone together. I look at the lean, Asian man next to me. "I'm Muriel, I'm sorry I forgot your name."

He gives me a sober glance, "Ping."

I use two fingers to point out to open space, "How good are you at controlling where you're going?"

"We are in space right? All restrictions are off." He gives me this matter of fact gaze.

I give him a smile, "Yeah."

He adjusts his grip on his paddle, "Shouldn't be a problem. What is your plan?"

I laugh nervously, "That is the question isn't it?"

He sighs and runs his hands through his hair nervously.

I am scrambling to figure out what to do. An idea comes to me. "We could ride up on either side of him and dialyosefos him back."

Ping gives me a sarcastic look, "The aether is thin out here. Maybe he doesn't need saving."

I smirk, "No other solutions from your end then? It seems hopeless, why bother?"

Ping snorts, "He is an arrogant idiot, to just go fly in space with magnetized molecules in his skin and no experience! "

I flip my hair out of my eyes. And expel some air, "So you stepped up to help because?"

He frowned, "Because, everyone fucking matters, even arrogant assholes! I would want the help, too. I've been an arrogant asshole in my day...but it needed to be said."

I chew on my lower lip as I try not to burst into laughter, " OK, we will ask him if he needs to be saved."

Ping shrugs, "I will take your direction."

I take a moment and watch Anthony. He is heading closer to the center of a cluster of asteroids. He is distracted, his paddle keeps sticking to his body.

I take a breath, cock my head at Ping, "There is enough aether to get us there and there is enough to get back, so dialyosefosing him out of danger shouldn't be too hard." We both start heading towards Anthony.

He is in a weird dance trying to disengage the paddle from his body. It would be comical if he was not edging closer and closer to the asteroids that were knocking into one another.

It takes some effort to get our inertia at the optimum speed and trajectory to parallel him. We were getting into a tight area. Ping and I had to jump some to stay on course and not collide, to get close to him. He was blissfully unaware, fighting with the paddle.

My mind was in a constant state of agitation, trying to predict all the movements of the asteroids around me. Then I saw it! He was on a collision course to be at the apex of seven huge colliding asteroids. We had seconds to act. I don't want to head in that direction. All I want to do is head the other way. I speculate creating a net, then realize a net would be unwieldy and I couldn't predict its movement.

I was going to have to go in and dialyosefos him out. I shout to Ping. "We need to get a hold of him and get out. Forget about the boards!"

He nods.

I point to the two asteroids farther apart from the colliding asteroids. "Let's anchor ourselves to those two asteroids. You take the right. I'll take the left then we throw out a tether and pull him away!"

Ping gives me a thumbs up.

We paddle out to our respective asteroids and reach out tethers. Anthony happens to look up from his struggles with the paddle and notice us.

Circe Syndrome

Timing is critical, we reach out with tethers toward him. We wrap it around his torso. Just as we are about to tug him out of the way. I notice a small asteroid heading for my head. As I duck, it throws off my grab and Anthony's arm scrapes across an asteroid for a few seconds. He dragged to the right.

Suddenly the asteroid I'm anchored to changes trajectory, and starts to head toward the inevitable collision. Pings also veers off course and he and I spin our heads around. The three of us are about to be the creamy center of an asteroid donut. I release my tether from the asteroid and make a push with my paddle to create a fast forward motion towards Anthony.

Ping mirrors my actions.

We both jump onto Anthony's board. I make contact with his skin when my foot lands on his foot. This burning, scalding sensation ran through me. He had toughened his cells with steel. I wince and still grab onto him. It is like holding onto fire.

Ping makes eye contact with me and we dialyosefos away, leaving our boards. We land on an asteroid the size of a building about twenty feet away. We watched our boards be shredded by the asteroid collision. Immediately my feet began to burn. Even though the boulder was mostly made of Iron, that is a key ingredient in steel. So my irritation to the steel I just experienced now opened me up to an iron sensitivity. The moss that had lived in the board was hanging out in yard strands like unwrapped skeins of yarn from my feet. Anthony and Ping used something else for those needs in space, so they just gawked at the moss. The moss slowly retracting into me.

The moss made a bubble of air about us. I was about to mourn the living wood of my board when I noted the pieces were splintering and life existed in those parts. My mind filled with the speculation of evolution in those splinters, and the lifeforms they could become.

Anthony gasps, "What happened? "

Janette Bach

Ping shakes his head and still breathing heavily says, "That was such a sweet board."

"Yeah, it looked like you could maneuver it well."

He rolls his eyes at me and glares at Anthony, "I meant yours," he gruffly remarks, "mine was fine, I have another I like better."

I smile at him knowingly, "Yeah, but keeping a friend is more important. How are you, Anthony? "

He looks at me with eyes wide open. "I didn't, I mean, I had no idea!"

Ping crosses his arms, "Space has dangers, distractions can be lethal."

I lean over and though it hurts like hell, I give Anthony a hug. We sit there a moment, our breath returning to normal, staring at the glob of asteroids and splintered boards. A solar wind blows through, raining tiny particles of debris across our skins. Every part of me that has had contact with Anthony burns. Then I ask them both. "You ready to go back?"

Chapter 19

Cleaning and Ironing

It was four in the morning when my hand landed on the carved brass handle of my parents' front door. Its worn pattern familiar and mocking. I looked down at myself; my shoes were gone and the dress was full of shredded edges. We had all returned to Ceres after the incident and paddleboarded for a few more hours after I brought back more boards and paddles from my warehouse.

The familiar noise of clicking tiles and soft giggling welcomed me home. My mother and my aunts were still playing Mah-Jong. They all looked me over with extremely knowing and bemused looks. My mother got up as Aunt Shirley and Aunt Hannah started a verbal fight and a woman I didn't know watched in horror. Her features were similar to Morgan's, so I figured it was one of her relatives.

My mother gave me a hug. "Did you go to an after party?" She was glowing with the idea of me being that social.

I played with edge of my dress. "Hi, Mom. Kind of."

185

She started circling me and her fingers reached out and pointed out the frayed bits. She picked some grit and rubbed it between her fingers and closed her eyes analyzing it. "The asteroid belt? You were on the asteroid belt? What kind of party happens in the asteroid belt?"

I flip my hair out of my eyes. Aunt Hannah and Aunt Shirley had stopped their silly argument and were staring at me. I shrug, "Paddleboarding."

My mother's face whitens and looks away. "Alone? You went stand up asteroid paddleboarding in this dress?"

I scratched my palms. They were still a mess from the contact with Anthony. My feet felt like raw hamburger. "No, I wasn't alone. I went with a few old friends and new acquaintances."

I watch my mother start to calculate the ramifications of this statement, trying to decide how she feels about it. My Aunt Hannah picks up a plate of my mother's pecan and chocolate rugelach and offers it up to me like a waitress. She gives her sister, my Mom an amused glance. "Give her a break Maxima! She did what you asked. So she included something she thought was fun. No harm done." She pushes the plate at me, "You must be starving."

I can never resist my mother's rugelach. My mouth was watering before I grabbed one whole piece and stuffed it my mouth. I bit into the blended flavor of chocolate, pecan and cinnamon. The pastry was buttery and flaky. It almost melts in my mouth. I smiled wide and pulled another piece.

My mother gave a resigned sigh, and with a forced brightness said, "New acquaintances, any possible gentlemen callers?"

I began to chuckle, "I doubt it."

Aunt Hannah laughed, "Always the optimist, Muriel."

Circe Syndrome

Aunt Shirley held up old time looking calling cards. They were linen and embossed. "You're wrong of course, Muriel. These all have put requests to call on you. Any of these men with you tonight?"

My jaw dropped, I was shocked. There were a few dozen cards. As Aunt Shirley picked and dropped them like a shower of coins, I made out a few faces that would appear as the light hit them. My attention went to them. A few were at the asteroid paddleboarding event. "Yes, I guess so." I turned away; some started to play videos if I paid attention to them too long. I took a deep breath and yawned. "I really should go to bed; I'll see you all in the afternoon?"

My mother and aunts exchanged looks and giggled. They had some agenda going on. I had no time or energy to get to the bottom of it.

I took a breath and enjoyed the completely exhausted feeling my whole body radiated as I walked to the stairs and pulled myself up to my room. I didn't bother to undress, and collapsed into the bed. Sleep hit me hard.

I awoke with the sound of rattling at the area around my head emanating from the window. I looked in its direction and found Sarina pawing at the molding of the window frame. I yawned and rubbed my eyes. Blinked a few times, and stared out at the purple sky lighting up. "Good morning, Sarina!"

She sighed, exasperated "How do you unlock this?"

I yawn and sit up and prop myself against my head board. I cross my arms and look at her. "I think we established you are not good for Ecospa."

Her brow furrowed for a second like when she was a child, and about have a tantrum and try to hurt me. Then she went placid. A pleasant expression filled her face. I actually find this more terrifying sometimes. "Don't you have other worlds?"

I shake my head and play with the edges of my dress as I straighten the fabric. I don't look at her at first and in a calm voice I say, "No, I'm not going to enable you." I look at her, " OK!"

Sarina looks at me shocked, I rarely say no to her. Her eyes begin to tear and the next thing I know she is wringing her hands and sobbing. She sits next to me on the bed with her head buried in her hands.

I have this desire to reach out and stroke her head and tell her it will be OK. I don't, I take a breath and stare at my vanity which is still in mirror mode. Something I find annoying. "I ran into someone who asked about you last night."

The tears stopped and a curious expression filled her face and she looked at me, "Who?"

I give her a hopeful smile, "Anthony, Simon's brother."

Sarina became quiet and whispered, "Oh?"

There was an uncomfortable silence where I stare at the ceiling, and I feel all these random emotions emanating from her. Sadness, pain and most of all, loss. After a bit she stands and moves down to the end of the bed, and she pauses, "Muriel?"

I look up and meet her eyes. "What?"

She has this look of someone really concerned, "What happened to your feet?"

I can feel the raw exposed skin and open wounds and the steel and iron radiating. I try to bury them in the blankets. Sarina reaches out and grabs my ankle. "Don't tell me dancing on air does this to your feet."

I smirk "Depends on how high you are."

She is dead serious and concerned, "They are covered in gashes, cuts and rashes, why haven't you healed yet?"

188

Circe Syndrome

The first wave of nausea hits me as the steel poisoning runs through me. I feel the blood drain from my face. I groan, and push my feet under some blanket to stop the air from hitting them. I want to curl up into a ball now.

There is a no nonsense knock at my door and before I can say enter, the door opens. My mother walks in.

Sarina looks at our mother expectantly. This tells me she summoned her telepathically. I eyeball the necklace and consider removing it from her out of spite. I don't want to have this conversation. Sarina pulls my foot back out of the blankets and points at it.

My normally pretty stoic mother winces. She comes and sits on the other side of me. She feels my forehead like when I was six. She talks to Sarina, "Sarah, did your little sister tell you what she did after the dance, yet?"

Sarina has this gleam of satisfaction, like when we were kids and she actually caught me breaking a rule. "Uh, no." She looks back out the window. I see her light of satisfaction waver, even though she has caught me not being perfect she is confronted yet again with my power.

My mother pulls my other foot out and starts tsking. She examines my hands. "She was asteroid stand up paddleboarding. Do you know one of the main elements found in asteroids?"

Sarina scowls at her mother with an, "I really don't have time for a teaching moment," look. "Let me guess; it's a main component of steel?"

My mother takes a big breath, and sighs, "Muriel, you managed to poison yourself last night."

I look up at her with lowered lids. "No shit," I think.

She gives me an amused wink, and shakes her head. She points at the door and it opens. In flies an array of fairies nattering at one another. The iridescent colors fill the room with rainbow light. The swirling colors make my stomach churn more.

My mother puts her right hand out in a sweeping gesture, "Luckily some of Morgan's extended family came to see the new blessing. They can help heal you so it is only a day you're incapacitated for, instead of a whole week."

This cloud of glowing two inch beings swarmed about my feet and hung there. They gasped in unison and then preceded to argue quickly in extremely high pitched voices.

I raise my shoulders at the room. "This is pretty odd. I usually only get a rash from asteroid exposure."

A fairy puts its hands on its hips and stands in my face. "You have carbon steel poisoning, too. If you were over exposed to that yesterday, then spent that evening around unrefined iron you were asking for trouble. Your body can't handle all that unrefined iron when your immune system is dealing with the steel!"

I am also trying to not bring up handling a person with carbon steel embedded in their skin, I rub my eyes because this creature's sparkling nature makes my stomach swim more. "Whatever."

My mother frowned, "When were you exposed to steel yesterday?"

I am thinking about Anthony. But I keep my response brief, "Headquarters."

Mom becomes thoughtful, "Oh, yes, the defenses. So the vampire had to help you home?"

I frown, getting the unsaid dialogue. "Yes, I was defenseless around opportunistic organisms," I think.

My mother frowns, "That steel defense, it seems to be an open opportunity for defining peoples' abilities."

I think about what Thomas had learned from my blood. I nod, "You have no idea."

Circe Syndrome

My mother's frown deepens and she leans in. "Perhaps later, we can discuss this subject further."

I nod.

My mother scratches her chin, "It is curious, you usually only get a rash from asteroid iron? Did something different happen?"

I thought about rescuing the steel skinned Anthony, winced and said, "Well, I had to stand on the asteroid barefoot for a bit."

She cocked her head and gave me a very focused stare. "Why?"

"My board was shredded." I watch a frown fill her features. I quickly and nervously say, "I had to help someone out of trouble. I got them out, but our boards didn't make it."

My mother sighs, shakes her head and lets out a breath, "No good deed goes unpunished."

"You can say that again, Mom." I say with an exhale.

"Why were you bare foot in space? How did you not explode?" She gestures with her hands.

I am watching the fairies don hazmat suits. They fly close to my feet and start examining them. Steel poisoning is contagious for magical creatures. I find myself distracted by these bright yellow hazmat suits and wondering where they are made. How does the manufacturing work for three inch suits with room for wings? I wonder how they stay in flight with the wings in that bulky material. I watch them unroll coconut bark. They lay it on my feet, all the threads activating nerves. I wince. Another fairy hands me a redwood rod. It feels soothing.

I start to involuntarily answer my mother as I follow the wood grain on the rod. "It is how the moss and the boards work."

"Moss, what moss?" She frowns and examines the shapes on my blanket.

I know she is looking away to get me to speak more. I comply, "It's this moss I found on another world and genetically engineered."

She looks at me interested and gestures for me to continue.

I look at my sister who has a brief look of fear, then returns to a look of indifference. The fairies are quietly working but look up at me now and then. My mother leans in to get my interest. I know she wants me to continue. "It works with the wood in the board, which is also alive. The moss produces oxygen and pressure in a symbiotic relationship with the wood, and the person it inhabits. My carbon dioxide helps its replicating cell process. The board also modifies sound waves. It feeds off the carbon dioxide also."

My mother blinks. "Are you telling me you have a piece of alien moss living in you?"

I sigh, of course, that would be the part she would glom onto in my explanation. "It is fine, Mom."

She shakes her head in disgust, "How do you know? What is this creature's agenda? How do you know it is you who likes to paddleboard in space? Maybe it's the moss in you telling your brain to enjoy it?"

I chuckle and hold my chin in thought, "I would probably paddleboard more often. The last time before this was over a year and a half ago. I only thought about it staring at the Columbia and looking at the reflected stars. If it was a planted desire, I would be thinking about it constantly."

Sarina looked out the window and grinned, then looked at me with a smug look, "What do you think about constantly?"

I am grateful for her changing the subject and grin back, remembering what went down in EcoSpa. "Not what you think about, judging by what happened recently."

Sarina's face flushed, and the fairies gave each other knowing looks.

192

Circe Syndrome

This is when Aoife, unannounced, walks into my room. The fairies had left the door open. Aoife stares out my window in a daze.

My mother stands and in front of her and, with a forced smile, says, "Yes, Aoife?"

Aoife adjusted her gaze to meet my mother's eyes. "Ummmm, Maxima, I was just wondering where you kept…" Her eyes wander to me and she takes in my tattered dress and abrasive feet, hands and other areas. "That is horrible steel scoring."

The fairies all chirp in agreement.

Nausea runs through me as the coconut bites further into my feet. I address her, "How is Morgan this morning?" I want the topic off me.

Aoife raises one perfectly manicured eyebrow. "Afternoon, Muriel, afternoon. She is doing well, as uncomfortable as a woman at nine months can be. How did you manage to cut yourself up so badly?" She crosses her arms.

Sarina giggles, stands and walks to the head of the bed. She ruffles my hair. "After the dance last night she decided to paddleboard in the asteroid belt without a board."

Aoife gives me an incredulous look, "That sounds unwise."

I chuckle, "You have no idea!"

I see Aoife's eyes narrow and her back straighten. She is about to say something condescending and authoritative. My mother stands in front of me and addresses her. "You were looking for something Aoife?" My mother escorts Aoife out of the room.

Two of the fairies fly up to my torso with a bowl. I'm grateful and mumble thanks as I take it.

The fairies' voices were incongruous with their message as they cheerfully say, "This next part might hurt a bit."

As they say this they push the coconut bark deep into my skin. I feel the steel in my body cycle toward it and cling to it. They twist the bark and rip off more of the flesh and blood clinging to it.

The pain shoots through me and I start to vomit. I am so thankful for the bowl as I feel the bile gush out of me.

Sarina squirms, "Ewwwww!"

I wipe my mouth with the back of my hand. "With the company you keep normally, Sarina, this should be nothing."

Sarina gives me an amused smile, "I'm usually long gone before this part manifests, itself."

I shift as I watch the fairies roll out a beech bark and lay it on my feet.   One flies to my face. "Don't worry Miss Muriel, we won't be ripping this one off for a while. If you're lucky, your body will just incorporate it into you."

They lay the bark on my feet then wrap them in leaf bandages.

I exhale and cock my head. I address the fairies, "If it doesn't incorporate itself, will you be ripping those off too?"

They exchanged mischievous and knowing smiles. They all shrug.

"Great," I think. I scowl. "Good to know."

Sarina chuckles, "You might want to have buckets instead of bowls."

This is when my mother, looking harried, walks back into the room. She looks at the fairies. "Well?"

The one who had informed me about the bark chirped, "She'll live. Keep her off her feet today and take the bandages off tonight. We will come back later to check her feet."

My mother nods, "Thanks for your help, Arial."

Arial gives her a gracious smile, "No problem, Maxima. Aoife annoying you at all?"

She gives her an endearing smile, "No." There is a pregnant pause. "Everything is going well."

I know none of us buy this. I bow my head to the fairies as I speak to them. "Thanks so much, normally I would be put out for a few days."

Arial's hands go to her hips. "Do you normally poison yourself with steel?"

I sigh, "It is a more common occurrence than I would like."

Arial shakes her head as if in disgust, "Oi! It's really easy, girl, avoid steel and iron!"

I want to ask about the iron in everyone's blood, but thought that would be a bit too smart ass at the moment. "Yes, Ma'am!"

She points at me, "And! Stay away from Morgan in your condition! You got it?"

I say cheerfully, "Got it!"

The fairies raise in unison. Their wings created a buzz that became high pitched as they flew out of the room.

I notice the metallic, bile taste in my mouth and stare at the bowl, still in my hands. I look at my mother. "Thanks, Mom."

My mother nods.

Sarina stands, "You ready to go down stairs?"

I finger my dress and the grime from asteroid dust and the sweat from vomiting between my fingers. "I should take a shower and change. Mom, do I have permission to hover in the house?"

My mother gives me a kind smile and nods her head. "Sure, Why my dear, when you were in space, didn't you do that?"

Janette Bach

I laugh, "That is the question, isn't it?"

Sarina smiles her cat that ate the canary, smile. She is so happy when I mess up in any way. "Your brain is not always working is it, sissy?"

Mom and her start going into the story from when I was six and tried to swim in snow. They leave the room together engrossed in the tale.

I sigh, and set the bowl on my night stand. I cover my face with both of my hands and take a deep breath. I stare at my bandaged feet, and move them back and forth a second. I wonder if I can get them wet? I guess I could just spell them water resistant for now. I coat them with a force field then cover that with wax. It's about three millimeter distance of air about my feet. I sit up and swing my legs over to the side of the bed. I consider an urge to scratch my left foot where the bark is embedded more than the other parts of the bark.

I tentatively stand on air. It is not easy to balance, and feels a bit like trying to stand on a moving conveyor belt. It takes me a moment to find balance. I take a step with my left foot and fight my ankle's urge to turn, then bring the right foot parallel. I try to not over overthink and just walk.

I walk into the bathroom. I lean into the tub to turn it on and almost fall in. I get the temperature where I want it then I change the spray from tub fill to shower spray. I take a moment to undress, pausing to examine the fraying edges of the dress lace. My skin goosebumps in the exposed air, and I notice different spots of abrasive rubbing on my body from the matter in space.

I bend my neck back and forth and then step into the misty, moist air of the shower. I lean against the wall and let the water run down my back and I breath in the air. I hadn't realized that my lungs had felt dry before. I soap myself down and rinse off and wash my hair. I find myself distracted by the water drops on the wall. I take a moment and just watch how they seem to flow at a consistent, slow rate. Then one drop will just spontaneously run down the wall to join with the bigger mass of water pooling in the tub.

Without much ceremony or thought after watching this awhile, I wipe my hand across the wall causing more racing drops. I make a clear, foot long smear of water condensation on the wall. I think about this fledgling galaxy I tinkered with a few months ago. Its image appears in the condensation on the wall. I am scrying it there. Like a video on a screen.

It is a spiral galaxy with one electric blue Sun. There are ten planet's spinning around it. Three of the planets are gas giants. The other seven were made of rock and had volcanic potential. As was my tradition, it was the third planet away from the sun that I started tinkering with.

I located it in the image and placed my thumb and forefinger on it, and pulled them apart from each other causing the planet to enlarge into view. At the planet's edge along the arch I tapped my fingers in a sequence. Stats menus on the conditions of the planet appeared.

I was curious. I had left this planet with a series of bacteria, plants and creatures. I was wondering how the eco system was doing? Were the Biomes thriving? I started tabbing through the organism database. I paused. The results were startling. I zoomed in on the planet surface. My jaw dropped involuntarily. I was flabbergasted. The landscape was wall to wall fungus. Any signs of wildlife or forests were gone. The fungus was varied in cap size and included two types of earth.

I sigh, bewildered and mesmerized at the same time. The mushrooms had this metallic sheen and a silver pattern. They were varied and unique. This part was intriguing. A shudder began at my foot and ankle, and up ran my body I drew a circle in the right corner of the water drops of the original swipe. I tapped another sequence in the space with my right hand. My creature database appeared. I see what I had downloaded there. All are now missing on this planet.

I tap my chin, thinking. I close my eyes and put my face in the spray of the shower. I thought about the different types of creatures I had put in the mix. A question comes through my mind as I review the mix. I take my right index finger and draw a straight line parallel to the bottom edge of the swipe. Tool Icon's appear in that space. I have one that scans chemical compositions. I use that on the mushrooms. It takes a minute to break it down into a chart of chemical compositions.

They contain a low amount of carbon which is odd in a life form. It has a high concentration of metal, water, sodium and some unknown element that seems to be half an atomic number. I shook my head, bewildered, and scanned it again.

I went to my database, found a spec for a tortoise, and put in a craving for this type of mushroom. I tweaked an Ivy plant to populate like the mushrooms and played with a few other species. I have this lab outpost I made in the vicinity. To make the embryos in. I sent an order for them all to be made and sent to the planet.

I washed my hair, and finished washing myself off. Ran a hand through the scrying, making it disappear. I turned off the water, still puzzling over the mushrooms and the disappearance of the other animals and plants.

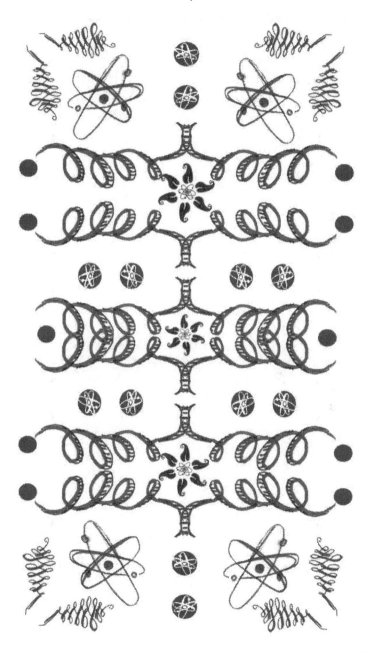

Chapter 20

Holding Cards Close

When I make it to the main floor, the first being to meet my eyes was Clay. His literally sapphire eyes twinkled, and his giant clay hand pointed to the game table. The mah-jong pieces were gone and my mother and aunts nowhere to be found. My uncle Mordecai was shuffling cards. I sat down at the table. He always has a frown but gave me a grin. I looked at him expectantly. I never know what he is going to do but I always learn something new from him.

He winks as he shuffles, and then smirks, "Poker?"

I shake my head and laugh, "No, I'm not seven anymore. Plus, I'm broke."

Clay comes and sits between us.

I watch Uncle Mordecai pretend to pout. "Come on Muriel, just a couple of hands?"

I cross my arms. He cheats badly when money is involved. I sigh, "How about Rummy 500?"

He brightens, "A penny a point? All you lose is 5 dollars."

I look at Clay. The massive golem shrugs. His baritone voice sighs, "Against my better judgement, I'll say yes."

Uncle Mordecai sits back beaming, shuffling and marking cards.

I reach out and take them from him.

He ruffles, "In my day younglings respected their elders!"

I give him an amused grin. "Just let me cut." I push a wipe spell across the deck removing all the magical markers. I cut the cards and hand them back.

Mordecai frowns. "Spoilsport." he says deadpan.

Clay snorts and smiles, causing dust to come out of his nose.

I meet his eyes with an amused smile.

As Uncle Mordecai deals he calls out to the other rooms, now populated with my relatives and tons of Morgan's, I don't know. "We have room for a fourth, anyone else want to play?"

Sarina looks up from a Vogue magazine. My mother and my aunts look out from the kitchen.

Aunt Hannah's eyebrows raise regarding her brother. "What are you playing?"

Aunt Shirley nudges her in the ribs, "We should ask Muriel why she has bandages on her feet and is hovering about the house."

I look at her and shake my head, "No, really you don't need to."

Tons of cheering comes from the family room where my father, surrounded by Morgan's relatives, is staring at this big screen watching some sporting event. It looks like they are playing Lacrosse on hovering skateboards. A flaming dragon just filled the screen and Morgan's family cheered. One of the fairies chose that moment to fly through the doorway. It gives me a judgmental look and crosses his arms. "Steel sickness! Your niece makes some interesting choices."

As Aunt Shirley starts loading the fairy with a leaning tower of tortilla chips and salsa, Aunt Hannah approaches me. "You don't usually get steel sickness from asteroid paddleboarding. A few abrasions yes, but poisoned?"

I adore Aunt Hannah, she knows this. I am going to answer her. As I examine my cards. "I went to Collective headquarters earlier in the day." I look just above my cards and meet her concerned eyes. The warmth floors me a second. I forget my family cares. I get myself under control before I tear up. "I guess after that exposure, there wasn't much to keep me from over saturating with steel in my blood. Even the unrefined iron could poison me."

Aunt Hannah's creases between her eyes softened, "Hey, Morty, did you hear Muriel got a few cards from gentlemen last night?"

I want to strangle her.

Mordecai makes a show of taking the king of diamonds from the discard pile. He nods at his wife Aunt Shirley. "Yes, I did. Quite a haul, I understand." He adjusts his cards and nods to Clay.

As I blush, Clay lays the king, queen, and jack of spades on the table. He discards the two of diamonds. My hand has the three of diamonds, and the four of diamonds. I pick up the two of diamonds and play the run. I shake my head, "Please, stop. I was uncomfortable going. This conversation is terrifying to me."

They all laugh. I scowl at my cards and take a breath, then put on the fake smile I'm good at. It always begins the same.

"You're a pretty girl, if you would just try a little more. You could be living like Yacob and Morgan." Aunt Shirley calls out.

Mordecai gives me a wink.

I don't want to yell at them all. I want to be loved for me, not some illusion of me. I know the right boy won't care what I wear. I let my terror generate a laugh, "It's your turn, Uncle Mordecai."

The doorbell rings and my mother wipes her hands then hangs a dish towel on her shoulder. She pushes past her sister and sister in-law, and heads to the door. She smiles as she opens the door and greets the newcomer. "Hi!"

It's a well cultured British voice that says, "Hi, Mrs. Anahat, I'm Jasper Underhill, Morgan's cousin on her father's side."

My mother smile widens and gives him a hug, "Jasper, I remember you. How is darling Isabelle doing?"

He gives my mother that look she always gets. The I like her look. "She is doing well. May I come in?"

My mother steps to the side and shuts the door as she checks the wards. The family around the TV call out "Oi, Jasper!"

He laughs and calls back, "How are the Beefeaters doing?"

A boy with bright orange curls and freckles runs up to him. "They are ahead by three points." He gives Jasper a high five, and goes back to the family room.

Jasper makes his way around the family room, high fiving and hugging a few of his kinsmen. He looks up at me and walks up to the table. "Hey, what are you playing?"

Uncle Mordecai gives him an appraising look, then a predatory smile. Really friendly. "Rummy five hundred. Only five dollars at stake."

Jasper scratches his head, "You play Rummy 500 for money?"

I throw up my hands, "A quirk of my Uncle's, he only plays a game if there is a wager involved."

Uncle Mordecai gestures to the empty seat, "You want to play?"

Jasper takes the chair turns it around and straddles it. He places his long manicured hands on the table. He exchanges a knowing smile with me and gives my Uncle a challenging look. "Yeah, OK."

I give Jasper a fond smile, thinking about his gambling hobbies.

He leans in toward me conspiratorially, "What?"

"I don't believe I've ever seen you sit so ungentlemanly before."

He playfully turns his palms up. "What do you mean?"

I almost whisper, "In my mind, you're always a gentleman rake from the Jane Austin period."

Jasper picks up the cards Clay dealt him and fans them in his hands. His deftness with them tells me he has some similar experiences as Mordecai. I might be witnessing a battle of two artists. "How so?" He says with a straight, puzzled voice.

I shrug and examine my cards, "I don't know, maybe it's the longer sideburns and the British accent. The high collars?" I take a card. It's a spade. I discard it.

Jasper picks it up and discards a three of clubs, "Sideburns, you define my character by choice of my facial hair choice?"

"Well there are also phrases like 'define my character' Who uses the word 'character' in modern conversation in that manner?" I involuntarily snort.

Clay laid all his cards down, "Rummy!" His course, gravelly voice making me smile.

Mordecai wrinkles his nose, "What?"

As we all add up our scores Uncle Mordecai addresses Jasper, "Why are you here again? To see Morgan?"

Jasper looks startled by my uncle's directness. "Well, yes, I am. Will she be around shortly?"

A few fairies flew over and stood on the table in front of Jasper. A male one squinted up at Jasper and said accusingly, "No!" He points at me. "She is steel scored." He uses a theater whisper, "Too contagious for the unborn to be around." He then backs away from me like I'm carrying the plague.

Jasper frowns looking me up and down, "Where?"

I slide a foot from under the table and the fairies fly to the other room.

Clay begins to shuffle the cards.

Uncle Mordecai pulls out a cigar. He clips the tip and starts to ignite it.

My mother storms into the room with her hands on her hips. "What do you think you're doing?"

He sighs, "Relax, sis." He pulls out an ash tray. "It's spelled to not smoke in your house. Only my lungs and this." He pulls out a glass mason jar with a lid on it. "In here." He lights his cigar and sucks on it. He expels but it doesn't appear in the air the mason jar accumulates smoke. When he sets the cigar down on the ash tray the jar continues to fill as the cigar burns.

My mother sighs, shakes her head and says, "Fine!"

Mordechai winks at me and smirks. He calls out to my mother as she walks away. A brother teasing his sister. "How about some coffee? Sis?"

Jasper is staring down at my feet. He swallows a moment. "Saving Anthony. Do you normally react so intensely to unrefined iron?"

I reach up and start rubbing the back of my neck and consider my cards. "No." I take a breath. "Was over exposed to some steel yesterday, before the dance. Started making me more sensitive to the metal molecules that make it up."

My mother had paused on her way to the kitchen and was waiting for a moment to interject into our conversation. She looked pointedly at Jasper. "Would you like something to drink, too?"

He looks to me. He had just watched the animosity between my mother and her brother. He is wondering if this was a good idea to accept the offer. He didn't want to offend her.

I smile encouragingly, "She doesn't mind, really. Uncle Morty is just her brother; you know, sibling stuff."

A knowing smile of understanding fills his features. "Sure."

My mother squeezes my hand in amusement and addresses Jasper. "Tea?"

He nods, rearranging his cards. "Yes, please."

Clay and I exchange looks and say in unison, "Me, too."

My mother nods and heads to the kitchen.

Mordecai coughs, "So young Jasper, you're seeing this Isabella, yet one of your cards ended up in Muriel's basket?"

Jasper nods casually, "Yeah, that's right." He stands and changes the chair back to the normal position, winks at me and sits straight in it.

I imagine the chair turning back around is a comment on being interrogated.

Clay deals the cards.

Jasper cocks his head as he examines his cards. He flashes a look at Uncle Mordecai then meets my eyes. "I don't know if Isabella even knows I'm in love with her, I think she thinks were just friends with benefits."

I laugh at the expression on my uncle's face, it was slack jawed.

"What? "He sputters, "Does that mean what I think it means?"

Jasper examines his cards, "I don't know, what do you think it means?"

I pull a card from the stack and discard it. My mother shows up and gives us all drinks, she places sugar and cream on the table, too.

Uncle Mordecai grasps his coffee cup. "That means you engage in" there was a pause and a stutter, "In," another pause, "Intercourse with no commitments to each other."

Jasper nodded and chuckled, "You got it."

Mordecai frowned "Muriel, didn't you just say you two were friends?"

Jasper gives him an amused leer.

I was drinking from my teacup and choked. The blood rushes to my cheeks. "Yes, but I didn't say we were that kind of friends. " I hold out my hand and gesture down ward. "We are just plutonic friends."

Jasper meets my eyes with a raised eyebrow, that I interpret as, "Well that can be renegotiated."

I close my eyes and shake my head in a negative fashion.

Jasper shrugs and discards a card. "So Morgan is not coming down? I'll have to go to another room?"

I nod toward the stairs. "They have an apartment on the third landing."

Uncle Mordecai studies his cards and puffs on his cigar, causing smoke to swirl in the jar.

"Say, Muriel? Do you know anything about the troll clans in town?" Jasper is looking thoughtfully at the stairs as he asks.

Clay just discarded the jack of hearts. I have two jacks. I pick it up, and place the jacks on the table. I muse how Portland is the city of bridges, and the troll population is quite healthy. "Yeah, why?"

He frowned at his cards. "One of my brothers did a deal with a troll family and lost a family, heirloom. I would like to negotiate getting it back. What would you recommend to begin my approach?"

Mordecai scowls, "Forget about it, that heirloom is lost forever."

I wobble my head and adjust my cards, "Goat Cheese." I say succinctly.

"What?" Jasper is looking at me like I have gone crazy.

"Goat cheese, preferably from a local farm. There is a great goat cheese spread sold at the farmer's market."

He sighs, "Not a goat, but goat cheese?"

"You know, it's Portland. Most of the trolls here were influenced by the communes of the sixties. They are all vegetarian. They still love goat flavors, and because it's Portland, they like to keep it local."

Uncle Mordecai laughs, "Really?"

I give him an emphatic nod and consider my cards.

Jasper cocks his head appreciatively, "That is some useful information. How do you know the trolls?"

I wave a hand as I say, "Oh? You know, childhood adventures."

He gives me an expectant look.

I don't want to talk about it and look to Uncle Mordecai to find a way to distract this conversation. He is looking at me expectantly, also, as he puffs on his cigar. I shift my gaze to the mason jar. I find the smoke moving in the jar mesmerizing. I see a tiny shadow figure outlined in smoke. I gesture to the jar. "What is that?"

Uncle Mordecai picks up the jar and examines it, squinting his eyes. "What did it look like?"

I fidget and shake my head, "I know this sounds weird, but I could of sworn it was a tiny dragon."

He nods absently, and puts the jar back on the table. He flicks ash into the ash tray. "Damn, smoke dragon nits. It gets infested with them on a normal basis."

He swirls the jar, causing the multiple dragon nits I can now see to collide and combine in one smoke dragon about one-inch long.

I gasp, "Is that normal?"

He looks at me puzzled and chuckles, "It's like you never played with smoke dragon mites before."

I mesmerized say, "I haven't!"

He puffs on his cigar in thought. "I guess you never spent time with elders who smoke. Your mother has some strict rules, that used to be considered really odd." He considers the end of his cigar. "But now considered rather wise." He sighs.

I look at Jasper, "Were you aware of this phenomenon?"

He shakes his head, and squints at the jar in wonder, too.

"So? You grew up playing with smoke dragons? That was a normal childhood pastime when you were a kid, Uncle Mordecai? When was that exactly? Did you know Moses?"

Uncle Mordecai snorts, and the smoke in the jar storms, causing the dragon to break back into smaller dragon mites again. "Funny niece! Funny! Not smoke dragons. Damn it! Just the mites. You don't want to come face to face with an actual smoke dragon! They will suffocate you as soon as look at you!

I cock my head, remembering something. "Is that why you smoke, Uncle, your work with the dragon treaties?"

He takes on a reminiscent, thoughtful look as he taps more ash into the ashtray. He then regards the smothering tip of his cigar. "Some."

Jasper cleared his throat and regarded us both a second lost in thought. He stands, stretches and yawns. Through the yawn he tries to cover, he says, "Upstairs?"

I give him a positive shake of my head. My sister, Sarina, must have been paying attention, because she sidles up to him at that moment. She gives him an impish smile and gestures to the stairs, "I'll show you."

Uneasily, he smiles back at her. She gives me a wink and takes his arm. He looks a bit blown over. She leads him away.

I look at my hands and then back at Uncle Mordecai. "The dragon treaties?"

"Tarnation child! How did you angle this conversation to be about me when I wanted to talk to you about...," He nods toward the stairwell, Sarina and Jasper climbing in animated conversation, "that boy?"

I shrug, I don't know what to say. I have no idea what he thinks could happen between Jasper and me, but I am sure he is exaggerating my friend's esteem of me.

"That boy is trouble with a capital T! Friends with benefits, pah, the unmitigated gall of him!" He swirls the jar again.

Tyring to convince myself as much as my uncle, I reply, "He was just looking for advice on handling Isabella. It really wasn't about me or you."

He snorts, "This a common occurrence with you, Muriel, people trusting you with intimate secrets?"

I shake my head up then down and flick the green felt on the table in front of me with my right hand.

He lets out a lot of air and states, "He gave you an inquiring look."

"You brought that up, and besides, he is male. You bring up certain opportunities and they will take a chance." I say exasperated.

He laughs, and gasps on the smoke in his chest. "He is a young man. It is all he thinks about."

"Right!" I shake my head in disagreement.

Uncle Mordecai gives me a nurturing smile, "Let's play another hand."

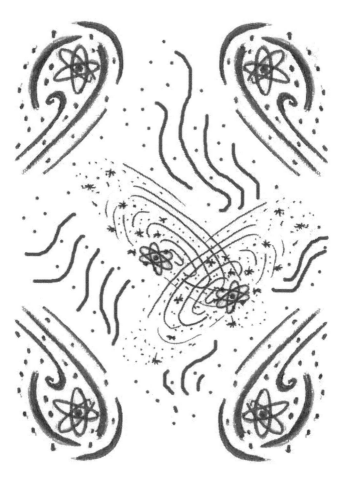

Chapter 21

Waking

An hour later, the game on the main TV ended, and people streamed through the house. My Uncle stubbed out his nub of a cigar, "Thanks for the games, Muriel." He stood and stretched and walked over to Aunt Shirley.

I twisted in my seat and bent at my waist stretching out my arms. A pair of unfamiliar, worn purple sneakers appear in my line of vision. I blink and sit up. I pause, lock eyes, with this young man who has a body builder body, and long, red, curly hair, tied back in a leather thong.

His dark, purple eyes with tiger type irises made me hesitate, and he did a double take toward me and grinned a dimpled smile. "Hey there, love." His voice had a Scottish brogue.

He wore a horizontal striped jersey that had purple, green and white stripes. It made his huge frame seem bigger.

I give him a wimpy wave and signal to the empty seat next to me. "Hi."

He pulls it out and starts examining the construction. He nods his head toward the stairs. "That bird that took Jasper upstairs. She your sister?"

"Yes."

An eyebrow raises, "What is her name?"

"Sarina, except when my mother is around, then it's Sarah."

He scratches his chin and smiles wider, "So, is Sarina single?"

I tap my fingers on the table. I am so used to this conversation, there are days where it is the only one I find I ever have. "I believe so."

He raises a palm, "You're her sister, you don't know?"

I look away bored, I'm not going to go into my sister's beliefs on relationships. I know that is her job in these situations.

He seems lost in thought as he puts the chair back.

Sarina appears back in the room. He straightens and approaches her. The room is starting to stretch, as more and more people pile in. The house is filling with relatives. Sarina makes her way through the throng, gives the boy a smile before she walks past him and puts a hand on my shoulder.

I give her a knowing grin.

She pauses. "What?"

My eyes flicker to the young man and back to her.

She follows my gaze, and looks at him appraisingly. Her cat smile of anticipation fills her face, and she meets my eyes with a raised eyebrow.

This conversation requires no words between us. I nod.

213

She looks over at him and as she meets the man's eyes, she flips her hair. A self-satisfied smile still on her face. He is starting to move toward her again as she leans down and says, "The fairies sent me. Morgan is going to come down. They want you to vacate the room."

I give a non-verbal agreement.

She has turned and gone to meet him, a good three yards away from me. I marvel at her ease and comfort in these situations.

I take a breath and stand with myself hovering a centimeter from the ground. I feel a bit unsteady and remind myself to not think about it so much. I have to imagine it is the ground and not the air I am walking on. I swallow when I see the number of people swelling into the room. I make my way to the stairs as a hole opens for me in the gathering of people. I hear mumblings of steel contagion. I focus on finding my way through the people.

I am stopped by my father just before I reach the bottom stair. I look up at him with his beaming, amused smile. "Oh, hi, Dad!"

He reaches out and ruffles my hair. "Muriel, dear, I haven't seen you for a few days. Things are really happening in here now, why are you leaving?"

I nod and shrug. "I have been ordered to evacuate the common room."

He murmurs and frowns, "I'm sure everything would be fine, but these modern medical practices are so hypochondrial. Let me escort you up."

" OK, Dad." I start climbing the stairs.

Dad paralleled me. "Did I tell you I got a new assistant?"

My mind is in a free fall thinking about the mushroomed planet, but I bite at his topic. "No, Dad, what is their name?"

He gives me this huge grin, "Schmooey." He lets the end of the name go up in a playful way.

I involuntarily roll my eyes, "What? That can't be true!"

He chuckles, "Hand to God his name is Schmooey."

I throw up my hands, " OK." I say deadpan.

He nudges my shoulder with his, "I'm trying to tell you a story here, we aren't even at the funny part yet."

I know my expression on my face is non plussed. "Tell me about Schmooey. Why did you hire him?"

He shakes his head, "I'm telling this story, Muriel. Not you."

I dip my head, "Sorry, Dad."

He frowns at me, "You OK?"

I give him a smile, "Besides the steel poisoning, yeah, I'm fine."

He rolls his eyes, "Yeah, that is believable!"

"Schmooey?"

He stares at me speculatively; I know he is wondering if he should dig into my response. But he nods, and regains the appearance of a storyteller. "Schmooey's learning how to do the math on circuit boards so he stops burning out transformers and circuits."

I meet his eyes showing I am listening with interest, "That is an important lesson."

He shakes his head, "Crazy, the amount of transformers he went through before I figured out his weakness."

I giggled in wonder, "How many transformers?"

He looks deflated and self-effacing, "So many I noticed."

I start to laugh. I start to cough when I laugh and speculate, "Billions?"

He shakes his head with a mock sorrowful face, "More."

My mind does an image of a supernova when I try to comprehend a number that big.

"So anyways, Schmooey and I were working on this circuit board for a new project of your brother's."

I give him a questioning look. "What kind of project?"

He winks, which means it's a secret he will not tell. "Schmooey is covered in electric residue from a burnt out circuit. He says he is going out to get lunch. Do I want anything from Fleshmen' s deli?"

I can see my door. As we are climbing the last stair flight and I give him a quizzical smile.

"I give him my usual order, a pastrami on rye, with pickles and onions. He nods and writes it down. Then heads out, his hair frazzled and all. He is this short pale guy with blond dreadlocked hair. The dreads bent all electric and heading everywhere. He wears these oversized pinstriped oxford shirts."

I find myself trying to not laugh out loud at the image this paints in my mind.

"So Schmooey goes out to get lunch. I look over his work. He has these wild ideas sometimes. He puts resistors before and after the processor, some type of faster than slower current theory. " Dad shakes his head and rolls his eyes. "But the economy of space is interesting."

I have a vague idea of what he is talking about, but me and electronics don't always get along, one of the reasons I am not in the family business. But listening, that I can do. Sometimes I ask the right questions. "Slow current theory?"

He starts to laugh "Yeah, he is convinced that unfettering the current will help the chip work faster."

"If it's too much for the chip to handle it will burn it out, won't it? Quickly!"

Dad head goes up and down emphatically, "Anyways he has a lot to learn. He makes it back a half hour later with my sandwich and this bag of microprocessors."

I am at my door, nodding...

Dad ruffles my hair, "Schmooey says to me, 'here is your sandwich and a bag of chips.'

I wince and groan. "Really, Dad? Really?"

He laughs, "Come on, it's funny!"

I shake my head and laugh, "Nope."

He pauses, and taps my shoulder as I make to open my door.

His face full of tenderness and concern, "You'll come visit me in my workshop soon, right? Tell me what is going on in your life."

I grin, "I am sure mother keeps you well informed."

He shakes his head, "It's different from the individual's mouth, dear heart!"

I give a positive cock of my head, " OK, Dad, I will, soon,"

I push open the door to my room and see purple dolphins jumping in the window. I can smell the seawater, and I think of Gregor's eyes. My dad looks in and shakes his head. "Such a bizarre window. You know you're lucky your mother lets you keep that, after..."

I look at him, the mourning probably still fresh now in my eyes and he backs away. I try not to cry. "It's nice to see you, Dad. Yacob and Morgan are going to need you downstairs. I will see you later."

I watch him struggle, but realize that he can't leave Mom to deal with everything alone. He gives me a quick hug and leaves.

I take a breath. I look at the vanity and play with the nobs, changing it back into a drawing table.

I pull out a sheet of paper and start to sketch the scene from the window. My mind wandering to the planet of mushrooms. Why did that happen? I seeded my standard 5832 species on to the planet. My private joke of chai cubed. But now there was only one species, one I never created.

I absently wonder at the taste of a metallic mushroom. Would butter be useful?

I play with all of this as I draw, then bring out a canvas and transfer the sketch to it. I start to paint.

A few hours later there is a knock on my door. It's the shave and haircut knock my mother can never resist. I just will the door open without getting up, as I mix one of the purples I need for the dolphins.

Mom gives me an appraising look as she brings in a tray of food. I assume she and dad had had a stilted, polite conversation about me surrounded by family. Then wince when I realize it was probably just a mental conversation. I am still baffled by how they can stand each other when they can access each other so easily.

She sets the tray at the end of my desk and sits on my bed. She is playing with the stitching and I assume she is just drinking in the quiet.

I create an arch for a dolphin back and say over my shoulder, as I notice the roasted chicken with mashed potatoes and spinach, "There are a lot of people in the house, huh?"

She chuckles and snorts. "Just a few. I have no idea how typical humans handle this situation. They can't make their own homes stretch and add rooms as needed."

I wink, "And keep the space on the outside the same. No they can't do that, technically we shouldn't be doing that either."

Mom laughs, "Multiple dimensions are accepted in science circles."

I give her a look then paint some more, "Yeah, OK Mom, Luckily I didn't take my vows to The Collective that seriously."

218

She snorts and points to the window. "That is a complete violation of several laws and treaties."

I blush, "Yeah." I change back to the subject on hand before I lose the one thing I feel I need to get through my days. "I believe typical people don't have everyone stay in one house when a baby is born. They don't require as much protection, either, when first born. Just the birth parents handle it."

Mom has stood and is examining the windows with her hands behind her back. She is actually a member of the council, the ruling body of The Collective. She rarely talks of her work and I know I owe my life to her.

She wistfully waves, "We used to be that way, too. Maybe, us all being egalitarian and letting all kinds of species live does have some downsides."

I clean my brush, and wipe my hands and grab a leaf of spinach, "Everything has down sides and up sides. But I don't want to live in a world dictated by the whims of only a few."

Mom is who I inherited the planet talent from. She gives me a heartwarming grin and laughs. She leans into the window, letting the breeze move her hair and coat her face. She lightens and asks, "How is EcoSpa doing? Anyways?"

I frown and adjust the brushes on my desk. "Well, too well, I am going to have to leave it to its own devices soon."

She crosses her arms and chews on a lip and looks at me. She knows how attached I am to the planet and the memories I have there. "Why?"

I groan, "A species has developed magic."

She turns thoughtful, "Ahh! That was quick. You will have to show me your formula sometime. That is the second time and quicker, too. Have you started another?"

I bend my neck and play with my earlobe unconsciously, "Yes, I might need your thoughts on it soon. Something bizarre is happening."

Mom had walked to the head of the bed and started fluffing a pillow. Her head cocked, "Sure, I would love to take a look. Say, did you meet this man new to our world, Irving, at the dance?"

I blink at the change of subject, "Yeah. He went paddleboarding with us."

She paused and raised an eyebrow, "Hmmm, I imagine he sent a card then." She exhales and looks at the door in to the hallway. "I guess I should get back out there. Heal quickly, Merlin believes the big event will be in two days."

I narrow my eyes confused, "I thought it was going to be a week."

Mom shrugged, her curls bobbing, "I think Aoife helped change his mind."

I review my schedule in my head, "I'm on duty for the next five nights."

Mom nodded, "I will let Merlin know."

I laugh, "He doesn't need me."

Mom giggled "I believe Morgan will, you know how to be calm in the midst of drama. She will need someone sane besides her mother, her mother in-law and her rookie-father husband."

I begin eating the chicken, "OK, Mom, I will attend."

She stands next to me, "Good girl, nice painting by the way." She heads out

Eventually, I head to bed. The next morning, I awoke to a swarm of fairies. My head was swimming trying to focus on one being, and my groggy mind couldn't focus. Stars shoot through my vision as they start ripping the bandages off my feet. I gasp then sit up and look at my feet. They are completely healed with the silverish color of birch bark, and the bandages are filled with tiny metal specks. They take this green smelly salve and slather it on my feet. The sensitivity falls away and they feel numb.

Circe Syndrome

Arial hovers in my face with her hands behind her back and paces. She gives me a fierce look. "You are OK to go back to your normal activities, but avoid large quantities of steel!" Her voice rose as she said the last five words.

I nod.

She gives me a weary look, "Muriel, do you hear me? I analyzed your blood. You keep doing this and you're going to be incapacitated!"

"I understand Arial. Thank you for your help."

The fairies exchange looks and fly out of the room.

I take a moment, swing my legs around, and make a tentative stand on the ground, solid contact. Nothing hurt.

I went about starting my day.

Chapter 22

Dog Gone

That night I head to work and to Sangria. I am hoping that Mr. Grout had a great time with Thomas and will show up. We can always use another agent in The Collective. As I walk down the streets, the wind blows the leaves about making them dance. The ones falling from trees and floating down through the air remind me of the dance at Multnomah Falls.

Suddenly, this pack of all types of dogs stream around me. This pokes at my brain as I fight to stay standing in the current of canines. I remember the briefing on dogs and a possible Circe manifestation. This stream is coming from a corner bar with a green door and two windows flashing Rogue Beer signs. I make sure the camera on my retina is on. Two young men manning my feed say, "Woah!" in unison.

They play with the camera, change lenses and one addresses me. "We are sending back up Muriel. Do not. I repeat do not engage."

Circe Syndrome

Jack's voice enters the conversation, "Take a look, Muriel. Shield yourself, but go take a look."

I splay my fingers as I thicken my anti-magical shield. Something always about me in public. We Heska must always be on guard. There are things that live in the aether that hunt us. I try to take on a casual air and then I walk into the bar. I blink in the dim light.

My feet stick a bit to the floor and there is a smell of years of smoke. The orange seventies wall paper above paneling is peeling a bit. It looks pretty deserted even though all the tables have empty glasses on them. There is a forty-year-old man with thinning hair and a loud Hawaiian shirt sitting at the bar. He is staring at his beer. I tall, willowy blond women with curly hair polishes pint glasses, mumbling to herself behind the bar.

I take a seat at the other end of the bar and pull out my sketchbook.

The blond bartender wearily comes over to where I am sitting and mops up the table top. She pulls two half-drunk glasses, dumping them in the trough. Her voice is that of one tired and wanting no nonsense, "Can I get you something?"

I meet her eyes, "You have any cider?"

She tosses the rag in her hand from one to another. "I think I have some Finnegan's, will that work?"

I smile, as I arch the pencil, "Yes, that would be great!"

She grabs a glass and fills it and sets it in front of me. Then she starts moving about the room bussing tables.

Jack's baritone voice echoes around in my head. "Do you think it's him or her?"

I consider them both under lower lids as I keep my face turned to my sketchbook. I think back to Jack, "It's more common in females then men, right. I say it's her. She seems unaware. There is a puzzled air about the empty tables and half empty drinks."

Jack's voice is impatient and his eyebrows are stern, "You can see energy signatures right? Give them both a look with power site on."

I take a breath as I think to myself, "Big Brother, this is so much trouble. That he knows this." I do realize that having access to my optical nerve opened this knowledge to them, but what I know about what they are doing with my blood I have reservations to consider. I comply and look with aether sight. Energy is swimming around the woman in a bubbling mass. It starts to spike with lightening.

It almost struck the man on the bar-stool. He is staring at his beer glumly. I reach into his mind and trigger a melatonin surge, giving him an intense need to go home and sleep. He yawns and reaches for his wallet and drops it. As he bends down to get it the ball of lightening in the aether strikes the stool he was on. He pulls out a twenty and sets it under his glass and stands. He makes to leave and the bubble strikes again.

He freezes and he drops to all fours. Fur pushes out of him and he shutters and shakes shedding his clothes. He begins to bark.

I send a thought to Jack, "I believe that is confirmation."

I don't wait for permission I reach into this woman's mind. One thought is that there in an ever repeating loop. "Dogs, all men are dogs!" Beneath this were onion layers of stories starring her with the same theme. She would fall in love with one man after another. Without really knowing them. She couldn't recognize the signs that the men were un-genuine. Eyes blanking out when she would talk, it is common later in a relationship but not in the beginning. In the beginning, a man will pay attention like they can't get enough when the pursuit is on. I look deeper, and find the unattending father in her childhood.

Circe Syndrome

I notice the miasma of energy around her is starting to spike again. I am trying to figure out how to neutralize it. The terrier is whimpering and pawing at the door. The bartender frowns, puzzled. She says out loud "Where are all these dogs coming from", as she heads to open the door. She lets it out and returns to the bar and starts to clean up where the man had been.

Jack clears his throat. "Get away from there, Muriel. We know what to do. Get out of the radius of that energy. We will keep others from coming in."

I took a couple sips of cider to continue my ruse as a patron. The sweet taste tickled my tongue and the liquid slid down my throat.

In my head Jack's voice was frustrated and his eyebrows bounced up and down. "Leave, we have things set up outside. Please get out of there. Do not try to engage her on your own! I repeat: do not try to engage her on your own!"

I spindled the amber liquid into a bracelet. There was no way I could drink a large quantity in a short time so this at least gave the illusion that I did. I put a ten on the bar under the coaster beneath the drink. I stood and started to head outside.

The bartender barely noticed me leave. Outside there were a group of people. Madame Kay, Jack Oppenheimer and ten different women in flowing gowns and eccentric clothing. There were also around fifteen other people in cargo pants and dark t-shirts sporting headsets and smart phones.

Madame Kay and Jack approach me. Jack issues a command into his headset, then his focus goes completely on me. His eyes measure me as he looks for confirmation on what he says. "What I saw through you was a one room bar with four pillars and about fifteen round tables, with two chairs per table and a worn, tacky wood floor."

I find myself narrowing my eyes in bafflement, "How did you get the floor was sticky from my visual." Suspicion fills me, since I know I thought about it, but not in my public mind.

He looked beyond me in thought," It is. Isn't it?"

I acerbically say, "Yeah."

He frowned in thought, "It was the audio, that sucking noise every once in a while with your steps." He gives me a measuring gaze and watches my reaction.

I let my gaze wander to the assembled people. The women in eccentric clothing seem to walk and preen like birds.

Jack cleared his throat and crossed his arms, "Can I continue? With the description?"

I clear my mind of suspicion and give him a casual, "Sure."

He gives me a sarcastic smile. "Thanks. The bar is at the back of the room in an alcove. The features of the room are all decked out in elaborate wood carvings and gilding. The young woman suspect is the only one in there now."

I watch a truck full of dogs back up close to the door of the bar. I bob my head in affirmation.

Madame Kay gives me a nurturing smile. "How old did she look?"

Jack stiffens.

Madame Kay gives him an amused tilt of her head. "We need to know if she needs a mother and a crone or a maid and a crone."

Jack rolls his eyes at the traditional wiccan philosophy. "Answer her, Muriel."

I went through the traditional references to witches, with the original covens consisting of a maid, a mother and a grandmother. Mirroring fate, the three big stages of life of a woman in society. "I'd say she is more of a seductress then a maid."

Madam Kay snorted and sighed, "Ah, if she is in this frame of mind she didn't do any seducing, she is still a maid."

"That sounds true." I bowed my head in agreement.

Jack looks at his clipboard, "Do you have everything you need, Mrs. Kay?"

Madame Kay gestured to a middle aged woman with almond skin and straight, black hair. "Chang, let's go give it a go."

Chang gave her a warm smile and nodded. She started walking next to Madame Kay. They didn't exchange a word as they walked together, as if this was a casual, companionable outing then disappeared into the bar.

"Do you have a feed on Madame Kay?" I asked Jack, I was curious.

He shakes his head in a negative direction, "Electricity messes with witch magic. I'm totally blind right now. You have the big recruitment tonight, right?"

I nod, "Mr. Grout. I have no idea how it's going to go. Did Thomas check in with you?"

Jack begins to frown into his clipboard, "Nothing from Thomas, but that is usually a good sign. Good luck with the recruitment." He turns and walks away from me.

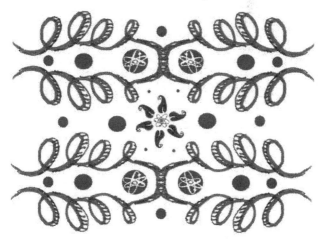

Chapter 23

Exotic Escort

When I got to Sangria, it was full of activity. Thomas and Viper were standing at my normal booth. Thomas was scrutinizing his cell phone, and Viper had his arms folded, staring at Thomas in admiration. He kept trying for a stoic expression when Thomas looked up.

I nodded to the bartender and went and slid into the booth. Viper slid across from me and Thomas came in next to me. The bartender slapped down a few napkins and asked. "The usual?" I nod as I detangle the satchel off of me and sit it down.

Viper leans in toward me. He gives me an amused, satisfied grin. "I'm in."

I look at him, "You sure? It is not a bunch of free days like you had with Thomas, you know? It's a military unit. Orders will be issued. There will be major consequences if they are not followed."

He looks at Thomas, puzzled.

Thomas reaches out and squeezes my leg. "Muriel, wants to give you every chance to exit. Doesn't want to hear she didn't warn you."

I squeeze Thomas's hand, trying to ignore the sensations that causes through my body, and move it off my knee.

Viper looks back at me and nods. "So, how do I join?"

I reach into my mind toward headquarters. No one is manning my feed. It's all about the Circe Incident, conversations about how crazy women are. There is one person kind of paying attention. I send him a thought. "Paperwork?"

I overhear some jokes about the men pouring out of the bar looking exactly like the dogs that went in. A young voice cracked, "Paperwork? Oh yeah! Hold a minute." I hear paper shuffling and muffled whispers of people asking him what he is talking about. My satchel suddenly starts to vibrate and I open it up. There is a stack of around fifty papers that weren't there before.

I exhale annoyed, pull the papers out and pull out a pen that has a syringe compartment. I take his arm. "These type of contracts are filled out in blood." I raise my eyebrows at him in a challenging look.

He swallows and looks to Thomas, who gives him a nonchalant shrug.

I wince as I touch the pages. This is paper grown out of human cells. Specifically for these purposes, but eerie never the less. It is made from an amalgam of Heska genomes. I stick the pen syringe into Viper's arm and fill up the reservoir.

I take a deep breath. It takes me an hour and half to go over it all with him, and to sign and dot everything. I watched the various spells activate all over him. The contract had all types of charms and compulsions.

It was two a.m. when I looked at my watch. Viper looked wiped at the end and Thomas was bored flirting with a couple women at different tables. I wanted another Shirley Temple.

Viper rubs his hands together, "When do I get more blood?"

I pull out two more syringes, and pull some of my blood. This will bind him further.   I give them to Thomas. He gives me a salacious smile and injects Viper then himself. I nod toward Viper, "He needs to report to the training center by noon."

I am listening to the chattering in my head. It is distracting. So busy, and so many talking at once. I hold my head and indicate I am listening to headquarters. "Protocol dictates two agents take a new recruit to boot camp."

He bobs his head, "Is it going to be hard right now to get someone else? Are you OK helping?"

I lean back but give him a smile, "Headquarters is busy, yeah, I can help. How do you want?"

He interrupts, "I got a convertible."

I chuckle, "Very practical in the Northwest, very practical for a vampire too."

He meets my eye with a smirk on his face, "Nice optimistic view, Muriel!" He beckons me to follow him with his right hand as he scoots out of the booth and heads to the door.

I put a twenty on the table and nod to the bartender. I stand and follow Viper, heading to the door.

Outside the door was a red, sixty-nine mustang with its top down. I squint through the misting rain. Thomas has generated a rain shield over the car. This is real flashing and energy draining magic. "Why don't you just put the top up? This will be noticed!"

Thomas shrugs with a sheepish, smug smile, "It works."

I shake my head admiring the lines of the car, "The amount of energy for this spell is going to burn through your blood in twelve hours instead of twenty-four hours." I note all the steel, "I can't ride in that."

Thomas frowns, "Why not?"

I wince, not wanting to admit how vulnerable I am at the moment. "I got steel scored two nights ago. I'm under strict orders to avoid any contact with steel. Why do you think the modern car is more plastic then steel these days?"

Thomas scratches his chin, "The Collective has been influencing car manufacturing?"

I give him a wink.

He frowns, "Wait, you're distracting me with this fact. What does steel scoring mean?"

I exhale, look down and kick a pebble on the sidewalk. "Essentially I got steel blood poisoning."

Thomas looks incredulous, "The trip to headquarters did that to you?"

I bob my head, "Headquarters and after."

Confused Thomas frowns, "You got steel poisoning at a dance?"

I point at Thomas, "Funny you should ask. Not the dancing. After the dancing."

He leaned in with raised eyebrows. "Are you going to tell us what that activity was?" Viper was listening intently now.

I sigh and run a hand through my hair and look away, "It's childish really, a throwback from high school years."

He crosses his arms.

I look up at him through my lashes, with a grin, "You won't believe me."

His voice is deadpan, "Try me."

I take a breath; I wasn't sure I wanted to say this. There is this moment when a being who thinks they are comfortable with Heska realizes that there are parts of our reality to which they can never go, have never thought of, and we become "other" in a major way. The relationship will change; some eventually adjust, but some distance themselves. I have a moment of devil may care and have an urge to see the look on his face. "I was asteroid paddleboarding."

His annoyed frown changes. He blinks and shakes his head, "What? What's that? How do you do that? Where? I've never heard of that."

I smile wide and take a breath while I shrugged "I would have been surprised if you had."

Thomas snorts, "Open wounds and steel poisoning? Sounds marvelous!" He crosses his arms and steps away from the car.

I shake my head and watch some leaves blow down the street, "Someone was being stupid. I had to intervene."

"So, it was more then you doing the paddleboarding."

I nod, "Yeah, it's suicidal to do it alone."

Thomas rolls his eyes, "Of course! Who?"

I shrug and meet his narrowed eyes, "Acquaintances from the dance."

He smirks, "From the dance? So your mother was pleased with the results of the dance?"

I give a non-committed head shake, and stare up, squinting trying to find the stars in the sky. The city lights and the overcast clouds create a barrier. I want to go back up. "She would have preferred I had not gone paddleboarding. But, interacting with others, yes, she was happy about that."

He stepped close, and leaned in whispering, "I want to hear more about this. But, how are we going to deliver him to training if you can't get in the car and I shouldn't drive him alone."

My subconscious had been chewing on this question. I could only dialyosefos one being at a time with thirty minute breaks in-between. That would violate the two beings escort rule. My thoughts were interrupted when the switchboard in my head flared up. A warm, bear feeling filled my mind, and I was linked with Creok, the animal mystic. He had this nurturing smile as he sent thoughts directly to me. "We are sending some giant eagles to pick you three up."

I pointed up to the top of the nearest building, "We need to get to a higher location, a different type of ride is being sent."

Viper and Thomas' eyebrows raise and they exchange looks, then stare at me. Viper's gaze to Thomas was speculative. Thomas shifts his shoulders and looks forlornly at his car. He starts putting the top up.

We head into the stone building and find the stairwell. The stairway was concrete and steel. I avoided the rail and stayed in the middle of the stairs without holding on. We started climbing the ten stories to the roof. Viper looked at me. "Can't you turn this into an escalator or something?"

I laugh, "If the elevator wasn't made out of steel we probably could have used it."

"You really didn't answer my question."

I pause and say deadpan, "Do you really want me to explain the chemistry and physics it would take to turn concrete into wood then motorize it? It really is just quicker and less energy to just walk up the stairs."

Viper sighed, "Quicker than explaining, or doing?"

I wobble my head, amused, "Either."

We reached the last stair, and arrive at a door fitted with an alarm that would sound if opened. The fluorescent light in the narrow space is burning out, creating this strobing effect. I pause, feeling dizzy and close my eyes to adjust to the strobing light. I opened the plastic door on the control panel to the door alarm. I stare at the wires. I review stuff Dad and Yacob have taught me over the years. I turn to Thomas, who was taking advantage of the situation to rest a hand on my hip. "Do you have a Leatherman on you?"

He sighs, "Which wire?"

I point to a yellow one.

He just reaches over and snaps it with his fingers.

We all pause and wait a beat. No alarm sounded.

Viper pushes through the door. The wind gusts in, blowing in huge feathers and the smell of the city and a spicy musk. As my eyes adjust to the night sky and lack of strobing light, I start to make out three huge, dark, large shapes. Each one a story high.

Viper manages to go paler and backs toward the door. The one in the middle screeches at us. I walk forward and curtsy. "Hey, thanks for coming. We need a ride to the coast. We need to stay in sight of each other."

The one on the right shrills and Creock's voice fills my head. It is a baritone, "Muriel, Creock here, that eagle to the right is Tristan and he says all three of them are Collective operatives."

"Any Heska?" I ask back. If one was, I wouldn't have to go.

Creock's voice sighed, "No."

I bow at them "I understand you're all operatives, but this is a class twenty-seven recruit, he requires at least one Heska in sight at all times till he reaches the training facility."

The middle bird caws at the other two birds. Creok chuckles, "They understand."

Thomas sighs and shakes his head, "What is this, the Hobbit?"

234

Circe Syndrome

Viper gives him an amused glance and I involuntarily grin.

Viper dusts some soot from his sleeve, "In your reality does this kind of thing happen frequently?"

I exchange glances with Thomas, "Ride giant eagles? Or climb ten flights of stairs?"

Viper gives me a nonplussed expression, "Sure, but I meant out of context, save in the midst of an odd problem?"

I shrug and meet Viper's eyes, "Well, yeah, that is kind of the point you know."

Viper looked at Thomas, who shakes his head emphatically.

Viper's lower lip raises as he considers, "Oh, cool!"

My mind hiccups reviewing the question, and I shake my head when the three eagles hiss at us. Creoak mumbles, "They want to know what is taking so long?"

I curtsy apologetically at the eagles, "Sorry, Nobel Avians, Thomas and I like to banter, and Viper seems to be enjoying that too. So how do we go about catching a ride with you?"

The eagle on the right bent its head and pushed Muriel toward the feet of the middle Eagle. Thomas and Viper each stood at the foot of the other two eagles. My heart stops and I forgot to breathe as the huge bird backs up and unfurls its wings. It starts this gentle beat where it hovers moving air all over then it swoops down and grabs me by the shoulders. The talons are the length of my body. The pressure is almost enough to hinder breathing, but I am silent as I look down at the building falling away from us. I turn to see Viper and Thomas in similar grips.

The air traveling quickly past me creates the sound of waves in my ears. I relax, and put my trust in the bird above me. I take in the view. The cities and suburbs light web out and disappear into a sea of dark shapes and dazzling stars. I think about a board and space, the moss in me twitches. A hunger to paddleboard again gnaws through me.

It takes about twenty minutes for the air to become salty. And there are sounds of waves beyond the blood in my ears.

Eventually, the birds start this spiraling decent, to set us down on a grassy hill with sharp cliffs leading to the ocean, on its west side. In a nearby hill a round steel door was inset into a cave.

Viper guffaws, "We are in the Hobbit!"

As I stare at the steel on the door, Thomas meets my eyes. Seeing my hesitancy, he asks, "What?"

I shake my head, and stifle a gag, even the thought turns my stomach, "I really can't handle going in there today."

Thomas frowns, "The five-yard steel entry?"

I cringe, "Yes." I say softly, "Exactly."

A three-foot-tall man with a beard, armor and hammer steps out of the door. He grins at me, "Hey, Clumsy Anahat. Back for retraining to be a real operative?"

I smirk, "Yeah right, Shamus." I cock my head towards Viper, "You have a new recruit."

Viper stands with his arms at his waist and looks down at Shamus. Shamus is amused and looks toward Thomas, "Thomas."

"Shamus.", Thomas nods back.

Shamus moves the huge hammer in between his hands suggesting the violence he is trying to contain. He meets Viper's eyes, "Back up, son!" He barks.

Viper jumps back, "What are you? Someone from Asgard?"

Shamus juts out his chin and laughs, "Right idea, I'm a dwarf of the Steelwood clan." He nods at me and Thomas, "Come on you two there is paperwork, of course!"

Viper groans, "We just spent several hours doing paperwork."

Shamus smirks, "Ah yes, but there will be different paperwork for this facility."

I kick a pebble on the ground, "I can't follow you in today, Shamus."

He narrows his eyes; I feel him examining me. He is appraising me and his eyebrows rose, "You were cleared to work with that amount of steel still flailing around your system?" He sighs, "Ah, steel girly, no wonder you look prettier to me."

I laugh, "Always the blacksmith."

He shakes his head, "If I could suck that stuff out of you I would pay a lot for it. The magic swords I could make with the steel exposed to your blood."

Viper licks his lips and gives me a famished look, "Do you want me to try?"

Shamus, pulls back to the moment, regards Thomas and Viper, "An unfortunate choice of words."

I look out toward the ocean, "Should I just head back home?"

Shamus scratches his chin and pulls his beard. "Wait till we process this young'un and I'll send Thomas out to go back with ye."

I nod, then watch the three men disappear behind the round door.

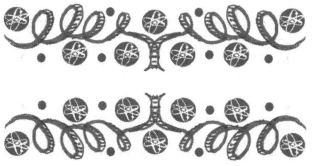

Chapter 24

Serious Selkie

When the door closed, it made this tinning sound that echoed through the ground and traveled up my leg.   I turned and looked out at the vast Pacific Ocean, listened to the birds call. I breathed in the salt air and walked toward the edge of the cliff.   I sat down on the edge and watched the waves smash against the boulders, creating fanning sprays that foamed and created images in my mind.

I take a breath. I count to three. I take another breath.

I sit there. After twenty minutes of this quiet contemplation, I hear a seal bark out. I look down, since the sound seems to be coming from that direction. I take in this huge, sleek, fit grey seal. Its head is raised in my direction and I pace.   Its head moves with my motion.

I deduce it is watching me. I raise a hand and wave.

I pause as it raises a flipper and waves back. The air about it seems to blur and there is no longer a seal there. A muscular man with curly black hair.

My mind registers he is a selkie. The transforming creatures of Celtic legend. Seals who decide to turn to humans from time to time.

He raises an arm and beckons me down.

I look back at the door. I send a spell on the threshold. It's a speaking spell, to que up when Thomas goes through the door and to inform him I'm down on the beach.

I look about the cliff's edge, searching for a way down. I take a breath and gaze straight down the cliff face, then turn and peruse around me. Checking to see if there is anyone else around. There wasn't, so I walk straight ahead and let myself fall. I take a few seconds and just feel the air rushing by me as I fall and tumble. It feels like cords of rope sliding by. But firm air instead of rope fibers. I watch the sand coming fast toward me and when I'm a foot from impact I coalesce the air beneath me. My body sits there, suspended above the sand. My head was still a blur of images, processing all the input from the fall.

I blinked, shook my head, reached down and ran a finger across the sand. The grains were wet, stuck to my fingertips and pushed under my finger nails. I put down a knee, then another, then both hands. I let the air flow as I take on my weight, then stand.

I rubbed my finger and thumb feeling the grains shed away with the friction. As I approached the Selkie, I had so many questions in my mind. How did he know I would not be alarmed at the sight of him? Was he aware this was the location of a Collective training facility? What does he want? Is he hostile?

His lean form rested on the boulder casually, but his emerald green eyes revealed his inner conflict. He seemed to be taking everything in as if it was brand new. A magpie of sights.

This made my questions bigger in my mind. This was a being who was unfamiliar with the dry world. I suspect he never ventured out of the water. I note his feet firmly in the water not ready to venture out entirely.

He pulled on a forced smile then chortled out the guttural deep sound of seals bark. It was a greeting.

I stand before him and bob my head then watch the spray frame him. His attractiveness wowing me a minute. "Ah, hi." I say in a small, tentative and casual voice.

He burps, and his voice fluctuates a couple octaves, "Ah, hi. Sorry about that. You're a Heska, right?"

I cross my arms, flash an amused smile while I note his pelt lying on the boulder behind him. "How did you know I wouldn't be alarmed by the sight of you and your transformation?" Internally I'm thinking, "Especially since you are unfamiliar with the dry lands."

Color drains from his face and he moves in front of the pelt defensively. He clears his throat and a rich baritone flows from his voice. He shrugs, stares out over the horizon and at the gulls flying above. He glances back at me. "The Salmon foretold you would be here, and able to help me with a problem."

I walked next to him and leaned on the boulder. A pocket of barnacles dug into my shoulder and I readjusted my position. I cocked my head, "The Salmon?"

He mirrors me and says with a contagious, knowing smile, "Surely, you have heard of the Salmon of Knowledge?"

I nod recalling the myth, "Yes, it was eaten by Finegas the Druid."

He shakes his head, his wet, black, curly hair sending out a spray, "No, it was not just one fish. All salmon contain the knowledge of the world."

"So the expression the Salmon of Knowledge is talking about something plural?" I say puzzled, kicking at some sand.

"Aye, the fish Finegas ate was a Salmon of Knowledge, not the only one!"

"Oh!" I start to trace the barnacles on the stone with my finger, "So, salmon can tell the future?"

Circe Syndrome

He looked incredulous, "Of course!"

I shook my head, "I had no idea." At this moment the tide advances, soaking my shoes. The icy cold crawled into my shoes, stinging my feet. I lean down, take off my shoes and peel off my clinging socks. I wiggle my feet into the sand, letting it massage my toes. The chill runs through me.

He frowns at his own feet and wiggles his toes, "Not very efficient, are they?"

"For what?" I ask puzzled by the question. "Oh, swimming." I shrug, "I wouldn't know, it's all I've ever known."

He crossed his arms and gave me a speculative glare, "I thought Heska can change shapes."

I wiggle my toes in the soupy, cold, sandy water, "Can they? It's never occurred to me." I pause, recalling the recent trip to Ecospa. I shrug, "I've made adjustments now and again."

He scratches his head and looks at the sky, back out and the water then back to me, "You're an odd creature."

I give him a smile while I was thinking, "You have no idea!" Out loud I say, "Talk about the kettle calling the pot black."

He frowned, "What?"

I struggled a moment trying to find an analogy that he would understand, "A jellyfish calling a sea cucumber squishy?"

His eyes narrowed, "What are you talking about?"

I shake my head, "Never mind. You need help?" I start transforming my shoes into a backpack. I put my socks into it. I sling it to my back.

"Whoa, that is distracting. Do those items normally do that?" He reaches out a hand.

Deadpan I say, "You live completely in the sea don't you?"

He shrugs and looks about suspiciously, "This fur-less-ness is bizarre!"

I give out an exaggerated breath, "Will I need to go underwater?"

A seagull flew overhead. He watched it. Then looked back at me. "Yes, there are these cage things with no walls, that dig into the ocean floor."

I rub my palm trying to figure out what he is talking about. "Cage things with no walls?" An idea comes to me. "Hey, could you just imagine what you are talking about," I pause, fidget a moment, this is uncomfortable to ask, "and would it be OK if I look into your mind?"

A relieved look passes across his face, "Seems much easier."

I reach out and enter his mind. It is thick and extremely liquidy, like being submerged in water. It takes me a moment to understand what I'm looking at since it started with an underwater view. The view slowly changed to an aerial view, and swimming away from the item in his mind. It was a beautifully decorated oil platform. I nod as I shake my head from side to side, "That is called an Oil platform."

He wrinkles his nose, "Oil platform? Weird, it's not made of oil!"

I exhale a chuckle, "No, it's used to mine oil."

"Oh, well this one off the coast of Long Beach, California is about to break in three hours, according to the Salmon, and cause some major health issues in the ocean and on land." He runs a hand through his hair.

I swallow, "That is horrible news." My mind is whirling. Those rigs are made of steel. How am I going to help? A sound permeates through my head and I am reminded of the internal wiring. It seems the stir from the Circe had settled down. An unfamiliar face with a young voice says, "Agent Anthony has been alerted, and is on the way."

The air five feet in front of me shimmers. Blond hair begins to appear, then the muscular form of Anthony appears before me. He doubles over and clenches his stomach. He dry heaves and I run to his side to steady him. "Easy. So Anthony, you not use to dialyosefosing?"

He groans, "Cell jumping? No."

I stand back and watch him, checking his vitals, "Give it a minute."

He rubs his face and growls, "That stings!"

The selkie frowns, "Cell jumping?"

Anthony moans, "Particles linked form a body to another particle at a distance. Essentially all the cell information is transferred to those particles and the cells I was composed of became cell-less pieces of air. My mind followed. Quantum mechanics. I prefer Newtonian physics."

I smiled thinking about what he said and gaze out at the ocean. The universe is an extremely weird place. The beauty of it all floors me.

Anthony sighs and stands straight, "So, I hear you need a metal Mage."

I turn to and regard the Selkie. "Ummm, I'm sorry I don't know your name?"

He cocks his head, "Aaaar Nah Snort!"

Anthony's eyes widened, "Ahhh"

I cross my arms and stare at the Selkie speculatively, "Arnold? OK with you?"

The Selkie shrugged, "What is your name?"

"Muriel."

Arnold smirked, "Mmmmmmm Ahhhhhhh Riaa Snort, OK with you?"

I give him a grin, "Touché, Aaaar Nah Snort."

He turns green, the color of a blushing Selkie, and nods.

I look at Anthony, "Why didn't you just jump to Long Beach first?"

He pauses and stares at me, "Good question. I will need your help with the underwater breathing spells." He kicked the sand. "I guess we could have told you to meet me there?"

I look back at the Selkie, "Ummm, Aaaar Nah Snort, do you have any ideas how the drill is going to break?"

The Selkie frowns, "Drill? I was talking about metal cages."

Anthony raises his eyebrows and meets my eyes. I wiggle my toes, "That contains a huge long drill that goes deep into the earth and pulls out oil."

The Selkie frowned, "Oh? No idea."

I bite my lip, confused, "About where it will or how it will break?"

He laughs and shakes his head and reaches reassuringly toward his pelt, "Both."

Anthony exhales, "Do you know the location of the cage?"

The Selkie gestures toward Anthony with a finger and gives me a look that says, "See, he knows how to talk." As I shake my head the Selkie says, "Yes, it's 500 body-lengths from a tuna trail."

Anthony nods, with no expression, "A tuna trail?"

"Yes." The Selkie blinks.

Anthony gives me a speculative look, " OK, Muriel, any ideas?"

I nod and address the Selkie, "Is it close to land, or still boats?"

The Selkie runs his hands across the boulder to illustrate his point, "It looks like an island, and is visible from the fancy houses on the cliff, behind the beach."

" OK, I have an idea where that is." I look out at the ocean and watch the seagulls circle as I think about logistics.

Circe Syndrome

Anthony taps my shoulder, startling me. He points up at the cliff, "Someone is trying to get your attention."

I look up to see Thomas waving and looking down the cliff face, trying to find a path down. I debated climbing back up. Dialyosefosing would make me wait a half hour before we came back down. I was deciding to carve a stairway into the cliff face when the voice in my head, headquarters man, cleared his throat, reminding me I'm wired. "We can just loop you into a call with him." I rub my head and laugh at myself, complicating procedures unnecessarily. I said OK, and looked at Anthony and the Selkie. Out loud I said, "I might look a little dazed and out of if for a second."

Anthony nodded and walked to the boulder and stared out to the sea. The tide was coming in.

"Hello, Muriel." Thomas's tentative voice sounded through my head.

I was way too happy to hear his voice in my mind. I had to quash the emotions, there was a seductive quality even to how he said that. I didn't want headquarters or him to know how much he affected me. I focused my thoughts on brick walls and robot emotions. Then sent back the surface type of curiosity. "Hey, Thomas, sorry to not be where you left me. Something weird has come up."

His mental voice was full of amusement, "So it would seem. Do you need my help at all?"

I sent back the image of me shrugging, "I don't know, what can you do about a leak from an oil platform?"

A disappointing breathe emitted from him, "Not my usual skill set, love."

I looked at the Selkie and Anthony exchanging glances, " OK, thanks for the offer, I think Anthony and I will figure something out. Do you have a way back to Portland?"

There was a smug smile in his mind, "I'll figure it out."

As the call ended, the voice from headquarters said, "We'll get him back and debriefed ma'am."

I waved and sent another thought toward him. "See you later, Thomas."

He waved down at me and replied in my mind, "Yes, Miss Muriel, you will." He turned and walked from the edge.

Anthony jumped down and landed next to me with a splash. "A dead guy? They partnered you with a corpse."

I look back out to sea, "I'm not an agent, therefore I have no partner." I look back at Anthony, "You're an agent, shouldn't your partner be here, too?"

Anthony laughed, "Medical leave."

"Oh?" I look at him expectantly.

He shakes his head, "Nothing I did, honestly!"

I smirk and give him, "A sure you didn't," look.

He rolls his eyes. "So how do I make myself breathe under water?"

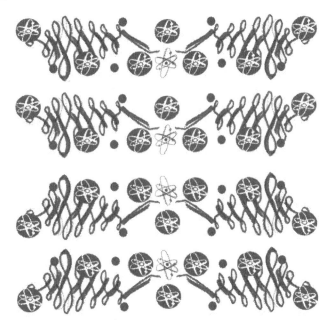

Chapter 25

Heavy Water

A half hour later, I dialyosefosed Anthony to Long Beach. We startled a couple making out on the beach.

I blush and call out, "Sorry." I send out a current of energy to disrupt their short term memory. They return to necking, covered in sand. As Anthony gives me an amused grin, we head away from them.

Anthony turns to me, "So? I make the gills first?"

I pull at the hair the air currents have pulled across my face and nod saying nonchalantly, "Yeah."

"Will we be able to talk?" He scratches his chin.

I put up an index finger, "We could also communicate telepathically."

He frowns, then gives me a self-ingratiating smile, "Not my strongest ability."

247

I scratch my head thinking, I understand how hard it is for him to admit to things he is does not do well at. " OK, we can just talk." I look out at the water. "A few whales and dolphins might come and check us out." I tap my finger in thought, "Hmmmmm, I should send out a warning so they don't come too close. Help everything from going purple."

He cocks his head, his gaze had been on the water line, in concentration. He stares back at me, "Purple?"

I giggle at my own turn of phrase, "You know, some people think that problems can be solved with a one or a two. But then something so outside what was talked about happens. The solution is so outside the box. It's not a number. It's a color. Not even a primary color. Everyone's purple is a little different."

He shakes his head, "Sure."

I fan out my hands and move my shoulders.

We both walk to the water's edge. I weave an image into the water particles moving the air to make it look like we walked in the opposite direction from wherever someone looks from.

Anthony dips his toe in the water and shivers. I put my toe in to the surf, too, and the cool water sends shivers up my leg and goosebumps across my skin. Anthony's teeth start to chatter. He sighs, "Do you know how to make yourself warm in the water?"

I look at him, "You can just turn your cloths into a wet-suit." I run my hand down my clothes, I make a show of the fabric changing as my hand down glides my body. The tightening neoprene: the hydrogen electrons and the carbon electrons I joined create the change in the fabric. "I also increase my heart beat by ten beats while I'm underwater."

He scratches his head, "Is that a covalent bond or hydrogen bond?"

"Covalent! It helps the whole elastic response of the fabric when it goes back to its original shape."

248

He points at his chin, "So gills at the neck?"

"I find the transition is easier if I walk in up to my neck first. Then I transform, so I don't flail trying to get to the water."

He gives me a nervous ascent. As we walk deeper into the water, I keep the image of the empty patch of beach in the mist around us. We are in a shell of illusion empty of scenery.

The sluicing sounds of the water as we walk deeper reminds me of Gregor. We had spent so much time together on Ecospa and in the water together. The tears threatened, my love for him still present, raw and real. The fraying edges of my soul poke at me. I knew I would never completely recover from him, he was my first love. I looked out at the harbor, at the boats and the man-made islands. I smiled thinking about how he would be puzzled in this world I live in. We had a lifetime together and it was only three months here. Fifteen and a half years there. My mother never let me go back to say good bye before he died. Thinking about his Suman society reminded me of Sarina and her complaining about the water transformation stinging.

I reach out a hand and tap Anthony's arm, "Oh, ummm, Anthony."

"Yes, Muriel?" We were waist deep now. His exaggerated movements sloshed water about and he looked at me.

I stared out at the island, "It will sting when we start to breathe differently."

He sighs, "How much?"

I winced exaggeratedly, "Like a spear through your heart."

He stares at me a moment.

I gaze back at him, his copper eyes are full of fear, "I thought you should know."

He runs a hand across his mouth and looks away, "Yeah, that is good to know. Any other advice?"

I give a crooked smile at my absent mindedness, I run my hands through my hair in thought; then skim them across the water's surface, enjoying the sensation of the water licking my palms, "Probably, I just can't remember at the moment."

He exhales and splashes me, "So it won't be comfortable?"

I shake my head, thinking about the pull of the moon in the water. I'm up to my shoulders now. I had just blinked away the splashes in my face. I take a long breath and place a memory of breathing air in my body for later.

After we both reach our necks in deep, he stares out at the man-made island that contained the well. We were ninety-five percent sure that this was what the Selkie was referring to. I had stopped and he was a few feet forward of me and up to his neck now. He gives me a fearful look as he asks, "Should I transform first so you can spot me?"

I nod, "That's a good idea. Before you make the gills take a huge breath and make a memory of yourself and how you're breathing air. Like when you map out your cells for dialosefosizing."

He takes a big breath and lets it out slowly. He breathes a moment. He lowers his neck into the water and shuts his eyes. His skin turns red and the flush of pain travels about his face. He gasps as if trying to breath.

I step closer and paddle water. "You got it. Breath with your gills. Move your neck through the water. Strain the water for oxygen."

He coughs, does some irregular gurgles, calms and then winces. "That is an odd expression, but it totally makes sense with the gills."

"Yeah, it's bizarre, I don't know if fish feel the same way, or if it's just something we experience because we are normally air breathers. I wonder if filling bags of air would be bizarre to them?"

He snorts, "You weren't kidding about the pain."

"It's unnatural, we aren't meant to be in this form and the universe likes its rules to be listened to. We'll be slightly uncomfortable and slightly paranoid that we will drown through the whole experience." I think about the coming experience with detachment. I do this with anything unpleasant. Create a space in my mind shielding me from the immediacy.

"Now, you tell me? Come on, it's your turn!" He ducks his head under and I feel a tug on my leg.

I take a long breath. I bend my knees, lower my neck into the water as the searing rip of the gills returned to my neck. I try to choke on air and encourage my gills to move in the water and swim forward. The oxygen returned to my burning blood and relented the piercing pain.

This all happened as he pulled me under and I felt the pressure of the water around me. Anthony's blond curls surrounded his head in a tendril crown. Strands of my shoulder length, auburn hair caught in my gills causing me to cough. I moved my head to help untangle my hair from my neck. I ripped a strip of fabric from the end of my sleeves into a circle. I pull my hair into a ponytail and tie it back.

Anthony looks about the cloudy water. "Which way to the drill?"

His voice sounds richer and louder in the water. I squint into the sedimentary milky water. "When we were above the surface it was at a diagonal, to the left of us." I felt the slant of the ground under me. I point behind us. "The beach is behind us, So..." I made a diagonal shape with my left arm. "Hopefully, as we travel beyond the surf, the water will be clearer." I shake my head to clear it, "We can always check from above. It seems just as murky."

Anthony starts to swim in that direction.

I follow and eventually we hear the crunching noise that helps us locate the drill.

I try to stay distant, but realize that the water around the platform is saturated with steel particles and rust. Anthony is circling the drill. I don't want to distract him. He has a hand on the metal caging and his gaze and expression is that of someone elsewhere in their mind. I speculate that he is tracking the stability of the metal. I keep watching him to make sure nothing approaches while he is occupied. The steel infused water is starting to make me feel nauseous.

It takes ten minutes and he looks up. "We lucked out. This is the drill." He frowns, "It has a hairline irregularity near the crown that meets the head of the sand. It is about to shatter with fatigue."

I hope I'm not looking green as I nod, "Can you prevent the shattering?"

He seems lost in thought, as if mapping something internally. He smiles, "Yes, I think so.   Can you block the force of oil flowing up?"

I send my awareness into the ground. The wellspring is full of black oily slime. The pressure is intense. I look at him, "Not long. How much time do you need?"

He looks at his left hand and cast out fingers one by one as if counting. "In the air it takes me about forty seconds to melt steel. I think I need to double that under water."

My head is dizzy and the metal tang is in my mouth.   I wrinkle my forehead. "That amount of heat can ignite oil right?"

He gives me a grin, "No, air. And if we keep the outside cool and you keep the oil back."

I run a finger through the sand trying to settle the sickness with my colored mind. "Could you try and melt some scrap steel underwater to see how long it takes you? Before you try the bit?"

He looks at his watch. "We are running out of time. I say the least amount would be three minutes, and the most five."

I'm grasping for measurements and how long I will last. "Three hundred seconds of holding the oil off. What was the density of crude oil again? Something like 700-1000 kg. Multiply it by the height and density of say 1000 feet of water?"

He chuckles, "A butt load of pressure."

I smile, "What kind of butt do you have? I'm thinking a 500 story waterfall level of pressure here. We are just talking about my mind after all."

He shrugs, "Just try some push, see how it feels. It won't be long."

I rub my neck and look around for jellyfish and leopard sharks. The water seems clear of wildlife, but it was hard to tell in this sediment encrusted water. The mental warning I had sent out seemed to have been heard. "Yeah, OK, here I go." I went on all fours on the sea floor and put my hands flat on the sand. I realize because of the steel I can't even mess with the molecules in the pipe itself.

Anthony settles in the same position on the other side of the pipe his gaze is directed at me but his eyes are glazed there is no recognition of me. His awareness is down the pipe.

I send my awareness down into the sand to the shale level, and direct it towards the opening the drill created. I tentatively push back the current of black liquid. I gather up the oxygen bubbles into one large bubble that I nudge into the stream of oil. It punctures. I push the oil back, it hurts. The pressure is like a vice on my mind, a sledgehammer of pressure. Meanwhile I keep the bubbles going down into the oil. It creates river of bubbles that collide into a river of oxygen to be sent up the shaft to fill the vacuum that was sucking the oil.

When the oil is suppressed, Anthony screams, "Yes! Three minutes!"

Janette Bach

My head is burning. I can't reply. It's just me directing the flow and pushing the oil down. I start to count the seconds. The vice in my mind pushing harder and harder. I know my face is flush with exertion. If I tried to move I would collapse.

Two hundred seconds later, I hear Anthony scream, " OK, release!"

Relief and no elegance, I let it all go. The release of pressure and adrenaline takes hold. The iron in the water sickening me. I see black.

Chapter 26

Wet Dreams

I woke up submerged in a giant, round tank in the middle of a craftsmen decor living room with a circle of men and women mumbling incantations surrounding the outside. I blinked, turned and looked up at the exposed brace of the ceiling, feeling the water slosh in and out of my eyes. The water tasted sweet and the air had a canned quality through my gills. I see Anthony's copper eyes soften, his head peeking down from the top of the tank worry, lines across his forehead.

As I scratch at my gills and yawn, I feel heavy and groggy, as if I have slept a millennium and could sleep more. I take in the other head staring down at me. He has curly red hair and curly horns out of the side of his head. I follow his torso down through the curve of the glass and note his goat legs, I realize he is a satyr.

I take a moment more to take note of my body, and then raise to a sitting position and swim to the surface of the tank. I sputter in the air. I find that memory from the beach and

255

Janette Bach

transform my gills. The undercurrent feeling of needles in my lungs leaves me replaced by this weight of breathing, feels so foreign at the moment. I cough up water as I grasp the edge of the tank. Anthony reaches out to touch me and I shiver in pain and nausea.

The satyr steps forward and gestures him aside and holds on to me. He looks at Anthony, "You are covered in steel. Let me get her." I feel like a child as he grabs me under the armpits and halls me out of the tank. He sets me on a wood cot. He crosses his arms, and looks me up and down with a serious appraising look. "So? Steel scored, huh?" He hands me a wooden bowl.

I nod as I feel myself turn three shades of green. The blood in my head makes it feel like a bowling ball hitting a bunch of pins. I take a breath, and just let what is left in my stomach go. It's all the sharp and hard bile, and hurts because I'm retching and there isn't much to come out. I feel self-conscious with the over a dozen people in the room staring at me. I wipe my mouth and scrape my hand on the bowl. Tons of questions flow through my mind, but one important thing needs to be voiced now. I can wait on everything else. I look at Anthony his face full of concern and paralyzed on the spot. "Anthony, did we prevent the problem?"

He shakes his head and smiles at me, "Yes."

" OK." I exhale in relief and lay down, keeping the bowl upright and next to my head. I am laying on my side facing him. I start to notice I'm naked. The cold air licking at my wet skin. "How long have I've been out?"

The satyr pulled a cotton blanket from a nearby couch and unfolded it and laid it on me as I started to shiver.

Anthony stared at his palms, then looked back at me, meeting my eyes. "Two days."

Alarmed I sit up. I know my mother would have started to panic. "Ah, my mother!"

256

Her warm comforting tones chuckle, "Is here!" The TV screen I hadn't noticed before comes on. It's on the wall.

I lay down and relax into what is an unsettled feeling and look at the screen and calmly say. "Hey, Mom."

She is tapping a finger on the table in front of her. "Nice to see you conscious, kiddo."

I raise my head and turn to look, "Nice to be conscious." I gaze at the bowl, "I think." I rub my head, the bowling ball still crashing around in there.

The satyr looks at the screen and in the matter of fact voice of a doctor says, "She should not dialyosefos for another two days. I am not even sure she could if she wanted to, anyways. She should take it easy longer than that. For real! Who cleared her for this endeavor?"

Anthony gives a brooding breath, cleared his throat, "Headquarters has been distracted by another incident."

The satyr rolled his eyes. He meets my eyes, "Little one, none of us can bring you back if you die."

My mother sighed, "Luckily, Merlin decided to wait." She then hit herself in the face.

I let my remorse show through in my eyes as I reanalyzed my decisions. I knew with the time constraints and other events, I had to do what I did. Mom letting anything about her unborn grandchild out in mixed company was a slip revealing her worry. "Sorry, Mom."

She rubs her eyes as tears threaten, "I love you, Muriel, rest please. I'm not kidding. Just rest! I'm going to let you sleep." The screen shut off.

Their were random people who were speaking a cantrap, a spell activated by speaking and strong intent something that makes magic available to everyone. To make it stronger they are speaking in unison. Their access to the aether is tenuous revealing them to be a group of hedge witches. What they have been doing has taking a great deal out of them, they all looked bedraggled. One women with a black bob and sophisticated dress shuffled up to the Satyr. "Gino, we are honored to be included in this, but may we go now? We're all tired."

I realize I am still in Long Beach and I am shocked that there is a satyr and witches here. California is known as a place low in having a magical population since all the ley lines are all eaten up by the entertainment industry. These six women and six men, are just borderline witches. Hedge-lines, beings, mostly human with an occasional view of foresight, telepathy and or telekinesis. It would be so much work for them to hold a circle.

I take a moment to meet each of their gazes, "Sorry to inconvenience you. Thank you all for your help. I owe you all."

The woman who had spoken gives me a tired smile. "We were happy to help and Gino here is in our debt."

They gather their things and shuffle out of the room.

The satyr pulls up an ottoman, sits next to me and extends his hand. He bends his head reminiscent, of a bow. "I'm Gino."

"I'm Muriel." I give him a smile and hold out the hand I hadn't wiped my vomit with. He gives me an amused smile as he shakes my left hand. I moisten my lips, "Thank you, Gino. You had them hold a circle for two days?"

He sits back, rolls his eyes, and put his palms up in supplication, "I had an unconscious Heska, not just any Heska mind you. An unconscious Anahat on my hands, to be precise. Young lady, do you know how many hurly burly things came out of the wood work? You dropped every defense you had!"

I wince at the thought of being unconscious and defenseless as I acknowledge hearing him. Internally I am not letting my mind play the what if game. For me a question remained, "How many?" I closed my eyes as I saw his remembered fear coat him.

Circe Syndrome

He laughs to hide his fear and to show his relief, "About five different beings, you are such a true American hodgepodge, my dear,"

I open my eyes and grin back at him.

He uses his fingers, counting out as he lists the beings with climbing volume, "Fomorri!"

I shake my head in ascent. A creature of the sea makes total sense, and with the selkie already involved it made sense.

"A gremlin."

I wince and groan, burying my face into the cot. Technology and oil, two things they love. Our house can get infested from time to time.

"Sneffel!" He paled.

I stared at the floor. That was alarming.

"Dark Raven!"

I shudder.

"An ice giant!"

I sat up and he pushes me down. "In the general public? In Southern California?" I take a breath, "How is the general public."

Anthony came up next to Gino and gives me a smile. "Unaware."

I scratched my head. " OK. Ummm, no offense , but I don't think you two could handle an Ice Giant on your own. And that coven was barely a coven. Who helped?" My mind wondering who else I owed.

A gravelly voice came from the other room. Two cyclops entered followed by a robust looking man supported by golden robots.

I adverted my eyes. I had not been given leave. "Vulcan? How can I?"

His voice, coarse from inhaling centuries of smoke, chuckled deeply, "I'm not in my glory. You may look at me. I would have incinerated the bungalow if I had appeared in that way."

"Pardon me, sir. What do I owe you?"

He gives a paternal smile to Anthony and pulls him into a headlock. "It was a favor for my godson, but we helped take that metal out of your blood. I have some great ideas for some clever weapons with that stuff. If a planet of gold appeared somewhere near Auriga Galaxy, I would see us as settled."

My mind is hazy, and I'm trying to not think too hard about that conundrum. I note Gino's face go stark white looking at Vulcan, as if comprehending what a god has asked of me. That the god had no qualms in asking and that he thought I was capable of that. Anthony rubs his chin in thought. I am trying to distract them both. As I look at Anthony and Gino as gratefully as I can. "I seem to be in a big debt to you two." I yawn.

Gino frowns, "You have your shields in place? Are you well enough for your normal sleep?" He looks about the room, alarmed, as the god chuckles and pats my shoulder.

I take a breath and evaluate myself, and check my subconscious systems. Everything is back up and running. "Yeah, I think it's just a physical healing sleep now. Who knew talking could be so exhausting?"

Gino nodded, and gestured to the god and Anthony to leave the room. "She doesn't need constant supervision anymore." Just before I slip out of consciousness I hear him address me again. "Sleep, Muriel, just sleep. We will talk when you wake up."

I am lulled to sleep by the conversation in the other room: the Roman god, Anthony, Gino and two Cyclops.

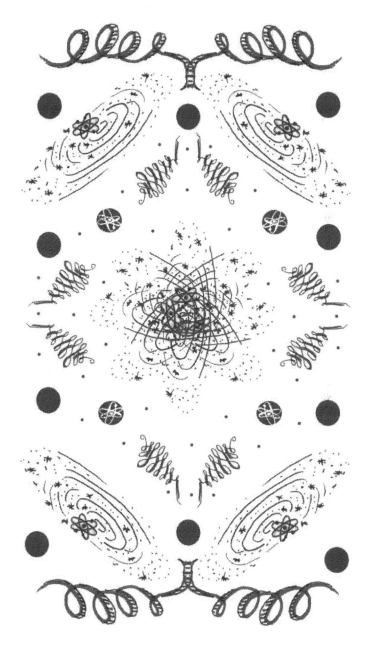

Chapter 27

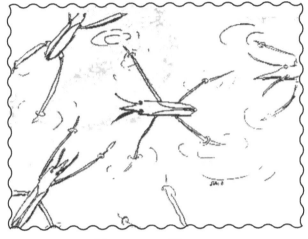

Skater Bugs

I am sitting on a dirt path watching the pond skater bugs skim across a pond. I am in the Japanese garden, at California State University Long Beach. Gino is chasing a maple nymph down the paths and Anthony is chatting on his cell phone.

I drop random dried leaves on the surface to watch their trajectories change. The ripples collide, creating patterns in my mind. I see the shape of a mushroom and find myself wondering about that planet that turned to mushrooms. This led to Hephaestus' request. I always prefer the Olympians in their Greek guises. I speculate about the Auriga galaxy and consider part of the Orion arc and the bunch of nebulous matter surrounding it. There are a lot of particles to work with there. This is a bizarre puzzle. How am I going to make a planet of gold? How could it sustain life? How could it stay together? How could it even spin? It would be a conductor. It could not be magnetized.

Circe Syndrome

As my gaze extends across the surface of the water, a thin line perpendicular to the water appears thread thin and gray. A slit in reality. My breathing pauses. I stay motionless. A mid-tone figure emerges with over elongated humanoid limbs and a gray pinstriped outfit like a magistrate from 1880's London. Its facial features masked in a non-descript human composition with a mustache. It is a yard in front of me, standing on air about five centimeters above the water's surface.

I school myself to remain calm. It has sensed my illness and weakness, so it has come. I look about me. Reality feels flimsy and tastes cloying. Gino and Anthony seem to be in a masked veil, it dims their appearance. The reason it stays a yard away from me is due to my shields. Even though it appears still, I feel it pacing my shields, testing them like a tiger stalking.

This is a trans-dimensional being, a Sneffel. It opens what looks like a notebook and clicks a pen that has all kinds of gismos attached to it. Its voice is thin, nasally slicing through the air sharply, "Muriel Anahat?"

I am lounging with one leg bent and the other up in a bend. I pull them both into a bend in front of me close so I could hug my knees and stand quick if I needed to. I moisten my lips watching every movement I can. As I check my shields. I respond, "Yes, that is me." I smile; this is a bit of a pantomime. The creature knows without a doubt who I am. It has my power signature to track me. That is how they worked.

It makes a tsking noise, and frowns at its notebook, "You are thinking of doing something."

I laugh, thinking to myself, "Aren't we all thinking of doing something?" But out loud I say, "Yes."

It closes the notebook and rubs its eyes wearily, causing his illusion of appearance to waver and all five of his eyes to appear. "Don't be rash in what you're doing!" Its voice had become richer and more pleasant for convincing purposes.

I stop breathing. My mother has warned me about these particular conversations. "Is that a command or a request?"

The creature starts watching the skater bugs. Its head jerks with their movements. It exhales defeated not looking at me.

I watch it for a moment, then throw a leaf into the pond.

The Sneffel looks back at me. "Come on!"

"What?" I ask, curious and baffled.

"I'm supposed to give you this message and you're supposed to question yourself! Not me!" It's left limb pointing at me when it says, "yourself" then shaking his head adamantly.

I rest my chin on my knees and cock my head, "Do you want me to build it or not? What will happen if I do it?"

"Besides the fact that it is bizarre? It won't be able to keep in any orbit or spin without an energy source." His manner devoid of pretense and mystery. He delivers this, flippant and frustrated.

I am thinking through the mechanics still, "An energy source. That is interesting. I owe a favor."

He regards his nails, I can see them change back and forth from manicured, emaciated hands to extended, jointed digits, with long thin blades as nails. He gestures in the air to punctuate this next statement. "To an outdated god? Who performs tasks mostly regulated to the art world these days!"

I shake my head in disagreement, "I believe machinery, which is the modern world, falls into his task set!"

In his hovering state, he starts to move back and forth in a pacing manner.

I rub my head, and speculate out loud, "Will it cause the universe to collapse or something?"

The Sneffel stops pacing and growls, "I'm just supposed to give you the ominous warning and you're supposed to think about it and?"

I raised an eyebrow, "And I'm supposed to do it, anyway. The Universe thinks a gold planet could be interesting?"

It let out a string of vowels that I was sure was some type of cussing noise, "How long have I been here, anyway?"

I look at my wrist and remember I don't wear a watch. I have no idea. I shrug, "Should we continue or are we done now?"

"Look, I put a lot of thought into that comment and I feel you're not giving it the proper weight and time to think about it." His voice in sulking and annoyed tones.

I scratch my ear and regard him puzzled, "I thought it was space and time that made up the universe?"

He harumphs, "Muriel Anahat! Maybe I'm not talking about the gold planet maybe I'm talking about Ecospa and its magical development?"

I frown. The current comment was about the gold planet, but I did change the conversation to that. I dig in the mud path with my index finger, "That is happening." I say deadpan and non-committedly.

"You are to cut all ties immediately! You know this!" His voice harsh and unwavering.

"Immediately? I'm not there now?" I exhale, startled by this veiled threat disguised as a request. Pondering why it feels the need to tell me this.

"Your window? In your room? You shouldn't watch it in any way anymore! No more tweaking that galaxy! Whatever planet you were going to enhance needs to stay as it is! Back out and let it be!"

I absently wipe my hands together, wiping the dirt from them. I was already backing off from the planet. The tweaking of another planet in that solar system was such a sub-level thought, it would most likely not have been acted on. I cock my head, "Sure, I'll leave it be."

He snorts, "You know if you just let down your barriers and let me devour you, you won't mess with the planet either!"

With that he sent this spear of persuasion at my shields. It was strong and I felt the compulsion to stand and walk to it. I shudder as I fight it. I throw another leaf on the water's surface to help distract the Sneffel. I stand up and back away. When I look back up at the pond the Sneffel was gone.

I turn and Anthony looks up from his cell phone, a serious expression on his face. His grip, white on the phone, anxiety he wasn't trying to show. "You OK?"

I feel like shifting cobwebs are in my mind as all the colors become technicolor again, and all sensation comes back online. I give him a blasée, sheepish smile, "I just need a nap."

He pointed with his cell phone at the pond. "What was that?"

I wince, fighting the urge to deny everything, a normal position I take. "What did you see?"

He crosses his arms, weary. I can tell he is wondering if I will tell him the truth. "Diffusion mist."

I raise my eyebrows, "I didn't think you were paying attention."

A weary expression crossed across his face, "I wasn't sure I'd be able to help you , but I made sure I watched."

I look back over at the pond, and say matter of fact, "It was a Sneffel."

He looks puzzled, "A what?"

I wobble my head, "Trans-dimensional being. They like to devour Heska. They believe they are part of some universal policing service."

"All Heska?" A note of hidden fear in the deadpan response from him.

I give him a wink, "Certain spell-sets."

"What type of spell-sets?" His voice shakes.

Circe Syndrome

I reach out and give him a reassuring squeeze on the forearm, "Not metallurgy."

Gino runs up to us out of breath. "Time to go?" He looks at me with fear.

"I don't want to interrupt your time with your..." I leave the statement unfinished not sure how to categorize the nymph he was literally chasing through the garden.

Gino gives me the biggest smile, like the cat eating a canary, "Conquest. Not today, but someday soon." Hope in his voice, rich and enticing.

A female answering giggle filled the air.

Anthony gives an amused grin, "So, Gino, did you see the thing over the pond?"

Gino is distracted by the answering giggle. "Ahhh, no."

I start to head toward the exit, letting my hands scrape against the leaves and bushes and manicured trees, creating this tickling sensation on my fingertips.

Gino's voice is bemused, he calls out to me, "What was the thing?"

Anthony's voice asked him, "What is the skill-set Sneffel's look for?"

I pause at the gate, and turn in time to see the humor drain from Gino's face. He glares at Anthony, "You don't want to know." He looks at me and with a serious voice asks, "Is it still here?"

Weary I say, "No, but I do agree we should leave. It may change its mind or bring a friend."

Gino's casual gate picks up and Anthony calls out, "Hey, wait! Don't leave me with the Snufflelufflapuss, either!"

Gino escorts us to a cerulean blue, four door Saturn Sedan. It was a car with enough plastic to keep me from steel exposure. I sat in the far back away from the engine. Anthony went in the passenger seat; he was looking at the floorboards. "I still don't know how you get the pedals to work with your hooves?"

I chuckle, "I believe you are the first Satyr I've met who drives an earth killing oil machine."

Gino looks at me in the rear view mirror and puts the car in gear, gives a defeated gesture with his shoulders, "There is no other way to get around in Southern California. My trotting leagues are not helpful for getting to the store."

Anthony messes with the radio and finds a channel where the singers scream the lyrics. "How did you end up in this concrete jungle? What are you doing here?"

Gino scowls at him and the radio. He pushes the radio buttons and Sinatra fills the car. Anthony reaches to change it again, and Gino slaps his wrist. "Bad hippie trip in the sixties and I got a gig blessing wealthy people's gardens. Pays well and I help all the local Nymphs. They are a lot more willing when they are starving for water and carbon dioxide."

"Charming." I snort and look out the window. The gray air seems to reek of despair and ruined hopes. Suddenly, the overly judgmental part of my mind hits me over the nymph comment. I wince, "Sorry, Gino, thanks again for saving my life."

He sighs, "You've had a hard couple of days, huh?"

Anthony laughs, "Busy and bizarre seems to be how Mind-worm Muriel rolls!"

"What?" I yell, resisting the urge to hit him in the back of his head.

He turns, and smiles at my agitation, "It's true." He shakes his head and looks out his window, "I've only started interacting with you for two days and somehow I'm stranded some 988 miles from home."

I shrug, "It's closer than when we paddleboarded. You can go back anytime you want, you're not ill."

"That, my dear, would be ungentlemanly! Especially after you helped me out!" He gives me a grin and gesture like tipping a hat, "So, have you told your sister about me yet?"

I meet his eyes and smile, "Yeah, I did."

He raises his eyebrows, "What did she say?"

I frown and look out the window, "She got distracted by my steel scoring, caused by me standing barefoot on solid iron."

"Oh," he said softly and self-consciously.

I only meant to tease. I felt bad at the uncomfortable silence that permeated the car as we drove the rest of the way to Gino's bungalow two blocks from the harbor.

Anthony holds the door for me to get out. He offers me his arm. I giggle, letting him lighten the mood. I stumble trying to get out on my own and take his arm. Gino has walked ahead and is unlocking the front door. We follow him in.

Gino looks around and then walks toward the back to check out his backyard. I follow, swallow hard, "Gino, do you need some time without your uninvited guests?"

He gives me a warm smile, "Just one more day and I'm clear of you. You're easy. You just sleep, mostly. Your shielding back in place has made it easier all around. " He gives me a hug and talks into my hair, "It's fine, it really has been my pleasure."

He then walks out his backyard door.

Anthony and I follow out the door because his garden is just amazing. Its center had a huge three tiered fountain decorated in the god, Pan, tales. The garden was set up in the classic four square pattern. Paths down the center and a path around the perimeter. In a rectangular space. Each quadrant had lush plants and trees, with plants in rehabilitating states. The garden looks to be two miles big, though the fence outside only surrounded 700 square feet. A dimension aggregation like my mother uses on our house.

As Gino gallops down the paths, some nymphs with scars, and ones with severe damage came out to greet him. Gino stops about five yards in and kneels next to a plot full of gourd like plants. They grew in bundles like grapes, and each plant had different colored gourds. He harvests three purple, two blue, one red and about ten green ones. As he approaches each wounded nymph, he take the grape shape gourds to his horns to puncture them.

I find this whole process fascinating. He had given me some of the yellow ones when I woke up. He called them satyr fruit. Only a satyr's horn could puncture the gourds to release each of the gourds healing nectars. Each color gourd had a different type of nectar for different types of needs. Mostly plant related. I could not keep track of their properties, even though Gino seemed to always know what was needed.

Gino was gentle and consoling to the nymphs in his garden. There was none of the carousing behavior that was present with nymphs elsewhere. I suddenly remember a conversation from one of my half-conscious moments the past day. This is why he stays in Southern California. He was the only one to help and heal these damaged creatures in this area.

I stumble on the path, remembering that conversation taxing my brain that was still healing. Gino and Anthony both look at me. I was unaware of Gino still being aware of me. Gino looks at Anthony, who reaches out and steadies me, "Time to lay down again, Muriel." I wanted to protest but let him lead me down the path and back to the bungalow.

My mind is slowly shutting down and the walk becomes more about steps, and the five steps to the door are daunting. He is firm and calm, and leads me through the kitchen dining area to a little room with a bed. It looks so inviting, I lay down and fell asleep before my head hits the pillow. I vaguely feel a blanket being laid on me.

An hour later Gino shakes me awake. He hands me a pink punctured gourd. "It's time to eat again." I take the gourd, I places it to my lips. It has this husky scent and feel. I tip the gourd and drink. It was the texture of watered down syrup and tasted of strawberry and mango with a hint of something beyond honey, but not honey. I sit up and swing my feet around. This wonderful smell fills the air. It is a spicy tomato smell.

Gino helps me to my feet and guides me to the kitchen table. "Anthony's been cooking."

Anthony has a towel over his shoulder as he stirs the heavenly concoction on the stove. The timer dings and he pulls fresh cornbread out of the oven.

I sigh and lean on my arm regarding him and chasing my dreams away. "Is that chili your making?"

He turns and gives me a grin. "Of course, two bean buffalo chili, to be precise."

I bite my lip fighting the drool, "Is that fresh cornbread, too?"

Anthony nods, "Yes!"

I know I'm grinning big, "Yeah, OK, I'll talk to Sarina about you again."

He shakes his head and grins, "I'll have to remember this particular currency with you."

I give him a sheepish expression, "Well, I haven't tasted it yet."

He laughs, "It will hit the spot. I promise."

Gino sits at the head of the table and puts a napkin on his lap. Two nymphs sit across from me. Anthony dishes out bowls and places them on plates with two by four inch chunks of cornbread. He sets them at everyone's place and asks what everyone wants to drink. He grabs me some milk on my request. He puts out a bowl of shredded cheese. He then sits next to me.

I put about five teaspoons of cheese in my bowl and crumble some cornbread into it. I stir my concoction and watch the steam rise. I take a bite and enjoy the savory tomato with the sweet cornbread and cooling cheese.

The whole table is quiet, everyone at their own chili ritual, and appreciating the flavors.

One of the nymphs leans forward. "Miss Muriel?"

I meet her green eyes and swallow, "Yes."

She gives me a shy look under her lashes and Gino smiles into his glass. "You live in the North West, right?"

I pull at my cornbread, "Yes."

She meets my eyes again, "In the area, where it is one of the most efficient places to grow trees?"

I set my spoon down and nod. "Yes, days of rain mixed with sunshine, we call them sun breaks."

The nymph exchanges glances with the one next to her. They giggle. I look back at Gino. He is trying to hide a smile as he stares into his bowl.

Anthony sighs, "Don't forget to mention all the environmental laws!"

I stir my chili. I was wondering if there was an unspoken question in this interaction. I point to the chili. "I didn't know nymphs eat meat."

They smile, showing pointed teeth. "We take all forms of nutrients from the soil from decaying living matter as plants so in this form we do the same."

I suppress a shudder. I found myself thinking about the trees on Eco-spa. Why had I imagined that trees would be peaceful creatures?

Circe Syndrome

Anthony starts to tell some jokes as the two nymphs asked is their trees can be transported to Oregon. I find out what types of trees they were and a great debate ensued about where would be the best area. We were tossing around the pros and cons of Tillamook forest, Crater Lake, Mount Hood, Hood River and Gorge areas.

Chapter 28

Aether-Verse

I feel unexpectantly winded after the two jumps, then the jump home. I steady myself in the shed and wait to get my bearings. I walk around to the front of the house, breathing in relief as I enjoy the lack of the bright, white light of California. The blue light of the Portland sun soothes me. The crisp fall air is refreshing to breathe.

The door opens with a bang and my mother gathers me into her arms and hugs me hard. "Why are you lolly-gagging out here?"

I hug my mother back and let her pull me inside, "Just enjoying the moment."

The robotic foyer arm reaches down to remove my internal communication and video device. My mother backs away with a scornful look on her face. I remember the Sneffel moment, wondering if that was transmitted. I look at the device and realize I hadn't heard much from it. It looked fried. I bob my head as the arm balls it up and tosses it. I realize I must have made it melt down in my mind pressure challenge.

My mother crosses her arms, glaring at the metal in it, her lips compressed tightly. "How much metal is in that?"

I sigh, "It's more silicone and gold than anything else."

She frowns, "What type of plastic?"

I cock my head, "I don't have a latex or rubber allergy Mom."

She harrumphs, "We will see, eventually."

As we go through the main door and out of the breezeway I exhale, "Let's face it, it is one of the sneaky ways The Collective is keeping tabs on me. They get to say it is just standard policy for their representatives, instead of mandating it as a negative item, like an electric ankle bracelet."

Mom takes a tense breath, "As long as you are aware of that."

"Just because I don't fight something doesn't mean I don't know what is going on." I pause and shuffle my feet. "Thanks for the home moratorium, by the way."

My Mom smiles and hugs me again. "We will get through this, kiddo."

The common family area had tripled in size and tons of family were mingling. A clump approaches me. They start barraging me with questions. I inch my way to a club chair, sitting down to answer questions. A swarm of fairy's, including Arial, swirls about me. They scan me. The air around me churns, causing my hair to fly up. Suddenly, they stop, hanging in midair. At the moment I find that creepy. Arial crossed her arms. "How did that Satyr clean you out so well?"

I suspect it was the gourds. I shrug.

"Well, you're cleaned out better than when you left. You may spend time with Morgan now!"

I nod, "Thank you, Arial."

My relatives around me start asking questions about the idea of a Satyr in California: how and why and where. I laugh and answer as vaguely as I can. Yacob and Morgan enter the room, causing all questions and attention to stop. I am so relieved.

Morgan looks uncomfortable, and Yacob basks in the attention following them across the room. Morgan sits in the chair next to me and takes my hand. "Hey, Muriel, whatever have you been up to?"

The room laughs and scatters to do what they were doing before. I watch. Uncle Mordecai maneuvers Aunt Hannah, Aunt Shirley and four of Morgan's relatives to the card table. A couple of the younger kids have created a miniature golf course, with changing challenges in a section of the family room. The teens are playing some complicated video games that appears in the air in front of them. They involve social skills, networking and battling skills. My father is showing off some new contraption and my mother is in a group of older women, including Aoife, quilting blankets in the air as they have a heated discussion.

The rumble of the family relaxes me. I sit back and lean in Morgan's direction, "Not much, you?"

Yacob snorts and sits on the arm of Morgan's chair, "We both want you at the birth, you know that right, Murry?"

I look at my hands, "I'm not trying to complicate things."

Yacob taps my arm, "I heard you went space paddleboarding without me."

I give Morgan a significant look, "You're kind of busy, Yacob. Besides, Mom wants me to be more social."

Morgan laughs and shakes her head, "Do you really understand what that means?"

I give her a mock baffled look, "I thought it was being in groups of people, having conversations. Sometimes doing activities together, like the dance."

Yacob covers a smile, "Nice precise definition."

I wrinkle my forehead, "How is paddleboarding different than dancing?"

Morgan wobbles her head, "I guess they are not. Just one is a safer activity."

I raise my eyebrows, "Dancing 100 to 600 feet above ground with gravity is pretty daring."

Morgan sucks in her upper lip, suppressing something, and shakes her head, "OK, why were you on the coast in California?"

I scratch my ear and look away, "Oh, that! That is classified." We sit in silence. I take a breath, lean forward, clap my hands together and give them a smile. "Enough about me! How are you and Merlin doing?"

Morgan sighs. The exhaustion about her is palpable. "I'm ready to begin! I'm tired of everyone telling me to get sleep! Because in this shape, there is no way to be comfortable! I have to get up every half hour to pee!"

Sympathetically I say, "Sounds trying."

About twenty minutes into this conversation I feel my attention waver and beg to be excused. I head upstairs and find my mother at my door, waiting. She gives me a hug and mentions a snack she put by my bed. Then her hand grabs my arm. She is fierce as she says. "There are spiders crawling through your aura, you saw a Sneffel in California!"

I just want to go to my room. I'm ready to be alone. I look at my door longingly, "Yeah, I did. It was a real ass, too." I say it matter fact and with exhaustion.

Mom opens my door and gestures me in. I walk in, she follows. I walk to my bed and stare out of my window at Ecospa. I'm not ready to say goodbye to it. I know I should. I take a breath, hold it for a count of three, and let it out slowly.

My Mom echoes the sigh. I turn and look at her. She has closed my door and her arms are crossed. "How many things crawled out of the aether-verse?"

I plop on my bed and hold my head, "According to Gino there were about five. Aether-verse?"

She gives a mischievous smile, "My nickname for the various hide-y-holes strewn across the universe and mortal collective unconscious."

I give her an answering smile, "So, real, imagined, and un-thought of. I like it. I will use that."

She gives me a bemused smile, like, "Of course you will." Out loud sheepishly she says, "Great, darling. What were the five beings, dear?"

I look over my shoulder, back out the window. I know I'm going to miss the view. I have taken some photographs, but it is never the same. I take a breath and begin the list. "There were Fomorri, a gremlin, Sneffel, dark raven and an ice giant. Hey, that reminds me, have you ever made a planet of gold?"

My mother sits next to me. "No, I haven't. Why would you want to? It would be hard to keep it in orbit or spinning. How does a satyr handle an ice giant? What is an ice giant doing in Southern California?"

I kick off my shoes and run my soles together. I shake my head, puzzled. "I don't know how one could manifest there. I was nowhere near a mountain top. That is why I'm asking about a gold planet. Anthony's Godfather is Vulcan, so he asked the Roman God to help out."

"Anthony? Anthony who?" Mom turns and looks me in the eye.

Circe Syndrome

I exhale raggedly, "Anthony Phoenix." I watch my mother's pleasant and caring demeanor change. Suppressed anger filled her. Anthony's older brother had broken Sarina's heart.

Her mouth has become a straight line. "Phoenix? Is he related to Simon?"

I nod, "Yeah, his little brother."

Mom turns and looks out my window. "Why? Why was he there?"

I turn and look with her. The dolphins were jumping again. "He's a metallurgy mage. Headquarters sent him to help me deal with a problem."

She huffs, "Dear heart, I'm on the council. If I don't have security clearance no-one does. Why are you handling problems? You're only supposed to be a recruiter. What problem?"

"I was helping drop a new recruit on the coast." I laid back on my bed and stared at my ceiling.

She gives me a big smile of pride, "A new recruit? Congratulations!"

It amazes how this thrills me, still, to please my mother, "Thanks, Mom, I ran into a selkie. He told me about a leak problem on the California coast that was about to happen."

She looks thoughtful, "How did the Selkie know?"

I sigh, "Salmon of Knowledge."

Her forehead wrinkles, "The one eaten by Finegas the Druid? How is that possible?"

"No, it's really weird, I guess all salmon have knowledge, you just need to swim with them. No consumption necessary."

She frowns, "That's fine and all, but why were you sent and not someone else?"

I show my palms in bafflement, "I suspect the whole 'Circe incident' had the whole organization distracted."

She nods, "I recall that report. Didn't you have a hand in that, too?"

I look away, "Kind of."

She gives me a look that says she doesn't believe I'm divulging everything. "Alright. Why does Anthony and Vulcan mean you need to make a planet of gold?"

I refuse to meet her eyes, "Anthony called Hephaestus to help deal with the Ice Giants problem."

She frowns, "Didn't someone else take care of the debt. Is he really asking you to make a planet of gold?"

I bite my lip, "I'm not in his debt. More of a favor."

She shakes her head, "Toe mat toe, Too mate toe, child! So, did the Sneffel: at your visit, come about the gold planet?"

I roll on my side and look out my window, "I thought so, but it was really about Eco Spa."

"Oh?" Mom says quietly, "It's been a year in our time since you last saw Gregor. It's been around sixty-two years in his time. He is most likely dead."

Tears fill my eyes. Leave it to her to touch this sore spot. I sniffle, "I loved him, mother. I know it's been a year, but I don't know if I'm ready to move on."

She pats my arm, "You were there with Sarah recently. Did you look at his community? Is he still alive?"

I wiped my tears. I had checked on him recently, but I had not over the past year. Mom playing this game of speculating he is dead then asking is a way to get me to leak information to her. "He eventually married and had children."

"That is for the best, believe me. My friend, Rosalind, has a nightmare to deal with. Remember her daughter."

I wipe my eyes, wondering at this change in topic. "Lydia?"

She points at me with a thankful smile, "Yes, that is the one. She is on some other dimension on some planet, with the assignment to make it magical. She decides to have a child with the natives, tying her family to this other dimension and planet."

I pause, thinking about the ramifications of tying a family through dimensions. Planets happen a great deal, "What do you mean make it magical? I thought we didn't know what causes that?"

Mom eyebrows raise, "Naturally, we have no idea, but some Heska have this talent to create magical eco-systems."

I sit up and get in her space, "What? Who assigned her? The Collective?"

She nonchalantly cocks her head, like I'm being silly, "No, there is this trans-dimensional council called the Obyx. You were almost recruited till the whole mind-worm thing."

My mind is awash in shock, "What? Trans-dimensional council? Recruit me, why?" My mother had this habit of dropping this type of thing on me casually. Stuff I knew nothing about and she acted like it was common, uninteresting information.

Mom is looking at the dolphins, "Your ability to make habitable planets is superb, but your talent in becoming an aether transformer and generator would make you valuable to a magical field generating team."

I frown, so confused. "I just run the current through my body instead of containing it. Anyone can do it."

She gives me a mischievous grin. "It doesn't feel natural to many Heska, I never told you this. Some go crazy from doing what you do."

I shelve this thought, overwhelmed by it. I will ponder it later. " OK, this council, are they elected?"

"Some are." Her voice is that of one distracted, she is not totally in this conversation. It will be easier to get information out of her.

I have so many questions, I wish I could ask them all at once. "So, my planet, there? Has someone been assigned to make it magical?"

Mom shakes her head no. "No, if you check your aether controls on your monitoring station, you should be able to see that there is no alien life currently on your planet. Should be a log of all the visits, and you will find it's only been you, me and your sister."

My eyebrows rose, "Aether controls?"

Mom's focus suddenly is completely on me, she bites her lip, "I've never told you any of this, have I?"

"Nope."

Mom leans toward me, "Do you have some system set up here to monitor galaxies you're working on?"

Annoyed at her hiding information from me, I fib, "I'm not really a plural worker."

Mom, detecting the lie, raises her eyebrows and a glint appears in her eyes.

I let out a long sigh, "You know we never talk about this." I wonder how things would have happened if I would have had been guided.

"I know."

I frown at my hands, "It's all spells, Mom."

She messes my hair like I'm six, "I know, dear heart, but you made a physical manifestation of them so you don't have to think about them all the time, right?"

I wobble my head, deliberating what to reveal, "There is more of an idea matrix set of them."

"Just manifest them in a way I can perceive them, child." Her patient mother voice present.

I stand back up walk to my vanity and pull a drawer. It transforms into a computer consul. My mother gestures me aside and sits down. She toggles through the spells. " OK, see the spells that direct aether for manipulating elements, just add some frequency detection spells."

My jaw drops, it never occurred to me to monitor alien life visiting my planet. I monitor native types all the time. "Oh, OK!"

My mother gives me an encouraging expression. "Make me an aether matrix map of EcoSpa to look at."

It takes me a moment to wrap those spells together and get a display of what she is looking for. The screen fills with wavy lines across the planet.

My mother gives me a patient smile, "See where the lines look to be knotting." She gestures at the screen.

"Yeah."

"I imagine that is where your portal is?" She points back to my window.

I squint at the screen and compare continent shapes to a map in my mind of that location. "You're right."

I zoom in on this spot on the screen. A little way from my portal, there are some smaller knots.

My mother points to them, "Most likely, those are the creatures that have been manifesting reality changing abilities. Hmmmm, they are close to your portal. Curious." She looks back at my window. I can see her eyes changing to perceive different energies.

"Yes, they are close," I notice. "Do you think the portal is creating the aether feed? Will they lose their abilities when the portal closes?"

Mom is tapping her chin with her index finger. "Good question. I'm not sure. Do they have butterflies there yet?"

I nod, "Yes." I go to a species inventory. I back up startled, "Hey, I only designed, like, five kinds of butterflies. Now there looks to be over a hundred different species, now!"

Mom says sagely, "Most likely the planet has its own source now."

I cock my head at the screen, "This spell seems to only show what is currently happening, not what has happened over time."

"Remember all matter has memory built in, just access it." She taps her forehead.

"Matter and memory, sure Mom." I tweak some of the spells to access cellular molecular memory. A series of buttons appear on the screen. As I toggle through them, I say out loud, "It looks just like you said. Except for a few bacteria traveling on asteroids and landing as meteoroids."

Mom stands, "Are the meteoroids available for analysis?"

I shake my head in negative fashion, "Looks like they have all been broken down at this time by erosion."

"That makes it hard to determine if the asteroids were aimed or just happened then." She cocks her head.

I stare at her blankly, trying to comprehend everything that she has just said to me. The idea of an asteroid aimed and the ramifications weighing me down.

She shrugs under my scrutiny, and sits at the end of my bed again.

"So the Obyx? Huh? I was being considered?"

Mom suddenly stands and shakes her head as if clearing cobwebs, "Yeah, I need to go help your father with something. You OK?"

I feel completely turned inside out and confused. "Sure."

Circe Syndrome

My Mom stands and makes her way to the door. She pauses and stares at the handle, "The key to gold is something to do with salt water." She opens the door and leaves.

I feel ridiculous, confused and just exhausted. Grief over Gregor suddenly hitting, I just want to climb into bed and sleep. I wonder why mother has never tutored me in planet manipulation before. What else she knows that she doesn't talk to me about.

I collapse into my chair before the vanity screen again. I bring up that galaxy I was tinkering with three days ago. I add the spells I just added to Ecospa. There is a Spartan amount of aether on this fledgling planet. I go to the species inventory and the hair on the back of my neck rises. The ivy is gone. There is only one turtle left. I zoom in to see this creature. What meets me is terrifying. It has quadrupled in size. It is covered in mushrooms and it has a metallic sheen to its eyes.

Perplexed and more confused I turn the consul back into a vanity. So many more questions. What is aether? How do I get a large volume of gold together to make a planet? What was with all the mushrooms? How mystical are butterflies really? What is the Obyx?

I lay back on my bed and turn my neck so I can look out the window. I flick my wrists causing the windows to open. A breeze of saltwater and the smell of pineapple encircle me. I hear the birds caw and the wind. This lulls me to sleep

Chapter 29

Dashing Diner

Bang! Bang! Bang! "Muriel, are you in there?" Sarina's voice calls out from behind my closed door.

I groan and sit up, "Yeah, I'm here."

As I rub my head I hear her pace outside the door. She grunts and says, "Dinner! Come on down."

I take a breath and sigh, " OK, I'm coming."

"Let me in!" She bangs on the door more.

I spell the windows closed, "Why?"

Sarina's voice, more annoyed, "Muriel! Don't be a pain! Just let me in!"

I gesture to the door and it unlocks. Sarina must have been leaning on it because she looks surprised as she stumbles in. She gets her bearings looks up at me and scowls. "You look awful, sit up!"

I rub my eyes, "I was sleeping."

She rolls her eyes at me, "Of course you were."

I laboriously sit up, "I just got home."

Sarina walks to my vanity and finds a brush. She hands it to me.

I take it and start to run it through my hair. "Thanks, how are you doing?"

Sarina leans against my vanity, crossing her arms. She looks about the room and asks, "How is your room always such a calm place?"

My mind is still digesting things my mother said to me. My mind doesn't feel calm so my room doesn't feel calm to me. I laugh, "I don't know what you're talking about!"

Her voice is acerbic, "Every room is full of family, but this room is just you!"

I raise an eyebrow, "Isn't your room just as clear?"

Sarina smirks, reminding me of that cousin of Morgan's who had asked about her. I rub my forehead, "It does help that I don't invite people to my room."

She shakes her head and walks to the window, her fingers tracing the boulders in the distance, "These young men don't seem to understand that, just because I slept with them, doesn't mean I want to spend more time with them."

I set down the brush and think about moving off the bed. "Most people don't assume that, Sarina. Most people believe physical intimacy goes with social intimacy."

Sarina glares at me. Old wounds apparent on her face. "Most men don't!"

I giggle, "But you're intoxicating Sarina! Men always want the one who doesn't want them. I bet you even tell them in the beginning it's just casual!"

Sarina throws up her hands, "I warn them."

"You love their adoration. You know what you're doing."

"Muriel!" She shoves me, then pokes me in a ticklish spot. We digress into a wrestling match.

My mother's voice in our heads stops us cold. "Muriel and Sarah come down to dinner. Please."

I am gasping for air from laughing as I back toward the door. Sarina gives me a gasping grin, "I guess we really improved your appearance."

I look over at the mirror and wince.   I go back to the bed and find the brush. I run it through my hair quickly. Sarina runs out the door and I run to catch up. I end up one flight behind her the whole way down.   I pause at the bottom step. The dining room had grown to the size of a small banquet hall. There are three long tables. One is filled with older people, the one in the middle has young married people and the last one has all the unmarried people ranging from eight to one hundred years old.

Sarina was sitting at this table in the middle across from an empty seat. She was surrounded by eight young men. Two to her right and left and two to the left and right of this open seat. I look over at my mother and raise an eyebrow. She makes a shooing motion with her hands.

When I, sit, my father begins the Motzi, the prayer over bread and drink.

Morgan's family watched with interest as my father rips off a piece of bread from a huge six braided challah. Other loaves start down the tables.

I rub my head. "Is it Shabbat? I think I'm missing some days."

Sarina was flirting with three men at once. She always marveled me. She gives me an amused glance, "It's not Friday. Dad just thought it was rare to have so much family together so we are doing the challah every day."

Circe Syndrome

"Oh?" I sip some of the sweet wine when the Kiddush finished. I fill my plate with roast, bread and cooked carrots. The young men around us are laughing at a story Sarina is telling. She had made a levitation app on her phone that actually levitated things. When a thief took her phone, she had to rescue him from the ceiling of the Rose Garden Arena.

Her voice is full of amusement, "So, I had to climb and levitate up to the top of the Rose Garden to get him down. He was pale as a sheet and soaked with sweat and urine!"

The men around us give her amused expressions.

I fiddle with my silverware. The room is buzzing with conversation. The red haired man to my right accidently hits my elbow when he reaches to refill Sarina's glass. He apologizes and I give him a shrug he doesn't look at me long enough to see. Kiddy corner from me a young man with curly brown hair meets my eyes and smiles at me. I smile back at him.

He then asks Sarina some questions that set the whole table talking. I listen, eat and enjoy my meal.

The room goes silent when the doorbell rings.

My mother stands and speaks to me in my mind, "Come along, dear."

I feel clumsy as I stand drop my napkin, go to retrieve it and hit my head on the table. I knock over my wine glass and send my fork flying. I mumble apologies as I disentangle my pant leg from the chair leg. The room chuckles, and they all start talking at once.

I catch up to my mother and ask, "What is this about?"

She gives me an appraising look. I'm in a t-shirt and jeans. "You went to the Gorge dance Muriel, remember? There were a lot of cards. A few of the gentleman have shown up over the past few days. One was quite persistent."

I give her a weary look, "Who, Mom?" I just want to go back upstairs and go to bed.

289

Mom's expression is thoughtful, "His name is Andy."

Not the boy from the MAX, I think, and groan involuntarily.

She snorts, "What? He's nice and not bad to look at."

She escorts me to the front room that she has partitioned off from the rest of the house. There were similar to our regular size rooms here, just larger. She gestures to the right of the front door where an elegant table, chairs, tea set and a tray of treats appeared. "Have a seat, Muriel, I'll bring him over."

"Mom, I don't think…" I stammer.

"Shush, Muriel, I know how these things are done. Go sit down, dear." She gestures in my direction. I feel my clothes shift. I look down and find myself wearing a lace dress inspired by the Victorian age. Sitting down suddenly felt like a great idea.

My Mom opens the door and escorts Andy to the table. He is wearing a gray pinstriped suit with tails and an ascot. Mom, blasé, says, "I know it's customary for her to make you wait. Since you have been trying for three days, I decided you waited enough."

My eyes widened, "Mother!"

"It's true dear." She walks up to me and adjusts my hair like I'm six.

Andy shifts his hair and smiles at me while he bows to my mother. "Thank you, Madame Anahat."

She giggles when he hands her a bouquet of small white roses.

He turns to me and hands me a similar bouquet of orange and light pink roses.

I blush. My mother taught me some of the language of flowers. My mother gives me a pleased satisfied smile and leaves the room. I direct him to sit as years of training from childhood taught me. I smell the bouquet and notice their thorn-less state. "So you desired me on first sight. Are you sure you were looking at me?"

"Modest, aren't you?" He laughs.

"Practical." I say as I look about for a place to set the flowers. I notice my mother had thought ahead. There was a vase with water in it. I gently set the flowers down.

He raises an eyebrow and speculatively looks at the tea things. "Wow, I don't think I've ever done this!"

I giggle, "Why? Perhaps because you live in America in the twenty-first century?" I sigh, shaking my head at my mother's presumptions.

He fingers the bone china, "Do you do this often?"

"Not since I was eight. Bet even then it was more toned down. You know, we could have just met at a coffee shop. Sorry for the pomp. Do you want me to pour?"

He presented his cup to me. As the smooth black tea poured into the china cup, he said, "No worries, this is fun and kind of civilizing. I definitely was not very gallant when we met, exposing you in front of all those people."

I poured myself some tea and added two lumps of brown sugar and cream. My eyes wander to the treat tray. My heart stopped. My mother's shortbread was on the tray. I gestured to the tray offering him, the guest, first choice. He took some fruit. I took a piece of shortbread and dunked it into the tea. I brought the softened, buttery dough soaked in tea to my mouth and closed my eyes in pleasure as I took a bite. It melted in my mouth tasting of sugar and butter. With my mouth full I say, "You got to try the shortbread!"

He cocks his head at me amused, "Is the dunking in the tea a Miss Manners thing, too?"

I shake my head, "I doubt it, but it tastes heavenly. Sorry you had to interact with my mother about this."

He leans forward, all interest, "Where were you?"

I pull back and trace a pattern on the lace table cloth. "Oh, here and there, mostly fighting illness."

He leans back, "Anything contagious?"

I watch him a bit, noting his body language change to backing away, "No, not anymore at least."

He raises his cup, "Oh, what was it?"

Steel sickness was a tell on magical ability so I was creative, "A stomach bug."

"Ewww, I think between your cookie dunking and illness talk, I think you have uncivilized this conversation!" He chuckles.

I chuckle, "You may be right."

He takes a piece of shortbread and dunks it. I watch his eyes light up as he places it in his mouth. "Awesome!" He mumbles as he chews on the cookie.

I grin, happy he is enjoying it. I take another sip of tea.

He devours his shortbread, "So you work for The Collective?"

I move my head in acknowledgement and wait. I wonder where he is going with this line of questions. I waited for him to tell me what he did. It's impolite to ask what someone else does for a living.

"I work in the tech industry. My family owns a Nano-tech company called Tesla-tronics. Have you heard of them?"

I nod, thinking about the name and remembering where I've heard it before, "I believe they have licensed some of my father's patents."

His curiosity suddenly looks forced and unnatural, "Your father? He is?"

I give him a bored expression, "Daedalus Anahat."

He hits his head softly, miming harder, "Oh! I didn't make the connection."

Sure, I think. I doubt this.

He bites his lip then looks at me as if he was thinking through this next question. "Is Yacob Anahat related to you?"

"My brother." I say, as I pour myself some more tea and hide my face with my cup.

An over eager expression fills his face, "Oh, their inventions are fabulous."

"Are they? I had no idea." I take another sip, hiding my smile. If he was going to lie, I was going to, as well. I was wondering what information he is actually looking for. Dating me was not his objective.

He was looking at me expectantly. I begin to fidget, "So, have you ever helped with any of your brother's or father's projects?"

I give a negative shake of my head, "I wish, I focused on other things growing up."

He suddenly looked bored, "So you have no idea what they are working on right now."

So corporate secrets were his game. "So Tesla-tronics! Is Tesla your family name?"

He gives a stiff nod, letting me change the subject, as he stares forlornly in his empty cup. I refill it as he says, "Yeah, a family member found out we were related by a distant cousin fifty years ago. So as a point of Scientific pride she renamed herself and her descendants. She even started the company."

"Your grandmother?" I grab some cheese.

He shakes his head, "No, mother."

I was surprised, "Oh?"

He nods, "I'm forty like you. Typical Heska growing cycle. Two years equal to one year. That's why we both seem to be in our twenties."

I chuckle, "That is quite a gamble, assuming a Heska age."

He laughs back, "No one is sending twenty year olds to the Gorge dance!"

"Nope, that is true."

"So what do you think? Do you want to try a real date? I'll pick you up Friday night around seven?"

I give him an overconfident smile. I'm not sure, but I've never really dated. "Sure, what did you have in mind?"

He gives me a mischievous smile, "How was asteroid paddle boarding?"

I cocked my head, "You paddleboard?"

"No, but I heard about it. Why didn't you invite me?" He bats his eyelashes.

I stifle a giggle. I count out my reasons with my fingers, "First, I don't know you. Second, it was supposed to be an exercise in blowing off steam from meeting new people, like you. Third, you don't know how."

"You want to teach me?" He asks, with a wistful expression.

I give him an amused smile, "I really don't know you that well. Let's stick to an earth bond place for our first date, OK?"

He sighs, "Alright, does it have to be this continent?"

I adjust my hair, "Were you thinking dinner or something else? Because breakfast in Bangladesh might throw me! And, I don't think anywhere is open in France at three in the morning."

He guffaws at that, "How about a walk on the beach in Honolulu and a meal at a hotel there?"

" OK."

We both stand. He bows, "Till Friday, my lady."

I show him out, I turn and stare at the arch leading back into the chaos of the dining room. I think about the MAX conversation and how dubious a beginning that was. I know first impressions are rubbish. The room was full of chatter and it was the sound of dessert being served. I enter and dodge the hovering trays after I snag three chocolate crinkle cookies and sit back where I was before.

Circe Syndrome

My Mom walks over to me, "How did it go?"

The men around me listening.

I put my napkin back in my lap and nonchalantly say, "It was fine, Mom."

She puts her hand on my shoulder, "Will you see him again?"

I look back up at her, "Yeah, we are going to try a date."

She claps her hands together and the people around me are all hiding their amusement, "Good."

I shake my head, "Don't get too excited, I think he is more interested in pumping me for information on Yacob's and Dad's projects."

A line appears on her forehead. "Oh? Well you are at least getting yourself out there, dearest. That is good."

She walks away.

I watch her go, and eat a cookie. People are getting up from their seats and the room has become more of a party atmosphere. The dishes were moved to the kitchen with hefty cleaning spells. The table cloth rise and ball themselves up, heading toward the laundry. The tables start detaching into smaller ones. They became gaming tables. Empty chairs galloped about finding empty spaces at tables to sit at. Groups of people move together to different tables.

The tables have Icon's that appear on their surfaces, little labels of words beneath them. A person could press an icon and the table will become the ideal space for the chosen activity.

My mother's table became a Mah-Jong table, while my father's ends up as a pool table. Wait, no, it is a billiard table, there are no pockets. Some young people's table became a multi-faceted video game cabinet. Sarina has a group of men and her table becomes a poker table.

The brown curly haired young man who caught my eye earlier approached me, with a young woman with similar features. As I watched them move and interact I suspected they were twins. He reached out his hand to shake mine, "Hey, I'm Gideon."

I shake his hand back, "Muriel."

I turn to the young woman and offer my hand.

She smiles warmly and exchanges glances with Gideon, "I'm Glinda."

I snort involuntarily, "So your parents had a thing for alliteration."

The both roll their eyes and chuckle. Gideon adjusts his collar, "Jasper said your jokes were hopeless."

I gesture to the table, "Ah, so you are forewarned."

They look at each other and back at me. They sit.

I sit down, "So what game do you want to play?"

Gideon gives a puzzle smile, "What exactly is Canasta?"

I shrug, "A game from the forties."

Gideon leans in conspiratorially like sharing an inside joke, "Ever play?"

I shake my head, "No, you?"

Glinda looks between us. Noting our amused attraction to one another, she nods toward the icon, "Let's try it." She gestures to another young man passing by, "Hey, Sean, come join us."

Gideon pushes the icon. The table becomes a standard card table with green felt and a fresh deck of cards.

As we settle down for the tutorial, Morgan gasps really loud. We all stop and turn and look at her.

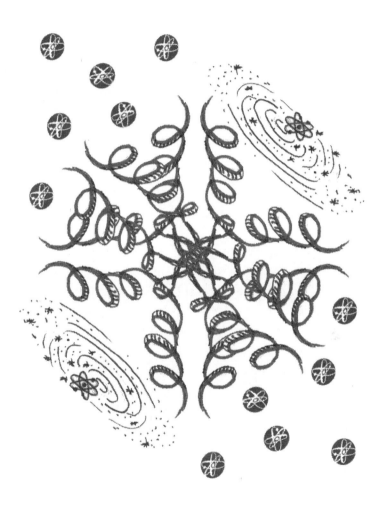

Chapter 30

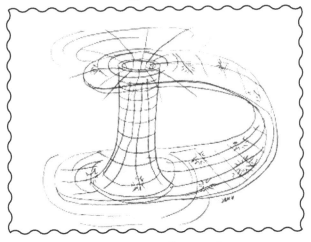

How Close?

I was out of my chair and next to Morgan before her next gasp. My mother, Aiofe and Yacob were there, too. The room is holding its collective breath. Morgan's family has started a low hum. I could see the tendrils of aether about the room start to form a base of shields.

Softly Aiofe addresses Morgan, "How long have you been in labor, child?"

Morgan looks at her warily, "I started yesterday."

My mother takes Morgan's pulse, no surprise in her manner. Aoife watches, digesting her daughter confiding in her mother-in-law, before her. My Mom asks, "How long between contractions?"

Yacob helps Morgan stand and they walk toward the stairs.

I tap my mother's shoulder; she looks at me. I gesture to the stairs, "You are not going to make her walk up the stairs are you?" I mumble.

Circe Syndrome

My mother gives me an amused smile. "It can help labor sometimes." I watch the door to Yacob's room appear at the foot of the stairs. We enter the door, I take Morgan's other side, as the room moves back in space and vertigo takes hold of us.

My mother directs us to the birthing room. When the door is sealed behind us, I feel the wards beyond the room slide into place around it from the family below.

Before we get her to the birthing chair, Morgan gasps for a breath. I feel something unexpected and terrifying in this moment. Her body was trying to harmonize with a different dimension. I just reacted. There was no time for thinking, I started weaving a rope of aether and wrapped it through Morgan as an anchor to keep Morgan in this dimension. The cords of this dimension echoing through us.

When Morgan's contraction pauses, she is breathing hard. I look at my mother, then directed a question at Yacob, "So, Morgan's a wormhole maker?"

Yacob and Aoife both nod. Morgan screams, "Yes, is Merlin OK?"

Mom and I exchange the looks of, "Did you know this?" We both realize neither of us did. Mom looks at Aoife as she talks to Yacob, " OK, Yacob, I'm going to need your help. Aoife, I thought you said multi-dimensional stuff never happened in your family."

Aoife shrugged, "It doesn't manifest till one is thirteen. She got it from her father's side. He never mentioned labor trouble with women."

Yacob frowns and looks at me, "What do we do?"

I look to my mother, she smiles at me reassuringly, "Muriel, you and Yacob anchor Morgan. Aoife and I will anchor Merlin."

As my mother and Aoife start a heated discussion of the how's and why's, I rub Morgan's back. I look at Yacob " OK we need to sever ties with Sarina or she could be pulled into a void.

Janette Bach

Then we need to anchor ourselves here, then tie Morgan in and close all holes she opens. I bite my lip. "Um, Morgan, is all this involuntary?"

Morgan is tensing, "It's going to happen again! Yes, my body does it to avoid pain. It's not used to internal pain."

I use soothing tones, "Have you ever opened a hole voluntarily?"

Morgan exhales, "Yeah."

I think a moment, " OK, so you can try to close them, too. If you can, between pains."

I send my distracted thoughts to Sarina. "We have to leave you powerless. When we are done it will resume." I vaguely hear her protests as I pull my power from her and sever our ties. I hear a wormhole opening.

My mind swims to close the wormhole. I gather the aether into strings. I sew it around the perimeter of the hole in a running stitch pattern. Then I start running it across the hole that is opening in a gathering stitch anchored on those running stitches. In my mind, it's like repairing a hole in a blanket of reality. When I was done sewing it up, Morgan is panting.

Mom and Aoife are both frowning at Morgan's abdomen.

Yacob and I share concerned looks, "How did you do that?"

I cock my head, "You know anything about sewing?"

He gives me a pained look, "Not the fancy stuff."

My mind races trying to find a techno analogy. I start explaining how I think about aether. "Try to remember it's about a tear in reality. How do you normally repair holes?"

He gives me a smirk, "Soldering."

Morgan screams, "Really! You two are going to have a philosophical discussion right now!"

An idea comes to me as I wince at the pain I know Morgan is feeling. I turn and look at my mother. "Mom? If you hold on to Merlin and we let Morgan and us slide down the wormhole would that really be a problem?"

Aiofe is scowling at me like it's the worst idea she has ever heard, and Mom is looking thoughtful.

Morgan's breath becomes ragged. Before Yacob and I close the resulting hole, two non-corporeal beings enter the room. They circle around the ceiling. I stare up at them as I take a moment to breathe. The closing is taxing my thoughts I send out a tendril of thought towards the non-corporeal beings. They were ghosts. Morgan's family. I clear my throat and say out loud, "Um, Morgan, Aoife, a couple of old family members have come! They want to merge with Merlin! What do you want to do?"

Yacob frowns and squints up at the shapes. "How did they get in here?"

I gesture toward Morgan, who is in rapt conversation with the specters. "Wormhole goes right through all the shield spells. Luckily these are friendly spirits!"

Yacob's face loses all color. I look at my Mom, "So, Mom? What do you think?"

My Mom looks at me and the ghosts speculatively. She knows I'm asking about the traveling question. I am thinking the visitors can only get worse. I didn't want to deal with a Sneffel here. "How would you get back? How do we detach the umbilical cord?"

Morgan starts another contraction. I brace. This time, one of their families' ghosts came forward.

Yacob yells at Morgan, "Where in the hell are you opening to?"

Morgan groans and pants, "I have no idea!"

I move hair out of my face. "They are not necessarily coming from there. The hole creates spaces with no barriers. Things from our world can use the space between to get around the protection spells." Morgan's breathing changed. I braced and counted internally up to a hundred, then Morgan's body relaxed. I noticed secondary holes were starting to form and wander the room. Another thought struck me. "Um, Mom, how about if we just dialyosefos the three of us five feet to the right, while you hold Merlin?"

Aoife smiles, "I like it!"

My mother nods, "Make sure the umbilical cord ends up out an orifice."

"Ewww! Thanks for the visual Mom!" said Yacob.

Mom shakes her head, "You are old enough to make a baby, you are old enough to handle all the details."

I look at Yacob and Morgan, "What do you two think?"

They exchange glances. Morgan nods, "Let's try it!"

I did a complete scan of the two of them and mapped out the difference between Morgan and Merlin. The umbilical cord was problematic. There was a constant blood exchange happening. I tried to think about what would happen when the cord was cut. "Mom, how do we handle the cord?"

My mother gave me a frown, "You over thought it didn't you?"

I looked down.

"Just relax kiddo, you three can do this." My Mom's hands are glowing blue. She is humming and puts them on either side of Morgan's hips.

"Won't the transparent blood create a problem?" I asked.

The four of them yelled at me, "Muriel!"

I take a breath and remember how fast the dialyosefos would be outside the normal event. It would be less than a second. The baby would be fine. "OK, I'll count to three."

Yacob gasps, "Wait," he grabs a chair from the side of the room and puts it five feet from us.

" OK, on three" I begin the count, "One," I take a breath. "Two," I take two big gulps of air. "Three!"

I was keeping an eye on Morgan as I started to dissolve. Morgan and Yacob are dialyosefosing together. I note the umbilical cord. I position it to be in an easy place when we solidify, suddenly a hole opens. We were all non-corporeal, we swirled together. I note my mother cutting the umbilical cord as Aoife closes the hole. Yacob, Morgan and I swirl into it.

This was a wild ride. It gives a sensation like rushing forward in a never ending race. I was trying to keep my particles together. I feel as if I am swirling down a drain. At some point Morgan and Yacob's consciousness touches me. Yacob sends me a thought, "Umm, this is taking family closeness a little too far!"

Somehow I laugh, and feel Morgan giggle, then cry. Every emotion available in each other.

It seems like days, but eventually we land in a bunch of sand. I pull myself together and find I am missing about six percent of my particles. I knew that human cells were only human one of every ten molecules, so I incorporate the sand into my body. Mostly on skin, looking like I have patches of sand on my skin. I blink in the white light. My vision wasn't clear for distance yet. I could hear waves and feel the sand going way beyond this spot. The air tasted of salt. I smell the clean fresh air with an undercurrent of decaying fish and pine trees.

I watch Morgan and Yacob reassemble themselves. I feel so sand blasted and fried at every nerve. Overexposed in every way. I want to scratch the sand patches on my skin, and force myself to stop thinking about them.

Morgan blinks, tilts her head and looks at me. Since her body had generated the hole, I ask, "Do you have any idea where we are?"

Morgan shakes her head and dissolves into sandy tears.

I stand and look at Yacob, "How about you? Any idea about our location?" I was subconsciously starting to analyze the air for aether flow.

Yacob tries to speak, but he had made his tongue out of sand and it crumbled. I wince and look away. It was unsettling to watch. I feel the currents of aether move about him as he readjusted his form. "No, but we have you, Muriel, with us. Mom says you can find the way home no matter where you are. How do you do that?"

I chuckle, thinking how I usually control the trip and know how I got somewhere. I run my hand through my hair. I used to wander without thought. I take a breath and remember how that worked. "Sometimes it takes a while. I use the song of our sun."

Yacob brushes at his elbow and pieces of skin return, sand drops. "Sun song?"

I send a replacement order to create new skins cells throughout my body. It doesn't respond as quick as his did. "You know how all matter is made of small vibrating particles. Well, they all have their own individual song. Our sun has a particular song. In the universe, you listen to the suns and find what region has a similar song to what you're familiar with, and head that way."

He shakes his head in disbelief, "The stories I've heard about you Murry. What about dimension and time?"

My vision is widening slowly, and more sand dunes appear. I see the edges of ocean lapping the sand. I ponder that my brother has heard stories about me. Those were conversations for other days. I answer the specific question, "Dimension is kind of like different sound volume and time is the melody stanza change."

Morgan gasps and I kneel next to her, "We'll get back Morgan. Are you still in pain?"

I scan her body and see that she had not recreated the baby, but has made all the empty placenta and cord out of sand. The wind is stirring. I hold my breath and start inventorying my parts. The wind didn't coalesce into a wormhole and I relaxed.

Yacob has been bracing, and looks at me puzzled.

I squeeze Morgan's hand, "Your body really doesn't like pain."

Morgan gives me a tired, amused smile, "No, it doesn't."

I raise my eyebrows as I look at her, "I think your body is trying to deliver the placenta which you've made out of sand. Do you want me to just turn around while you stand and shake out your pants?"

Morgan gives me a puzzled stare and turns her gaze inwards. "Wow, my subconscious knows what it is doing, sometimes."

Yacob scratches at the sand on his head, "Why didn't a hole form on her last twinge of pain?"

I look up at the sun, squinting, modulating my hearing to hear it. "Not sure, maybe the pain's not so bad, maybe she used up all her aether stores. Maybe there is not enough aether here to generate a hole."

Yacob looks up. I watch him hide his panic at my last statement. He squints.

I look out at the horizon. My vision takes in a farther scope now. There is a huge rock in the surf. It is covered in a net of mosses and trees. The top has a swirl of birds. Life, I think. Good. Aether is here. The birds are swirling and landing. The rock is huge, with rounding sides with a pointed middle. It looks familiar, really familiar. I realize I know where I am and I begin to laugh. "I know where we are!"

Morgan and Yacob look at me.

I turn and see the sprawl of human habitation, and make out the Wayfarer restaurant's huge windows in the distance. "We are on earth! We are on the same continent and the same country! We haven't even left the state! We're in Cannon Beach!"

Morgan and Yacob look at each other and back at me. They blink in unison. Morgan addresses me, "Should we head back?"

I walk next to her, "How are your contractions?"

"Tapering quickly." She says, wistfully.

I look at Yacob, "We should give it some time. Do you have a phone on you to call Mom?"

Yacob gives me a sarcastic head bob and calls Mom. I was sure, with all the shields in place, mental contact would be problematic.

Morgan stares at all the houses beyond the sand dunes. "Good thing I didn't take my pants off."

"So Morgan, wormholes and pain, very insane combination? How far away do you usually end up?"

She gives me a sheepish grin. "Usually there is a time, space and dimension combination."

I nod, "This is impressive with the wards going on around us, the room and the house. Maybe that is what kept us in the here and now and not too far away."

Yacob ends his call with Mom. "Yes, an hour and a half drive isn't too far."

I kick at the sand, "What did Mom say?"

He shrugs, "Time the contractions and find the safe moment to dialyosefos or wait an hour."

We both look at Morgan, who was looking out at the sea. She was shaking her pant legs, spilling sand onto the beach.

"We need to get back as soon as possible. I want to hold my son! I really haven't felt another contraction!"

I look at Yacob, "What are your thoughts?"

He points to Morgan, "She is functioning on adrenaline right now. If she waits an hour she will be exhausted. So, let's go for it!"

Morgan smiles, "Yes, please!"

I watch Morgan's body reach out to the aether to refill her stores. "Morgan, don't." I say hastily.

She frowns at me, "Why?"

I sigh, "Don't fill up. Let Yacob or I dialyosefos you. That way if you have a bit of pain you won't…"

"Create a wormhole." Morgan finishes, her face thoughtful. "I see." Morgan looks at Yacob, "Are you up for it, dear?"

Yacob's features fill with tenderness, "Yes, always."

I look away, suspecting this is a private moment with memories from some other day. As I stare at this huge piece of driftwood I feel them embrace. I focus on the sunlight and enjoy the idea of them happy together. I wonder about my future. Will I ever know anything like that? Yacob clears his throat and I turn and look at them again. "You two ready?"

They nod in unison. I wish I had a camera to take a picture of this moment. They were glowing with love. I found a spot in my brain to make a marker for the image and I planned to upload it when I'm home. " OK, on three. One." A bird started flying to us. "Two," It was almost over us when I said, "Three!"

The shed for dialyosefosing shook as we arrived. Morgan and Yacob held hands and dashed out the door. I steadied myself and followed at a measured pace. When I turn the corner, they were already at the front door. It closes behind them. I take a couple breaths and watch two maple leaves spin together down to the sidewalk. A small man with a baseball hat sideways addresses me from the gate.

"Miss Muriel? How did you get out here?"

I smile at the gnome, "Oh, hey, Gnasher."

Gnasher, our lawn gnome, has a gray beard, silver eyes and his hair hidden under a Winter-hawk's baseball cap. The cap has two raptor eyes staring out from the face above the brim. He wears a red plaid shirt with blue jean overalls. In his hand he has a white pipe shaped like an air drake. He puffs his pipe, creating smoke rings that change into the shapes of squirrels and swallows.

He points to the Fort Knox type wards and squints at me. "I expect that means good news. But is it bizarre to see the parents-to-be walking in? And, I don't recall watching you exit?"

I nod and go through the gate, I crouch down next to him. "That is true."

He puffs his pipe thoughtfully, "You're not going to elaborate, are you?"

I look at the sky and the shadows about, sensing all kinds of things. "Nope, not at the moment."

"Are you going to hurry in?"

I was taking time to collect and process all that had just happened. "After a moment, sure." I was trying to shake all the terrible things my imagination was telling me could have happened. I was trying to focus on that, they hadn't. The street was quiet and the wind swirled more leaves. Even though Gnasher wants to know more, he wouldn't press me like the beings inside.

Gnasher starts to mumble about the rose bush, a fairy species of aphids and the lady bug rebellion.

Chapter 31

New Edition

Five shadows gather outside the gate and coalesce into ten Sneffels. I stand. A weariness so profound and complete fills me. I walked to the center of the garden and cross my arms. I stare at them.

They look at one another. They all stare at me. Their illusions wavering.

I swallow and hide all fear. I imagine a well and dump my fear down there. It would just feed them power, I think of my family. I know I must not waver. My voice is even and emotionless as I address them. "So, there is ten of you? A minyan? Are you conducting a religious service?"

The voice was oily that replies, "Just a witnessing of something dangerous to haunt our dreams."

Gnasher scowls and stands next to me and frowns at them, his hands on his hips. "They feel unnatural, what are they?"

"Multi-dimensional beings." I kick a stone as I ponder his statement. I realize they are probably more natural then I am. "They are usually pretty grumpy and deadly."

They give me a smirk, the ten of them. As if reading my thoughts and judging me. When the voice resumes it's a different head that says each word of the sentence. "Your family has unleashed something dangerous into existence."

"Dangerous for whom? You? How?" I have no patience for vague rhetoric.

They start to mumble to each other and disappear. What I hear in their last words is, "Unchecked dimension creator."

Gnasher frown up at me, puffs his pipe. "I've been around for a hundred years and your family still rattles me."

"Hello, Miss Muriel?" I glance up to this voice. Behind the gate is now a wispy woman with blond hair, clothed in purple swirly cloth. She waves at me. Her voice was light and airy.

I smell lilacs emitting from her. I know what she is and know my mother will be annoyed. The last thing my family appreciates are wishes from fairies for newborns. Fairy Godmothers are trouble.

Gnasher's features light up in wonder, "Well hello there, love!"

The fairy giggles, "A blessing on this house is in order, I understand."

I cock my head to the side. "There are already several fairies in there." I gesture with my thumb.

She brushes her hair from her green eyes and gives me a knowing look. "Not, wishing fairies, dearheart. Even if there were, family members can't give each other a benediction wish, it must be from another family."

I think of the ridiculousness of this statement. We were all related, but I nod. I head to the gate, scan her and her area. I

311

let her in and close the gate quickly. I hear the door behind me open. There is music, clanking glasses. My head follows the sound and I watch four fairies fly out the front door in drunken spirals.

One lands on my shoulder and belches something strong in my face. I wince and wrinkle my nose. I look at it. It winks at me and wipes its mouth in my hair. "Muriel, what are you doing? Let Trina in. She is a great wish fairy."

I walk toward the house, as the other three pepper Trina with questions and hand her a flask. "Are you sure? How do you know she hasn't imp-ed out?"

The fairy burps again and laughs. The other three start to laugh with her. The one on my shoulder slaps my ear, "It be OK, steel score girl, every family can handle some black sheep."

I can't help but giggle at that reference to my unwelcomed qualities. I look back at Gnasher. He shrugs, taps his pipe thoughtfully. I go to the front door and open it. I look at Trina again with second sight, "I invite you in, Trina. As long as you respect the wishes of the Anahat family."

The fairy on my shoulder screeches in my ear and pulls my hair. "Insolence, you limit her power!" She flies away muttering and Arial meets her with a stern expression.

Trina enters and gives me a reassuring smile, "You're a savvy aunt. You can never be too careful these days with the very young's safety."

I nod at Gnasher, who gives me a go on gesture. I follow Trina, who is being swarmed by fairies wanting to know if she is going to change form.

My father walks over and wraps an arm around my shoulder. "How does it feel to be an Aunt?"

The house is alive with warm yellow light. There was singing. It sounded like the "Rock" pub song. The lines were getting really complicated. There was dancing and laughter. "Have you seen him? How is he?"

He gives me a big grin. "Perfect, he is grateful for your help in getting his parents back to him."

I flash my father a smile and move my hair from my eyes, "How does it feel to be a Zadie?"

He glows, "Amazing!"

I point to Trina, "How is Mom going to handle that?"

He winces then smiles, shakes his head, "You know the usual, as gracefully as possible.

I look up to see Mom at the end of the stairs. She catches my eye. She gestures me forward. My father and I move through the throng. Jasper runs into me and spills a few drinks on me. His voice slurs. "Hey, Muriel, What's the word? Muscle top?"

I give Jasper a nurturing smile, "Hey Jasper, when did you get here? The word is Mazal Tov."

"Muzzle tuft. About an hour ago." He gestures toward Gideon and Glinda. "The twins say they met you."

I look over at them and they raise their glasses to me. I nod, "Yes, we didn't get to talk long."

Jasper stands straighter, "You should definitely fix that."

I bob my head politely, doubting he will remember this discussion, " OK, my mother is motioning me, but perhaps later?"

"What? Oh, yes, later." He turns and walks back to the twins.

My father clears his throat, "What was that about?"

I shake my head, "I have no idea."

He gestures for me to walk in front of him. I weave through the celebrating extended family members who create a path for him. My Mom gives me a hug and takes my father's hand. They share a warm smile as their eyes meet. Then Mom looks at me fondly, "Thanks for bringing them back quickly."

I blush and wave a hand, "They would have figured it out."

Mom becomes serious, "Muriel, it's OK to take a compliment."

My blush deepens, "Did you have any idea that…" I suddenly remember I am in a highly populated room, so I don't say that Morgan is a portal maker.

Mom, knowing what I'm editing out shakes her head, "No idea. I can't understand the incredulousness in the earlier conversation about the equipment in the room."

"There is the whole age activation and the paternal side thing." I shrug.

My mother eyes brighten, "Good thing she married into our family." She gives my father a peck on the cheek. She looks at me, "Have you two seen Sarah?"

I show my palms symbolizing I have no clue, my father smiles, "I just retrieved Muriel, but Sarah is probably over in that corner full of young men doing stupid things."

Mom gives a resigned exhale and gives a forced smile, "Of course. Why don't you two head up and I'll fetch Sarah."

I put out an arm to stop her, "No Mom, you and Dad go ahead and I'll grab her. Where do you want us to meet you?"

"In front of Yacob's and Morgan's suite."

I feel a tinge of anxiety, "Do we have to all witness the fairy blessing?"

"Heavens no, child. Only the parents and the child get to witness that. It's for their own safety, since it always opens up a way for another vulnerability."

I nod, " OK, I will be quick."

Circe Syndrome

Mom and Dad start a discussion together and head up the stairs. I survey the room. It had stretched to the size of a ballroom, with crowds of people drinking, singing, playing games, dancing and talking in highly animated fashions. I want to avoid the corner my father has mentioned the most. Young men are daring each other in to do impossible stunts at a fervent pace. Lava pits, snake pits and odd obstacles courses appear and disappear at an alarming rate. I take a breath, put on a calm demeanor and walk that way. At the same time, I send out a mental call to Sarina. I am surprised when the response is not coming from the direction I am heading toward.

She isn't in the family room at all. I turn around and walk to the stairs. Three stories up and to the left of my room is Sarina's room. I knock on the door.

Her voice is muffled, "Who is it?"

"Muriel." I say calmly, staring at her door.

Her voice is petulant and a whine, "Can I have some magic back? Now!"

I feel a bit of guilt as I reestablish the link.

Sarina sounds physically relieved as my magic spilled into her. The door opens. She is standing at a full size mirror smoothing her dress and changing her hair color. She is adjusting her facial features in subtle ways. She looks at me, puzzled, "What happened."

I chew on my lower lip, comprehending what I just saw. "Labor for Morgan was complicated."

Sarina gives me a pained look, "You two have never both cut me off before at the same time."

I sit a second gathering my thoughts, "It was an out of control multidimensional gate. We didn't want you pulled in and ripped apart." I watch her to see if she is comprehending what I am saying. "We were pulled in together; we are all lucky that all we lost was about seventeen percent of our body mass.

That was due to the fact we have each had enough experience to completely not dissolve and spiral out in a wormhole." The gravity of it all hit me and tears were threatening. The fear for which I didn't have time in the moment.

Sarina's petulant tones changed to ones of concern, "I guess it's good you did that." She put a hand on my arm and sand dissolved into her fingers, "Ewww, Muriel, don't you use moisturizer?"

I snort, "I try. That's sand, not my skin, by the way."

"What?"

"We landed on a beach. It was easiest to replace missing mass with sand particles until the different cells can replace those areas." I suddenly find the idea of moisturizing sand skin amusing and begin to laugh.

Sarina sits on her bed and gives me a fond smile, "I know I tell you to try some of the spa treatments, but this is taking a mud cleanse to the extreme! Does it itch?"

I shake my head emphatically, "You have no idea."

Sarina fiddles with her hands, "How long will it take to replace with typical cells?"

"A normal person would take about three weeks. I have some cells I keep in a cryogenic state I can change it out with, when I get a chance. Just magic. I can probably do it in three days but it would take me going to sleep for the whole period. It isn't like regular healing, since I actually lost cellular mass with my cellular memory."

Sarina frowned, "You have cells frozen? Where?"

I think of my workshop in space. I chuckle, "You don't want to know. Mom wants us to meet her in front of Yacob's door."

" OK."

Circe Syndrome

I cock my head, still flummoxed by what I witnessed when I came in. "So? You alter your appearance so much, you don't feel comfortable in a room full of family?"

Sarina's expression becomes cold, "Shut up, Muriel! I'm not having this conversation with you!"

"The body image conversation? You are so far down the road to denial you don't even want to talk to me about it?"

Sarina pointed at the door.

" OK, I'll let it go. But if it angers you this much that means you aren't as comfortable in yourself with this decision as you would like to be." I walked out the door with Sarina fuming behind me.

Sarina huff as she shuts the door behind her. We walk in cold silence to Yacob's door.

Morgan's immediate family is outside the door, her mother, father, three sisters and four brothers. They are chatting amongst themselves. Our parents are to the right of them.

My mother looked between us and noted the tension, "What happened?"

Sarina crosses her arms, her gaze falls away, "Nothing, I'm here."

Mom gives Sarina a speculative glance. Mom looks at me and I shrug. I put my hand down in a cooling motion out of Sarina's sight, but where Mom can see asking Mom to ignore the tension.

At that moment the door to Yacob's room opens. Trina steps out. "Hello." Her wispy voice echoes in the hall.

"Hello," My mother replies cheerily.

Trina was preening, "I'm finished." We stand to the side as Morgan's family mobs the fairy with hugs and escorts her down to the party.

Sarina watches them trail off with interest, "Mom, you let a fairy in for a baby blessing?"

Our mother gives a long exhale, "Yes, we must honor all of the family history Merlin has been blessed with."

Mom heads to the door, does a perfunctory knock and enters. We all follow her. Morgan and Yacob are both still staring with horror at the door. Morgan's last words from what she was saying were still in the air, "I think we can work with it." She looks down at her son who was suckling and staring intently at her.

He is adorable and a perfect mix of Morgan and Yacob's features. Involuntarily I say, "Oh!"

My father and mother give me an amused look. Sarina looks bored and wanders to a chair.

"He's beautiful, Morgan." I watch his tiny head with intense green eyes look through me. He seemed to stare into my soul, then look back at his mother.

Morgan sits down in a club chair cradling the baby with a serene daze on her face. Yacob moves to stand next to her. His gaze unwavering from Merlin.

I feel unbelievably happy for both of them.

My parents coo over Merlin and we all visit for about half an hour.

Outside Yacob's door. I mention to my mother about three days of sleeping to rejuvenate my skin cells. My mother scowls, "You can't miss your date. Even if it's Shabbat. I'm waking you for it."

I wrinkle my nose, "Yeah, OK Mom."

Mom squeezes my hand, "Why don't you finish talking to the rest of the visitors before your big sleep?"

I really don't want to but I nod, "Sure Mom."

Mom pats my cheek, "Good girl. " She then takes dad's hand and they stroll down the stairs together.

Circe Syndrome

Sarina scowls at me. I open my mouth to talk to her. She raises her hand, turns and heads down the stairs.

I pause on the last landing that had a full length mirror. As I take a breath, I look at my appearance. My hair is windblown and clothes messy. I smooth my clothes and my hair. I practice a serene, non-committal smile.

I head to the main floor. The party is still in full swing. The crazy young men are now fawning over Sarina. I stand by the wall and edge about the room. I have a few non-sequitur conversations with inebriate people and find a space between the dining area and living area to observe. My mother brings in a huge birthday cake. This marks the beginning of a speech competition between my mother and Aiofe. Both of them illuminating how great this event was.

The curly haired boy taps my shoulder. I turn and look at him and his sister both smiling at me.

Jasper was with them and whispers in my ear. "How did you and the expectant parents get outside? The dialyosefos seals on this place are tighter than a steel drum?"

I meet his eyes with a grin, as I give him a negative nod, letting him know I won't answer, "That is a great question. What have you been up to? What have you been telling your cousins about me?"

He chuckles, takes a sip of the pint in his hand, then offers it to me.

I shake my head, "How is Isabelle?"

"Fine, as always." He says with the confident smile he always gets when he talks of her.

Glinda gestures to a felt table. "Do you want to try a game again?"

I scratch my chin, "Did you two figure out Canasta?"

Gideon laughs, "No, we want to play a game we like. It's called Munchkin."

My eyebrow raises, "Munchkin?" I think about how Ginda's name is the same as the witch in the Wizard of Oz, and wonder if I'm about to be the butt of a joke.

Glinda smiles, "It's this crazy, card slash board game that is like battling in Dungeons and Dragons, but a lot sillier."

" OK, let me get a drink and I will be with you. Do either of you want anything?" I ask Glinda and Gideon.

Jasper sputters at me, "What about me?"

I flick his pint glass and look back at him.

He laughs, "I might want more. I will probably finish it before you're back. What kind of hostess are you?"

I apologize, "I'm sorry, did you want more?"

He gives me an enthusiastic nod, "Yes, Guinness please."

I give him a knowing smile.   Glinda and Gideon both speak up. The night ends up being fun. I am hopeless at the game and can't get past the first level.

Chapter 32

Coffee Anyone?

I am awakened by a call from Isabelle the next day. She invites me to meet her and Irving at Stumptown, the local coffee shop. I agree to go. I check with my mother on Merlin's rotation, to verify I wasn't on it today. My Mom tells me to go out with my friends. She also tells me she had been fielding calls from The Collective. She has the fairies tell The Collective to give me the rest of the week off. The idea that the organization keeps exposing me to steel is unforgivable to her.

I find myself wondering about Jasper. Is Isabelle serious about Irving? I pull on a pink overcoat. I hold it close on the thirty-minute walk to the coffee shop. The sky is a mix of dark and light blues, with what looks like brush strokes of white clouds feathered across the sky.

Irving is in the coffee shop when I get there. No Isabelle to be seen. He waves to me.

I smile and wave back. I go and stand in line. I order a hot chocolate with whipped cream. Then I sit down at the table with him. I notice he looks like himself but with flattering adjustments.

He ponders his coffee self-consciously, "Do you know when Isabelle is going to be here?"

I glance at my watch and out the window. "Any time now. This is when she asked me to meet you and her here, she tends to run fifteen minutes late."

He exhales slowly, "I tend to run thirty minutes early."

The barista calls out my drink. I stand to get it. I return to the table. I try to take a sip of my drink but realize it is too hot and set it back down. I turn back to Irving, "How has your week been? Have you been talking to Cleo at all?"

He nods, "Yes, and several others. My phone has been ringing off the hook!"

I blow on my cup. "That must be exciting."

"Yes, and quite surprising. I was never a person in high demand."

I swirl my cup. I look out the window and watch Isabelle jaywalk across the street. "That's great, not that you were not in high demand before, but that..."

He looks up and watches Isabelle entering the coffee shop. He holds his breath. Two seconds later, Jasper enters. Isabelle sits next to Irving. Jasper waves, he walks up to Isabelle and kisses her then asks her what she wants. He gets in line.

Isabelle gives Irving a big grin. He lights up.

I meet Isabelle's eyes, "Thanks for the invitation."

She gives me a slight smile and nods to Irving with raised speculative eyebrows. "I've been chatting off and on with Irving, I thought you two should chat."

I watch the shock go through him. Isabelle was half siren and never realized the effect she had on men. Because of the siren blood a lot of females hate her. She has this problem making female friends. I try my hot chocolate again to see if it is drinkable. It isn't; I set it back down.

Irving leans forward, "Why don't you cool your drink with you know?" He waves his fingers.

I laugh, "You've been in the community for, what, two months and you think it's a good idea to just casually throw magic around?"

Jasper sits down at the end of my statement. "What now?"

Isabelle reaches out and takes his hand and looks at him adoringly. She gestures to me amused, "Muriel is teasing the newborn."

Jasper gives her an answering smile, he squeezes Isabelle's hand and gives me a wink. "She is just a member of our police network. She's Collective."

Irving pauses and sits back. "What?"

Jasper laughs, "You've heard of The Collective, right?"

He gives me a pained expression, "You don't come across as authority."

I shrug, "I'm not really an officer." I am starting to regret this trip. It is a setup, second one this week. I look up at Isabelle, to see her and Jasper staring into each other's eyes. I direct my question at the both of them, "So, tell me why you two went to the Gorge dance?"

Isabelle blushes and answers me. "I wanted to make sure I had explored all my options." She took Jasper's hand, "Jasper's family wanted him to do the same."

I take that in. Jasper's family didn't approve of Isabelle, they demanded he look around more. Isabelle took umbrage with that and took it as an opportunity to show her desirability. I readdress Irving. "I don't use magic every time I feel like it. So when I need it and its not available, I will be able to do things. It does go with the whole Collective mantra of simplest force can move mountains."

Irving frowns, "Mountains?"

I chuckle mysteriously, "You can create an avalanche by just moving one stone.   It just needs to be the right stone."

He takes a drink of coffee and gives a speculative glance to Isabelle and Jasper. He seems to be asking if I am always like this.

At this lull in the conversation I stare at my cup and wonder again about a planet of gold. I carry on the conversation, "Hey, do any of you know anything about how gold collects over time? How it groups itself together?"

Jasper raises an eyebrow, "Gold?"

I start tearing at the heat sleeve on my cup in thought. "Yeah."

"Collects?" Jasper taps his fingers on the table top.

Irving frowns, "What do you mean?"

I suddenly remember he is from a family of jewelers. I throw up a hand, "Well I know it's a basic element."

He chews his lip thoughtfully and sips his beverage. "Yes."

An order calls out and Jasper stands. Isabelle follows. They take their drinks to the condiment station.

I tap my fingers on the table, "And I know that it is one of the elements that helps form the earth, and it is present in small amounts of salt water."

"Sure," Irving turns, watches Isabelle and Jasper together.

I spin my cup, "How does it go about clumping together? It's not magnetic. Is it like water and just wants to clump together?"

He tips his head toward Isabelle and Jasper, "How long have those two been together?"

"Off and on as long as I have known them." I frown at the table thinking about gold.

"How long is that?" He asks uneasily.

"About twenty years. We have been out of touch for fifteen of them." I lean my head on my arm and regard him.

His mouth becomes a straight line. "I see."

I stare at a painting on the wall of a rabbit in a monk habit.

"Why this interest in gold?" Irving taps the table.

I sit back and give him a mysterious grin, "I like to make myself these mental puzzles and work them out. I was wondering how to make a solenoid out of gold." I say to cover the truth.

"It won't keep a magnetic charge. It won't work. How does the clumping question relate to that?" He asked amused.

Jasper and Isabelle return to the table. Jasper gives Irving a sympathetic look. "You know who you should ask that gold question to, Muriel?"

"Who?" I give him a curious smile.

He gives me a cat eating the canary grin, and sits next to me conspiratorially, "My cousin Gideon, his hobby is chemical magic!"

I involuntarily smile, thinking of the young man who rained mischief down on me during that game last night. I couldn't mention anything about the night before, we were in mixed company, "Do I know him?"

He gives an exaggerated gaze at Irving then winks at me. "He's visiting from Scotland. I'll introduce you."

I nod, " OK." I start puzzling over the fact that gold could not hold a charge. It was a good conductor and low on corrosiveness so it was used in high end electronics to stave off corrosion of connections. Could I make a motor to turn the planet and send a current through it? How was I going to get that much gold?"

Jasper nudges me and passes a hand in front of my face. I look up at him, "What?"

He shakes his head, "You were not listening. Where were you?"

I take a breath and meet everyone's eyes, "Sorry, what did I miss?"

Isabelle giggles, "Irving was telling us his life story."

I pause and widen my eyes in surprise, "What, I missed all that? I thought that I just tuned out for a second."

Jasper gets all proper in stance, "How insulting!" He says in a emphatic tone.

I wince and look at Irving, "What, I'm sorry."

Irving looks at me serious and annoyed, then looks at Jasper and Isabelle. A smile breaks across his face, "No, we were all silent."

I chuckle, "Oh, OK."

He bends forward conspiratorially, "Do you want to hear my life story?"

I look at Jasper and Isabelle, we all lean in. "Sure." I say with a chuckle.

He laughs, "Let's wait, I really don't know you all that well."

I shrug, " OK, what should we talk about now?"

Jasper nudges me, "You have been unavailable. Where have you been?"

I thought about the vampires, Circe, Selkie, Satyr and the nymphs. I couldn't talk about those things. I thought about Merlin, another forbidden topic. "Mostly, I've been sick." I rip the insulator on my cup some more. I look at Irving, sparking another idea. I ask him, "So, what did you think of the dance?"

He frowns and sets his cup down. "Weird, exciting, and the after party, do all of you paddleboard in space normally?"

Jasper smirks, "No, it's like surfing in the ocean to most people. Not everyone does it."

"Is it tribal like the Polynesian tradition?" Irving asks.

I almost spit out my cocoa thinking of a tribal culture paddleboarding in space with regalia. "It is pretty modern, but similar to the original concept. Some people thought it would be fun. So they tried it."

Jasper gives me a glance, "Wasn't it your brother and you who decided to try this?"

I blush and look down. I am debating telling them this story but proceed, "We were watching a Gidget movie and discussing a project I was working on. And one thing led to another."

Isabelle gives me an incredulous look, "Yacob was watching a Gidget movie?"

"No, he was teasing me watching a Gidget movie, OK?"

Jasper looks at Irving and back at me, "What's a Gidget movie?"

Irving looks puzzled, too.

"The Original movie was made in 1959 starring Sandra Dee. It's about a girl who moves to California and learns about the surf culture there. At that point, it was unusual for girls to surf. It also has a romance woven through it." I look imploringly at Isabelle.

She snickers, "The characters have great names too, like Moon-doggie and Kahuna."

Irving looks at Jasper and they both roll their eyes.

Jasper guffaws, "I can't imagine why your brother was teasing you about that movie."

Irving looks askance, "So a project and this movie about surfing led to asteroid paddleboarding? What kind of project?" Jasper and Isabella exchange amused glances. They all give me a curious look.

I wasn't going to tell them the truth, that I had been stirring the contents of several comets and the left over products of a red star to create the solar system EcoSpa resided in. I was essentially analyzing asteroids for their elemental contents, "I was working on paper on calculating the path of asteroids in the asteroid belt."

Irving's eyes widens, " OK."

Isabelle lowers her gaze and swirls her cup. "It is fun, though."

"Calculating the path of asteroids? Yeah, I like it." I replied.

Isabelle shook her head, "No, silly, the paddleboarding."

Jasper taps the table, "The lichen is quite a nice invention. Was that you or Yacob?"

My brow knits; this line of questioning was a bit probing. "It's a moss and kind of both of us, along with the moss."

Irving's mouth hangs open a second before he asks, "The moss has opinions?"

I nod as the bit in me squirms sending tingles up my legs, "Oh, yes." I pick up my cup and take a sip.

Jasper taps my shoulders, "How does a moss speak and think?"

I take a breath to give myself a moment to digest how to explain, "It's a chemical language, kind of like invertebrates. Like snails and mollusks."

Jasper gives me a puzzled look, "How many invertebrates have you talked to?"

"What do they like to talk about?" Isabelle looks like she smelled something bad.

I decide it was time to make everyone laugh, "Oh, fashion!"

It works, they all break out into snorts and giggles.

Isabelle gasped between laughs, "Who's their favorite designer?"

"Hands down, they love Isaac Mizrahi. What he does with form and detail excites them."

"Funny," Jasper pokes me, "I didn't realize invertebrates had hands."

"Let alone shape or wear clothes." Irving's expression was pained.

I moved hair out of my face. I was happy, they were distracted.

Isabelle taps Irving's shoulder and nodded at me, "What do you think? Funny, right?"

I exclaim, "Hey, I'm right here."

Jasper pats my hand. "You're such a good sport."

Irving groans and turns, "So, do I have a chance with you Isabelle?"

I am fighting dropping my jaw. He is being bold.

Jasper takes Isabelle's hand and stares into her eyes, "Does he?"

She gives Jasper a sly look, "Not really. I just wish your family would accept me more."

I give her a sympathetic look. It was so hard to find love in the world and his parents were being ridiculous. "I was unaware of this set up, too." I say to Irving.

Isabelle acts innocent.

Irving sits up straighter, "So, Collective? What do you do for The Collective?"

I stare past him to a couple of hipsters chatting adamantly. I have to be careful here. "I'm a recruiter."

He looks curious, "Like military service recruiter?"

"Yes."

He shakes his head, "I'm not interested."

I give him a wink, "Thanks for that. I have a species specialty and newborn Heska isn't it."

Jasper leans in closer to me. "Specialty species, I'm intrigued. Oh, wait, at the dance your aura had been salted. That means a malicious creature."

I give him an encouraging chuckle, "Guess."

Isabelle giggles, "Zombie?"

I shake my head, "Ewwww, no."

Irving pauses and looks between us, "They are real?"

Jasper and Isabelle nod.

Jasper starts observing the hipsters, "It's not demons, that demon totally lost it with you."

The blood drains from Irving's face, "What?"

"Ghosts? How effective would they be?" Isabelle wrinkled her nose.

"They are great information spies. Transparent, and can go almost everywhere. But no, not ghosts."

"Werewolves? They seem a little rough for you, though." Jasper gives me a head to toe appraisal.

"No, I do work nights though."

Isabelle's eyes sparkled, "Vampires?"

"Yeah." I point at her.

Irving sputters, "What, where, here in Portland?"

I bite back a laugh.

Jasper gives me a doubtful look. "No way! You're far too delicate for vampires. They are violent, hunting machines. When I think of their speed, thirst and some mind manipulation abilities, I shiver."

I laugh, and blink my eyes quickly with my words, "Vampires just want to dominate. They are easy to bait. Act helpless, then let them know they are no longer in control. It's like catnip to them."

Jasper rubs his chin thoughtfully. "Explains your weird hours, but damn, vampires! I would never have thought."

"What? I paddleboard in deep space but some earth bound creature with fast impulses would be a problem?" I give him a non-plussed look.

Isabelle laughs.

Irving was patting his shirt where he had spilled coffee. "All these creatures and vampires are real?"

I cock my head at him, "You just found out you were a wizard and this is surprising you?"

Isabelle reaches out and touches my hand so I would meet her eyes, "I must know, where do they hang out?"

Irving was pointing at the table, "Here in Portland. Your saying all of this is here?"

I absently scan his body metrics. He is anxious. I nod at him calmly, "They hang at a few bars and clubs."

Isabelle gasps, "Which ones?"

I put up a stopping hand, "That is classified."

She put her hands together, "Please!"

I raise my eyebrows, "No, but by all means do a reconnaissance mission to check out every club and bar in the Portland Metro area. You'll figure it out." I shudder at the thought of a Siren vampire.

"How did you fall into this job?" Irving looks crushed and defeated as he asks for more information that is challenging to him.

"What? You don't imagine a child growing up doesn't dream up a career in operative recruitment involving vampires?"

He winces, "No."

Jasper gives me an inquisitive look. He is asking if he can tell about my past. I nod. He leans forward, "Remember in the eighties how computer hackers ended up working for the CIA? Muriel started as a criminal."

Irving gives us puzzled looks, "She's a hacker?"

I trace the liquid residual on the table. This is a point where I find out so much about the people around me. I then smile, it kind of was a hack.

Jasper straightens, "She violated the second law of magic."

Irving's eyes rolled, accessing visual information he had memorized, "Don't bend a person's will with magic."

I smile wide, "Yes, good memory. Three months, that is great retention!"

He blushes, "So, somewhere you got caught bending someone's will? The Collective thought that would make you a great recruiter? You're not bending the mind of the vampires to work for The Collective, right?"

I think of the nightmare that would create, when they became strong enough with the blood to see through all spells. My smile broadens, "No, they have free will. We don't want vampires hyped on Heska blood realizing their decisions might not be their own." I watch the three of them have their eyes widen as they digest the words.

Irving's voice was sarcastic, "If you're a criminal how can we take your word on that?"

I nod, acknowledging and noting in my mind that he was a shallow person who took labels really seriously. "I'm monitored the whole time. There are at least four other people telepathically linked to me and watching video camera feed from the video camera in my head."

They all stiffen,

Circe Syndrome

Isabelle adjusted her hair. "Are we being observed now?"

"No, I'm off duty."

Jasper gives me a studied look, "Is that why sometimes you seem distant and keep conversations light?"

I give a non-committal gesture.

Isabelle chews on her bottom lip. "Maybe, we should develop a sign for you to tell us when you're…", she raises her hand in quotes, "plugged in."

Irving frowns, "How do we know for sure she isn't plugged in now?"

His paranoia intrigues me. I wonder what he wants to hide. "I'm not."

Jasper scratches his chin in thought. He was thinking about last night, I could tell. "How do you know it's really off? I mean, couldn't they just tell you the thing is off and still use it?"

I nod, "Sure." I drink my chocolate. "I take it out after every shift. Besides Mom does not let it in the house."

Isabelle's jaw dropped, "Ouch! How much does that hurt?"

I move my head side to side in a wobbling manner, "It's more uncomfortable, there are no nerve cells in the brain."

Irving winces, "How? " He shakes his head, "You still live with your parents?"

I blush, "Yeah, part of my parole."

Everyone at the table is still wincing, "It's really small, it's not that bad."

Irving looks thoughtful, "I pretty much still work at the family business. Making jewelry and selling it. The power has been great for all kinds of things."

"Such as?" I ask, grateful that the conversation has moved from me.

"I don't need to heat metal. I can just tell it to change its state of matter and enter a mold or take on the design in my head."

I give him a look of admiration, "Very nice."

A throat clears causing everyone to look up. A white pale hand takes mine. I turn my face up to see Thomas. His smile was predatory and infectious, "Excuse me."

I am surprised. He snuck up on me. I act as if I am unaffected, "Hi, Thomas." I glance around the table. Isabelle's color has drained; her charm aura had responded by going more intense. A defense mechanism for a siren. Jasper was rigid and guarded. Irving hadn't caught on. He was examining the pale skin.

I point at Thomas, "This is my," I pause weighing the terms, "friend." Thomas's eyebrows raise. I then point to my table companions and point to each as I say their names. "Irving, Isabelle and Jasper."

He meets each person in the eye. To Irving he says, "Hi." To Isabelle he says, "Enchanted," and to Jasper he cocks his head, "What's up?"

Thomas grabs a chair and pulls it up. "What a lovely surprise running into you Muriel. I had no idea you had actual friends."

Isabelle and Jasper look bewildered and Irving is starting to make the connections in his mind. I could tell he was still puzzling out why Thomas felt welcome to sit down.

I laugh and nudge him, "You're right, I'm a hermit."

He leans in on his elbows toward me. "Are these from the dance you wouldn't let me attend with you?"

I watch Isabelle and Jasper stiffen in reflex. That implies what they were. They weren't used to being identified as Heska.

He gives me this imploring gaze dripping with vampire compulsion magic. "Where have you been? I hear you are out for another week?"

I look around the table and back at him. Trying to remind him I can't really say much. I frown and made sure none of his compulsion was influencing my response. The time I took to respond showing him it wasn't working and I was weighing his words. "I've been unwell. I keep being exposed to an allergen. I need to recover and get what's in my system out before I risk more." I am sure he is aware of this. I wonder if he had been following me. He is starting to feel like a handler. I am pondering if my job is changing even though I am refusing promotion.

They had court ordered the operative training. I had to do it. I am starting to doubt he is my partner. I keep doing activities outside my original brief.

Isabelle recovers her composure, "Out of what?"

"Work." Thomas replies.

"Oh!" Irving gasps, finally putting the pieces together, "Umm, the sun is out. How can you be here?"

I raise my eyebrows at Thomas. His gaze weighing Irving and finding him useless. "Classified! Speaking of classified, I need Muriel here, for something."

I frown, "Really? You do? Are you sure?"

His smile is big, "Oh, yes!" He motions towards the door.

My hot chocolate is empty and I am annoyed with being setup anyway. "Yeah, OK." I look at everyone who seem to be in shock, "Thank you for a nice time." They smile politely. I stand and walk to the trashcan and throw out my cup. I wave at them as I walk out the door that Thomas is holding open for me.

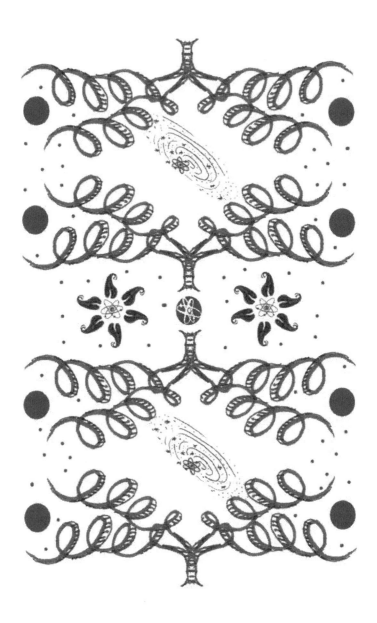

Chapter 33

Why Not?

When the door closes, I give Thomas a weary expression. "So, something?"

He directs me toward a parking structure. "This way." He tugs my arm and me across the street.

"I'm not plugged in. I know you know this." I say acerbically.

He pulls me into the stair well and looks about. He steps close. His grin is huge. "Perfect." He leans in and envelopes me into a kiss. His mouth is firm, warm and my lips tingle with what feels like buzzing bees from the contact. He pushes me to the wall and slips a hand up the back of my neck.

I let this happen, until I can't breathe and my senses come back to me. I push him away. Between breaths I say, "I understand the classified part. Now."

He gives me a huge grin. He leans in and kisses me again. I start to feel dizzy, I groan and back away. I rub my head, a bit confused. "Wait, give me a moment to think here."

He steps close again and strokes my hair. "I think you do too much thinking. You were very receptive."

That is the problem, I think. I back away and out the door to the public sidewalk. My arms crossed in front of me. He steps in step beside me. I look at him, trying to remind myself this is just a hunting tactic for him, "You need some blood?"

"Yes, please." He matches my pace. Then scowls at me, "No, that is not what that is about!"

I rub my forehead with my left hand. Realizing he was warm to touch, he just had blood. "Of course, I'm receptive, you have been laying on the charm for a while now. I am just in an emotionally vulnerable position. I think the third setup in the last forty-eight hours. But, you, me, it can't happen."

He stares at me insistently, "Why not? You want to. I want to. Why not?"

I give him a sarcastic huff, "Very articulate, no."

I look up. We are standing in front of a hotel.

He puts an arm about me and whispers in my ear. "Your conscious mind says no. But, ah, Cheri, your subconscious has other plans. Shall I go in and get us a room?"

I take a breath and turn around, "No."

"Where are you going?"

I look up the street. "Powell's."

"A book store. I throw my heart at your feet and you want to head to a book store?" He stands in front of me with a hurt expression.

I walk around him. "I doubt it's your heart. I can't do this. I'm not built this way."

He is dripping into sarcasm and the charm is melting away with his frustration, "What do you mean? I'm pretty sure you have all the parts!"

338

"I'm a monogamist, I can't emotionally handle casual sex." I state.

"It's not a philosophical decision. It's a physical decision, besides maybe I want a relationship." He looks at me under lowered lids.

I snort. "Yeah, I believe that." I shake my head no. "The only reason you're interested is that I keep shooting you down. Things will get weird. Besides, I need to have an actual human lover this time."

His eyes widen. "A human lover this time." He draws it out in staccato and stops walking.

I keep walking and say over my shoulder. "Yeah."

After two blocks he catches up. He made to speak and stopped again. "You've had a lover before?"

I shake my head, "It's amazing what you retain from a conversation."

"Not human? Not Heska?" he strokes his chin, "You don't come across as someone who would like a werewolf."

I laugh, how was I in this conversation again? "No, it was not a werewolf, and you won't be able to guess for a million years." I smile looking up at the Powell's sign. "Now, if you will excuse me, I'm going to do some hunting of my own." I give him a peck on the cheek. "Thank you for rescuing me from the mechanizations of others."

Before I step off the curb. His hand shoots out and grabs my arm. I stop moving and face him. His mouth was in a straight line and his gaze was fierce. "If you were ready to go off species once, you can go again. I'm not substandard in anyway."

I let my grief show. His expression softened. "We're not together, not because of a tiff. We are not together because he is dead. It's too soon for me."

He let me go. His eyes wild and looking away. "There is so much I don't know. I don't know you at all, do I?"

I inhale, "No, but how well do we know anyone anyway?" I cross the street.

I take a breath and walk into the bookstore. I go to the sci-fi fantasy section and get lost browsing the books. After thirty minutes of browsing, I look up at the end of the row of bookcases to find him holding a Charlain Harris book. He gives me a crooked smile. "I can recommend some reading."

I cock my head. "I didn't know real vampires read her books?"

"We read them all. But, these happen to be well written." He gives me a smirk as he pages through the book in his hand. "You could be Sookie."

I laugh, "Who would you be? Bill or Eric?"

He struts, "You wouldn't have to choose, I could be both."

I throw up my hands, "I am pretty sure you're Lystat."

He chuckles and shakes his index finger at me, "Ah, author jumping! Feisty girl!"

I take a book from the shelf in front of me, "Anne Rice started it all."

He walks closer, "No, Bram Stoker did."

I nod in concession.

He jiggles the book in his hand in front of me. "So, have you read this?"

I give him an amused glance, "Yes, you?"

"Of course, that is why I'm suggesting it. We could read certain scenes to each other."

I shuffle through the four books in my hands. "I'm going to purchase these and grab something to eat. You want to come?"

His grin is predatory and triumphant, "It was the book suggestion, right? Got you all hot, right?"

I roll my eyes, thinking no you get me all hot with no help of anything else. "No, I just thought I'd give you a chance to redeem yourself. The cheese is pretty thick at the moment."

He crosses his arms, "How about after the meal?"

I roll my eyes, and walk to the registers.

We walk to Jake's Bar and Grill. After a pleasant meal and conversation, he invited me to his place. I was curious about where he lived, but I didn't want what he was offering. "Maybe some other time."

He wants to say something else. I have no doubt it would be charming. I never hear it because I look up at the moon. I dialyosefos at that moment to the dark side of it.

Chapter 34

Mooning Around

I startle a little girl with curly, blond pigtails. I move from the landing square as I apologized.

Four adults regard me. I step forward and consider the pressurized dome that was a popular campsite for Heska families. It contains a forest that is an experiment The Collective is working on with NASA, for future planet colonization.

I see the tents and twenty kids in scout regalia.

Realizing being here alone could seem odd, I think back to my old responsibilities as a volunteer when I was younger; before my sentencing. Previous volunteers were always encouraged to do spot checks when in the area anyway. I approach the adults, while I motion to the forest life support system. "Just doing a diagnostic check, then I'll be out of your way."

342

Circe Syndrome

A woman crosses her arms and makes an announcement toward the kids, who stop running to listen. "Anyone working on their herb or life-support badge?"

Five kids raise their hands.

She beckons them to move closer to me and reaches a hand to me. "I'm Anne, a couple of us would like to watch what you do. May they ask you questions?"

I shook her hand back as I nod, "Sure, I'm Muriel, anything in particular we need to cover?"

She gestures to the gathered children. They all have books out and are reading through requirements. "They will ask all the questions they need. Right guys?"

I give an assent and turn to my right and toward the forest. I stop at its edge as the children gather around me. I take a moment and just take in the site. I think about my workshop. I scratch at the dirt floor revealing the spongy surface that is the barrier between the upper forest from the root forest. Each tree is anchored from below to stick out of this flooring.

A little girl with red braids and freckles clears her throat. In a stilted voice she reads from her book, "What are the challenges with growing a tree in space?"

I smile, "Gravity, pollination and separations of nutrients in the soil and gases in the atmosphere."

Six set of eyes blink at me.

I clap my hands together, "Any ideas of what I'm talking about?"

The little girl who raised her hand, "There is less gravity here. Shouldn't the trees be bigger and wider in shapes?"

My head moves as if on a loose spring bouncing up and down, "Yes, it does affect that. See how the leaves have more pointed shapes and there are more of them. This is an oak and it has twelve ridges rather than the normal six. The branches seem to widen more from the trunk than on the earth."

A curly haired boy speaks, "But gravity is also needed for water to mix into the soil?"

I laugh, "Yeah, there is some gravity here on the moon."

"So slime is sprayed on the roots?" asks the curly haired boy, again.

I give a gentle shake of my head, "Yes, a nutrient slime."

"How does that work?" asks the same boy.

"Hey isn't there a problem with the roots? How does that tree stay up if they are not in the ground?   Why don't the trees topple as we walk through?" The red headed girl asks.

I cock my head, "Kind of a spongy soil with brackets at the base of each tree in a gold coated wire mesh, supporting each base." I see the confusion in their expression as they all blink at me in unison. "I'll take you below in a few minutes. Have you thought about the air?" I gesture with my arms about the space.

They all show similar expressions of concentration. The creepy mimicry of the Sneffles comes to my mind. I stand there a few minutes and let them fidget. I listen to the big fans go on and off. I put an index finger in the air. "Listen, what do you hear?"

Puzzled expressions cross their faces and they shift.

I face my palm upward, "Do you feel the fan?"

They all look in every direction, then smile.

I shudder with the flashback of the Sneffles. "The fan helps move the air so different gasses don't just hover in one spot. Why do you think that is important?"

Pigtail girl chortles, "To keep the trees cool."

The other kids giggle and I chuckle too.

A boy with red hair speaks up. "To create the gas combinations trees need to use?"

I point to his nose. "Yeah, and helps us have the compositions us Earth dwellers need also."

Circe Syndrome

A squirrel jumps from one tree to another and some quail amble out startling us. I smile, "Animals live here to help provide carbon dioxide when there are no people here." I motion them to follow. I lead them to a panel on the wall listing percentages and numbers. "This is a real time feed of the air and soil percentages. We make adjustments based on these numbers."

As I lead them to a service door that says, "Personnel Only," and open it, one of the male leaders joins us. I lead them down two sets of stairs which opens to a huge room, showing the grid of gold coated wires that creates the mesh that keeps the trees anchored and upright. I pause; this view is awe inspiring.

All the long three to four story tap roots were a purple color from the nutrient glaze. This inverted forest of roots is inhabited by foot long golems. The golems are brown and oblong with two dozen tiny legs beneath. They have ridges down their backs, three eye stalks, two sets of arms with brush hands and two sets of arms with wrench hands.

I step into the room, which has a large Plexiglas window separating the maintenance equipment from the root area. I tap at a monitor with a monochromatic green screen from the seventies, and watch it come on. Nutrient levels look good and I look up when a tapping sound comes from the Plexiglas. Three golems have their eye stalks extended and were signaling me closer.

I am surprised that they seem to remember me. I hadn't been here in four years.

I tap Morse code on the glass in a greeting. They tap it back. After a few minutes of these exchanges the restless kids asked me what I am doing. I explain Morse code, where it originated and how it was used. They seem shocked that golems could be communicating their own wants to me.

I forget that most of the magic community thinks golems have no internal thoughts. The golems have a specific request. I had wired their root room for music and left them with a few hundred songs play-list. No one had changed it since I left. As I explained the limited amount of music, I am getting more and more annoyed with myself for not arranging a way for the golems to change the list themselves.

While the kids debate if the golems have feelings, I find the newest computer terminal in the area. I navigate to the web and I interject in the middle of this debate, "I consider being bored a feeling. They claim to be bored and want some new music."

I want to figure out a way for the golems to set up and control their own music themselves. Morse code is out of vogue and others most likely think it is a quirk of the golems. I need to give them a way to communicate with anyone.

The kids become quiet as I set up an account on Amazon. I peruse the objects in the root area. I sigh, thinking the cliché magic mirror spell on the window would be the best in this situation. Where the glass works like a touch screen and a computer interface appears when touched and disappears when not used for a period of a time. Technically, in space, all the American science rules don't apply. I tap on the wall all my intentions. The golems surge to the window. One indicate where it wants a window. I realize I could just spell the whole window so anywhere they touch they could access a magic mirror control panel. It will be about one and half foot wide and one foot high. I remember to put a command that will not let the panels overlap but keep a clear inch buffer around each screen. I enable chat access and net access. About twenty-five touch the screen all at once and different windows open.

The kids' mouths are wide open as the panels all open and different screens appeared on each rectangle peppering the glass with various stages of screens.

I program a chat window from the side we are on and a speaker spell so the golems can chat with whomever is in the room.

A girl pulls my elbow, "How are they going to get money to pay for things through Amazon?"

I look at the floor. "I guess I could give them twenty dollars a month. I'll talk to the director of Heska Parks and Rec and get them a stipend. They deserve some compensation for all the work they do."

Multiple voices from several speakers at once say, "Cool!" This was interspersed with a few responses of "Excellent!" and "Yes!"

I give them all a big smile. "I didn't type that. Have you already hacked the system so you can hear what is going on in here?"

Their eye stalks nod in unison.

I roll my eyes as I chuckle heartily and uncontrollably.

The kids shuffle because the man is scowling at me. "Compensation! For un-living creatures?"

I look at all the kids and meet this man's eyes. I read the room and my smile passes my normal corners. It hurt. I take in his furrowed brow and tight lipped expression. He seems wound tight. I speak succinctly and politely, "Interesting classification. They have needs, they perform a service. Shouldn't they receive compensation?"

He shakes his head, "They have no rights! They're just mindless automatons."

I raise an eyebrow, "That get bored?"

The girl with pigtails grabs my hand. "How does this relate to a life support system?"

I grin in appreciation of the girl trying to change the subject. I direct my gaze at the window of curious golems watching them all finding unique screens. Their stocks waving in various patterns, a kinetic conversation going on I wish I understood. Under my breath I whisper, "It seems we are not sure what life is."

The little girl gives me a curious smile, "Did you say something?"

I act like I didn't hear her. I point to the golems. "These lovely beings monitor all the roots. They keep tabs on them and mix the nutrients."

Unexpected, my phone rings. I blush and note it is my parents' house number. I answer and my mother's voice is sharp. "Muriel, dear, how is being on the moon helping you rest?"

The kids start talking about Pokeman cards.

"Are those children's voices?" Mom asks puzzled.

"Yeah, there is a scout troop camping here." I say cheerfully.

"Scouts?"

"Science Scouts." I correct her.

"Oh? You're helping with achievement badge requirements?" her voice is gushing now.

"Uh huh." I say causally.

Mom resigned says, " OK, come home when you're done."

I give her my business tone, " I was kind of on my way elsewhere."

Mom's voice is now punctuating every syllable. "Elsewhere? Off world? Have you really thought this through?"

Wincing, I rub my forehead, "Perhaps not."

"Muriel, come home." In this pregnant pause I imagine her rubbing her own head. "And by home, I mean our actual home, not just the planet."

I give a long exhale, "Yeah, alright."

"Bye, dear."

"Bye." I hear her disconnect.

The kids give me a bemused look. I send a link to several online radio services to the golems. I had a problem I was chewing on. The one adult's anger reminds me how thoughtless others are about golems. I need a way to give them another solution to have their needs met if some random person decides their communication is tedious and disables what I put in place. I directed the golems to bring me a glass piece from the other end of this room, something they can move away and hide. As they went to fetch it I addressed the kids, "Looks like I need to wrap this up and send you back upstairs."

The man is fuming and takes heavy footsteps up the stairs. The children all thank and wave to me and leave in their ramble scramble way.

There is a tap on the glass. I look back at the window. A couple of them are holding various shards. I mime them taking the shards and holding them flat against the window glass. I put a hand on the window parallel to each on. I send the terminal spell into that glass and encompasses each shard. I include in those spells a link to Clay, my Aunt and Uncle's golem. I explain who he is and direct them to take their shards back to the other side and hide them. I explain that they are safety communications devices in case something happens to this big glass. I send a quick email to Clay. I explain how I don't want them isolated again with no one listening. That it is a safeguard for them. I have also included an added spell that if any of the shards break to send an email to Clay to check up on them.

I wave at the golems and head back up the stairs. The door locks behind me. A black and white lemur does a three spin jump from one tree to another. The adaptability of life hits me and I can not help but grin wide and silly.

Janette Bach

I walk to the dialyosefos spot. I nod at the troop, as the angry faced man rants to people who are acting patient with him. I wave and reach out to the aether.

Chapter 35

Semi Lucid

I stumble in the shed and cough for a few minutes.

My mother catches me when I topple out of the door of the shed. "How you feeling?" She touches my forehead with her palm. She shakes her head, "The moon? Really?"

I let her take my weight and she starts to escort me to the back door. As we walk, I see the undulating cobblestones accent my mother's Azalea plants. I note the moss forming between the cobblestones. This coupled with my mother's familiar gate is comforting. When we turn the corner to the backyard, I look up, as I hear the sounds of excited shouting. It wasn't a large backyard but my parents had added interesting features.

If one walked through the ornate arched portcullis covered in jasmine, the person shrank to the size of an ant making the yard open to all types of possibilities. Some of Morgan's and my cousins were playing that skateboard Lacrosse game in an

351

octagon field surrounded by grass. I look at the greenhouse that has a set of fountains that become a water-slide park at the micro level.

I cock my head toward the green house, "Have they checked out the grottoes?"

My mother shrugs, "They have been so focused on that game, I haven't brought it up."

I try to carry my own weight and stumble, "What is it called anyway?"

"Fatigue, dearie, you really should do that three-day nap." Mom adjusts her grip on me.

I roll my eyes, "I wasn't talking about the stumbling. I meant the game of flying skateboards and Lacrosse."

My mother gives me a bemused smile, "Levi-toss."

I pause, " OK."

"Your Uncle Mordecai is speculating and starting a regional league." Mom shook her head in bewilderment.

I looked at the octagon again. "That is what this world needs. Another licensed sport."

Mom chuckles, "You and I are of one mind, child. Your dad's excited though. If Yacob wasn't so preoccupied, I bet he would find it interesting, too."

I cock my head, "And Sarina?"

Mom gives me a stubborn puzzled look. "Who my dear?"

I take a breath, "Sarah."

"Oh, she is always delighted with another reason to watch fit men contest each other." Mom smirks.

I nod, "True."

We reach the door and Mom holds up her hand flat parallel to the door and twists her wrist, causing it to open. A breach in standard practice since the skies are now full of camera satellites and droids. I marvel at how the shrinking solution has opened up our yard to all types of shenanigans the satellites could not pick up on.

My mother opens the back door that leads to a wind closet which feeds to the basement door, where my father's workshop is. The other door leads to the kitchen. Mom levitates me, now that we were in the house, to a chair at the kitchen table. She heads to the refrigerator and gestures to the cupboard. A glass flew to her hand and she fills it with water. She gulps it down.

I wonder how I taxed her nerves. Then remember the is house was filled with all types of people.

Someone clears his throat, startling me. I look up to notice we were not alone in the kitchen. I looked up into Gideon's hazel eyes. I give a casual glance in his direction, "Oh, hey." I frown as if trying to remember his name as he drinks some coffee and peruses a newspaper. "Gideon? Right?"

He gives me an almost unperceptive bob, keeping his eyes on the paper.

I lean back, and look about, "Where is your sister?"

My mother snorts. That is uncharacteristically rude of her. He seems quite comfortable in my mother's kitchen. How much time has he spent with my mother? Mom sat a teapot on the stove and opens another cupboard bringing down cups and saucers. "Tea, darling?"

I gave her a nod.

Gideon ruffles his paper and clears his throat. He flips it back, then halves it and sits it down. He leans back and openly observes me. "My sister and I are not always joined at the hip."

The phone rings and my mother takes it. "Gideon, could you help Muriel with the tea. She will not ask for help and try to do it on her own." She leaves without waiting for Gideon to acknowledge her.

I sigh and look out the way my mother had gone, "Mom seems quite familiar with you?"

The teapot whistles. He looks back at his paper and waves a hand. Without looking, the stove turns off. The hot water pours into a waiting teapot. The tea tins open and a tea strainer dives into the tin then flies to the teapot.

"It needs to steep. I can hurry it, but it never tastes as good as just leaving it the four minutes." He returns to reading the paper.

I scan the room, then stare at his bowed head. "You didn't answer the question."

"You asked several, which were you wanting an answer to?" He flips the paper.

"There were two. I would like an answer to both."

He takes a sip of coffee and sits back, frowning at me. "Technically, it was one question and a declaration. I did answer the question about where my sister was, I just didn't tell you where she is. As for the familiarity with your mother, I've been staying in her house for over a week now."

I trace the wood grain on the table, "It's more than that. What is it?"

He looks longingly at the paper. "We've done a few Merlin shifts together and are in a linked static net spell together."

I am reminded that those spells require a level of emotional intimacy with no secrets, "Oh, that makes sense. That is a hard thing to agree to do with someone you hardly know."

He turns his cup and sighs, "Not anymore, that is for sure. Your mother and I know each other well now, there is no separating." He meets my eyes. "My sister is in trouble. Your mother, Jasper, Morgan and Yacob all think you can help me. Why?"

I rest my head on my hand and look past him to the steeping tea. I rub my thumb and index fingers together. "There are times when I am considered creative in terms of constraints, and following them while breaking them." I meet his eyes. Currently they had a blue cast with purple and green spots. "What kind of trouble?"

He takes another sip of coffee. He looks around the room and over his shoulder confirming it is empty. "She has a relationship addiction."

I run my hand through my hair, speculating, "Relationships are addictive for her, or there is a chemical component with the subject of the relationship?"

He taps his fingers and glowers. "The latter."

I sigh, "Elf?"

He scowls, "Yeah."

"Oh." I look at back at the table making calculations. Elves give off pheromones that give Heska a euphoric feeling. They feed off the magic in Heska. As they feed, the pheromones raise with the magic harvested. Eventually, the beginning high isn't enough, and the Heska begs for more and more draining until even their life force leaves. "How long?"

He turns away, "Off and on for five years."

I take a breath and examine the teapot. "So this can wait three days, right?"

He gives me an incredulous glare, "That is an odd question."

I put my hands out with my palms up. "Take a look at my aura."

He squinted, color drained from his face, "Oh? They are all sure you can handle this."

I point, "Do you think the tea is ready?"

He leers, "We all have our vices." He stands and prepares the cup. "Sugar?"

"Yes, two cubes." He turns and frowns at me. I avoid meeting his eyes and study the cupboards, I have a question for him, "So, how does this work with your family? Over half of you are fairies and I imagine there are elves also?"

He raises his eyebrows, "Milk?"

"Yes, please."

He stirs the tea and sets some shortbread on the saucer. He sets it in front of me. As he saunters back to his seat he answers, "That is a great question. Yes, we definitely have both. With what I've seen in Merlin, so does your family."

"I don't know much about dad's side." I shrug.

"Unfortunately, relation does not give immunity." He laments.

I take a sip of tea, "So, is that where Glinda is right now?"

"Yes."

I pick up some shortbread, "Is it a male or female elf?"

"Male, how does that matter?" he gives me an annoyed look.

"The approach." I dunk my cookie and spin it around. "He lives in Portland?"

He gives a quick assent, "Up by the Rose Garden at Washington Park."

"Hmmmm, swanky." I took a bite of the cookie, savoring the buttery, melting, crumbling dough.

"What's swanky?" Sarina silkily asks Gideon.

Gideon raises his paper and rustles it, "The steak house by the theater."

"You asking my little sis on a date? How cute! Such an upscale place, too." She pats my head like a cat's.

I run my hand across my face. "No, but thanks for making us both uncomfortable!"

Circe Syndrome

Sarina grabs a cookie, "I'll take a date to Morton's restaurant. What time are you picking me up?"

Gideon snorts, "No."

Sarina sighs, "Nine?" That is quite late."

He stood and pored himself more coffee and brought me another plate of cookies.

I took the cookies and looked up to see Sarina mesmerized by Gideon. I nudge her, "I'm surprised you're not out watching that game in the yard."

Sarina gapes down at me. "Game? What game?"

"That Levi-toss thing the cousins were watching. They are all playing now."

Sarina gives me a huge grin, "Thanks Murry, "She ruffles my hair, grabs three cookies and heads out the back door.

When the door slams I look at Gideon, "Why didn't you ask her to help you?"

He frowns at the door. "I know she is your sister, and you love her, but I do know trouble when I see it."

"No kidding." I give him a smile. "Have you been to the elf's house?"

He nods, "I've met him, too."

I sip of my tea, "Charming?"

He takes a breath and let's it out long, "Extremely so."

"How did they meet?" I set down my cup, "You guys don't live in Portland, right?"

"He used to live in Edinburgh. He was a professor at University." He wrinkles his nose.

"When did he move here?" I watch the crumbs float in my cup.

"A year ago. We all thought it would help Glinda. But, when we came for the birth, I realized she knows the area well, visits weekly." He groans.

"I see. Have you noticed ill effects yet?" I'm not trying to jump to conclusions.

"She forgets commitments. She hasn't finished her degree, or been able to hold a job."

I tap my fingers on the table, "Sounds like she isn't managing it well. Some can you know."

He snorts, "Not forever. She did fine in the beginning."

I take a breath, "This is the most important question. Does she want to stop?"

His eyes are forlorn, "She says she does. I really don't know, though. She might be saying that because she thinks I want to hear that."

I touch his hand, it feels electric.   He meets my eyes; I give him an imploring look. "Good, to know you're honest with yourself."

"Always an excellent trait!" My mother's imperious voice fills the room. She is followed into the room by Clay.

I watch my mother walk up to a metal bowl. "Were you listening long?" She lifts a plaid dishcloth from the top of the bowl and pokes the dark dough.   She begins to punch it down and flip it.

Gideon gives me a reassuring squeeze on my hand, "She just walked in."

She spins the bowl, "What's the concern? I told him to consult you after all!"

I look askance, I've never seen my mother make bread this way before. My mother shakes the bowl back and forth and spins it the other way.   When she tilts it up for a few moments I see there are a spiral of a white components that looks like they are swirling, colliding and randomly flowering stars. She spins it the other way again. Then she punches it down. She starts it spinning the other direction and covers it with the cloth again. She turns away from it and gestures to Clay. "I brought Clay to help carry you to your room."

I study the Golem, "Are you OK with that?"

His clay face takes on a huge grin, "Yes, thanks, for friends, Muriel."

Mom gazes at me, questioningly.

"You're welcome, Clay. Thank you for being available to help them and me."

Gideon clears his throat, "I'm at a loss."

Clay grins so wide cracks appear in the clay about his mouth, "Muriel made me moon friends."

Gideon and my mother exchange glances, then both in unison consider me.

Self conscious I turn my tea cup on the table as I speak. "The golems on the moon needed some help. So, I gave them some tools and access to Clay to help them out."

"The moon? You were on the moon today? In your condition?" Gideon scrutinizes my mother for verification. "It does explain your exhaustion; I could not fathom how a coffee date with friends could drain you so completely."

I regard him, "Your keeping track of my schedule?"

He chuckles, "Yes, no, everyone tells me to chat with you, but you're hard to pin down."

I shake my head, "You were not forthcoming when I sat down."

He shrugged, "You wouldn't have been interested otherwise."

"What? You know nothing about me. I thought I've been quite receptive when we talked in the past."

He blurts, "If there wasn't something else distracting you!"

I shake my head at this pointless discussion, "Jasper just mentioned to me today that I should talk to you about a puzzle I'm working on."

He gives me a curious look, "What type of puzzle?"

"Chemistry." I raise my eyebrows in supplication.

My mother clears her throat. "Muriel, you need to go sleep now, dear. Did you eat today?"

I yawn involuntarily "Yes, I had breakfast and lunch later at Jake's."

"I'll prepare you a snack for dinner. Clay take her up. Gideon would you mind keeping her up 'til I can get there with some food?" Mom is pointing fingers.

Gideon nods as Clay picks me up. We all turn when an explosive noise comes from the bowl with the dough in it. The dish cloth flies up.

Mom says the words that are her closest equivalent to swearing and exclaims, "Oh my!" Then she gestures for us all to head out. Gideon stands and follows Clay who is carrying me in his arms. The house is eerily quiet as Clay starts up the stairs.

I yawns, "Where is everyone?"

Gideon scans the room, "Most likely, the game, Merlin duty, off exploring Portland. Some may be back to their lives and will come back for their shifts."

"I haven't done a shift yet." I announce.

He raises an eyebrow, "You did do the birth and you haven't recovered from that yet!"

The motion of Clay's walking was lulling, like riding on a boat or swaying in a hammock, "True." I yawn again as I fight to keep my eyes open.

Clay pauses at my door. Gideon opens the door for him. Clay ducks and gets through the door and sits me on the bed. Slack jawed Clay walks to my window and stares out at the waves and purple dolphins. Gideon's gaze sweeps the room and lingered on the window as well. He then turns and looks at my drafting board which has a painting of dolphins on it.

I fall back and stare at my ceiling waiting for questions. I don't have the energy to share information or make up anything to answer them with.

Gideon clears his throat, "Your drafting board is beeping."

I blink, sits up and stare past him to the drafting board. I try to stand and I stumble instead. Gideon catches me. Clumsily, he helps me to a chair. I turn the handle on the drawers. The unit turns into a vanity/computer console again. It is the fledgling galaxy and it is all mushrooms again, except there is the turtle figure covered in mushrooms. I frown, hold my head.

Gideon sits on the edge of my bed behind me. He pauses and pulls out a wooden disc from his pocket and suspends it at the seat level, just to left of my shoulder. Tendrils of wood extended from the disc down toward the floor and embedded themselves into a chair of woven wood with flourishes. He sits down, wrinkles his nose, and looks at the screen. "What is that?"

I look over at the chair, impressed. "I'm not sure. It's completely baffling." I support my chin with my hand and exhale flustered. My mind is reeling; I remember introducing a few thousand more species to this planet just the other day.

Clay yelps, "There is a kitty at the window."

Gideon turns to glance that direction, "You're right, big guy, it is a feline of some type. That rainbow calico is as unique as those purple dolphins out there."

Grogginess threatens my mind as I toggle through images and charts of the planet.

Gideon clears his throat, "Does this involve the chemistry question you had?"

I glance back at him, "Yeah. No. Kind of."

"OK?" his voice puzzles, he readjusts his seat.

I wobble my head, "It wasn't about this planet."

"This planet! There are other planets?"

I wince at him, "Neuro net, right?" I stare at the species numbers again.

"Muriel?" He runs a hand in front of my face.

"What?"

"You turn planets into eco-spheres?" His voice cracked a bit.

"Yes." I say, deadpan.

"How long have you been doing this?" He taps my arm and points to the screen.

I scratch my ear, "Awhile." As I think, my whole life, and I make more than habitable planets.

He sucks in, "What chemistry question do you have?"

My mother walks in, carrying a tray, which she places on my bed.

I gesture to the screen. "Has this ever happened to you?"

My mother looks at the screen, "That isn't a very diverse system. That isn't like you."

I glance nervously at Gideon then back at my mother.

Mom pats Gideon's shoulder, "Don't worry about him dear. He is family now and with the spell we are entwined in, the secrets are mutually assured."

Gideon gives me a smirk, "No one would believe me anyway if I were to reveal what goes on in this dynamic." He looks out my window and back at me.

Circe Syndrome

My mother giggles.

I roll my eyes and exhale as I talk exasperated, "I started out with my standard 5,000 species variations two years ago and left it alone. I went to check it out a few days ago, and it was all mushrooms. So I add a few thousand more species, with a turtle variant that consumed the mushrooms, and left an alarm to let me know when the mushroom mass happened again. It was just beeping. This is the result."

Mom frowns at the screen. "That is troubling. But, dear heart, you need to rest." She turned a handle on a drawer turning the desk back into a drafting table. She reaches out an arm, gesturing to the bed, "Come on, eat some food and rest, I will wake you for that date."

Gideon stands, and grabs his seat that retreated back into a wooden disc. He puts it back in his pocket. He and Mom maneuver me to bed. Mom points out the corn beef sandwich on dark rye with a side of Matzah ball soup. There is also some soda water.

Hunger hits suddenly and fiercely. As I devour it, I made plans with Gideon to check out his sister's situation and hopefully get to ask my metal questions. My mother talks about different situations going on in the house full of people. My mind keeps wandering to the mushroom planet. Exhaustion hits me as I finish my food. It becomes harder to keep my eyes open. My mother guides me to the lip of the bedding and helps me lay down.

Just before I fall off, I hear Gideon talk to Clay and a feline voice. Gideon and Clay are leaving. I turn and blearily see a rainbow mass in Clay's arm. My Mom gives me a pat and parting smile. She turns off the light and shuts the door.

I start to dream of steel mushrooms with calico cats prowling through the depths.

Chapter 36

Orbits

I wake with an awful taste in my mouth. I wince from the light streaming in the window. I glance at the clock, and it reads 5:20 PM. I wonder what day it is. I sit up, stretch and run my fingers over the sections of my skin that had been sand. Bloodied sand flakes into my bed, revealing pink skin. There are several holes in some spots still, but over all, I am mostly healed. I think it's been a least at couple of days.

My Mom clears her throat and swivels the chair from my vanity. "It's been three days, dear."

"So today is?"

"Thursday, dear, actually Thursday evening."

I sink back into bed. I sweep at the sand. "I'll go back to sleep then."

"No, you won't", my mother taps on my feet, "you made a commitment to Gideon."

I sit up and turn with my feet dangling over the edge of the bed. I rub my eyes. "You're right, I did." I look through my scraggly hair and survey my mother toggling through screens on the vanity, "What-cha doing?"

My mother snorts, "What am I doing?" She enunciates each word clearly and with exaggeration. "I do believe, you were taught to speak properly." She gives me a wink. "I'm observing this planet you're colonizing."

"Cool, give me a second." I stumble to the bathroom. When I finish I return to the edge of my bed. "Find anything useful?"

"You're using a satellite mass off a dormant gas giant."

I nod, "Yes."

She gives me a patient smile, "Did you check out its orbit before you started tinkering with it?"

I chew my lip, I can't remember, "Umm, no, I didn't."

Mom taps the mirror and pulls her index and thumb apart zooming out so the colonized moon and gas giant could be observed in one image. She flicks the screen where the swirling gasses on the huge planet, "It looks like it might have a synchronous orbit with the gas giant."

"What?" I run my hand through my hair from my brow to behind my ear. I stare past her not seeing her, trying to remember what this concept was.

My mother gives me her playful grin and a kind twinkle illuminates her eye. She turns back to the screen. I know she is waiting for me to ask the question. I sigh. I want the answer so I ask, "I'm sure I covered this in an astronomy on physics class at one point. But currently I'm at a loss. What do you mean?"

My mother turns, clasps her hands together and stares at the floor as if referencing a visual memory. She then turns up her right palm and a grapefruit sized hologram of the earth hovers at eye level distance above her palm. "You've noticed when looking at our moon we seem to always see the same side. You were just on the dark side." She raises an eyebrow asking me non-verbally if I understand.

A moon the size of a ping-pong ball appears next to the earth. "The moon still spins one cycle as it orbits the earth. That takes about 29.5 days. Even though the moon is always there we don't always see the sun shining on it. "She gestures to the far wall creating an illusion of space and a huge segment of the sun. She sends the planet and moon spinning, showing the effect. "It spins but at the same speed as our planet. Because of that, parts of the moon do not see the sun for weeks."

"Oh, so you're saying this planet doesn't see the sun part of the time. And it's longer then a twenty-four-hour cycle." I'm embarrassed, I cover my face. I think about the size of the gas giant and the planet moon. It could be several weeks for the sun to show up in some parts, and overly exposed in other areas. Fungus could definitely handle the variations better. "So this planet should be called Fung-Mungus. Maybe I could develop some mushrooms with bio-luminous fibers and some plants that can use that light with the sunlight for photosynthesis?"

Mom nods, "That is an interesting idea."

I glare at her, "I was kidding."

"What could be the harm in trying?" She shrugs.

I yawn, "Did Gideon and I come up with a time and place?"

Mom starts shutting down the screens and jiggled the nobs, turning the vanity into just a vanity again. She gives me a cool look. "He's picking you up here at eight. I guess the professor is having a party."

I internally note the elf that Glinda is addicted to is a professor and it must be "his" party we are going to, " OK."

Mom stands and examines the sand in the bed. "I'll take care of this. Just clean yourself up and dress up. Oh, and the professor won't be the only elf at the party."

I cock my head in understanding, "So go plugged in."

Mom smiles, "Definitely, make sure you let your handler's know that Gideon and Glinda are to be kept anonymous."

Even though I could snap my fingers and be completely clean and dressed, the actual process of showering and getting ready was a great way of centering my mind and waking up. I stand and stretch a couple times. "Should I be worried that Gideon might turn on me?"

Mom's look was bemused and knowing. "No." She gestures to the bathroom.

I pause just to reassure myself at my door, "No?"

"No!"

" OK.", I slip into the bathroom and get ready. When I come back into my room, Mom is smoothing my bed and there are three outfits laid out.

"Really, Mom, I think I'm old enough to dress myself."

My mother gives me a dismissive expression, "I'm just trying to be helpful. It's more formal then you usually do, but not ball gowns and suits."

I wrinkle my nose. Honestly, people make assumptions, "I thought I would just wear this robe."

"You don't want help, fine! I made you dinner so come down to the kitchen before you go. " She stands and leaves.

I watch her leave, and then stare down at the clothes. They are all great choices. I decide on the plum slacks and black peasant top with gold details. I put on some black stockings and black flats. I looked in the mirror and run my hand through my hair, drying it in loose, wavy curls. I tint my eyebrows and put color on my lips. Then I head downstairs.

Circe Syndrome

The house is less expanded, now it is only twice the size it normally is. I head to the kitchen and am stopped in the dining area. About fifteen various family members are there. This included my parents, Sarina and Gideon. A chair next to Gideon move out of its own volition.

I look at my mother who nods toward the chair. I smile, and sit down and pull in. Mom places a bowl of chicken soup in front of me. I look longingly at the roast chicken in front of everyone else.

Mom tuts at me, "You haven't eaten for three days. Let's begin slow."

My mouth waters at the smell. I start with a delicate spoonful of my mother's homemade chicken stock. I can taste the carrots, celery, onions, and chicken blended in a warm liquid. I finished my bowl. It automatically refills with huge Matzoh balls.

Gideon looks uncomfortable, "What are those?" He points at the dumplings.

I blink and try to look at them as unfamiliar. Gray color lumps with a moist texture. Hmm. Maybe not the most appetizing to look at. "Matzoh balls."

"What are they made of?"

I cut a dumpling with my spoon, "Matzoh."

He pauses, "Ummm."

"Matzoh is unleavened bread. If you are ever here during Passover, you'll get really familiar with it."

"Really?" He cut some of his chicken.

I look up at my mother's amused eyes. "Mom." I nod toward Gideon's place. My Mom turns to look at my father and a bowl of Matzah ball soup appeared in front of Gideon. There was a spoon next to it.

He looks over at my mother and pouts jokingly. "You two going to gang up on me?"

I take another bite, "Yeah."

He tentatively picks up the spoon. He gazes at it as if trying to plan the attack.

I gesture with my spoon as I suggest, "Try a spoonful of broth first then slice off a piece like this and scoop in the broth and try it."

After he takes a tentative bite he digs in and devours it. His cousins watching started complaining to my mother that they wanted to try it, too. Then my family chimes in. The table fills with steaming bowls of soup.

I finish my soup but I am still hungry. I glance at my mother. She gives me a bemused smile and my bowl dissolves and my plate fills with roast chicken, mashed-potatoes and green beans. I mouth thank you and scarf it up.

Sarina waits until my mouth is full to ask me a question. "You look nice, are you going somewhere, Murry?"

Gideon takes a drink of water. Then speaks, "We are going to a party."

"Oh, I love parties!" she bats her eyelashes at him.

"That's nice." he says noncommittally and takes a spoonful of soup.

Not use to disinterest, Sarina stares daggers at Gideon then turns to talk to the person on her left.

Then she looks at me again. "So, Murry, are you and Gideon dating?"

I laugh, "We just met." Let's face it I thought, I'm not that attractive.

Gideon snorts, "Maybe we aren't ready to talk about it yet."

"Why? Are you embarrassed to be seen with my sister?"

I stand. "I'm full, you ready to go?"

He stands with me.

Circe Syndrome

My mother gestures to the kitchen, "I made dessert."

"It's OK, I'll try it later."

I look at Gideon and appreciate his harlequin gray sweater with black slacks and crisp white shirt. As we turned to leave I whispered to him, "You look nice."

He stammers and says, in the foyer as the camera was being reinserted, "Umm, you too. Even at this moment."

I blink as the cameras adjusts and clamps onto my ocular nerve endings. "So what do we expect at this party?"

He winces, "Casual opulence."

" OK?" I am curious what that means.

He leads me to a vehicle completely decked out with a wood interior, "Jasper lent me his car."

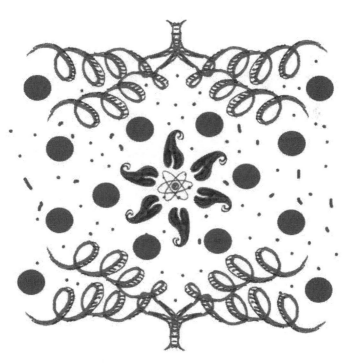

Chapter 37

Take Me Home

Gideon holds the door for me. I sit down. As I say, "Thank you," he smiles. I put on my seatbelt. He walks around to the driver's side.

He gets in and starts the car. He looks at me, "By casual opulence, I mean some will be barefoot and sprawled about the room that is richly furnished and scattered with caviar, champagne, brie, fruit and wine. Servants will not be seen but will be present, picking up and cleaning things. Some guest will be talking, gaming and watching TV."

I cock my head. "So like home with fancy dress."

He gives me an inquisitive smile, "Yes, I am curious as to what else you will notice."

I study my hands wondering about my conversation with my mother about him. I ask, "Mom seems to think I need not worry about you being taken in by the elves. "Why?"

He adjusts his hair. "I'm hard to fool."

Circe Syndrome

I am curious, "What does that mean?"

"Forefront in my mind is what is happening to my sister. It keeps me focused."

I give him a hopeful grin, "You two must be close."

"We are twins. How about you, why won't you be swayed?" He gives me a sly look.

I shrug, "I seem to not be easily swayed by persuasive beings."

He laughs, "You sure."

"Well, it happens, I'm aware it's happening, then I pause and think everything through, and when I understand the consequences I choose not to be swayed. It is a matter of choice in the end." I turn to peer out the window and think about the trees of Eco Spa.

He turns on the radio and the song "Radioactive" by Imagine Dragons starts to play. He drives to a house across from the Rose Garden at Washington Park.

Strangely the vegetation around the dwelling had not started to turn for fall. The house is white with column like rectangle pillars almost too chunky for the two story structure. By the front door, I notice a spider spinning a web. It reminds me of a tip a masseuse had given me about fairies and elves. I must avoid making skin contact. Apparently, their pheromones are even harder to resist once burrowing into the skin.

I pause by the spider web, making Gideon wait and raise an eyebrow at me. I have a favor to ask, actually more of a deal to make, with this spider. It takes a couple minutes of us chirping back and forth before we came to an arrangement. I am going to provide an extra protein and it will spin me a pair of elbow length gloves on my hands using drag line silk.

I do a quick spell over the web and it became a pile of trapped moths. It tickles when the spider climbs onto my arm and begins to start weaving. I wince trying not to laugh and squirm as the feet make tickling steps across my arm. When she finishes I moved my fingers and arms staring at the gloves, transfixed by their silkiness and lightness. Gossamer comes to mind.

Gideon pulls out my arms and examines the tight weave and he seems overwhelmed. "Wow! Can you have some made for me?"

The spider's mind is already overwhelmed by what it has done and is in a bit of shock. So I take some leaves and transfer the molecular signature from my gloves to them and make him hand length ones.

His grin is huge as he puts them on. He admired the gloves on his hands, wiggling his fingers. He pushes the doorbell.

The doorbell has a pipe melody and the door opens. It reveals a tall, thin man with plastered dark hair and a black suit. "Yes? May I announce you?"

The foyer opens to a modern style home decked out in Dania furniture and track lighting instead of chandeliers. The expansive room was filled with elegantly dressed people and tinkling glassware. The art on the walls was all themed out with mythological subjects, original covers from fantasy books Rembrandt, Caravaggio, and Klimt paintings. Some I have never seen before. I stop to examine one by Klimt with dancing fairies surrounding a flute player in a forest area.

Gideon nudges my shoulder and does a head nod toward the approaching gentleman in tails. With long, blonde, curly hair tied back and high cheek bones, he approaches us with his hand outstretched. "Gideon, so nice of you to join us tonight."

Gideon reaches out his gloved hand and shakes this gentleman's hand. "Thank you for inviting me, Professor Opiate."

"Vic, please, Gideon, call me Vic. And who is this fascinating creature you brought with you?"

Circe Syndrome

Involuntarily, I blush.

Gideon chuckles, "This is Miss Muriel."

I don't know what came over me, I curtsied. "Nice to meet you, Professor Opiate."

He smiles "Charmed, welcome to my little abode. Please help yourself to some refreshments and enjoy the dancing." He waves casually with his hand in different directions. Then he excuses himself and walks off toward another guest.

There are groups of people, hedge wizards, witches, fairies, elves and other magical creatures scattered about the room. I stand a moment to stare a little longer at "Midsummer Eve" painting by Edward Robert Hughes on the divider. The center figure of the fey women, watching, the smaller fey dancing around her. As she stands leaning in. Gideon finally clears his throat, I turn and look at him. "Did you find your sister?"

He nods and cocks his head toward the dance floor.

The pipe and harp music is lively. The dancers are creating a beat with their feet and in the swirl of movement I catch a glimpse of long, curly, auburn hair highlighted in golden streaks.

I am about to squint and do a power gaze when an inebriated elf brushes up against me. "Eeeee-x-cuuuuuse me! Would you like to dance?"

I wince at his breath and stepped closer to Gideon. He responds by wrapping a possessive arm around my waist and nuzzling my neck. The warm, unexpected sensual feel throws me a second. I try not to completely melt into his arms. "No, she promised me her first dance." His voice a possessive male.

The elf blinks and smiles at Gideon, "Yeah, we can all do it together."

Gideon stares at him for a quiet count of ten seconds. "Not now." He says it quietly and authoritatively.

The inebriated elf starts puffing up as a voice calls out, "Muriel! What a delightful surprise to see you here!" The approaching silver haired elf crowded out the inebriated elf.

My face lights up, I can't help it. An old friend is here. "Fin! How are you doing?" There is a beautiful, young blond man standing next to Fin scowling at me in disgust. "Is this Steven?"

The man then gives me an smile of wonder and shakes my hand. Him comprehending, I understand their relationship and respected it. Fin grabs my hand from Steven, and starts examining my gloves closely, "Whoa, where did you get these, they are fabulous!" Gideon clears his throat and Fin gives me a wink, "Who is this brooding figure of manliness at your side?"

I reach out and squeeze Gideon's hand affectionately, "Gideon this is my friend, this is Fin who is an amazing masseur, if you are ever looking for one."

Gideon and Fin shake hands. A server walks up and offers us Pomegranate martinis. I look to Fin, who shakes his head. Gideon reaches for one and Fin speaks, "Steven, what was that story about Persephone you were telling me?"

Gideon pauses in his reaching, "No, thank you." Persephone had to stay in Hades because of three pomegranate seeds for part of the year. It was a subtle way of warning us about a trap.

The server seems disappointed and moves on. Fin nods toward the martinis, "Vic likes to be dramatic sometimes." Fin takes a hand and touches my ear as he pretended to brush something off my shoulder. He uses this skin contact he to initiate a mental connection, where he asks, "Muriel? I know what happens when you go places you had not planned on being. Should I be leaving?"

Circe Syndrome

I meet his eye and nod my head slightly as I say out loud, "Thanks." He is actually a member of the collective, an informant. The people using the monitors, in my head, start to pay attention. Fin and Steven start to withdraw and my sight changes to energy vision.

I direct it at the dance floor. It is a churning energy through the floor into a detailed mosaic on the wall. The elves around the room are getting a slow drip, while the host is harvesting mega doses of magic and filling the walls. It is in this beautiful spiral mesmerizing pattern. It nags at my memory but I can't place the spell construct type yet. I study the floor mosaic and lose my breath. It is a dimensional gate spell. "Shit!" I think. I note how close to activating the spell is; it is big enough to take the whole house with it. Displacing this much matter was going to create some major residual effects.

I take a gulp of air and count to three. Then I start to think. What is the defensive strategy against elves and fairy magic? We didn't eat the food; that is good. No physical contact. What is the other thing? The music pumps up a notch. This music is great, it would be so much better with lyrics. That is when the light bulb goes off in my head. Sung music renders them immobile. Elves and fairies would go into a kind of trance state with sung music. One of the reasons most cultures sing prayers. I look at Gideon, who is watching the dancing uneasily. "How is your singing voice?"

"What? Are we going to get my sister out of here or not?" He growls at me.

I patiently say, "Bear with me, do you know songs you can sing the words to?"

"Ummm, sure." He is still glaring at me but is slightly puzzled at the same time. "What?"

I want to lead him to the realization himself, "At family gatherings on your side of the pond, do they have vocal singing, out loud?"

"Sure, but only if the guests are told in advance. Why?" His facial features pass from annoyance to wonder. "Oh? Yeah! Got it now!"

I cock my head at him. "Have you done a power perusal yet?"

"Power Perusal? I know you think you're speaking English. But sometimes, I seriously doubt it."

I laugh, "Look with vision that sees the streams of energy flowing through the room. I would focus on the dance floor."

He nods. I can tell he is holding back a retort. He must have done what I suggested, because his eyes widen.

I acerbically ask, "Did you plan to go to fey land tonight, because I did not?"

His body language changes as the comprehension rolls over him and his voice has hints of stress, "I don't know. Do you think our mobile plans will work there?"

I wrinkle my nose and bite my lip, "I don't know, mine worked on the moon the other day."

"Really?" He looks at me, curious.

I give him a look of nonplussed wonder, "I know the satellites are up there but the beams aren't aimed that way."

He gazes around the room and gestures with his arm, "Interesting question, should we stay focused on saving my sister and some of these other people's lives?"

I shrug, "Sure, let's start dancing, then start singing. What songs do you know?"

We discuss song options and surprisingly find one we both know. We start to dance. We weave through the crowd to where an exhausted looking Glinda is swaying with glazed eyes.

Gideon starts singing, "Take me home...."

The room shivers and all eyes turn and stare at him. I join in, "To the place I belong."

Another person in the room picks up the song and sings, "West Virginia."

The musicians started to follow the song and more and more people begin to sing. The elves all freeze. Glinda's eyes slowly began to look clearer and she clutches at Gideon's arm. She starts to sing along. I help guide them off the dance floor. I encourage other singers and people off the dance floor. We all sing. I get us to the back door of the room to a beautiful set of walnut French doors.

They open to a picturesque backyard swimming pool that appears as if it was formed from nature, with a waterfall feeding into it. We stop singing and make our way around the pond/pool and all its decorative foliage. Some of the plants are extremely active. Snapping flowers and sticky leaves, creating another defense for the elf.

Other people are streaming out behind us. To the far left corner there is a side gate. We are heading toward it when hear this huge shuddering sound.

We turn. It is a low growling sound like you hear before a storm or an earthquake. Deep and crunchy as if very world is breaking. The house shudders.

Glinda pauses and pulled at Gideon, "Gideon, wait, I want to go back in!"

Gideon's features are pained, he stares down at her, "Why?"

"I love him, Gideon."

I turn to the back door. I don't want to see the pain on both of their faces. I feel it emanating and have the snapshot from this moment etched into my mind.

Vic storms out the door with a red face. "What do you think you're doing? She's mine! I have plans for her!"

"He loves me too, see." Glinda limply points.

I feel bad for Gideon and I try to hide that as I look at him. Gideon swallows hard. I look back at Vic and stand in front of Glinda. My hands at my side. I yell out to Vic, "What type of plans?"

Vic frowns at me as he scans me in an appraising way. "Stop being a nuisance. It's taken me five years to break down that girl's defenses! She's mine now!"

I put my hands out in supplication, "Let it wait a night."

The power throbbing through him and the house is at an explosive stage. I am pretty sure the elf's self-control wouldn't extend to the emotional at this moment. I cross my arms and glare, I ask, "You love her?"

He snorts, "What? She's a disgusting, uncouth animal like the rest of you primates! I don't love her, but I have uses for her! My wife is expecting and I need a nursemaid my children can suck raw magic through! I'll sacrifice myself and get her pregnant to get the milk flowing!"

Glinda gasps as if she had been hit.

Gideon tightens his grip on her. I put up a barrier as a snatch spell tries to cross the pool. "Get her out of here!" I yell.

He gives me a panicked look, "What about you?"

I raise my hand in a casual manner to block a spell Vic lobs at me. When it hits, I stagger. "I'll be fine!"

"You don't seem..." Gideon stammers.

I interrupt him, "Gideon, get you and her out of here. These things are easier to do when I only need to defend one instead of three."

Glinda tries to move toward Vic.

I catch her. "Sing Gideon, sing and don't let up until you're at least three miles away!"

Gideon started singing, "Twinkle, Twinkle."

Circe Syndrome

I smile at how charming I find that.

He still doesn't move with her.

Vic lobs another spell my way. It is bone shattering. Protecting the three of us was going to fatigue my mind. I stagger again. "You've got to go."

He still doesn't move.

A smooth cadence comes from the gate. "Come on, do what she says. I got her back."

I smile involuntarily I knew that voice. It is Thomas.

Gideon wrinkles his nose and guides Glinda to the gate. He pauses there and stops singing and has to tighten his grip on Glinda. I am still blocking spells. Gideon calls to me. "Are you sure Muriel? He's a vampire."

I call back as I stumble again, "Yeah, it will be fine. And keep singing."

Vic had started talking about his plans for Glinda and the others he planned to transport tonight. "See this house, I will show my noble in-laws how well I can provide for their princess!"

This explained why he was transporting the whole house. I created an illusion of Glinda leaving my shield and running toward Vic. I had her stumble and pause, out of breath. He stopped lobbing spells at me. "See, my pet still loves me! You should really..."

I stop listening and look at Thomas as I rest a moment. "How did you find me?"

He gives me a huge smile, "You actually had the foresight to walk into this wired up. I can't believe you got him to monologue." He looks at Vic whose mouth is still going.

I shrug, "It's a talent."

"Why isn't he walking to meet the illusion or to confront you directly?" He scratches his chin.

"The spell to teleport the building is in motion. It will activate soon. He wants to go home. He's at the end of its radius."

He points to the pool, "He's not taking this. Why?"

"Yeah, it's beautiful, but large volumes of water can't go in a fey transport spell unless performed on water."

He has a confused expression, "What?"

I say in a no nonsense way, "It's a matter thing and an old belief."

He raises an eyebrow, " OK."

I make the illusion of Glinda stumble. More people and creatures stream out of the house. It shudders three more times. I back up and motion Thomas back. The illusion reaches Vic. He tries to gather the illusion in his arms and finds his arms empty. His face flashes red. The house appears to suck in on itself as the transport spell takes hold. Vic is sucked into the house. The wind blows. The pool swirls into a whirlpool cracking its bottom and allowing the water to escape.

"Duck!" I drop to the ground and plant my fingers into the moist dirt. I feel a worm slither by rushing to the commotion. My skin feels sandblasted from the debris shooting out from the crack in reality. This huge old oak behind me rips itself from the ground and is sucked into the maelstrom.

Thomas winces, "I got here too late, I would have loved to attack an elf. Their blood is like chocolate. And the energy it produces, stellar."

It all happens in a manner of three blinks and the grassy lawn with a ring of mushrooms glistened in the moonlight. The yard fills with collective operatives, who wrapped blankets around the stragglers and separate the human from the magic population.

I sit up and examined my dirt encrusted nails. Thomas stands over me and offers me a hand.

"Stellar, Huh?" I take his hand.

He guides me to standing.

Thomas gestures toward the gate. "That man wasn't going to leave you alone. He didn't think much of me. He wasn't at the coffee shop the other day?"

I watch as the stragglers gathered together. They are treated with medical care and as they were being debriefed, the human ones are having their memories altered. "I'm opening my circle."

"Is he your boyfriend?"

I shake my head and wipe my sleeve, "I just met him."

He kicks at the grass, "Quite a favor, for someone you just met."

I stare at mushrooms and think about my planet. "He's technically family. Morgan's cousin."

"So is that Jasper character, right? But they are both by marriage. So as far as dating goes they are game."

I frown at my nails, "Jasper is in a relationship even if he doesn't know it. I don't know Gideon's status."

"You're hanging out with a lot of extended family?"

I let that hang there. I can't talk about why. "It happens." I respond nonchalantly.

I watch as a wizard comes in and dissolves the concrete pool and fills in the land, turning the whole lot into a flat piece of land. Another pulls out a digital print from my first view of the property. "Should I build it again or let whoever buys it make their own design?"

I turn to Thomas and he points to the gate. I called over my shoulder. "Just throw a forget spell over the lot and let the new tenant create their own home."

The agents around us give us amused confirmation smiles.

Janette Bach

Thomas gives me a smirk, "So, was it an elf?"

I give him a bemused smile, "That was just here? Yes."

He brushes my arm with his, "No, the being you had a relationship with?"

We start walking to the gate. I shake my head, "No."

He gives me a wink, "A selkie?"

I meet his eyes, "No."

He bites his lip, "A centaur?"

I pause at the gate and stare at him and shake my head, "How would that work?"

"How would what work?" Anthony meets us at the gate. He has a clipboard in his hand.

"You can physically transform yourself or them." Thomas laughs.

I glare at him.

Anthony clears his throat, "Transform who?"

I say exasperated, "That's true. No, it wasn't a centaur."

Anthony frowns in confusion, "What are you two talking about?"

Thomas is grinning ear to ear. Muriel pulls a loose strand behind her ear. "Nothing."

Anthony sighs, " OK, I've been asked to debrief you."

I nod, letting him know I understand.

Thomas sighs, "Can we go to a coffee shop or something?"

Anthony looks at me and Thomas. Nonplused says "This is classified."

"Yes, I understand that. Can't you two just make a spell that keeps people from listening or has them hear language they don't understand?"

I nod. "I could drink something. I think it is only classified in the norms world. This is already going to be blowing up the social sites."

Anthony sighs, "Let's go to that bar you hang out at, Muriel. So was there or was there not a centaur in there?" He points at where the house use to be.

I raise my eyebrows, "You mean my recruiting hang out? It's a bit rough."

Anthony shrugs and stares at Thomas.

Thomas nods, "Sounds fine. As long as this isn't some species thing."

Anthony snorts, "I just want a drink and I figure those occupants won't care about what we talk about. They think they are all-", he makes air quotes, "functioning", then dropped them, "On a higher plain then the rest of us apes."

I interject, "Boeing 747!"

Thomas shakes his head, "No my dear girl, Mars probe."

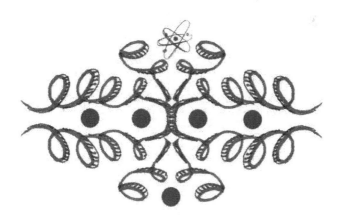

Chapter 38

Clubs

I spin my pint glass of Angry Orchard Cider and watch the striped condensation appear around its side.

Anthony stares at his clipboard and takes a sip of Rogue Ale. "You did this on some personal request right?"

I straighten and nod.

"You know the chief is recommending you for agent?" His fingers move across a paper with the doodles and notes responding like apps. He pulls up a file. "You do know vigilante-ism is frowned upon in the Collective?"

Thomas snickers, "Frowned upon? I believe it is downright discouraged."

I give them a grumpy deadpan glare, "Is this where you do the not so veiled threat that if I were an agent, I could be protected from potential litigation that may arise from these situations? If I don't become an agent the evidence you all have collected could end up in less generous hands?"

Anthony puts down the clipboard, "I helped you with that oil debacle and Thomas here has helped you with a couple of things. I would love to have you as a partner."

Thomas lightly punches him on the shoulder, "Me, too."

I take a drink of the cold liquid. "You both seem to handle yourselves well in a crisis and I would be honored. I just don't want to be an agent."

Anthony eyebrows cross and become stern, "Are you sure? These notes don't speak of an individual who doesn't want to step up and help people in need."

Thomas leans in "Come on, pet. It would be fun doing stakeouts together."

I take a breath and ask, "Is this an official request?" This is the last thing I want. My life would belong to The Collective.

They looked at each other. Anthony wipes his hand across the clipboard. "No, one will happen though. Take the next week to think about it." He taps his fingertips together and looks at Thomas, "So, was there a Centaur there?"

I break out into laughter and point at Thomas, "Look at what you started."

Anthony sighs, "So the centaur conversation wasn't about this event."

I look at my pint, smile, thinking about Gregor, "No."

Anthony taps his fingertips on the table and asks, "You two going to fill me in on that conversation?"

In unison we say, "No!" and bust up again.

A slip of a woman with stringy blond hair comes up to the table. She is a new waitress. She ignores me and Anthony and makes a beeline for Thomas. "How is your Chianti, sir?"

Thomas swirls it and looks at her in a full charm mode. She moves closer.

I look away beyond the booth to Mothius's regular table. Samantha and he both had human guests that look a bit high. Samantha and Mothius are chatting with their guests and each other then casually, quickly, feed off their guests.

Uneasy, Anthony follows my gaze. He frowns. He speaks into his glass. "That is illegal. It's a public place."

I give him a cooling motion with my hand and swipe parallel to the table. "We are out of our territory in this place. These are regulars here. It's fine."

He sighs and softens his eyes and plays with his glass, "But, it's illegal."

I wrinkle my forehead, "How do you expect vampires to eat and survive? The humans will live when the vampires are done. The vampires will make sure. It's easier having willing regular prey then having to restart every day different people. Kind of a farming thing. "

He snorted and takes a drink of his beer.

I look at Thomas, who has the waitress leaning closer to him in conversation. I take another sip of my cider, observing him, then look back at Anthony. "So the report is done? I can leave right now?"

Anthony gestures to my cider, which is mostly full. I shrug, "I'm a light weight. I really shouldn't have anymore."

I suddenly feel eyes on my shoulder and turn to see Thomas staring at me. I met his eyes. He is moving fast and wrapping the waitress's wrist with a wide bandage. "You two aren't supposed to drink alcohol, right?"

I let my gaze linger on the waitress's wrist, then I look back up at him, "When on duty, no." I suddenly check the equipment in my head and note no one is really paying attention. They are all still at the elf site. I toggle, it off. Wondering if it really does go off.

Anthony looks back at Mothius's table.

388

Circe Syndrome

I inhale slowly and give measured glances to Anthony and Thomas and capture both of their eyes, "We are not on duty right? This is a personal thing I let you guys know about."

The waitress leaves a folded sheet of paper on the table next to Thomas. I could see part of a handwritten phone number.

Anthony gives me a grin, "Your personal life seems calm."

Thomas snorts, "About as calm as a hornet trapped in a pair of trousers."

I giggle at the image, "Pleasant thought."

Thomas raises an eyebrow, "You are ready to go?"

He has a drop of blood on the corner of his mouth. I mime wiping the corner of my mouth. "Are you?"

He takes a thumb and dabs the spot and then sucks on his thumb. He smiles, "Yes. You want to come over to my place?"

I sigh, "No, I should head home and check on my family members."

As I ready to leave, Anthony raises and index finger and asks fro clarification. "Glinda and Gideon, should not be named in the report?"

I give him a grateful smile, "Correct."

Thomas leans back in the booth expansively and points to Anthony, 'You want to go clubbing?"

Anthony gives me a mock worried look, "Should I be concerned?"

I look around the room and meet the waitress's eye, she nods with confirmation that she understands I want my check. "I don't know. I've never been clubbing with him." I laugh over a joke internally that is too terrible not to share. "Hopefully, in this day and age, it doesn't involve an actual club." I mime whacking something with a large object.

The waitress hands me a bill and I set my card on the tray. She takes it away.

Thomas is fighting a smile as he stares at the table. "Puns, you've resorted to puns. It is definitely time for you to go and you have definitely had too much to drink."

Anthony winks and smiles.

I put my hands up in resignation, "See, light weight all the way."

Anthony clears his throat, "So, your sister Sarina, she still single?"

Thomas does a double take and looks at Anthony, "I've never met the woman, but are you sure you want to go down that road?"

Anthony goads him back. "You stood behind Muriel in the middle of that shit storm tonight and you're trying to get her guard down, now?"

I shake my head, "Yeah, it's definitely time for me to leave." The waitress gives me my card and a slip. I write out the tip for an equal amount to the total. I look into the aether and grab a line and say "See you later, boys." I wince as I evaporate into air. The last sounds I hear are Thomas gasping and Anthony groan.

Chapter 39

Mindworm

It is dark in the shed compared to the warm light of the bar and the stream of aether. I stumble and my fingers catch on a rough board, giving me a splinter. As the stinging sensation pokes at my mind, I halt at the sight of Gnasher. The gnome's hands are on his hips and he is puffing his pipe intently. "Your mother has had to deal with a bunch of council members coming in and out to protect the...", He stops and looks around cautiously and leans in so he can whisper.

I raise my hand in a stopping motion. "I understand who you're talking about."

"What did you do?" His look is pained and accusatory at the same time.

"I helped some family. Should I enter through the front or the back?"

He exhales, shakes his head and starts mumbling under his breath, "Back!"

"Thanks!"

I start down the cobble stoned and moss encrusted path. I pause at the back gate. The fountain is in a shower of light and noise. I breathe in the cool air and stare up at the stars. They call to me. It feels like an eternity since I floated there. I shake my head and wince. I walk to the back door, open it and note the thwacking sound of the screen door that I let flap behind me. In the breezeway, a wooden robotic arm appears and the door refuses to open. The electronic voice buzzes at me. "Unauthorized surveillance equipment present." I sigh and went through the unhooking process and enter the now open door.

My mother is by the stove pulling a kettle off the heat and pouring it into a teapot. She gives me a smile and comes over and hugs me. "Thank you, darling."

I breath in her scent of yeast and star-fire. It brings on a feeling of comfort. "You're welcome. Is that pot for Glinda? Can I take it up?"

Mom nods and adds it to a tray with two teacups. Then she adds another cup. There is a stack of chocolate chip brownies and some hazelnut caramel bars.

"Where did those come from?" Food can be made from magical transformation but it never tastes as flavorful as when a person actually takes the time to make it. My mother is great at making batches and saving them with preservation spells.

"I have a secret stash for emergencies." She points at the stove causing it to widen. "Which reminds me. I'm going to need to replenish my chicken stock supplies."

I start speculating about dimensions and where Mom keeps her baked goods. I walk toward the stairs, with my mother following me. I turn and ask, point blank, "How is she doing?"

My mother strokes the hand rail of the stairs, lost in thought. "She's... she's a mess."

"She's not alone, right?"

Mom has a gentle look, "She's with Gideon."

I start up the stairs and then I turn around, "I don't know where her room is."

Mom gives me an amused look and her eyes twinkle, "I know, that is why I'm here."

"Thanks, Mom."

She reaches out and ruffles my hair like when I was a child. She hesitates recalling my age, "Sorry dear."

"It's OK, Mom."

"I put them on your floor." She pauses again. "How did you get him to admit all that horrible stuff?"

I adjust the tray as she peers down at it. "He was channeling enough power to gate a house full of people to Fey-land, he couldn't spare any mental control to stop spewing the rancid thoughts germinating in his brain. All I had to do was ask."

We make it to the third floor and Mom gestures to a door that led through a wall that was normally an empty space.

I squint do a double take, "Mom, that's a gated door to Scotland!"

She nods, "Everyone needed to get back to their work and projects, and still be able to get here for Merlin duty. So I created house simulacrum for the cores and gave them access."

I frowned, "Can anyone go through those doors?"

"Dear-heart, how naive do you think I am? I have been around a bit longer, dear, then you. Certain people are keys. Now stand still a moment."

It feels like I am being coated with a gelatin-like substance on my aura. Then it sinks in and disappears from tactile touch. I turn to Mom, "This mean I can open the door now?"

She gives me an amused nod, "Yes."

I reach for the handle and pause, "Any passwords included?"

Mom raises an eyebrow, "Quit stalling."

I open the door and walk into a hall with mid-morning light streaming in. The hall was full of doors, "Which door, Mom?"

"The first on the left."

I adjust the tray in my hand, and tentatively knock on the door. Gideon answers the door with a weary look and then a look of relief passes over his face. He whispers, "You made it out!"

I give him a turn of my head nonchalantly and walk in. He adjusts, opening the door wider. He waves to my mother and shuts the door. Glinda is curled in a quilted coverlet in a fit full sleep. The skin around her eyes is red and puffy, and a basket of used tissues is on the floor by the bed. There is a crumpled up one in her left hand.

I set the tray down on the table by the bed with tea and sweets.

Gideon walks to the window that contains a window-seat strewn with large books, and sits down. He curls a book in his lap. I pour some tea and gesture for sugar and milk. He shakes his head "no." I walk it to him, then make myself some. When I turn around he is sprawled across the seat with his back on a pillow supported by a half hexagon wall. I remember the unanticipated embrace and nuzzle at the party. I know it was a pretense, but it had stirred some unexpected warm feelings inside me.

I try shaking my head to wipe the feelings away. That doesn't work. I sit on the other end of the window seat, next to his feet. I look out the window, taking in the view. It looks like a country estate. Leaves blow and the sun shines through drizzling rain.

Circe Syndrome

I take a sip of tea and look back at Glinda. Talking isn't always what people need after trauma, so I wait.

Gideon is shuffling through his book "Do you? I mean, have you heard?"

"What?" I turn and look at him, meeting his eyes.

He swallows, "I hear the first week is the hardest."

I nod, take a sip of tea, and wince at the heat of the drink, "Me, too. I understand it takes a good three months to a year to recover from, but it's never a complete recovery."

He buries his face in his hands to cover up his tearing.

"Look, if you want to go take a shower and rest a bit, I can watch for a while." I reach out and squeeze his forearm.

He sets the book next to him, and stares at the floor. I can tell he is weighing options, " OK, but check her aura every fifteen minutes, there are these..." He pauses mid-sentence and his face takes on a mask of disgust, "Energy ticks that appear and start harvesting. Then these emotional worms try to stir up more despair."

I frown, " OK, what do I do with them?"

He sighs, and sternly says, "Just destroy them. My mother," He gestures to a stack of mason jars, "wants a sample of each, every hour. I personally could care less. Just destroy them. I burn 'em."

I understanding his rage and offer no resistance, "Go rest." I change my vision to power vision. Glinda's aura is a mess. The colors are all over, but free of foreign creatures.

Before he leaves, Gideon leans over and kisses my forehead, "Thank you, I'll see you in an hour."

Butterflies catch in my stomach and I watch him leave trying not to read anything into this affection. I remind myself that he is European, and this is a common greeting and leave taking.

Glinda whispers, "Thanks for getting him out a minute."

I kneel close to the bed next to her. "I have some tea and brownies; do you want some?"

Tears stream out of her eyes. "It hurts so much. I feel like my heart has been shredded to pieces."

I levitate the tray to Glinda's eye level. I take a plate and sit the chocolate brownie on it and place it in front of her. Then I make a cup of tea for her with two teaspoons of sugar and a lot of milk. I set it on the corner of her night stand. I put the tray back. "I know it hurts." I find it hard not to tear up watching and feeling the emotional pain going through her. I look away a second to get myself under control. "I find it won't solve it, but chocolate always helps. And homemade good help more."

A look of wonder passes over her face as she looks down at the brownie, "Homemade?"

"Mom." I smile letting my pride in my mother out.

Glinda wipes her eyes. She reaches out to take the dark, moist, crumbling, edge brownie. She sits herself up a little and I watch her eyes widen in pleasure as the rich theobromine hits her. "Whoa! That is, that is something." She takes a sip of tea. "Can I talk to you, Muriel, about Vic without you scowling like my brother does."

"Yeah," I sit back on the floor, my back to the mattress and stare out at the sky in the window above the seat. Clouds move about making patterns. Glinda's voice is soft and plaintive. Things she says reminded me of Sarah. Essentially she was a thrill seeker. She craves excitement like a fish craves water. She wove her story, talking about it as if she had it all under control. Vic had played on her arrogance and thrill seeking.

I have no idea how long she talks and I listen. The light outside changes. I have removed a few aura parasites and they are in mason jars. Glinda has devoured all the bars and finishes the pot of tea when Gideon walks back in. Glinda was crying.

Circe Syndrome

My heart aches for her. People deserved to be loved and not be used in this way. An idea is tugging at my mind. I have this idea to help abate her depression to a lesser level.

Gideon stands at the end of the bed and glances at me on the floor, and then at book he had cradled on the window sill. "I've been backward and forwards in the family glimory, and there is nothing about cures for this besides being vigilant for a certain amount of time."

I bite my lower lip, take a breath and speak, "I have an idea."

I feel them both look at me. Clumsily, I stand and take the teacup and plate of crumbs from Glinda to the tray.

"My dear girl, you can't drop something like that in the air and not finish." Gideon's voice was full of amusement.

I scratch my head and sit back on the floor crossed leg style, where my eyes can meet Glinda's eyes. "It's a bit illegal." My back is to the window seat and I'm facing both of them.

The siblings stare at each other. I have no doubt they are having a telepathic conversation between them. I wait as I examine the stitches of the tartan woven afghan sticking out on the edge of the bed.

A decision must have been made, because Glinda speaks softly, "Maybe it's not illegal here."

I frown, "Oh it is. It's a treaty violation between nations."

Gideon is impatient, "Just tell us."

"Well, that is part of the problem. Just mentioning the idea starts its influence in motion. You have to ask me. I can't bring it up."

Gideon rubs his forehead, "Lovely."

Glinda is interested, "I understand. Gideon, call the family solicitor and Mum."

Gideon raises his hands, "What?" He tunes out a moment and summons the people requested.

Glinda sits up straighter. "What is she called outside the family circles?" She points at me with an index finger in an unflattering manner.

I watch Gideon as his features change from confusion to understanding. I am surprised that there was no disgust from the realization. He begins to pace, "The wording on this has got to be very careful."

I stand to sit on the window seat and scoot back until my back touches the window. I can feel the vibrations of the raindrops hitting it. The rain is coming down in sheets. I stare at the wooden baseboard of the bed and notice an elaborate carving of dragons and fairies. I am trying not to speak until more witnesses come. "Should I have Mom come too?"

Gideon gives me a reassuring smile, "I already asked her. She is your parole officer right?"

I nod, "And Dad."

He looks away, "They are both coming."

Glinda asks, "Parole officers?"

I follow a pattern on the glimory book on the bench. "Yeah."

There is an uncomfortable silence for ten minutes, Glinda finally breaks it, "Has anyone given you a time line?"

Gideon chuckles, "They're almost here."

There is a knock at the door. Glinda covers herself more. Gideon lets an assortment of people in. My Mom looks around, "Where's Muriel?"

I lift my hand against the window. My mother shakes her head at me and motions me to sit up properly. I sit up and hug my knees to myself.

One of the group of people is a gray haired, massive man in a formal, pinstriped suit. His shirt is crisp white. He has the faint smell of smoke about him. He comes to the window and reaches out his hand. "Hi, I'm the McQweston solicitor. My name is Mr. Stodge."

His grip is firm and efficient as we clasp hands. I feel him take the measure of me within legal limits. I do the same. He gives me a knowing smirk and returns to talk to a woman with similar features to Aoife who has also come. The twins' mother has auburn hair and pixie like features, she wears a tartan dress with a green knitted shawl. Aoife hugs her and calls her Megan.

Megan, Aoife and Mr. Stodge stand whispering to each other. My parents and Gideon move close to me. Mom gestures for me to stand.

Mr. Stodge clears his throat. "So no one has said out loud what we are all thinking, yet."

We all nod in unison.

He turns and looks Gideon, Glinda and I in the eye as he says, "Especially the three people in the room before everyone arrived."

The three of us nod again.

He takes out a device that looks like a metal cigar with holes along its side, and inscribed with restricted time magic sigils.

He fidgets with it nervously. "This will create a transcript of everything said in this room for the last forty-two minutes. Everyone copasetic with me using it?"

I look at Glinda. She meets my eyes, smiles and nods, and we all say, "Aye," out loud.

His fingers run along the holes in a combination and the cigar buzzes and starts printing a few pages. He shuffles through the pages. Aoife, their mother, and my father look over his shoulder to read it.

Glinda exasperated wonders, "May I ask yet?"

My mother, Mr. Stodge and Aoife confer. Glinda's mother

speaks up, "I am comfortable with you requesting this of Muriel Anahat as long as it is under your own volition."

Glinda looks at me. "Muriel, will you create a mind-worm to help me deal with this emotional situation I find myself in?"

Mr. Stodge speaks, "That is Miss McQweston, addressing Miss Anahat."

"Did you have anything specific in mind in terms of words?" I look out the window, not wanting anyone accusing me of influencing her, or them.

"I was thinking something to the effect of, 'Victor Opiate meant nothing to me.'"

I am staring at the cornice of this building on an outcropping. The water is being sliced then reconnects beneath its gargoyle face. The air is still palpable in the room. I think about the words and frown. "That would be a bad idea."

Everyone gasps.

Glinda frowns at me, "You mean you won't do it?"

"No, it is just that wording will cause trouble later on. You have experienced emotional trauma. That does not go away. You need to deal with it and heal. Otherwise, you'll have a psychological break later on that could be deadly."

Aiofe's voice is venomous and full of scorn, "Then what do you suggest?"

I bite my lower lip. I kneel next to the bed and look imploringly into Glinda's face. How I approach her begins the mind worm. "I was thinking more along the lines of everyone makes mistakes in love when young. Luckily you were already out growing him."

Glinda numbly repeats the words, "Out growing him."

I look at Mr. Stodge. He gives me a smile and looks at Glinda, "Yes, out growing him."

Circe Syndrome

I look at Glinda's mother, she straightens, nods thoughtfully, "Definitely, he is a whim of a childish heart. You were on the brink of out growing him."

Aoife stiffens when we all look at her, "Sure, even I let myself fall into the persuasion of an Elf in my youth. I eventually out grew him."

Gideon gives me an amazed smile and looks at Glinda, "You are definitely at the moment when you realize what you want out of life has nothing to do with him. You have out grown him."

My parents add similar comments with the same three words.

I reach out a hand to the back of Glinda's head. I look around the room and address them all, " OK, let's say it all together now." I give Glinda a wink, "Even you, Glinda."

As the words, "You have out grown him," fill the air, I look into Glinda's brain. I find a small new neuron net being created. I send power into it to strengthen it and encourage more connection paths.

I withdraw my hand and stand. I walk to the wall facing Glinda, that was lined with bookcases. I run my hand across it in a diagonal pattern. The books realign, creating the phrase over and over with the titles. I walk to the end of the bed and place my fingers on the coverlet, my mind focuses on the stitches. I map out a repeat pattern of the words. "I have out grown the need for elven company."

When I finish this last step, Glinda sighs, "The pain is still there, but it's not as raw, more of a dull ache than a bleeding wound."

I give her a reassuring squeeze on her wrist.

Glinda snuggles down and falls asleep.

Aoife and Glinda's mother walk to the other side of the bed and examine her with power vision. I walk back to the window seat and sit down.

There is a palpable tension in the room. A slow smile comes across Glinda's mother's face. Aoife still looks severe, but nods at all Mr. Stodge's questions.

Gideon walks over to his mother. She hugs him. My parents and I make eye contact. I grab the empty tray. I join them and we start moving toward the door.

Mr. Stodge stops me at the door. "I want to inform you that you are not to be alone with Miss McQweston without another Heska in the room for six months. It is believed that once a person successfully does a mind manipulation on someone, they are viewed to be more susceptible to that person's influence for six months. That was the cleanest mind manipulation I've ever witnessed, though."

I give him a puzzled expression, "How many have you witnessed?"

He gives me a mysterious smile and walks back towards Glinda's family.

Gideon breaks away and takes my hand and kisses it, "Thank you. Can I treat you to a meal?"

I look at Glinda.

He smiles, "Mum and Aunty Aoife are going to watch her for a while."

I turn, and see my parents have already left. " OK."

He takes the tray out of my hands. He closes the door behind us. "You know it's Friday here already. You have a date tonight, right?"

I open the door to my mother's house. My mother gives me a knowing smile and takes the tray from Gideon. "You don't have to come home yet." She closes the door.

I give Gideon an amused look, suspecting he asked my mother first if this was OK. "So, how do you know I have a date?"

Circe Syndrome

Gideon walks toward the other side of the hall to a grand staircase, ignoring my question, "It's almost lunch time here."

Chapter 40

Haggling Haggis

I make to follow him, and stall while stare out a window. This dwelling, looks out over a valley with a waterfall falling over its edge. I take a breath and let the awe I feel over the natural beauty fill me.

Gideon comes back and stands next to me. He rests his hand on the sill, which I realize is stone. I look around the hall, the stone structure and heavy carved oak doors. I'm in a castle. He admires me. "That was a brilliant idea, you know?"

"You should find a way to work the phrase into her day to day, for a month. How is she really? Is it true about twins' spiritual connection?" I move toward the stairs and walk down a step.

He cocks his head, "Kind of. She is lot better. The suicide watch won't be as intent as it has been." He walks next to me and starts down the stairs.

Circe Syndrome

I was scanning the family paintings lining the walls and making sure I didn't miss a step.

His voice is tentative, "So, that vampire?"his voice is stilted.

"Thomas?" I flip my hair out of my face and meet his eyes.

He gives me a serious look, "Is there something I should know? Your mother suspects, but she doesn't know."

I frown, "Not that I'm aware of. We work together a great deal. I work for The Collective these days. After what I just did in that room, I'm probably going to be going deeper in."

His eyebrows raise, "Deeper in?" He pauses at the front door.

"Yeah!" I changed the subject, "Where are we going?"

He opens the door, revealing a village street instead of the open wilderness that I saw from the window. He shrugs, "The local pub."

" OK." I nod.

At the end of the block of the cobblestone street is a little pub covered in shutters and ivy. The roof is thatched. The sign board has the picture of a Unicorn's head. "It's called Unicorn Head."

I look at the sign and look at him with a bemused look, "Ahh, I see."

When the door opens the air is filled with this sweet spicy smell. The floor is covered in sawdust. The decor was all dark paneling and brass details. He guides me to a seat near a window. Two grey haired men in kilts were bickering at the bar, while an amused young women polished glasses. She nods at Gideon. She comes to our table and sets down napkins. "Something to start yah with?" Her words run together to sound like one word. It takes me a moment to piece it out.

Gideon gives her a warm grin, "I'll take a coke."

I bob my head, "I'll take the same."

I look out the window, Gideon clears his throat, "Are you tired?"

"Not really, I just slept for three days. I'm definitely hungry."

"You also battled an Elf mage?"

I shake my head, "Not head on. I took advantage of a situation and distracted him. That was unexpected, though. I was just going to feel things out."

He takes my hand and looks at me, "We are lucky you decided to wake last night and not tomorrow."

The barkeep clears her throat and Gideon withdrew his hand. She gave us both amused looks and set down our drinks. She turns her head and starts yelling at the men at the bar.

I examine the menu. When I look up catch his eye, say sincerely, "I'm just glad we got her away. Fey-land extractions are tricky on easy days."

He leans in, "What did you just say?"

I scratch my chin and smirk, "You heard me. So what do you recommend?"

He sits back with a smug grin, "I think since I tried the matzah ball soup you should try the Haggis."

I involuntarily wrinkle my nose and wince, "And what is that again?"

He props his head on his arm, "Heart, liver, and lungs minced with onions and suet then boiled in a stomach."

I feel the color drain from my face and wait a beat as I digest this idea, "What animal?" I understand this is a trust game.

He takes a sip of his Coke, he gives me a measuring glance, "Sheep, It's really, um, good."

I nod as I trace the wood grain, "How long is it cooked for?"

His head bobbles in thought, "About three hours."

I look back into his eyes, "Should I be concerned about the pathogens transferred from the sheep's lungs?"

He snorts, "It's been boiled for three hours!"

I acquiesce, "What should I have for the side? Neeps and tatties?"

He gives me a big grin, "Perfect!"

I cock my head and play with my straw, "What exactly is a neep and a tattie?"

"Turnips and potatoes."

I run my hand through my hair and nod, "Yeah, OK. I'm surprised you didn't start me out slow, with like a meat pie or potato cake. It's not like I had you try gelfilte fish."

He gives me a thoughtful expression, "Gelfilte fish? I normally like fish. What's that?"

I think about the grey slimy lumps of fish particles in ball shapes. I laugh. I imagine his look of disgust in trying to eat some.

The barkeep comes back. She looks at me expectantly, "I'll take your order."

I look at Gideon, then take a breath. "I'll take an order of haggis with a side of neeps and tatties, please."

The bar keep gives me a big grin, "Very good!" She turns and looks at Gideon and snidely says, "And you Mi Laird?"

He sighs, "Cut it out Edith, I'll have the same."

She gives an exasperated sigh back, rolls her eyes, "Coming up!" She walks away.

Gideon taps the table, "Didn't you have a chemistry question for me?"

"I do. It's about gold. Is there a history of transformation of other elements into gold?"

He gives me a playful expression, "Alchemy? Lots of mythology around it. Some true, some not. It is not a question I expected from you? Why?" He crosses his arms and looks at me with lowered lids.

I debate some other excuse, but decide the truth is easier, "You're aware of my hobby?"

"Saving people?"

I blush, "The other one."

He sits back, "Oh, the planet one."

"Yeah, I owe a big favor. It's funny really the one hobby influenced the other. I was asked to make a planet of gold."

Gideon chokes on his drink, "What?"

I calmly repeat myself, "A planet of gold."

He throes up his hands, "What being would presume?"

I take a breath and exhaled, "Vulcan."

He stills, and swallows hard, "The Greek?"

I shake my head, "Roman."

"God! How did you end up in his presence? Why would he expect..."

I shrug, "He did me a favor. It was a request, not a requirement."

He shakes his head with his eyes closed, "So, you're trying to make a planet of gold?"

I take a sip of soda, "Yes."

He frowns "You would have to rob other planets of that mineral to get enough."

I play with my straw as I spin it in the cup, "Plus, getting it to spin?"

He frowns, "Why do you think he wants it?"

Circe Syndrome

I look out the window of the pub and notice the glass is old, that the bottom is thicker than the top. "He forges weapons for the gods. Only celestial gold can kill a god."

Gideon sits back. "It doesn't even break down well."

I tap my finger fast in thought, "It's real soft as metals go though?"

He shakes his head, "But deterioration is important to conversion of energy to matter and for life. Of course that is assuming you want life on the planet."

We started talk about fission vs. fusion. From there we discuss the theory of planet rotation. I tell him about my theories on particle vibration and the song of the universe.

He teases me about that idea and wonders if it made a top ten song ever. I think and laugh that most of the hits have parts of that song in it. We fall into silence as he considers his drink.

When the food comes an idea os starting to form in my mind. Fusion happens in stars. I shake my head and stow it away for later and let Gideon's voice and dark humor take me.

I tentatively took a bite of Haggis; I was surprised, it had a nutty flavor. The turnips and potatoes had been cooked in a soup stock.

Gideon starts devouring his, "What do you think?"

I take a swig of soda as I chew on the meat. "Not bad."

He gives me this ear to ear smile.

I return the smile, "So, what do you do when you aren't rescuing your sister?"

He gives a long off dreamy look, "Pharmaceutical researcher."

" OK."

"More entertaining than you think. It involves a lot of puzzles. One has to approach from different angles."

I stare at this odd picture of a man standing on the top of a log, end up, in a kilt doing a high kick. "I imagine it is. The whole figuring out the release time of medicine."

He fidgets with his fork, "So, saving people is a thing you do?"

I shrug, "If someone asks for help, I know how hard that it is ask, so I am going to do what I can to help. Anyone would."

He points at me with his fork giving me a serious measured look, "No, they won't! Is it part of what you do for the Collective?"

I tap my fingers on the table top. "I'm just a recruiter."

He raises an eyebrow as a baffled look crosses his face. "Oh, and the vampire?"

"My specialty is vampires. Thomas was my first one."

He winces, "How does that become one's specialty?"

"Well I really don't relate with college graduating Heska well. Weres are a bit rough for me. Zombies and ghouls make me squirm. Ghosts ignore me." I take a drink. I shrug, "I went to a vampire bar and I'm successful there. I really haven't tried other creatures since this venue has worked for me."

"Other creatures?"

I list off with my fingers, "Trolls, dragons, elves, fairies and of course abominables."

He points at me, "I had forgotten about the Bigfoot population in your area."

I chuckle, "They sure wish everyone else would."

He laughs, "I bet they do. So have you ever met one?"

"Met what?"

He cut his haggis, "A hairy humanoid creature?"

I cock my head to the right, "Oh, that would be classified."

"Really?"

I smirked, "No."

He squint, "No to the meeting, or to the classification?"

I gasp a giggle, "Both." I gesture at him. Changing the subject was a need now, "You and your sister's names aren't traditional Scottish names?"

"That is true. But yours is."

"Is it? I always thought Mom was trying to name me in a modern version of Miriam without naming me after someone still alive in our family. It means the same in both doesn't it? Woman of the sea."

Gideon frowns, "Why would that be important to the person not being alive?"

I look out the window and watch a child chase a ball bouncing irregularly on the cobblestone corners. "Mom's great aunt is named Miriam. In our superstitious moments, we believe the angel of death can get confused if more than one person alive has the same first and last name. So we don't name after the living."

He cocks his head, "Oh, I see."

"Why did your parents name you two your names?"

He shrugs, "I think my parents just like them. Mother like the tales of Frank Baum a lot so I think they named my sister, then wanted another "G" name for me."

"Does the alliteration bug you two?" I ask.

He gets a thoughtful expression and nods, "Sometimes."

The check comes and I reach for my wallet, he puts his hand up as a stopping motion. "It's the least I can do, and I offered."

He pays the barkeep and we head out the door. The wind sweep through the street setting leaves in motion and a drizzling rain soaks our heads.

I look at my watch, still set to Pacific North American time. It is four in the morning at home, "I should head home. I have a personnel report to write."

He gives me a plaintive look, "What were you doing before you came?"

I look away, thinking about Thomas and Anthony, "Reviewing the verbal report with two agents."

"I could smell the vampire and the metal tang guy, at the gate, permeating you when you walked in."

This makes me self-conscious, "Sorry, I should have showered."

He reaches out and squeezes my wrist, "No, I didn't mean it that way, I was just wondering about the metal tang guy, I've noticed it before."

"Another agent, Heska. I used to think he was obnoxious, now I just think he's really thorough."

He nods, "He have a name?"

I smirk, "Anthony."

"He a close friend?"

I give a matter fact response, "Nope, more of a new acquaintance and work colleague." I don't feel the need to go into the history of his brother and my sister.

"Interesting."

"Anthony? I don't know if he's your type, but I can ask? He keeps asking about Sarina. But he might be bi." I say matter of factly.

Gideon stops and shakes his head, "Please, don't trouble him. I'm not interested, but thanks for your offer."

I shrug, I am so confused now. I was finding him alluring and distracting, but now I am not sure if he is interested in women.

Circe Syndrome

He starts to walk again, and over his shoulder he says, "I'm personally not into men in a romantic way."

"Oh." One hurdle down I think, about fifty more to go. I suddenly feel light headed. I have not had a crush in a while.

He finally breaks the rhythm of the walk, "How about you?"

I smile, "Oh, I do like men in a romantic way."

He reaches down as he smiles and takes my hand. He has tough calluses on his thumbs and the interior padding under the thumb. We walk hand in hand in silence to the door of the house. I keep telling myself not to read too much into this. Nevertheless, my stomach becomes a mess of butterflies. He gives me a warm smile before he withdraws his hand and take out keys for the door. He opens it and holds it open for me. Aoife is there in the foyer as we walk in. She is yelling into a cellphone. She gestures for Gideon to wait. He stops. I suddenly feel out of place.

I walk close to him, "I'm going to head home."

He nods, "See you later."

I climb the stairs and walk to the end of the hall and open the door. I walk down the hall to my room. When I closed the door behind me it feels small and oppressive. I feel lonely. I thought about the smell comment. So I go, take a shower and change.

Even though I hadn't slept since noon the day before, I was not tired. Three days of sleep made me feel awake still. So I sit down at my vanity and turn it back into a drawing board. I grab a fresh sheet of paper.

I start drawing a mushroom drenched turtle while thinking about bio-luminescence and photosynthesis. I have to keep shaking my head to get the image of the curly haired, young man with the Scottish brogue out of my mind.

Somewhere in the midst of drawing the turtle, I start making notes on the page for plant DNA and algae DNA. I start playing with the idea of fireflies, really big and very bright fireflies. This evolves to other insects including bright moths, glow bees and disco ball beetles.

Chapter 41

Controls

I fill sheets with ideas. My mother sends me a mental note around noon. She is glad I am home and would like me to join my aunts and her for lunch. I try to refuse. I am enjoying the roll I am on but my mother let me know that she is being polite in letting me think I have a choice. I am expected for lunch.

I reluctantly left the sketches, and paused to stretch, as I realized I have lost feeling in my feet. I grab a jacket and go through my door. I arrive in the foyer as my mother, Aunt Shirley and Aunt Hannah arrived. "Where are we going?" I sigh.

Mom nods to her sister, "Aunt Hannah wants to go to the Wayfarer restaurant."

I put on a forced cheerful face, "That sounds great."

Aunt Shirley harrumphs at me. "Cannon Beach, isn't that the place where all those hippies did those weird rituals?"

We are walking through the front yard and around to the side.

I sigh at her, "There really haven't been any hippies for, like forty years, Aunt Shirley."

Aunt Hannah giggles, "If there are any still around, that is where they would be."

"Didn't some of those rites cause some of the newer magical families?" I ask.

My mother nods, "Yes, dear, it did."

Aunt Shirley scowls, "But they really wrecked havoc with the aether. My poor Morty had to go into debt to a couple of dragons and elves to balance it out and stop the coast from exploding."

This makes me pause. Dragon debt is a disturbing and scary thing. I think about the cigar and the jar of smoke gnats. My mother and Aunt Hannah exchange knowing looks. Mordecai is their brother.

At the shed my mother looks at me, "So, I'll take Hannah and you dialyosefosize Aunt Shirley."

I look to Aunt Shirley. She nods, "I've never been there, so fine."

To dialyosefosize safely, one must have been to the location before.

My mother and Aunt Hannah and sharing an intimate sister joke as they disappear. Aunt Shirley look at me, "It's weird how well those two get along!"

I nod, understanding that they are siblings. "Oh, they fight, it's just a subtle dance."

She raises an eyebrow and leans in, looking for more info.

I am not going to play. "Where are you and Uncle Mordecai living these days?"

Circe Syndrome

She shakes her head back and forth, "A little bit here, a little bit there. We have a regular rotation with the grand kids. Quite heavenly, really."

We walk into the shed. Gnasher run up out of breath, "Miss Muriel, there's a troll at the gate demanding to see you!"

I feel my eyebrows raise. This is curious. I look at my aunt and motion her to follow as I tail the gnome. We walk to the front and are face to shin with a troll casting a shadow on the yard and squinting. In a rough voice it grunts, "Miss Muriel!"

I squint up into his great silhouette. The voice is familiar. "Master Attila is that you?"

When he laughs, it sounds like boulders smashing, "You have grown, as have I."

I blink, and calmly say, "I see. Do you need help with something?"

He sits down and pokes the fence, then wipes snot from his nose across it. "Yeah."

I take a breath and step closer, into striking distance. My Aunt steps back. I address him again. "What is it?"

He scratches his head and then his armpits. "I'm trying to remember."

"Take your time." I sit down cross-legged on the side walk and pull on a piece of grass. I start analyzing its structure, and begin thinking about bio-luminescence.

The troll starts to sweat and glare at the sun. Trolls rarely came out on sunny days. It must be really important for him to leave his bridge.

Cars on the street have started to swerve since part of his backside extended into the street. Aunt Shirley scratches her head. She gestures at the road. "What do the norms see, with him sitting here?"

I am in a half meditative state and my voice is dreamy when I respond, "Only what they want to see. Probably a fallen tree."

Aunt Shirley nods in acknowledgement.

Twenty minutes later, Attila gives me a glassy eyed stare. "Oh? Miss Muriel? I was just thinking of you."

Aunt Shirley scoffs and mumbles under her breath, I can still hear it in the distance.

I raise a silencing hand and sneak a glare at her. Her diatribe stops. I don't want him distracted and taking another twenty minutes to remember why he came. "How thoughtful. Anything you need?"

He scratches his jowly chin and nods, "One of my father's prized crown jewels was just tricked away from him."

I have a vague memory of the conversation with Jasper a few days ago. "Was he a thin man, gaunt and elegantly dressed?"

"Fancy cloths, yes. Not a scrap of meat on him. Not worth eating, not that I do that sort of thing." He looks at the ground and whispers, "Every day."

Aunt Shirley snorts, "I bet!"

I walk closer to the gate and my aunt yells, "What are you doing?"

I give my aunt a "Cool it" hand gesture, and place my hand on the gate. "Have you seen it?" I am curious if he had seen the jewel his father was missing.

He puts a massive boulder size hand on the gate next to me and gives me an amused smile. "Yeah!"

I raise my hand and hovered it over his left pinky. "May I?"

He sighs, "Yes, Miss Muriel, please. Dah, ain't killed no one in fifty years, this might push him over."

Circe Syndrome

I lower my hand onto his calloused skin made of neurons. Memories fly into me from contact with him. It is a whirlwind of dubious sights, sounds, textures and experiences coloring my consciousness. I pause, take a breath and close my eyes. Trolls are multi-dimensional creatures and their consciousness swims in perceptions from these dimensions. That is why they are made of neurons and their speech is slow. They have to slow down to perceive humans and talk to them. The dichotomy of the real world and the remembered world in view, give me vertigo. "Think only of the jewel," I remind him.

I expect to see a ring. I was theorizing Jasper is going to propose to Isabelle, but it is not a ring. It is a golden arm cuff, woven with platinum and studded with thumb size rubies and emeralds it fills my vision. The configuration is of a lotus flower. It sparks a memory. It is the cuff of influence. Also called the Siren Lotus. The cuff had been lost centuries ago, actually the Siren Lotus was believed destroyed. Hitler was rumored to have the Lotus for a while, it gave its wearer the ability to sway crowds to his or her point of view. That would be extremely handy to a ruler. I withdraw my hand quickly before my mind bursts with the experiences downloading in a stream to me.

I blink, thinking he didn't just want something that looked like that, he wanted something that worked like that. Making enchanted items is something that required a license and a permit. There are inspectors, and forms in triplicate. There are also rules on what they shouldn't be able to do. I slowly move from striking distance of the troll. Trolls get easily distracted by the other dimensions and hit at things elsewhere. Most Heska are unaware of this and think they are just random killing machines. Few have spent time with them, as I had.

My right heel is almost crushed, and Aunt Shirley screams in terror as I looked back at Attila to talk to him and his fist lands a centimeter from my heel. "I have an idea but I'm going to need a few days." I have no idea. I am buying time.

He blinks and his glazes eyes stare past me to my screaming aunt. "Who, red hair?"

I turn and look at my aunt, who is accumulating aether energy in an alarming fashion. I stand in front, of her blocking the troll's view of her. "She's my aunt. I'll see you in a few days. Which bridge are you living under these days?"

"Steel Bridge. Two days, Muriel. Just two days. I'm calling in my favor." He holds up two log sized fingers.

I shiver. Trolls like having beings under their thumbs. They only keep you around if think they have something on you. Once a favor is received, a person is more likely to die. "Got it."

He stands, dislodging a branch from a tree and raining debris on the parked cars on the street. He lumbers down the road.

I turn to find my aunt almost completely purple with pent up aether. I moved forward quickly. Aunt Shirley is in a dangerous state. That energy needs to be formed and used.

My aunt backs away. Her hands are in a pushing motion.

I open up my aether receptors in my aura and closed the distance. There is fear in my aunt's eyes. She is about to lose control and she is terrified she will hurt me. I speak gently, "I can disperse that without it creating damage. Stop running, let me help you before you explode!"

The front doors bang open, distracting Aunt Shirley who looks to see her husband Mordecai shuffling down the steps. This gave me time to close the distance and get a hand on her arm. My grasp releases the flood of aether into me. I freeze, and channel the energy through a maze-like pattern I have designed through my body. I reach out and cause the oak tree to reach for me. As the tree and I touch, I send the now doubled energy through the tree cells. The tree lights up with green light. Buds of acorns coat the branches and the leaves began to glow. I map the trees flow, and with its permission, guide the energy it couldn't leak back into the aether during photosynthesis back into the ground. I direct this energy in the ground to find minerals. Because it is the last thing I thought about, I build a copy of the Siren Lotus cuff from the specs in my head. I leave it there in the ground beneath the tree with instructions for the tree to guard it.

A curious amusement goes through me. When the energy has been safely dispersed, I turn to find my uncle Mordecai hugging my aunt and whispering to her pale crying form. He is angry when he glares at me. "How could you have exposed her to a troll, Muriel? I thought you had more sense than that. You know she's a warrior mage!"

I stand my ground, still heady from the power I just wielded. Reminded myself to stay humble but not to give ground here. "I didn't invite him, Uncle. That troll came on his own volition. It seems Jasper moved on that recommendation I gave him."

Uncle Mordecai shakes his head, "Ahhh, no good deed goes unpunished."

I shrug, "So it would seem."

"She, she, she!" Aunt Shirley stammers and points at me. "How?"

Mordecai hugs her closer, he strokes her hair. "You're alright, dear heart. You're alright that is all that matters."

"Bbbbbbbut?" Her hand points as it waves at me.

Clay rushes out the door and stands between me and my aunt and uncle. This is interesting, he is sworn to them. Golems don't just protect someone else. Clay's back is to me and he is facing them.

It is time to de-escalate the situation. I sigh, "Do you still want to go to lunch?"

Uncle Mordecai stares daggers at me, Aunt Shirley sighs, "I suppose so."

Clay moves to the side. I puzzle what they were going to attack me with and which one it would have been.

Aunt Shirley gestures for a hug. I tentatively move forward and hug them. Uncle Mordecai pats my back. "You just scared her, Muriel. She didn't want to be responsible for killing us all and taking out a few city blocks."

Aunt Shirley gives me a sober look. "How did you know you could handle that?" She then peers at my Uncle, "How did you know she could handle that, you moved to distract me so she could do what she did."

I look at my Uncle expectantly. I am not technically supposed to say. He clears his throat, "It's a family thing. We spindle magic."

Aunt Shirley frowns, "What?"

I looked at the tree. I am having problems remembering something. I examine it, then look underground where my mind is telling me to. I analyze the root system then note this golden cuff with the root growing through it. The memory of just forging a Siren Lotus went back through me. I realize the tree has grown a root through it, the tree is now wearing the Siren Lotus. I am feeling a strong urge to put manure on the ground by the tree. I shake my head, I smirk about the advantage the tree is taking of the situation. This is going to be interesting.

Mordecai is still talking to Aunt Shirley, "Instead of being vessels for aether, we are more circuits or conduits. We create streams through our bodies that we can tap for spells."

Aunt Shirley holds her head and looks at Uncle Mordecai. "Did you teach our children this?"

He gives her a wink, "Of course, dear heart. "

She stammers, "But I thought that could drive a person insane?"

He nods, "It does, for some. Not all. There is a temperament check. Our son Freddie shouldn't, I shouldn't. But one of our children can. Caleb, it's as natural for him as breathing. Muriel here is another that it gives no ill effects to. I know how to use it, that is how I've helped you in similar situations."

She frowns, "Our son Caleb? You kept this a secret."

He nods, "It's a very big, need to know secret. In some countries, it is illegal."

Aunt Shirley shakes her head as she processed the statements. "There is something else she did. What was it?"

Mordecai gives me a speculative gaze. "I bet, but you can't remember and if she doesn't tell us we will never know."

I blink at the tree that is whispering with command magic not to look at it. I shrug. I make a hard note in my mental calendar to work on the magic item paperwork. Though The Collective will want it destroyed immediately. I send a thought to my printer to print the form.

Uncle Mordecai looks out at the now empty street, "Where were you two going?"

"Lunch at the coast with Mom and Aunt Hannah. "

He grunts and looks at Clay. "Let's go fishing."

They both saunter away to the house and Aunt Shirley gives me a nod toward the teleport shack. I smile and follow her lead.

Chapter 42

Several Secrets

I wince as Aunt Shirley and I land in the sand. I thought about how long it took me to have my skin grow back. I look about. My mother approaches us alone. She has a bemused look on her face, I am curious why. She nods to Aunt Shirley. "Thanks for the heads up about you two running late."

I look around for Aunt Hannah, puzzled. I hold out a hand in supplication. "Aunt Hannah?"

Mom jerks her head out toward the ocean. "She was called away also."

At that moment a whale with a huge horn crests and Aunt Hannah gets off and wades to the shore dragging a long spiral horn. Ivory and from an animal but about three yards long. The grin on her face is huge. The sunlight on the spiral horn makes it glow iridescently. I slip into magic sight and blink at the blinding light. I note its shape and the power while realizing the whale she just rode in on. Narwhal horn.

Circe Syndrome

I swallow, "Is that Narwhal horn?"

Her expression saddens. "An old friend passed away and left me this."

I reach out and hug her. I get soggy from her wet clothing. "How are you doing? Was it expected?"

She sighs, and runs a hand through her long wet hair, drying it. "Not really. I am going to miss him. I know you know how grieving is."

I shrug, "It's not about me right now. It's about you."

She gives me a grin and musses my hair. "You are always so perceptive."

I point to the horn, "What are you going to do with that?"

Her eyes twinkle. "I have a client who has been wanting to procure this type of thing. There is a pharmaceutical company I work with. It likes to incorporate the properties of magical creatures into their manufacturing equipment. Especially for certain Heska medications."

I cock my head in understanding. "Did your friend know what you planned to do with the horn?"

Aunt Hannah raises an eyebrow at me, "Yes, there was a contract exchange."

I raise an eyebrow, I wonder what a narwhal wanted in exchange for its horn being given to a major corporation. She shakes her head at me, signaling to not bother and ask.

I stare out at the water and watch the whales breach and swim away with a wave of their horns, spray creating rainbows in the surf.

My mother sighs at her little sister and fans her fingers at her soaked clothes. "You going to finish drying off?"

Aunt Hannah wrinkles her nose and tucks some hair behind her ear and twists her torso slightly. The clothes are dried and looked freshly pressed when she stops twisting.

I give my mother a once over. There is a windblown look to her hair. I squint, "What have you been up to, Mother?"

She reaches out and moves my hair and chuckles softly, "You miss nothing, do you dear?"

I cock my head, "You didn't answer."

She laughs, "I know." She winks and looks at Aunt Shirley. A concerned look passes over her face, "Hi, Shirley, everything OK?"

Aunt Shirley nods at me, "This one consorts with Trolls."

Aunt Hannah gasps and my mother raises an eyebrow, "Does she, now?"

I shrug, "Sometimes."

Aunt Shirley fumes, "You were so comfortable with that beast! It was terrifying!"

I draw in the sand with my foot, "They are not really beasts, they are really sophisticated creatures."

My mother smiles at me. She gives an imploring look, "Really?"

My mind replays the contact with Attila's skin, how the dimensions burn through my mind. I use the moving ocean to keep my balance and I blink at the screaming gulls. "Their skins are knitted neurons; they think with every limb."

Mom blinks, waiting for more.

I turn away from her following a seagulls flight with my gaze to act distracted. This part of my life I keep to myself. She has secrets, my time playing with Trolls was private. There are secrets that I was privy to that I could never reveal. Attila and I had been best friends as children for several years. I always had his back and he had mine. His family never understood and I knew mine would try to understand it more, which would not be good for the Trolls.

I turn toward the Wayfarer restaurant, "Is that where we are going?"

Mom nods and looks back at Aunt Shirley, "You going to be OK, for lunch?"

Aunt Shirley crosses her arms, "I just learned about your daughter's spindling ability."

Mom raises an eyebrow and looks at me. I shrug, and start walking toward the restaurant, stepping over a little current snaking through the sand. The resistance of the sand makes me flex my muscles more. I breath in the salty air and ponder what my mother has been doing.

We gather in the foyer of the Wayfarer restaurant and they escort us to a window seat. I look out at Haystack rock and watch the birds land and take off.

Mom pokes me, "Muriel!"

I give her a bemused smile, "Are you excited about your date?" she asks.

I find myself thinking about Gideon's eyes and curls and turn of phrase, trying to remember something about Andy. I shrug, "I don't know. I find excitement can be a problem sometimes."

Mom snorts, "I'm excited."

Aunt Hannah gives me a cool look; she was a confirmed bachelorette. "Men can be fun, dear."

I raise an eyebrow at her, "Really," I cock my head, "I don't think I have ever met a man you were interested in. Do you have a boyfriend currently?"

She laughs, "A couple."

I think about Sarina. And I smile, " OK."

Aunt Shirley shakes her head at Hannah. "Between Sarina and you, Hannah, people would think that men were nothing but toys to be used and changed out."

My mother chuckles and winks at Aunt Hannah. She exhales wipes her eyes and looks at me, "So what are you thinking about, Muriel?"

I look back at the rocks and shake my head. "Just flight, and how amazing birds are."

She gives me a grin, "Not about Scotland?"

I blink at her, "What have you been up to mother?"

She beams at me, as the waitress comes and hands out menus and takes our drink orders. As I listen to Aunt Shirley go into a tirade about her youngest's love life, I take in the view and marvel at the women in my life.

They all have opinions on what I should wear on my date tonight. When I return home, I stare at my closet for a good twenty minutes, before I choose an outfit.

It is still early and I return to my drawing board. I start tweaking creatures I had been drawing out. Eventually there is a knock on my door. I get up and answered it.

It is Morgan. I take in her dark eye sockets from lack of sleep and a whining Merlin. Merlin's fingers grasp at her hair and she fixes me with a tired stare, "Have you seen Yacob?"

I shake my head. I walk to my bathroom and wash my arms and hands thoroughly. I came back to Morgan and take Merlin. ""Why don't you lie down for a few minutes. When was the last time he ate?"

"Ten minutes ago, he's changed, fed and burped. I don't know why he is still crying."

I nod and gesture to my bed. Morgan didn't need to be asked twice. She goes over to my bed, collapses on it and falls asleep. I take Merlin out of the room and down to the empty family room. I turn on the TV. A BBC version of Pride and Prejudice mini-series is on. I start chatting to Merlin, he starts levitating strands of my hair, weaving them in and out. I start to sing, "Swinging on a Star" and he gives me a beautiful, big grin.

After twenty minutes of me singing, I look up to find my mother, sister and aunts beaming at me. I give them a wink and start to sing the preamble of the constitution. They all joined in. Merlin turns his head to see the other voices. Each of the other adults take turns starting a song. Merlin freezes when a smooth baritone joins in.

It is my brother, Yacob. He saunters into the room with a galloping step. He sits next to me on the couch. Merlin's face lights up at the sight of his father. His chubby arms reach for him.

I hand Merlin to Yacob who takes him and puts a stopping hand on my arm, "Have you sung the Shema, yet?"

I give him a grin and I shake my head as I say, "No."

He beams and catches everyone's eye in the room, and starts to sing, "Baroch A tah..."

My family and I join in and Merlin's face lights up. The room fills with the sound of the pinnacle prayer of the Jewish faith.

Merlin is chortling by the time we stopped.

Yacob cocks his head at me, "Do you have any idea where my wife is Sis? She is not in our apartment."

I gesture with my chin toward the stairs as I say, "My room."

His face becomes hopeful, "Sleeping?"

"Yes, how are you doing?" I ask.

He rolls his eyes, straightens and replies, "Fine."

I don't believe him and let it slip into my tone, "Yeah, OK. Why don't you go join her?" I met my mother's amused eyes. "We can hold the fort for a while here."

He cricked his neck and ran his hand over the back of it. "When was the last time he ate?"

I recall what Morgan said, "It's been about a half hour."

He looks away as if calculating the time.

I imagine how that is working in his sleep deprived state. I'm pretty sure it's hilarious in his mind trying to hold on to numbers.

" OK, just come get us when he is ready to eat. Do you know how to tell when he's hungry?"

I squint my eyes in thought, "Does he nuzzle and make sucking motions with his face?"

Yacob gives me a surprised look, "Ah, yes, he does." He gives our mother a look as he talks to me, "How do you know this?"

I chuckle as I watch the speculation that I might have had children pass across his face, "Sometimes I read stuff. Sometimes it's useful."

He suddenly looks exhausted as he bows to me and starts toward the stairs.

Mom gently cuffs his forearm, "Sleep for a while. Remember that spell you and Morgan fought Aoife and I on. It's in place. Get some sleep."

He looks down. "Yeah, alright, Mom." He looks relieved, gives her a grateful hug and heads back up the stairs.

She beams at me, "Thank you, darling girl. They have been running themselves ragged."

I adjust a strand of hair Merlin had moved into my face and tuck it behind my ear. I feel Merlin changing spells to capture it again. Impressed, I wrinkle my nose at him and tickle his chin. "Cool. One problem though, they are in my room and that is where my clothes are. That date you wanted me to go on is in an hour."

My mother looks at Aunt Hannah, Aunt Shirley and Sarina in a mischievous way. As my stomach drops I say out loud, "Lord help me."

Circe Syndrome

Twenty minutes after Yacob left the room, my mother stops talking and runs to my side. She snatches Merlin out of the air; he had just started levitating. "He is a little too clever for his own good."

Confused and relieved, I swallow, "Mom, how did you know he was going to do that?"

Mom gives me a knowing smile. "You and your brother were just as curious. I've seen it before. The problem is newborns don't always remember to keep spells going and fall. Sometimes, from scary heights and in scary places."

I chuckle, "Scary places? This house?"

With a completely sober face my mother gestures to the brick fireplace. "Ah, but really think about it." She was looking up at the glass chandelier. "Yacob liked to hover above boiling water. It was a nightmare."

"I imagine so." I look at Merlin in my mother's arms as he pulls at her collar. "How do you prevent it at this age?"

My mother is smiling down at Merlin. I wonder at the memories passing through her. "Take a look at his aura. I've made a lasso spell to keep gravity on him."

I change my sight and see this complicated woven spell a matrix of colored light strands cast on or around Merlin. "There is a lot going on there."

My mother gives me a wink. "Wait a second, it's about to activate."

As she says this, the thin, transparent, hinting at red and yellow stripe strands light up. They look like neon, and the red and yellow become brilliant. I blink at the after image, and form flashing purple and green in my blinking eyes. The form was an actual rope, like a lasso. Merlin arches when the new spell doesn't work.

We start to sing a few more songs to him. He becomes a cooing baby again. I look at the two and note the characters

431

talking to one another on the TV. "I have no idea what I'm going to talk about with mister Tesla."

Sarina comes over and sits next to me. "Andrew Tesla? You have a date with Andrew Tesla?"

I look past her to Mom, who shrugs at me. "Um, yeah, I do." I was unaware Sarina had an interest in this man.

"How? Never mind. It really is the man's responsibility to bring up topics." She shakes her head at me like I'm ridiculous.

I sigh and give her an incredulous look, "What? It's 2004 right? I didn't get to sleep and wake up fifty years ago? Right?"

Our Aunt Shirley laughs, "No, kiddo, thank the stars, no. The clothes were fun but the gender roles were way to rigid."

My mother laughs, "I believe the Regency period and Victorian were a little more versatile than the fifties."

Sarina smirks, "Yeah, Mom, you should know. You lived through them all."

I swat her knee. "She did not, she was born during the Victorian period."

Our mother sits between us and leans over Merlin, she giggles loudly, "It was a heady time."

Merlin's eyes are wide staring at his grandmother. I reach out my hand and he grabs my finger.

"What's all the laughing about?" A gruff voice calls from the stairs. It was Uncle Mordecai.

Aunt Shirley walks over to him and he wraps an arm around her back. They walk together over to us. Aunt Shirley points at me, "Muriel has a date and she is not sure what she will talk about with the young man."

He noisily clears his throat, "It's not that young man we played rummy with is it, dear?"

I give him an eyeroll, "No, Uncle, it's not."

Sarina shakes her head, glares at me, "I've heard it but I'd never believe it. It's always the quiet ones."

Mother fires her with a cold stare, "It's always the quiet ones, what?"

Sarina tightens up, straightens, "Nothing."

Uncle Mordecai raises an eyebrow at me. "Who is the young man? Where did you meet him?"

I make a funny face for Merlin, "His name is Andrew. I met him on the way to the dance."

Uncle Mordecai winks, "He danced with you?"

I move my fingers, making Merlin squeeze my finger harder. "Yeah."

He gives a goofy smile, "Then he left a card? Arranged to meet you at your parent's home?"

I blush.

His smile broadens, "I really don't think you need to worry about it. What did you talk about before?"

I shake my head as they all look at me with anticipation. "You won't like it. He was trying to cast a compelling spell on me." Their faces all turned sober. I fluster as I say, "It's fine, I shut him down. Apparently, he likes that."

"Wow." Says Aunt Hannah dumbfounded, shaking her head.

Mom frowns at me, "At the tea I set up, did he try that nonsense?"

"No, but I still think he is more interested in dad and Yacob's inventions, than in me."

Sarina sighs and sits back, "That explains it."

Aunt Shirley scowls at Sarina, "Explains what? Miss Sarah, explains what?"

Sarina sighs wearily and shrugs, "I've seen Andrew in social circles before and Muriel is definitely not his type."

433

I laugh, "Thanks, sis."

Sarina reaches around Mom and pokes my shoulder. "No offense intended Murry, but you know you don't change your appearance in the manner most people in your situation do."

I nod, "Yes, I actually want people to hang out with me because they are interested in what I talk about, not what I look like."

Sarina sighs and stands up. "Whatever." She heads toward the stairs. "See you later, I have an appointment of my own."

Aunt Shirley takes Sarina's spot. Mom hands her Merlin. He smiles up at her red curly hair. The curls started to boing. My mother makes a springing motion with her index finger. I set the spell for the lasso and Mom withdraw hers.

Aunt Shirley pats my knee reassuringly. "Your sister is jealous of so many things, child."

Mom snaps, "Don't Shirley!"

I cock my head, looking to the stairwell, verifying that she has gone, "It's OK, I know. The thing is, I really would rather do something else then go on this date."

Mordecai snorts, "Then don't go."

His sister, my mother, gives him a glare. "I appreciate that you're trying this out, Muriel. The only way to get past…" She doesn't complete the sentence and say Gregor. "You are meeting new people and that is great. Just don't write off this acquaintance till you have more data, OK?"

I give her a reassuring smile, "Sure, Mom, sure."

"Getting past what?" Aunt Shirley sharply asks.

I rub my forehead, embarrassed, "A past love affair. No, I don't want to talk about it. And no, I don't want to forget about it."

My aunt's mouth drops. "I had no idea."

Circe Syndrome

Mom ruffles my hair. "Muriel rarely over shares." She shakes her head in thought, "Even when she is asked directly, it's hard to get a clear answer."

I'm uncomfortable with this conversation. I shift in my seat.

Mom winks at Aunt Shirley, "What do you think? A wimple for the date?"

Aunt Hannah creates a simulacrum of my form with a corseted dress.

Aunt Shirley laughs, "Yes, but shorter." She cuts the dress at the knee and puts a lacy wimple around the head.

Mom stands and starts changing the colors and adding different stitching details.

I shake my head, "I'm not wearing this to a beach."

Aunt Hannah gives me a curious glance, "Beach? Where are you going?"

I laugh, "Honolulu, Waikiki beach."

Aunt Shirley groans, "That's so commercial." With a wave of her hand the corset part become a bathing suit.

I wince. "Ummm, I'm not sure I'm attractive enough or want to show that much skin."

My mother tsks, "Don't be so provincial, dear heart."

Aunt Shirley threw up her hands, "It's a one piece. It's not like it's a bikini!"

I change the light waves into an off the shoulder flowy top with big flowers and dark jeans.

Mom winks at me, "Put the bathing suit underneath. You never know what can happen on a date."

My aunts and I stare at her stunned.

Merlin tries to levitate again and I feel my strands keeping him in my aunt's hands. He begins bringing his hands to her face. I look at my Mom and gesture to Merlin. "Um Mom, does this mean?"

She nods and reaches out and Aunt Shirley hands him to her. "'Yes, he needs to eat."

I cock my head curious, "Should I go wake Morgan and Yacob?"

Mom shakes her head in a negative fashion. She grabs a glass globe from the neighboring table. It transforms into a bottle. It fills with a watery white liquid.

I scratch my cheek puzzled, "What's that? Formula?"

Mom gives me a wink. "Nope, it's Morgan's milk, and the nipple on the bottle will be..."

I wince and raise a hand to stop her. "I get it; you don't need to finish that sentence. "

Mom shrugs, "It's completely natural, Muriel."

I cover my face. "How? Morgan's not in this room."

Aunt Shirley nudges me, "Chill, sleep deprivation is horrible, when you go down this path, you'll be grateful."

I look past her and give her a stiff nod, "Yeah, OK, I'll take your word on that."

Merlin was gazing adoringly up at my mother. I find this all mesmerizing to watch.

"So, you think the young man is more interested in your father and brother?" Aunt Shirley asks.

"He's an owner of Tesla-tronic and did a bad impression of not being aware Daedalus was my father."

"I still am shocked how your father got away with calling the company Daedalus Do-Dads. It is so silly. I bet he wastes energy and time getting people to take his projects seriously." Aunt Shirley examines her nails.

Aunt Hannah nods, "Tesla-tronics does have a more majestic ring to it."

My Mom laughs, "Reminds me of the Titanic."

"Titanic-tronics?" I giggle, "For that sinking feeling or dread, try Titanic-tronic products. No warranties or guarantees."

The doorbell sounds and Merlin, who was thinking about closing his eyes, startles. He let out a cry. I feel like a deer caught in headlights as the three women surround me. My clothing is shifting. I go to answer the door but Aunt Shirley holds me back. "Don't look too eager, let your mother answer."

Aunt Shirley takes the baby. Aunt Hannah escorts me to the kitchen. My mother turns off the TV and gives me a wink, then heads to the door.

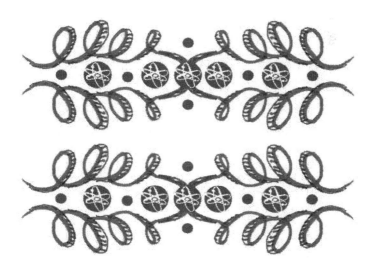

Chapter 43

Talk Story?

I feel clumsy standing next to Andrew in the teleport shack.

I move the strands of hair from my face and look at him. "Waikiki?"

His smile made dimples, "Yeah."

I nod and look up, "Where?"

He looks up also, in thought. "By the Cheeseburger in Paradise restaurant."

I nod, thinking about where that was on the main drag. "Yeah, OK."

He cocks his head, "I could teleport us both."

I squint and look him up and down, wondering if I trust him to take me apart and put me back together. "Nope, I'll meet you there." Before I can see his reaction to my slight, I dissolve into energy.

Circe Syndrome

The hotel area at Waikiki is usually crowded with people. So I go to the ocean and materialize under water. I wince as the saltwater pours into my lungs when I materialize and take an involuntary breath. I blink in the air and dialyosefosize the water out my lungs and take a deep breath. The white light sun of the tropics was scorching compared to the blue light of the Northwest fall. I wade toward the shore. My clothes had become a one-piece bathing suit, as I had changed them to when I appeared.

I walk toward the shore past swimmers and sea life. As I walk, I make subtle changes to my appearance. Once on land, slowly I morph my clothes back and started accelerating the drying process. By the time I made it to the sidewalk, my hair is dry and the suit has returned to a dress. In the three blocks time it takes me to get to the restaurant, I am wearing a floating, flowered sundress that hits below the knee and my hair has a hibiscus in it.

Andrew appears, ten minutes later, brushing sand from his clothes. He gives me a crooked smile, "You have a shadow!"

I look down to see a little girl dressed in clothes identical to mine. "Hello, are you lost?"

Her ebony black hair sparkled with a purple, opal-isk quality. "Ya smell stinky, you opake?"

My mind is spinning, her words confuse me. There was something other about this little girl. "What?"

Andrew narrows his eyes at the girl. "Ghost?"

She giggles, "Ghost? No, I'm not a ghost." She then sniffs the air around Andrew in an exaggerated manner. She wrinkles her nose. "Stinky, manna malinini!"

On a whim I change my sight to power sight and almost blind myself. This isn't a human; it is a supernatural being. "Mana?"

The girl is scowling at Andrew, but turns to give me a blank

439

Janette Bach

look. "Ya smell sweet, like Tutu and he's a stinky moke!" She points, disgusted, at Andrew.

I exchange glances with Andrew and look down at the girl, "Moke?"

Andrew exhales loudly and straightens. He is frowning, "Pidgin English."

I blink at him, not understanding.

He shuffles his feet and shrugs, then looks at the throngs of people, "She's a Menehune."

I repeat the word slowly, "Mini who knee?"

The girl brightens and smiles, sticks out her chin, "Yah, brah!"

I look at Andrew, "You know Pidgin English?"

Non committedly he says, "Some."

I note this, knowing there is a story there. But knowing it's not the time, I reach out to shake the girl's hand, " OK, hi, I'm Muriel. And you are?"

The girl raises an index finger, and shakes it back and forth, indicating we should not touch. "Akamai."

I look at Andrew. He sighs and grumbles, "I'm Andrew."

Akamai rolls her eyes, "Okay, Okay." she looks up in thought, "Come, wiki, wiki."

I look at Andrew. He rolls his eyes. I shrug and follow the girl, and Andrew keeps pace beside me. "What is a Moke and a Tutu?"

He chuckles as we ducked under a surfboard being carried through the street. "Tough guy and she called you a grandmother."

I find this startling, "What?"

"I don't think she means you look old, she was trying to say you seem as kind as a grandmother."

440

Circe Syndrome

I look to the water then back to the tiny form, "Oh?"

She leads us through a tangled path of the city-scape towards Diamond Head, to a public park. Akamai points to a huge Banyan tree and urges us to walk between some pillared roots. When we walk through them, a tingling sensation settles over us and we find we are on another part of the island.

I almost walk into this huge chain link, barbed wire and electrified fence. I stop before I make contact and look back at Andrew. He raises his eyebrows.

We both turn to look at Akamai, who is behind us. Her arms are crossed and there is a defiant glare on her face. She is in a half circle of other children. Menehune, not children, I think to myself. Akamai unfolds her arms and gestures in the direction of the fence, "No, talk story, what that?"

Puzzled at the question, "It's a fence."

Andrew nods next to me, "A very imposing fence."

Akamai scowls. She covers her face with her right hand. The shortest boy next to Akamai give me a wink and points up.

I look up and what I see makes my jaw drop. Involuntarily, I say, "Oh!"

There is a hole in the Aether. It is about two miles wide. We are standing on the edge of the circumference.

Akamai nods and shows her palms, "And then?"

I scratch my ear nervously, this is unsettling, "You want us to find out what's going on?" I narrow my vision and watch the electric current traverse the steel fence. All problems for me.

Akamai smiles, "Yeah, no."

I look at Andrew confused.

His expression is suddenly very guarded, "Yes, she does."

I mumble, "Alright." I turn and look back at the fence and the air around it.

Akamai yells out cheerfully, "Tanks, come back and talk story, here!" Her and her companions dissolve into the foliage, chattering at each other.

Andrew gives an incredulous expression, "I had a feeling that a date with you would not be boring." He reaches out and throws a palm leaf at the fence. The force of the electricity scorches it and sends it back in a direct opposite trajectory.

I stare up at the sky, bewildered. I kick at the earth, frightened by this anomaly. " OK, so we need to get in there covertly, without direct access to magic. Find out what is going on."

I am curious what that hole is. Is it something that is randomly occurring, or some anti-aether field? I pick up a stone and fill it with aether and toss it over the fence. The power stays in the stone.

Andrew stares at the stone then back at me. "How, how did you do that?"

I take in his nervous stuttering and note it. I cross my arms and stare at the rock. I wasn't going to answer this question; the answer would be too big of a tell on how I use magic. "What?" I respond naively. I gesture to the fence, "How do you propose we go through? No magic on the other side, only what you bring with you."

He starts walking away, "I'm not going in there."

I look down and nod at him, "Why not?"

He points to a sign mounted on the fence a few rungs down. It reads, Keep Out. Restricted. Felony For All Unauthorized People.

I sigh, "But the mini humans?"

He frowns at me and shakes his head. "Menehune and just because a magical being asks you to do something, it doesn't mean you need to do it. What would you do if a demon asked you to do something illegal?"

I frown and ask, puzzled, "Are Menehune demons?"

He frowns, exhales and looks away, "No, they are industrial natural spirits of Hawaii."

I gesture to where they disappeared, "Nature spirits turn you the wrong way before?"

He rolls his eyes, "Naiads will drown you given a chance."

I shrug, nod mentally thinking about the water spirits of lakes and streams that drown passing men. I shake my head realizing these are not like Naiads. "Look, I don't mind helping them out. I am also curious as to what is causing this. I'm going in. You can help or move out of the way."

He grimaces. "Fine."

I let out a breath, "I think it's a military base."

He sighs, shaking his head looking forlorn, "Yeah."

I stand back five yards from the fence and examine the soil. There is a myriad of volcanic rock tunnels. I gasp in surprise.

He looks at me, startled. "What?"

"Ley lines. Uncorrupted ley lines." My mind is reeling. This was weird in this day and age.

He scratches his head, "Ley lines?"

I rub my forehead as I grasp at my memories, "Old world mystical energy of the earth."

He frowns, "Is it aether?"

I shake my head, "Similar energy type, but unprocessed."

He sneers, "Raw aether? Does it have worms?"

I chuckle and feel confused trying to explain. "Sometimes."

He looks at his fingertips, "Do these ley lines extend through the diameter of that circle?" He points up at the sky.

I nod, "Yeah."

There is this moment of rage that passes across his features, then he looks at me calmly, "I have no idea how to harness that energy, do you?"

I sit down cross legged and put both hands down on the ground on either side of me. I push them flat against the earth. There is a lava tube. I created a stalactite structure in the tube. This will be my spindle. I remember it's like taking wool through a spinning wheel. I grab the edge of a ley line and encourage it to flow through the lava tube. Ley line energy acts like water as I create the trail, more follows each time. I guide the lumps down an incline and through the tunnel, and across the spindle. A line of aether shoots straight out through the tunnel, bisecting the building and the center of the aether-less circle. Parts of the refined power will immediately evaporate up and will be pushed outside the circle into the sky.

That is curious. I watch this cycle a little bit. Then stop this path, not wanting to waste the energy. I stare at the fence and muse over creating something to cut it, but then I realize the electricity did not go below ground.

Andrew is frowning, staring at the ground, "What, what did you do?"

"Creating an aether stream underground. It evaporates fast, though." I examine the rock I tossed in earlier. It has depleted half of it's magic. "I want to know what is at the center of that circle. Is it expanding?"

He frowns, his gaze is on where the line I created had been.

I move my hands in front of me, still palms to the ground. I start the ley line path again. I send this energy into a patch of earth beneath the fence. I create a perpendicular rectangle about two yards long on either side of the fence. I encourage the soil into a hole with stairs on either side. "What type of base do you think this is?"

He kicks at the dirt, and looks into the forest in thought. Absently, he says, "Air Force."

I nod, and note his fists tightening. I modify my clothes to Air Force fatigues. Where the insignia of rank should go, I put on a happy face button with an illusion spell geared to the watcher. It would show me as one rank above anyone addressing me. I stand at the tip of the hole. "You coming?"

Chapter 44

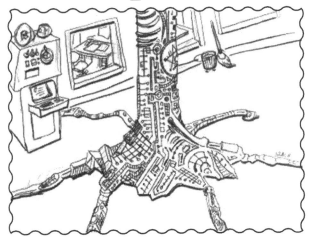

Dampening

He looks at me then in a guarded manner as his clothes changed similarly, but he puts a Testla-tronic insignia on his rank pin spot.

I fill myself with power and hold it. I rarely do this, so it feels bizarre. I walk down into the hole to the other side. I try to create an illusion spell over the hole, but it is picked apart immediately. This is getting curiouser. I pull some palm fronds to cover the hole and made a few other piles around. I remind myself that this is why I try to find other ways to do things instead of using my magic.

While I had been distracted by this it seems Andrew has entered the hole, because he moves a palm frond aside and stands next to me. "What's your plan?"

I stare at the hanger at the center of the circle. I point toward it, "I'm heading there."

He shakes his head, "People are going to stop us. How do you plan to get past them?"

I shrug, "I'll find out when it happens."

"Great!" He says sarcastically.

We walk toward the building that is a massive rectangle with humongous doors. I note the aircraft around. All jets, with a few helicopters peppered in. I realize the building must be a hanger. I keep the pace slow. Acting as a person that is supposed to be there, not in a hurry. "So have you seen that show Wonderfalls?"

He shakes his head, "Nope, I'm watching Lost. Have you seen that?"

"Not really."

We are quiet for a few moments. I finally sigh, "We really need to work on our small talk."

He smirks, "What are we accomplishing here?"

I note some small stones and the debris on the cemented ground. "To find the source of that abnormality."

He sighs, "Then what?"

I just shake my head, "You can go back."

He purses his lips.

We are at a nest of parked planes and I run into a man with a wrench in one hand and oil seeping down his arm. He takes in our clothes and goes back to work.

I head to the hanger and I am stopped at the door by a guard.

The man grabs his walkie talkie as he yells, "Freeze."

I stand still and feel off since I just realize that my spell is gone and the magic stores are nowhere in me anymore.

Andrew clears his throat. The man stares at Andrew and puts his communication device down. "Stand down. I'm just doing a spot check."

"Yes sir." The man salutes Andrew.

Andrew nods, "As you were Master Sergeant."

Puzzled and dazed, I follow Andrew into the hanger. He leads me to a metal pillar. It is strewn with circuits. All of them are Tesla-tronic circuits. "So, you know what is causing this?"

He walks over to a control panel and turns a few dials. "New defense contract."

I stare at the pillar and up at the ceiling. I'm evaluating this structure. "Does The Collective know you working with the unawakened?"

He snorts. "Unawakened, such a polite word for the uniformed and talentless!"

I was unsure of him before this, this disgust with others makes me hate him in this moment.

He adjusts some dials. "I must thank you for showing me the holes in this design."

I walk closer to the pillar, "How many of these do you have?" Blue electricity crawls over its surface.

He looks disappointed, "This is the only one. I can't seem to replicate it. We've used the same schematics as the designer used, but he was killed in the assembly."

My eyebrows raise in concern and realization, "So, he had notes he didn't write down." I was thinking this might be part of the mystery too. Maybe his spirit became part of the working prototype. The ghost in the machine that made it work. I look at the metal all over the inside of this huge hanger room. I look back at the pillar. There are a few of my father's chips. I note their numbers and groupings, filling my head with my own schematic of this monstrosity. I am staying calm and not letting any of my anger or horror show.

He gives me a sarcastic look, "You think?"

Circe Syndrome

I take a breath looking the pillar up and down, staying in the tone of a fellow problem solver, "Have you taken it apart?"

Andrew looks crestfallen, "That is one of the problems, when I shut it down, it doesn't turn off."

I am pleased the schematics are missing replicable parts and he hasn't been able to do any backwards engineering on it. I wonder why I am here. "OK, so this date thing, was this in the plan?"

He gives me an angry look, "No, I wanted you nowhere near this! You didn't want to eat in Paris at three in the morning! Why would you just follow any nature spirit's direction?"

"They have been around a great deal longer then I have. Sometimes, listening is the best way to learn."

He snarls, "That person who drowned when I told you the story about the river spirit, it was my sister! I have no love for these beings or what powers them! We would all be better without magic. It's not like you can do the most important thing with it."

I nod, comprehending his anger, but trying to get this under control. "I have an idea. Shut it down at your end."

He turns off the various computers and screens. I go to the wall and unplug it.

He laughs, "I've tried that."

I nod as I watch the pillar continue to crawl with electricity and aether. The arc of electricity grows. I feel a shudder from the world as it sucks in more life force. I find a crow bar and there is a bucket of water. I wrap my hands in plastic from a package crate, grab the crow bar then stick the crow bar in the water. I take the dry wooden handled mop from the floor and push the bucket to the pillar as he screams in horror, "Wait!"

The pillar lights up with lightening and then becomes a dead thing full of melted circuits. It makes popping and fizzle

449

sounds. I take the broom and wet it, then I coat the circuits with more water. It is like a wave crashing down when the aether fills the room and air. I use aether to cool the pillar down and start pocketing random chips and adding more holes, with random ground and power labels about the pillar board. All custom chips I could find, I melted.

He looks at me, stunned. Then in a very quiet voice he says,"Walk away from that."

I back away.

He walks around the pillar, his back toward me and holds out a hand. "Give those back."

I melt the random chips and resistors into a plastic mass and handed them back to him. He sneers and drops the mass in the bucket.

I cock my head, "You wanted it shut down, right?"

He gives me a disgusted sigh. He walks out of the building fuming, and I follow. I finally ask, "Are we still doing dinner?"

He won't look at me. I nod, knowing he isn't talking to me anymore. I head toward the spot Akamai asked me to meet her. I stumble out of the hole and Akamai gives me this huge grin. I fill in the hole and I explain the pillar to her.

Akamai touches my elbow and a shock goes through me at the amount of power this creature possesses. "Stinky mana moke." she says.

I return her smile, "Yeah."

Akamai gives me a nod, "Tak Muriel."

I nod and dialyosefosize back into the aether. As I was melting in, I felt, Akamai's presence. She gathered me into a ball of energy and said, "Let's goes swimming." We materialized at a beach surrounded by cliffs.

I look around, mesmerized by the beauty, "Where are we?"

Circe Syndrome

"Hanauma, Brah!"

I nod, " OK." I bend down and take my shoes off and bury my feet in the warm, white sand. I wrinkle my nose and change my shoes into a towel that I drape over my arm. It amazes me that Akamai has just materialized us to a busy beach and no one noticed. "Are we swimming for a purpose?"

Akamai walks deliberately toward the water and over the shoulder says to me, "Ya see."

I was thinking about how I should contact my superiors at The Collective about what just happened. Akamai turns and looks at me. "Wiki, Wiki, mana girl! Wiki! Wiki!"

Chapter 45

Sponging Off

At the edge of the water, I pause a moment and turn to look longingly at the people lounging in the sunshine. I have no idea what Akamai was asking of me now. I turn and follow her into the crystal clear, blue water. Huge gray fish twice the size of my head swim by in groups of two and five. An eel snakes between rocks, and black and white fish, the size of my hands, seem to be playing hide and seek with one another. The weightlessness of the water cushions my shocked nerves, and I take a stinging breath before I begin the stinging itch sensation of creating gills and changing how I breathe. Akamai pauses and gives me an beguiled glance. She beckons me deeper into the bay.

I inhale the fragrant water filled with coral spores, fish eggs and micro-plants. It is buzzing with life and aether. A low hum fills my thoughts that corresponds with the moving waves into the bay. I feel like I am sleep walking and have just woken up. Fish slowly move out of my way, and I follow the

Menehune deeper into the waves. There is an abrupt stop at a huge coral that glows brighter with aether then the coral around it. It is iridescent and massive. All types of fish move around it. I fight the urge to analyze the coral's DNA. This made me think about the light problem on the planet I was working on.

The coral's voice was an amalgam of middle range sounds neither female nor male. It sparkled in my mind. "Akamai just told me that you found the source of the blight."

I nod, look for Akamai and realize she disappeared. "It was a man-made device."

The coral sighs in my mind. A bizarre sound of whooshing water and almost farting noises. "Of course it is."

In the quiet that follows and I interpret as the coral processing, I look around. I let myself be distracted by several moray eels darting in and out of holes. They glowed like the coral reef.

Suddenly, the sound of the coral fills my head. "Will it happen again?"

I look up at the water above my head, the light streaming in. I think about the schematics of the decimated pillar and answer honestly, "I don't know."

I feel the coral waiting. It has no face, no expressions to gauge. I am amazed at how pregnant this pause is. I start to shift and clear the sand around me of rocks and shells. I sit down. It is an interesting feeling, my hair floating up and my fingers dragging through the sand and the struggle to not float. Some fish surround me, pick at my clothes and swim through my hair. I finally break the silence, "It was a prototype device. I really scrambled everything I could. They probably have specs. They can try to make another."

The coral's response sounds like a grumble. I feel it scan me, then sputter in my brain, "You, you, you are acting like a common magic user, but you're a planet builder!"

I stand at this caustic response and shake my head incredulous that it would scan me without permission. In retaliation I scan the coral as it invaded my space."What about you? You are connected to Gaia!"

The lights of the coral flash in a strobe pattern and the fish scatter. Its voice is stern, "Do those land dwellers have any idea what they are playing with?"

I frown, sit down, "Nope." I run my fingers through the soft sand and sift it between my fingers. In a calm voice I ask, "How come I can understand your language as you speak while with Akamai she has that pidgin English affectation?"

The sound of the voice in my head is puzzled by my question, "I'm a biochemical creature. What you're hearing is a chemical compound translation. She is also a creature of magic; she probably did that for a reason."

I thought about how Andrew understood what she had said. It was kind of a warning about how familiar with the island he is. "Oh!"

The coral chuckles, " That stunt has been going on for several moon cycles."

I scowl, totally aware that the coral probably doesn't pick up on facial expressions.

Two striped fish carrying a coral piece swim up to me and drop it on my wrist. It wriggles like a worm; a burning sensation envelopes me. The coral starts to burrow into my skin and I involuntarily yelp out with the pain. As the tear forms in my wet eyes causing an odd sensation of water displacement and pressure, I yell, causing the fish to scatter. "What? Man that stings!" I change my vision to waves that can see through skin and muscle. The coral mass had flattened out, cross-border to my bone. I notice the lichen in me envelope it. The wrist stings, though looking at it externally there is no sign of the trauma. I swallow and force myself to calmly asked, "Why did you do that?"

454

Circe Syndrome

Its voice was slightly puzzled, "You have other symbiotic creatures I thought you wouldn't mind having a way I can contact you the next time this happens."

I rest the wrist on the coral. My wrist lights up in a pattern with the great coral, "I would appreciate a request first."

The coral's mind retorts, "It's easier to apologize sometimes."

"Great." I mumble under my breath, "I always love hearing my sister's philosophy coming out of a centuries old creature."

It made a sound like a snort in my brain. "See what you think of pleasantries after your first millennium."

"I imagine you appreciate them. The fey seem to."

"Ah, but all you can do is imagine. Don't throw your human morality at me. I am an alien creature to your thought processes. In the future, I may need your assistance again. Do you think you destroyed that thing?"

"I really messed with the left over pieces, but I think, sure, they can try it again. They have schematics. In the modern world it's a little harder to destroy an idea. Especially if it has been written down and sent to multiple sources."

The coral is browsing through my mind at that incident, and pauses when it steps into another memory. I am not happy about it looking through this. It seems to shudder. "This request by Vulcan?"

I look out over the reef, "What about it?"

"It's a puzzle you're trying to figure out. I can help you with it. But I need you to think about why he wants a planet of gold first."

I run my fingers through the sand again, as I think about gold and why Vulcan would want it. "Well, Vulcan is a weapon smith and celestial gold is the only metal that can be used." I stare towards the deep blue depths of the ocean sea. I examine the shapes swimming there, puzzling them out.

The coral sighs, "Can what?"

I swirl my fingers in the sand, "Murder a god."

The coral harrumphs in my mind, making me wince and twist my neck. I notice the sand I am running through my hands starts to sparkle. It became gold.

Its voice is silkier, "You can make sure the planet is not purely celestial gold. You could spread a bit of our planet about to contaminate the spot."

"I'll take that into advisement. So far, I'm at a loss as to how to go about creating it anyways." I draw a circle in the sand.

"You already hear the songs." The coral muses.

I cock my head, confused about the subject change. "The songs?"

"The planet songs. All the elements working together to keep a planet functioning. That is how you navigate around the galaxy, right?"

I chew on this idea.

The coral continues, "Transmutation is all about quark and lepton vibration frequencies."

It was as if I was sitting somewhere solid and the floor was ripped from beneath me, and I was falling through the air like a leaf, back and forth. This information was making sense and flooring me.

"You have been doing it unconsciously for years, I do believe you're old enough to realize that."

I rub my head. This day was becoming transcendent. "So this bone graft is a two-way communication thing?"

The coral sighs, "No."

I exhale with water in the mouth it's odd, "Fine." I start thinking about dialyosefosizing home.

456

The coral's voice in my head manages to be irritated. "Don't check out on me yet. I want to talk to you about the bio-luminescence creatures you're working on."

I straighten, "Yes."

"You don't need to include the Luciferin and Lucirrerase in the normal DNA strands. Just insert some plasmid DNA. You're right about the photosynthesis just needing light. You might want to make sure the site starts with some oxygen instead of relying on the plants to produce it."

I scratch my chin, digesting the words. Luciferin is the light emitting compound fireflies use. Luciferase is the class of oxidative enzymes that produce bioluminescence from a photo protein. Plasmid DNA is an independent DNA molecule in a cell that is separated from the chromosomal DNA. This could be easier than trying to map it all together. All I say is, "Hmmmm, anything else?"

The coral's lights dance in amusement, "Don't forget to report this incident."

I shift the gold sand some more. "I wonder how unaware The Collective is?" I am nervous, I could be mistaken and this was a Collective sponsored weapon. The ramifications of that would be terrifying.

The coral's lights were green, "A very good question. An innocent way of finding out, right?"

I chew at my bottom lip and tense, "Sure, but what are your motives?"

The lights became rainbow and bubble, with a chuckle, "A direct question, do you think you'll get a real answer?"

I smirk, doubting, but stating the truth, "An answer would be nice."

Its consciousness seemed to turn completely away, "Go, I will summon you when it happens again."

I frown, "You sure they will use the same place? Maybe they will use a different island or take it to Alaska?"

The coral's voice is smug, "Anything that happens on this chain of islands Akamai and her brethren will know about. Isn't Alaska too close to another country and could violate some treaties?"

I sigh, weird in water, so weird. "Hopefully, the recreation will take a while." I stand and feel the gold sand slide from my clothes. "I'll await your page. Anything bizarre, you need to make me aware of or will it be obvious."

"It will be obvious." The coral lights creates a smile.

I find myself bowing, "Alright, I am at your disposal." I dialyosefos home.

Chapter 46

Pilling Debris

I walk around to the front of my parents' house. I stop and stumble at the astringent smell of manure. Gnasher is hovering at the base of the oak tree; he is finicky managing the arrangement of the manure at the tree's base.

I wince, thinking about the copy of the Siren Lotus cuff I left on its roots. "How's it going Gnasher?"

He turns and gives me a glazed look. He makes some incomprehensive noise. I really need to fill out that paperwork and remove the cuff of influence from the oak tree. I need to tell my father all the details of the aether damper before anything else distract me.

I send a wave of mental resistance to Gnasher hoping to help him fight the will of the tree, the glaze look leaves his eyes and he gives me a lucid regard before I go into the house.

I rush through the foyer. Nobody is in the front room. I head to the kitchen, it is also empty. I pause at the door to the basement that is in the back breezeway, between the kitchen and the backyard. I take a breath and study the handle. My father sometimes puts traps on the door that leads to his workshop. I see nothing and tentatively reached out a hand to turn it. Nothing out of the ordinary happens, the knob turns with a click and the door lets me open it.

A single exposed bulb hangs with a pull chain from the cavernous top of the ceiling. The walls are just institutional white. The stairs are typical unfinished basement stairs, with an added detail. Each step had a chrome oval with crisscross texture found on the back of pickup trucks.

I grab the chrome handrail and descend the stairs. The light has a blue glow. I shield my eyes immediately, I have no idea what my dad is working on and he could be arc welding.

His voice is soft and distracted, "Oh, Muriel? You're home?"

"Yes." I still kept my eyes shielded. "Can I look, Dad?"

His voice is full of amusement, "Yes."

I uncover my eyes and blink. He is sitting at a desk festooned with circuit specs, and five projects in different stages are being assembled around him. He has his glasses on halfway down his nose and he is looking at me with a speculative gaze.

I start to explain what happened on the island. As I go through my tale, one project would halt and sit on the floor. When I finish I find my mother standing next to me.

A chair comes out of the floor and under me. Another goes under my mother. A table with a pot of tea appears in front of us. My father rolls up the papers on his desk. "Can you draw what you saw?"

I lean forward, suddenly craving the tea. "Some, I also messed with the board before I left." I reach in my pocket and find a few microchips I hadn't relinquished. I dropped them on his desk. A little puddle of water surrounds the soggy chips.

Circe Syndrome

A drafting board flies to my lap. It has eagle board mapping software running on its screen table top. I take a breath.

My mother stares at her own cup and turns it in her saucer. "Have you told your superior at The Collective yet?"

I frown down at the surface of my tea, "No."

Mother's eyebrow rises, "Do you plan to?"

I sigh, "Yes, I'm on probation. If it gets out that I knew and they didn't, I would be in a great deal of trouble."

My father shuffles with the chips on the table as he opens a box of Nano-bots that swarm out and around the chips. He looks at me, "Do you suspect The Collective already knows?"

I watched the gnat-like robots surround the pile of damp chips I'd left on the table. One pulls out a huge fan and aims it at the chips. My father clears his throat and points to the board on my lap.

I concentrate on the screen. I close my eyes and reach for the images I made from those moments. "It was a lot to take in, Dad. My last images were of the sabotage I was performing."

He is gruff when he replies, "Try, child."

I toggle through the resistor directories. I sketch quickly trying to keep up with my memory. "Mom, I do wonder. It was a military base. You're on the council, have you heard anything about an aether suppressor?"

My mother and father meet eyes then look back at me. "No, I haven't."

I nod, and remember what else I haven't told them, "They have started to map out my abilities."

The room becomes silent. The air seems solid and there is no longer a current. I notice the fan had stopped spinning.

My mother's eyes are narrowed and fixed on me, "Mapping you how?"

461

I insert some CPU chips into the drawing. "That vampire"

"The one with the cloying smell that clings to you?" She crosses her arms.

I wince, "Um, yeah."

Mom takes a breath, "What about him?"

I stare at my palm where there is some residue from melting chips in my hand. "He has been given written permission to take my blood directly instead of through The Collective brew."

Mom sucks in her lower lip, "What is the justification used?"

"Reliability of abilities. During black-ops he knows what magic he can perform with my blood." I feel slightly shamed by being put in this position. Being made to feel it is OK to be used specifically for my blood and what it can do and violating the Heska right of magical privacy violated. Leaving me open for all types of ways I can be attacked.

Moms raises her voice, "Are you telling me, vampires can use our magic sustained by our blood?"

I put a strand of hair behind my ear and nod, "This one can. He is the only one I've ever talked to closely after they have been recruited."

Mom stares at my Dad. He starts a pendulum of the first ball on a string moving back forth. It was in an armature with four other balls suspended. It causes a reaction where the one at the end moves them back and forth. "Does he know what your dominant field is?"

I take a big breath, and exhale, "I don't know. He talks about the illegal spells he can do."

Mom chuckles, wicked and knowingly. "Ah, the pull of the phatasmical. He won't know how to balance that. It will strike him back in the end."

Circe Syndrome

I look up at her, "You sure? He is, by his own nature, a killer. He may balance it without knowing that is what he is doing!"

My mother gives me a sarcastic snort, "I thought Collective vampires no longer kill! That is part of the bargain for the blood brew?"

I sigh, "That is the agreement. I have no idea how it's policed. He is also doing black ops."

Mom is lost in thought. "That is true. Here is another question for you. Will you tell The Collective all you told us about the damper?"

I meet her eyes, understanding the subtext. "Not unless directly asked. I will not volunteer the information."

Mom nodded, "Alright."

My father is frowning at the chips on his desk. He examines the water drops on his fingertips from the puddle thoughtfully. "Have you voiced your concerns about the blood use to your boss?"

I raise my eyebrows at his fingers. "Not really, I'm not sure how to handle that. I wonder if I'm being paranoid, or just being critical of something harmless."

My mother looks thoughtful. "Find an indirect way to ask."

I sigh, "I suspect he will site the whole reliable spells for Thomas to work with being the reason."

"He might not have informed his superiors and might be being manipulated by the corpse. If you can hint at the latter without outright accusation, it will make him doubt his own reason." Mom taps her chin in thought as she said this.

My father just shakes his head, "Just put it out there. All this subterfuge is ridiculous."

I save the file I had been drawing. I set the board aside. "I agree with your Dad, but it is not the world I'm currently occupying. I'm not above reproach, and I'm swimming with sharks. Mom's subterfuges could keep me from trouble."

My mother gives me a wink, "So, how did the rest of the date go?"

My father chuckles.

I stand bewildered by my mother's humor, "I don't believe Mr. Tesla will be calling again."

My mother gives me a tight lipped disappointed look, "I see, dear. Do try to do better next time, Dear."

Suddenly all these things out of my control fill me with an overwhelming feeling of frustration. I'm itching to do something, in a place where I can control things. I remember Morgan and Yacob sleeping in my room when I left. "Is my room free?"

My mother nods, "Yes, dear, they have returned to their apartment."

I wave at them and head toward the stairs. I can hear their voices raise as they begin a discussion.

My Aunt Hannah is in the kitchen humming a tune and pouring a pot of tea. I wave and continue walking through. She stopped me with a question. "What type of cat is it that Clay got from your room, Muriel?"

I stop whirling in thoughts, "Cat?" The events of when I went to sleep for three days briefly passed through my mind.

Aunt Hannah stirs her tea and takes a sip. She smiles, looks at the cup, then me, "It's rainbow calico and talks."

I rub my head, "Are Aunt Shirley and Uncle Mordechai still here?"

She looks away thoughtfully, "No, they took Clay to see your cousin Moeshe's family. It's the triplets birthday."

Circe Syndrome

I sigh thinking about the craziness going on there and realize the cat can wait. Especially if it is Hestia. I nod, "Thanks." I head up to my room. The sorcery object permit request lays on my printer. I pick it up and examine it as I remove my shoes. I began to fill it out when my console starts to beep. I set the form back on the bed and sit down at the vanity. It is a nebula detection spell. There is a prime pocket of gases ready for some solar system molding and seeding.

I let go thoughts of the form, the fey, the aether dampening pillar, the power mapping, my failed attempt at a date, The Collective, Eco Spa, Merlin and think about paddleboarding in this nebula. I take down the coordinates. I run downstairs and let the front door slam behind me. Barefoot I run to the shed. The coarse wood threatens to give me slivers; I don't care. I want to feel the winds of creation and the crests of change and just be. I take a breath and reached for the aether. I dialyosefos to my workshop on Saturn's moon and grab a board. I reach to the aether and go to the coordinates.

It is an uncharted area, way beyond my home in the spiral of the milky-way. I found a thin ribbon of life and follow it to its end.

I stare in wonder at the effects of the recently exploded stars. Clouds of elements clumping and churning, spinning in iridescent colors. Some areas are so dense the stars behind just cause a strobing effect. I pull myself back to a space way beyond the heart of a reaction but where the waves will still happen. These rides are thrilling.

I modify my skin cells to work like armadillo skin. A chemical response with impact will cause them to harden. I stay still and listen to the current music of the vibrations of these particles. I hum with it, and slowly and deliberately mix the elements to change their positions and their songs. As the gases swirl and change, a symphony of complimentary rhythms surrounds me. In response, they spin and explode. I ride the currents and shock waves and eventually turn to see two stars and thirteen planets. I am still riding the currents with tumble in barrel rolls and head over heels as I ride my board. The forces start to simmer and cool. I surf to its center. I find an equal distance for the suns not to devour each other, and move them. I evaluate the planets and adjust their orbits to avoid collisions.

I take some time to lay on my board and just watch this newborn galaxy. My mind tumbling with ideas from the coral as I analyze the structure of each planet. I finally look at my watch. My personal time. It was showing two days. I wince. The deadline for Attila. I hadn't reported the pillar to The Collective. This had all only felt like two hours. I am in trouble now, I know. I sigh, the fatigue suddenly hits me. I am tempted, but remind myself that time travel is forbidden.

As if somehow knowing what I was thinking, my mother's mind calls to me. "Where are you? You have been gone a week! The Collective is furious!"

I resolve myself for a tongue lashing. I dialyosefos to the sixth planet here and cough in the nitrogen rich air and tell my mother the coordinates.

Mom just exhales as if resigned, "Don't use a time spell! Come home!" There was a pause, "Don't forget to set up your remote manipulation spells, then come home."

"Yes, Mother." I respond meekly.

Mom withdraws from my mind.

I steady the dark elements into a computer structure with remote access. I create a base for a nursery for seeding life. It is a remote genetic manipulation lab. I load my basic operating system into the computer structure. This all takes another hour or so and then I dialysefos home after stopping at my moon base.

Chapter 47

Into the Fire

I feel tired as I stand in the foyer and let the camera and The Collective's tech be inserted into my brain. It feels way too bright and it itches. I scratch my head and sent a connection to my direct superior, Jack. I put both hands on the wall of the foyer and stare at the oak tree outside through the window. Squirrels are stacking acorns into pyramid structures making a wall around the tree.

I am being put on hold. I yawn. The hold music is "Red Dragon Tattoo" by Fountains of Wayne. I slump to the corner, humming. I slide down the wall, trying to figure out how to account for not reporting the Hawaiian incident for a week. I keep looking out the windows, and watch how wrong it is for squirrels to be that organized. I run a hand over my face as I realized that I had not filled out the form about creating the cuff yet. I keep forgetting.

Jack's voice is calm, but has a razor sharp edge to it, as if waiting for me to say something to give him permission to yell uncontrollably."Where have you been?"

467

"Sorry, I was dealing with something off world and the time didn't seem as long there."

There is a shocked silence, I feel the shock escape out of his mind.

There is a hesitation, "What off world?" He seems to fume, "The moon stuff? The time aggregation wouldn't account for that!"

"Out of this galaxy, Jack!" I wondered how he knew about the moon excursion. Then I remember logging into their computers.

"You are on parole; you're not supposed to leave this jurisdiction!"

I sigh, "My parole has full travel rights, as long as I avoid certain countries and I must be in contact with my parents. My mother contacted me. I'm here."

A calculated mumble comes out, "Does it now?"

I decide to pull the band aid off, "Jack, I'm sorry to be late reporting this, but in my time off, I came across something extremely troubling."

I can tell he was still mulling over my previous words, "Troubling how?"

"A device is being tested in the Hawaiian Islands that damps the aether for about a mile."

His roaming thoughts stop. I feel more of his attention fall on me.

I trace the decorating motifs carved into the wood molding framing the window. I wait for the next question.

"Do you know who is behind it?"

"Not really. It was on an Air Force base, and a Tesla family member has been working with the Air Force, that is all I know."

His voice is full of questions, "Tesla family member?"

I bite my lower lip, then say, "Andrew Tesla."

His voice in my mind becomes all business, "Is it still there?"

"I doubt it."

He sighs, "How long ago did you see it?"

I drag my fingers through the window condensation, "I guess I've been gone a week."

There is a long pause, "A week? That is unacceptable."

I rub my forehead, weary, I run my hands through the sunbeams shining through the colored glass and watch my hand change color. "I know."

He sounds resigned, "I guess I will send a forensic team. Maybe there will be something left." He addresses me again, "Where are you right now? All I see is dark wood paneling with ornate carvings and colored light streaming rays on your video monitor."

"My parent's foyer."

Puzzled feelings again, "Oh, why aren't you inside?"

I patiently answer, even though I want to scream this, "Mom likes her privacy. The monitoring system is not allowed in the house."

"Oh" there is a pause, "Your cortisol levels look like you need sleep."

I nod, "I might."

An edge comes with this next question, "Were you in fairyland? That would be a breach of several treaties. Did we not get everyone in the raid?"

He knows what I have just told him, this question to reassure himself and try to catch me in a lie won't work, so I sigh and say, "No."

"There is no time for sleep. I need your help with another matter."

I laugh, "Yeah, alright." I find it amusing to be accused of wrong doing then asked to help again.

Concern fills this next phrase from him, "You are not using time spells, right?"

Exasperated I say, "If I were using time spells this whole conversation would have happened differently and a week ago."

I hear him staple something forcefully, "True!"

"With what matter do you need my help?"

There was a dismissal in his voice, and a loss in thought quality, "Thomas is on his way to you. He will fill you in."

"About Thomas, Jack?"

"Yes?" he sounds really distracted. I hear him call out in the office, "No, put Anthony on it. He'll assemble a team." His attention comes back to me. " OK, Anahat, you are being called to address a real agent's job, make us proud." He disconnects.

I speak to the empty room, "But I don't want to be an agent." Since I do not know when Thomas will arrive, I take the apparatus back out of my skull and walk into the house. I send a tandem mental communication of what I told The Collective to my parents. I walk to the kitchen.

I start rummaging through the refrigerator. I pull out some French vanilla Tillamook yogurt. I start the tea kettle boiling and scarf up the yogurt. It's bright sweet flavor sparking my mind out of its drowsy state. One of Morgan's cousins walks in. He grunts at me and pulls some apples from the basket on the table. He takes a bite, filling the air with a sharp crunch.

I look at him again, and realize that he is the same cousin with the long red hair and muscular build who had inquired after Sarina when I had finished that rummy game. "Hi, I don't believe we actually exchanged names when we spoke last."

He wipes some apple juice from his chin. "Shamus."

"I'm Muriel." I reach out my hand to shake his.

Circe Syndrome

He looks at his moist hand then at me. "The quiet one. The one who disappears all the time."

The water starts to boil and I stand. "Did you get to talk to Sarina? You seemed quite intent on that when we last spoke."

He gives me a wolfish smile, "Yeah."

I open the cupboards and pull down a cup.

"Hey, I'll take one, too."

I pull down a second cup.

I take the cup I got down for me and reshape it into a travel mug. I place an earl gray tea bag in it and pour hot water in it. He comes and stands next to me. So close but not touching. He selects an Assam bag and puts that in his cup. "So, are you as lively of a..." he pauses and leers, "...conversationalist as your sister."

He then brushes my hand.

I stiffen and walk back to the table. "Nope."

He turns as he dunks his tea bag. He gives me a seductive look and a wink, "I bet that is not true."

I stare across the room, "I'm sure it is. Has anything interesting happened here in the last week?"

He sits across from me. "People looking for you. There was a troll. A couple kidnapping attempts by pixies and these really odd creatures called Sneffels. Your mother and brother were both quite put out that you weren't here and hadn't told them something about those things. "He nods to the outside. "That gnome told them about some conversation you had, with some Sneffels on the night Merlin was born."

I frown at myself for letting them down, the timing never seemed right. "Merlin still here?"

He pales, looks down at his tea then back at me, giving me the impression that he experienced a sneffel since he had been here. "Yes."

I breathe a sigh of relief, "Good."

He licks his lips and stares at my aura, "Where were you?"

I think about the swirling galaxy and give him a mysterious expression, "Blowing off steam."

He leans in with his cocky smirk again, "Blowing who?"

I wince, shake my head, "Nope, just relaxing."

"With who?"

I laugh, "Not everything is about sex you know!"

He frowns, "What? You frigid?"

I nod, "Yeah, sure, that is it."

He smiles, "I can fix that. I'm a great time."

I give him an ingratiating smile, "I'm sure you are. But I'm not interested, thanks."

He leans back, I watch him try to decide if he is insulted or not.

The doorbell rings. I stand and put a cover on my tea. "That's for me. See you around."

He nods.

Chapter 48

Suidae Speculation

When I step into the foyer, I take a moment before I open the front door. I nod hello to Thomas. I retreat to a corner to install the camera.

He gives me a curious stare. "You look amused. Care to share?"

I was still tickled by the conversation in the kitchen with Shamus. I shake my head, then stand still as the camera is reinstalled.

Thomas's grin disappears, "You have to do this every time you enter and exit the house?"

I give him a deadpan look, trying not to think about how it looks externally. It is gruesome to watch, nevertheless feel. "Only when I'm on the clock."

He nods toward the door to the house. "So your amusement?"

I pull on a coat. "Oh that, it was nothing. Just conversation, out of context it would make no sense."

He opens the front door. I send a thought to my mother that I was attached to surveillance equipment and being sent on Collective business. I walk outside.

Thomas follows, pausing to stare up at the house. "It's always been very secure here, but lately it seems more so. Is there a reason?"

I stare at the walls of acorns around the base of the oak tree with squirrels holding sticks pacing on what looked like ramparts. "I think you need to ask the squirrels."

He follows my gaze and frowns, "That is extremely odd."

I smirk, "You think?"

He moves cautiously toward the walk.

I follow, "Where are we going?"

Nonchalantly, he says "The zoo."

Hair has blown in my face and I brushed it away. "Washington Park?"

He starts down the street. "Yes."

We were heading towards the streetcar. I notice several of the trees drop leaves and seed pods on my head. I brush them off.

He raises an eyebrow at me, "If I didn't know better, I would swear those random things that fall in your hand and on your head are not random."

I shrug and give him a mysterious smile. I try to remind myself to finish filling out that form and send it in. "Perhaps."

He frowns and blinks, "So, you were off world for a week?"

"Jack shared that with the whole office, or just you?" Annoyance flashed through me as I try to keep my tone curious.

Circe Syndrome

He meets my eye and raises both eyebrows, "Just me."

Another acorn hits me on the head and I wince. I send a thought to the surrounding trees. "Knock it off!"

Thomas gives me an imploring look, "I think he wants me to ferret out what you have been doing and where you have been."

I laugh and toss my head. I kick at the leaves on the ground. They crunch under my feet, "Good luck with that."

He shakes his head, bewildered, "Thanks."

"Why are we going to the zoo?"

He cocks his head and gives me a sly look. "So, you are going to need to find out from me. Maybe you will tell me where you have been? So you know it is a question for a question. Spill."

I laugh, "So me going in unprepared sounds like a good idea to you?"

"How badly do you want to know?"

Not feeling any pressure I call his bluff, "I'll find out eventually."

We wait at the street car stop. Wind blows by showers of leaves and I hear the trees rustling whispers to each other. More leaves and seeds end up on my head.

Thomas frowns a me, "Seriously, what is going on with you and these trees?"

I shake out my hair and brush it out of my face again, "It involves that squirrel trouble you saw at my house, I suspect, though I am not sure. I have been away for a week, I guess."

"What do you mean you guess? How long was it for you?"

I absently look at my watch, "My watch said two days. To me it felt like two hours."

He looks at me, stunned, "How does that happen?"

I shrug and dodge another group of leaves looking to fall on me. "Time is relative to what I am doing." I cock my head at him, "When you feed, doesn't if feel longer than it is?"

Anger flashes through his eyes, "Yes, how do you know that?"

"Actually, I didn't know. I speculate and ask. You confirmed it." I point at him and grin.

He scowls, "Is it a family secret where you were?"

I look at him silently, wondering what he is speculating. "I came when called. That should be all that matters."

A woman and child who had been talking to each other at the streetcar stop as we walk up. We stop talking. When the streetcar pulls up, we board. Thomas meets my eyes, "Have you ever read those books by Lloyd Alexander, The ones with the prophetic pig?"

I look out the windows in thought, watching the buildings pass by, "Not completely."

Looking around at all the people, he presents this phrase as if it were a hypothetical question. "Wouldn't it be interesting if someone wrote that a particular pig, what was the name Hen Wen happen to appear in the wart hog pen at the zoo? What kind of author would do that?"

I stare at my fingertips. This means it was a possible awakening of power event. That means someone who has no idea about magic suddenly has access to it. This kind of thing could be tricky to trace out from the zoo pen. All different manner of people came through the zoo. Many types of people work at the zoo. I give him a whimsical smirk, "An author with a fondness for humor and animals?"

He nods with a responding smile, "That is an interesting speculation."

I am pretty sure he is speculating, like I am, that a person is going through an awakening and has a fondness for animals.

I adjust my grip on the bar overhead. "Is there a known author working on such a book?" This is me asking if the person is a known entity.

He shakes his head, "An author talking about doing such a thing, no." He prods me with his foot. "So the Hen Wen story was alluding to certain types of events playing out?"

I involuntarily nod. "The sundae family, the pig species, has some odd connections with author events. I was just thinking about the Circe event recently. You know the original Circe turned men to swine not dogs?"

He flicks his fingers, "True, doesn't the wild hunt usually involve wild boar also?"

I find myself searching memories I try to forget, "Yeah, sometimes." We make it to Burnside. We get off and walk to the Goose Hollow stop for the MAX. We wait on the platform after buying tickets, then board. The light rail train takes us into the tunnel and we when get to the Washington Park stop we disembark.

We travel in silence, Thomas says, as if the conversation hasn't stopped, "That is such an odd connection."

We are the only ones to get off at this stop. The platform is pretty deserted and feels rigidly cold. I stare at the core sample that shows the different layers drilled through to get to the stop. The train rushes out pulling air through the tunnels, sending goose bumps along my skin. We walk to the end toward the elevators. I push the button for the elevator. "I know right." I looked around. No one else is there. "So a possible awakening in the area?"

He nods.

"What is the protocol on this?"

He reaches out and pulls a leaf out of my hair, "Didn't you go through training?"

"On recruitment, nothing on this. "I put my hand out in a flat motion.

The elevator doors ding open and we enter. Thomas nod, "If you can help with identifying, I will help with the interaction."

I nod, "Roger that."

He laughs, "Really?"

I shrug, "Have you investigated something like this before?"

He turns to face the other set of doors in the elevator and pushes the button for the stop above ground stop. "Not really. I usually do more violent things." His glance lingers on my neck. "I think you will be an asset here, though. The way you handled the Circe and the fey event show you have great social skills."

I laugh, "I doubt it. I'll give it a try, though."

Chapter 49

Just Prophetic

The doors of the elevator open. We step out onto the sidewalk, facing the entrance to the zoo.

Thomas gives me a sarcastic look, "Maybe this will be so fun you'll just feel seconds pass."

I tighten my coat and snuggle my neck into its collar. The wind feels like it is blowing through me. "Do we need ash sticks with runes on them?"

"No, there's a few animal speaking Heska there." He rubs at his fingertips as if the grime from the leaf was hard to remove.

I raise an eyebrow, "So if there are already Heska handling it, why are we being called in?"

He shrugged, "I think we are muscle. Someone can get in a heap of trouble deciphering the future and using it."

"I would imagine they would be long gone. Since they might know when we become aware of their talent."

He shakes his head, "You're such a kill joy."

We wait at the curb as a pick-up truck passes by. The entrance has random clumpings of family and friend groups. We walk to the office door and came face to face with a receptionist. She has horn rimmed glasses and her hair tied up in a gray bun. She is on the phone explaining membership policy. We wait. The woman looks bored until she takes a focused look at Thomas. She sits up straighter and ends the call quickly. She is breathless as she says, "How may I help you?"

Thomas gives her a quick wink. "Is there a zoo manager we may speak with?"

Her voice is puzzled, "What is this regarding?"

He gives me an expectant look. I give him a blank stare. He sighs and pulls out a badge wallet and shows it to the woman. I am curious, I don't have a badge. "We are part of the investigation team for the wart hogs."

"Oh?" She looks down at her desk and shuffles papers. Then looks at him as she grabs some visitor badges and hands them to us. "What names should I put in the logs?"

We give our names as she types them into the computer and stands to escort us to an interior zoo door. She hands us a map and leaves us inside the zoo. Then she retreats back to the office. The wind blows and I pull my coat tighter. I yawn, still feeling the effects of space travel and trying to ignore how long, technically, I have been up now.

We walk the twists and turns of the paths. We arrive at the wart hog pen. Madame Kay is there, talking over the rail to a reddish, dark coated wart hog. There is a sow to the side of the pen, squealing. Next to Madame Kay is a middle aged woman with curly black hair writing on a clip board. Some young men with black trench coats are holding up whirling gadgets that make random dinging noises. I look around the perimeter of this tableau. The general population is moving as if none of this is happening in their midst.

Circe Syndrome

I step up to Madame Kay, "I didn't know you spoke Suidae?"

"Pig? Oh yes, I've done the spell multiple times. It sticks with you after a while."

I adjust my language comprehension and apologize to the wart hog for interrupting its conversation with Madame Kay. It snorts at me and return to the conversation. Now, with this in effect, I can hear the babbling happening with the sow in the corner.

I point to the sow in the corner and the curly haired woman,

"Who is that?"

Madame Kay flicks her eyes in that direction, "Katie Doolittle. She is a visiting vet at the zoo.

The warthog sighs, "Sumi, she has been talking non-stop for two days now. She hasn't eaten anything in that time either!"

With sympathy I say, "Has she been able to tell any of you who was here when the prophecies started spewing from her?"

The male warthog puts his head down in the dirt and grunts, "Nope, and the rest of us were napping at the time." He walks off and lays down in the den.

Madame Kay gives a sharp hum and turns to me, "They are sick of the same questions over and over."

I nod, "Anything, else weird happen that day?"

Madame Kay shakes her head subtlety, "Not that they are aware of."

I walk toward Sumi and Ms. Doolittle while throwing out a calming spell on Sumi. She stops talking and looks at me. She goes to the food pile and ate a bunch of food. Then, she went to the den and collapses.

Janette Bach

Katie and the rest of the staff stare at me. "Why did you do that?"

I meet Katie' s eyes, "She's been up for two days. She needs sleep."

Katie scratches her head, "Couldn't you have had her tell of what happened that day, before you did that?"

I shrug, "Sure, but I just collected copies of those memories." I spread my fingers out with the index and thumbs at right angles. I spread out my fingers in a rectangle shape in midair to play out the sow' s sight from that day. It depicts all kinds of people from different ages and walks of life, until the moment changes. Surreal images fill the scene. I rewind to before those images. The people are all unfocused blobs. Four tall adult blobs and their smaller children blobs.

Thomas, who had been watching silently asks, "Can you focus better than that?"

I struggle, trying to explain a species point of view. I say, "How detailed do you see a warthog?"

Madame Kay grabs my arm, "How about the sound? Can you turn it up?"

I look at her puzzled, "Sure," I am positive it will be undecipherable, just as is our perception of Suidae language.

Katie interjects, "When she wakes will she still be prophetic?"

I take a moment to wonder if she is concerned for the sow, or wants to exploit the spell. "Yes, I didn't want to erase any evidence."

Katie scratches her chin, "Will she be able to control it?"

I shake my head negatively and sadly, "No, someone is going to have to cast her with a calming spell to get her to eat and sleep."

"Can you change that?" Katie blinks at me.

I rub the back of my neck, uneasy, and look at Thomas. "Didn't you say there would be other Heska here?"

He gestures to Madame Kay and Katie.

They both speak at once.

"I'm a witch." Madame Kay touches her chest, indignant, and slightly humbly.

"I'm just an animal speaker." Katie kicks at the rocks on the ground.

I want to bolster them but don't want to come across as condescending, so I look away. "Where's Anthony?" I ask.

Madame Kay grimaces. "He was going to come but then got called to a mission off continent. I heard discussion of surf and coconut oil mentioned. If I could get such a mission!"

I nod, understanding where he is. "All the Heska they could find went for that one, huh?"

Madame Kay looks at me a second and scratches her chin and nods. Her eyes appraising me.

"I'm willing to give Sumi more control, if Jack thinks it is OK and is sure I won't be tampering with evidence. What do you think, Thomas?"

He becomes stern and strokes his chin, "What kind of evidence?"

"Some magic users leave fingerprint type spell markers. No two spell casters lay aether the same way." I analyze the young men with the devices.

Madame Kay follows my gaze, "Mostly tech Heska."

I find this odd because the Hawaiian incident was about technology. Why wouldn't they be there?

Madame Kay harrumphs, reading something in my gaze, "Extremely green, tech Heska."

I speculate that might be a good place to learn and get more experience, but realize this is a decision outside my pay grade.

Thomas cocks his head at me, "Check with Jack. He is monitoring you, isn't he?"

I sincerely doubt it since that other operation is happening. I look back over at these young men and realize they were usually the screen monkeys at headquarters when supervisors were elsewhere. Everything in The Collective was being stretched thin.

I just nod and say, "Yeah, OK." I send out a call in my mind to Jack. No response. I pull out my phone and send a text to him. Then I put the phone away and jump the fence into the warthog pen. This causes Katie to sputter. The wart hogs all give me a wide berth.

Katie yells, "That is not OK! Humans are not to be in an enclosure when the animals are in the enclosure!"

Thomas grins at her with his fangs showing, "Remember, she isn't exactly human."

Katie crosses her arms and shakes her head, "They could hurt her!"

Madame Kay snorts, "Would do her some good."

"The animal's confidence and trust is being tried!" Katie fumes.

I acknowledge and hold up an index finger at Katie, "Excuse me, I'm going to examine Sumi." I start to snort and squeal in Suidae.

There is a chorus of "Thanks!" from the warthogs.

I meet Katie's eyes, she glares at me.

Sumi is snoring and shuttering in her sleep. I look at the male hog that had been talking to Madame Kay. "May I touch her?"

Circe Syndrome

He sighs, "Give it a try. I can't soothe her."

I place a hand on the shoulder of Sumi. I send another spell of relaxation through her body. Her muscles relax and her jaw opens wider. The big gulps of air quiet the snoring and a calmer rhythm spills from her heartbeat. I send my mind into Sumi's brain and quietly look. Jack has not texted back. I wade through the strands of time and space twined with aether rushing through the sow's cerebral cortex. I find the brutal switch that has tuned her into the weave of cosmic instances. The time reader is the only way I can think of. It is mangled, so that it slips forward, not just backwards and now in time. I take three dimensional pictures down to a quark level, then rebuild the cells. I pause to look back at the male wart hog, who is watching me intently. "Do you know if she wants to keep the ability or remove it entirely?"

He snuffles and paws at the ground, "I don't know. Can you leave her with it but give her more control when it's happening?"

I take a breath and consider the brain, "I think so."

He snorts affirmatively, "Do that. We will have Katie contact you if she wants it completely destroyed."

I grunt back in a positive affirmation, and create an iris shaped opening to the aether that connects to a conscious portion of Sumi's brain. I stand when done, as I do this I can see the sow's body is more relaxed. I walk to the gate and vault back over. Thomas motions to a moist stick covered in dirt sticking to my backside. I wiped it off. Madame Kay and Katie both give me questioning looks. I explain what I did as the young men stared at their hand held devices and back at me several times.

"So, we have a new Heska wandering about, who knows nothing of the rules. Only a hint involves an impressionistic view from a different species." I report.

Thomas frowns, "Are you sending your images to the forensic team?"

I nod, "Yes, but I think they are as distracted as everyone else."

Madame Kay raises an eyebrow, "Do you know anything about that?"

I look away so she can't read my face. I am an awful liar. "No idea."

Madame Kay harrumphs.

Katie, staring at the warthogs distractedly, says, "I guess I'll go type up these notes."

I nod toward the wart hogs I suggest. "You should probably assign someone to keep an eye on them for a while."

Katie grimaces, then walks away looking at her cell phone.

The young men pack up their equipment and nod to Madame Kay.

She hums and gestures to Thomas and me, "We are heading to

Starbucks. You two want to come?"

Thomas shrugs, "Sure."

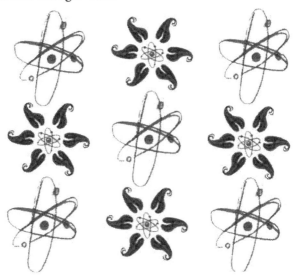

Chapter 50

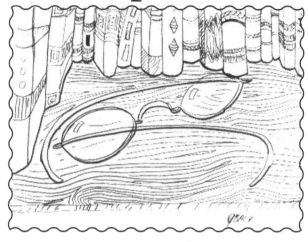

Spectacles

We walk up the main thoroughfare, then through the false cave past the sea lions swimming in circles, then up the path to the main gate. I catch scraps of the young mens' conversation that include red stone, creepers and slime. Madame Kay rolls her eyes and takes Thomas's arm. "How old are you, honey?"

He gives Madame Kay a sheepish grin. "Older then this country." He lets his voice take on an accent from another time.

I listen with interest as the two try to probe each other for information. They are each rewarded with vague replies from the other.

We all eventually file onto the MAX and ride to Pioneer Square.

I order a medium Earl Grey tea with milk and two sugars at the Starbucks stand. Madame Kay, the young men and

Thomas start heading to the headquarter entrance below at the Trimet office. I make to leave, "I'll see you later."

They all pause, Madame Kay frowns at me, "We all need to review our findings together."

I caught Thomas's eye and he nods. "Sure, but my health cannot handle headquarters right now. How about a library meeting room?"

Madame Kay exchanges glances with Thomas, "Let's go to my place." She guides us to a penthouse in a building off Burnside, by Powell's. When the door opens a rich, spicy, beefy smell fills my senses. My mouth starts to water.

Madame K hangs her coat on a hook and calls out, "Maribel, is that you? Hon?"

An amused female voice answered, "Yeah, Auntie K, it's me."

Madame Kay tastes the air and directs us all toward the hooks, then heads down the hall to the kitchen. "You need more onion and a bit more bourbon child. It's not Oxtail if you don't go, Oh! when you smell it!"

I hang my coat on a hook and follow the others to Madame's K's kitchen. It was huge, with an island in the middle where a gas stove churned a huge pot of heavenly smelling, boiling liquid. Madame Kay nods at me and gestures to a bar on the side where the others had sat. There was a young woman in a t-shirt and jeans giving her aunt a bemused smile. She raises an eyebrow at us all.

I wonder if the amusement is at the lack of introductions.

I looked at the young man sitting next to me and whispered, "I went, "Oh!", When I smelled the soup."

He gives me an understanding and agreeing grin.

Madame Kay rolls her eyes at me as she grabs a spoon and collects a bit of broth. She pulls it from the steaming pot and looks at the liquid. She gently waves it in the air. Her face is contemplative. "Hmmm, more of a yellow tinge. Did you use turmeric?"

Maribel winks at one of the young men and stirs the pot, "Maybe."

Madame Kay harrumphs and waves the spoon a little more. She runs the spoon under her nose and takes a deep breath. She closes her eyes. After thirty seconds, she places the spoon in her mouth and tastes the broth. A huge smile breaks across her face. "Fine, it's not mine. But this here is superb." She sets the spoon in the sink.

Maribel claps her hands and gives Madame Kay a hug. Madame Kay hugs her back.

I look toward the family room. It is all modern, clean lines. It is strewn with books and paintings from the Harlem Renaissance. There were some Palmer Hayden's, Archibald Motley's and Mavin Gray's works. I step down from the stool and go to examine the brushwork on Motley's piece. The geometric smooth figures give the work a sense of timelessness.

I hear Madame Kay talking on and on with her niece. The aura of the apartment takes on the serene feel of family life. It is similar to my mother's home, but different in its modernity. I smile at the paintings and return to my place at the counter. Madame Kay raises an eyebrow at me. She then looks at her niece's ring finger on her left hand.

Maribel starts scooping soup into bowls. Madame Kay is breaking a couple of loaves of French baguettes into portion sizes.

Madame Kay gestures to Maribel, "You got something on your finger."

An uncontrollable smile brakes across Maribel's caramel face and her cheeks redden. "Auntie you're such a snoop."

"Did that happen today?"

Maribel held her hand up and examines it some more. "Ah, yes."

Madame Kay starts placing bowls on plates with the bread next to them and fishing out spoons from a drawer. I stand to help and Madame Kay shooes me back to my seat. Maribel brings me one bowl while Madame Kay brings a couple to two of the young men.

Madame Kay looks over at Maribel, "Did you call your Ma?"

"First thing. She demanded to visit so I booked her a flight, she will be here in two days."

Madame Kay nodded, "Where is she staying?"

"I know she wants to stay with me and Ken, but well, Ma can be a bit much at first."

Madame Kay shakes her head, "Ah, so this soup is also a bribe. Does she know you two have been shacking up?"

Maribel takes a moment to pause and look dramatically around the room at each of us. "Really? You want to have this conversation now?"

Madame Kay chuckles softly to herself. "He's a doctor, your mother will forgive you. My colleagues wouldn't judge you. If they do, who cares! You're in love and making plans. Scream it to the high heavens!"

Maribel exhales, "So, is it OK if Ma stays here on her visit?"

Madame Kay looks thoughtful and looks at me. "Your family has all types of family visiting all the time, especially lately. How does your mother do it?"

I try not to be paranoid that The Collective is noticing the different people coming and going from our residence. As I give Madame Kay a questioning look and gesture toward Maribel. I don't know if her whole family knows about Madame Kays's abilities. I send out a thought to Madame Kay's mind, "Does she know what you are?"

Madame Kay's eyes widened, but she nods and speaks out loud."Oh, she knows child. She doubts, but she knows!"

I scratch the back of my neck in thought as I stand. I walk to the hallway. "So how many rooms do you have?"

Madame Kay follows me and sniffs, "Three bedrooms and one office. All occupied, except for my office, which I would like to keep my office."

I nod, "My mother uses a pocket dimension expansion spell on the house. It expands internally but the outside remains the same. It expands for need and contracts based on need. This helps so one isn't constantly cleaning hundreds of rooms."

Maribel frowns and squints her eyes at us, "What are you talking about?"

Madame Kay gives her a shushing noise and looks at me, "How could someone like me do that?"

"I could set you up a few spells that you could operate using a control panel." I look over at the young men. "Any of you work on a quark field manipulator spell?"

"So all these people indulge in the same delusions as you do, Auntie?" Mirabel points at each of us.

I find myself smirking. "You sure Madame Kay? There are rules about showing."

"Shh." She rose a finger and pointed at her niece, "You're about to learn something."

A young man with light umber skin, straight black hair and a t-shirt depicting a bear's slash marks stands. His demeanor is easy going. The movement of his arms makes me aware of the totem embossed bands on his wrists. "Sure, I've done a few of those panels."

I nod and look back at Madame Kay, "So, the heart of your home is..." I squint and look at the aether web of the condo.

"Ah, the hearth." I walk back to the kitchen. I look at the pot with soup and note the letter "f" carved into it.

Madame Kay follows my gaze, "I label all the pots, I don't want spell pots being used for food."

Maribel quips, "After her dumping some amazing food we have all learned to the use the right ones." She sounds, bemused like she didn't believe it.

Madame Kay gives her an annoyed look.

I examine the aether lines. I find a thread of aether leading to the rooms. I run my finger down the island. I looked at Madame Kay, who is watching my every movement as if trying to decipher it all. I run both hands down the strand of aether and pluck it. The sound is a rich but tinny noise. I take Madam Kay's hand and run the invisible to her strand over her fingertips. A look of wonder passes over her face.

I move ahead with my fingers following the strand. I looked back at her, "Don't let go." I walked toward the family room and Madame Kay follows. The strand twists around furniture and the book shelves. I find a spot by the hall.

I look back at Madame Kay. "Is there a song you hum?"

Madame Kay is still clasping the aether cord tightly. She looks puzzled. "Hum?"

I see an old pair of spectacles sitting on a book shelf. "Do you use those?" I point to them.

Madame Kay shakes her head right to left. "No, they're just a memory, my grandfather wore them."

I nod, "May I add a spell to them so you can see aether?"

One young man clears his throat, "Do you have a permit for magic object creation?"

"Nope." I think about the Oak tree. "I'll de-spell them before we leave." I give Madame Kay a wink. "Besides, this isn't creation this is bewitching."

Madame Kay gives me a big smile, "That would be great."

I wove the sight of aether and magical forces into the form and handed the glasses to Madame Kay. She dons them and her eyes widen. She looks all around the room. "Wow, it's like a fiber-optic display!"

I grin, "There is a lot of love and life here."

"Do you walk around like this all the time? How do you not trip?" Madame Kay's head is swiveling back and forth and looking in every direction.

"No, I would trip." I give her a wink, "I do all the time." I reach down and gently tap the junction of the glasses to the right of the ear arm and the front three times. "That should have dulled it down a bit. Sometimes, I do walk around like that. But usually, I only use that vision to find threats, do certain spells or trace aether."

Madame Kay smiles nervously, "How do I get it back to where it was?"

I gesture to the other side. "Tap on the same place on the other side."

Madame Kay does it.

I repeat my question, "Is there a song you hum normally when home and content?"

Madame Kay starts humming a song with staccato low notes and then staccato high notes.

The string is starting to vibrate and widen, "What is that?" I ask.

Madame Kay is staring at the filament, "Bamboula by Gottshcalk."

"Never heard that before. Quite cool."

Madame Kay continues the song and the thread vibrates more. Hee hand is starting to move wildly with the vibrations.

Maribel frowns and goes to her side, "Auntie are you having a fit?"

I gestured for Madame Kay to let the filament go.

Madame Kay does. The song is causing the vibration to create a portal size oval in the aether. I find some harmonic sounds and hum them till an infra sound is reached, creating a link to a pocket dimension. I move a painting on the hallway wall and use my finger to create a rectangle. The wall within that rectangle becomes a video screen control panel.

Maribel gasps as the wall transforms.

I tie the filaments into the contact points on the circuit boards. I make the screen transparent and gesture to the young man who stepped up to check my work.

He stares at it a minute following the filaments and contacts, then he shrugs, "I'm more familiar with the software side."

I nod and pull the screen back up. I spread out the filament and have it encompass the apartment and the portal at the hall. The portal sink into the walls and for a moment all the walls looked like molten light. The filament construct the current shape of the apartment on the screen. I assemble a menu on the side of the screen. One of the buttons is to add a room or subtract a room. I double check the safety protocols for living things at certain sizes to prevent room removal. It would automatically eject people and pets to the main room if it dissolved with a living creature in it.

The young man steps up and starts adding other useful features. He adds paint color changes, furniture design changes and even a cleaning spell. I check for safety codes to make sure humans and house pets are recognized and not hurt in any way by cleaning spells. Those could sting or worse, be fatal.

He double checks my work and when we were both done, I move away from the panel. "You're going to need to take the glasses off to work this.

Madame Kay reluctantly takes off the glasses and sets them on a shelf. She walka up to the panel and clicks through the interface. She adds a room. The hallway glows and expands. We walk to the door that appears and open it. Maribel, Madame Kay and Thomas walk into the room and look about it in wonder. I explain the safety features but I am sure none of them hear me as they walk about the room, their expressions varying degrees of awe.

The young man who helps with the programming laughs, "Watch this!" He starts changing the wall color and the floor.

I walk out and back to the soup, "Is it OK if I eat?"

The two young men who had been watching followme. The one at the control panel put the picture back in place. He looka at Madame Kay who could not stop smiling. "Do you have a printer? We need to fill out a sorcery form."

She gestures to the first shut door to the hall. He goes to the door and walks in. We can hear the printer going almost immediately and he calla out from the office, "You have a document box from The Collective, right?"

She laughs, "Yes, Jace."

Maribel is pale and stuttering, "Auntie, what just happened?"

Madame Kay sighs, "Child, I've explained The Collective to you several times."

Maribel swallows. She points at me, "Is she a witch like you? Can you do that?"

Madame Kay sighs, "If I could do that, do you think I would have asked that of Miss Muriel and Mr. Jace?"

Maribel frowns, "So they are not witches?"

Thomas took Maribel's hand and releases a bunch of calming hormones.

Jace and the other young men bristle. He isn't suppose to do that without consent.

Madame Kay pats Maribel's hand and gives Thomas a thankful smile.

Thomas says, "No, they are more different than that."

Maribel looks dazed but less agitated. "More different? Are you one of them?"

He looks at me with a glare, the anger of all he didn't know apparent to me. "Nothing like."

Maribel swallows, "Are you a warlock?"

Madame Kay snorts, "Let go of his hand, child. He is trouble, with a capital T."

Thomas flashes a smile with his fangs extended and Maribel backsaway. "So, you have never been deluded, Auntie."

Madame Kay smiles wide. "Nope, I'm a witch and so are you."

Suddenly, I understand why Maribel was being exposed to this

spectacle. Untrained magic can cause all kinds of problems for a

person. I take a sip of soup.

"This is amazing." I feel content after a swallow.

The other young men start on theirs and Thomas gives me a curious glance. "I thought I understood spell work. It seems there is much left from my education."

I nod and frown down at my soup. I am still uncertain about how I feel about him doing spell work, especially with no formal training.

Thomas sits next to me. He looks at the bowl in front of him and takes a spoonful. "Wow!"

Madame Kay nods at Thomas. "We have been lucky. Maribel's magic has been showing itself in her cooking. You will find the meal more nourishing than just food."

A couple of the young men are tearing up.

Maribel looks stricken, "I must be dreaming this." She shakes her head, "This cannot be real."

Madame Kay gives her a sad smile and leads her to the couch. She pulls an afghan around her. Madame Kay looks at me.

I nod and set a perimeter spell around Maribel. Maribel pulls the afghan close and stares out the picture windows to the gray, rainy skyline.

Madame Kay ladles herself some soup and sits across from Thomas and I. Between bites she starts asking questions. "So, the footage from the sow? Can you put it on more traditional media to watch?"

Jace places the form he mostly filled out next to me. I begin filling in sections that relate to me. "Um, sure. TV,computer, tablet, which do you want?"

Jace takes the form and places a device under my hand with a jump drive attached. "Which box in your office is The Collective document box?" He asks Madame Kay.

Madame Kay looks at Jace, "The one with the butterflies on it. It's in the bookshelf and looks like a book."

He nods and heads back to her office.

I look at the contraption he left in my care. I place my palm on it. A memory dialog box appears in my mind. I call out, "What format do you want for this?" This device is for downloading the video of the sow and I am addressing Madame Kay but loud enough for Jace to hear me.

Madame Kay looks at her niece staring out the window, "AVI or RM, I can use either."

Jace comes back out of the office and takes the machine back. He looks at Madame Kay, "Where do you want to review this?"

Madame Kay is staring at her niece, in thought.

I stand and take my dishes to the sink. I rinse them and start loading the dishwasher as the other men follow suit. Madame Kay stands and walks to sit next to Maribel. The men are all looking at their handheld devices.

Thomas catches my eye. His look says, "Do something."

I close the dishwasher and dry my hands. I walk over to Madame Kay and sit on the arm of the couch, "Do you want to watch the footage here? Now?"

Madame Kay gives me an imploring look, "Help me here." She squeezes Maribel's shoulders.

I take a breathe. I think this is a family matter. I am not sure why she thinks I can help in this situation. I have always lived in a world with magic. It has been a truth in my life always, not puncturing my life view like what is happening to Maribel now. "My name is Muriel. I'm a Heska."

Her caramel skin pales and she cringes, infinitesimal. "What does that mean?"

I chew on my lower lip, "What you would think of as wizardry."

"Heska? What kind of word is Heska?"

I smile, "A rose by any other name?" Maribel glares.

I become less light and more on task, "It means power. I am a person of power. I can manipulate the currents of power in the world."

Maribel frowns.

I get this is a lot and I am sure talking about something more famiilar would be helpful at the moment, "So, tell me about you. What do you do?"

Her voice is expressionless, "I'm a surgical intern."

I look at Madame Kay as she nods. I think of all the ramifications of this. I shake my head, "This is going to get really complicated for you."

Maribel frowns at me, "Besides messing with everything I know to be reals."

I chuckle at that, "It is critical you own your power and master it, or it will do things unchecked."

Maribel frowns, "Such as?"

I gaze over at the kitchen and the cookpot, "Right now, it may come out in your cooking, but eventually, it may do something during a surgery."

Her eyes widen, "What kind of things?"

That is unpredictable. I shrug and gesture to the glasses on the shelf. Madame Kay notices and stands to get them but they fly across the room to me. Maribel looks at Madame Kay, "Can you do that?"

Madame Kay shakes her head, "It would take me casting a spell and some time. I could take on the ability for a little while."

I clear my throat and hand her the enchanted glasses, "Try these on."

Maribel does and stands in alarm. She looks right and left and all around.

I study my fingers as I peripherally watch her with a bored tone coming from me, I do this to keep from pushing her charged emotional state to more excitement, "Do you see the swirling rainbow streams in the air?"

She gasps in wonder, "Yes."

I nod, "That is the aether. It is a bi-product of living things. It fuels most magic on this planet."

Maribel stammers, "Bi-product of life? Most magic?"

I grin, "Leave it to a scientist to focus on those two parts of what I said. That is a conversation for another time. Look at your fingers. See the spirals with the little lock valves there?"

"Yes." Maribel nods.

I gesture to Madame Kay, "Look at your aunt, she should look similar."

Maribel nods.

" OK, now look at Thomas." I gesture to him.

She exclaims, "That is weird."

I look at him with power sight. "Well, he is a walking corpse. That is why it looks like arteries and veins and heart. It is only in the blood he drinks."

Maribel raises an eyebrow, lites her lips nervously, "Corpse?"

Madame Kay scowls at me, "Honestly, child, quit scaring her. He's a vampire."

Maribel looks incredulous, "Yeah, like that explanation makes me more comfortable?"

Thomas laughs.

I nod, "Yes Ma'am, how about these gentlemen." I gesture to the three young men.

"They have power everywhere in their skin. Except him." She points at Jace. She stares at me, "He's like you. You're both blurry with it. Your forms are hard to make out."

I nod, "Yep, some of us are that way." Jace and I exchange uneasy nods. We both know some things about each other now. "You can take the glasses off now."

Maribel has more questions and doesn't want to take them off, "Why are you so blurry? Is it about moral ambiguity?"

I know it is because I don't hold power I just let it flow in and out. I'm not volunteering that information.

Jace steps up and has a placating smile, "No, it's not about morality. As a medical professional, you know there are just odd quirks that sometimes happen."

She frowns at him, "What do you know about being a medical professional?"

He sighs, "I'm a pharmacist."

Thomas laughs, "Aren't you also a..."

Jace frowns at him, "What?"

"A part of a tribe." Thomas exhales trying to not say what he wants to say.

"A medicine man? We prefer shaman." Jace shakes his head, trying not to smile. But it starts to crack, "It does go well with some pharmacology and psychology, too."

I nod at him, "So you understand all the rules The Collective lays down in those fields?"

He stares out the window, shaking his head, "The rules, oh yes, I know the rules." He looks haunted.

I suddenly really want a cup of tea.

Maribel looks between us.

"Too many people being healed magically opens up our community to scrutiny and mistrust. It also attracts otherworldly beings. So, the rules of moderation and balance are closely watched in healers." I explain softly and look at Jace empathetically.

Jace scowls, he changes the direction of the conversation, "It is really a discussion for another time. We are here to work on a particular problem. You need to accept that you are not completely human, and accept your aunt's tutelage. We need to watch some blurry video on this big screen TV. Stay or go to another room, it's up to you. Just don't talk about this with anyone outside this room unless given leave by your aunt."

He plugs the jump drive into the TV.

The room takes on a serious quiet.

The screen fills with crisp pictures of the different warthogs, their voices clear. They were discussing food, and Sumi looks at the Plexiglas window. Two small blob figures stand at the Plexiglas window. A structure that is most likely a stroller was behind them. Behind the stroller is a lean, tall figure thrusting a rectangular object at the littler figures. Next to that figure is another tall figure with an arm extended out toward the warthogs. To the left is another figure looking on. In that moment the scene changes. Surreal images appear. The screens is filled with floating mushrooms and tall grasses.

Maribel frowns, "What are we watching?"

Thomas cocks his head at the screen. "The prophetic gift, hitting a wart hog? Right?" He looks at me for reassurance.

I nod, "Yeah, the people are really hard to make out."

Jace walks up to the screen. He talks to it, "Rewind!"

Madame Kay lifts a remote and the mushrooms fly backwards.

He calls out, " OK, stop!"

It is back to the image before, he shakes his head, "Too far."

Madame Kay starts and stops it again.

The mushroom is in the shot. Jace tenses and walks to Madame Kay, he puts his hand out for the remote, "May I?"

Madame Kay rolls her eyes and hands it to him. "Please! By all means."

He holds his right hand over the remote with the palm down in a fist, and rubs his thumb and index finger together. Very slowly the image goes back frame by frame. He stops it when no grass or mushrooms appear in the picture. One of the small figures is leaning completely forward on the Plexiglas and the figure to the side is in the same position. The person behind the stroller's arm is down and the head blob looks like it was leaning toward the other adult blob.

Jace points to the solitary figure. "What do you think?" He looks at me.

"Do you think we can look at the aether in the figures?"

"I have no idea if that shows in film." I shrug.

One of the other young men looks at me, he has red hair and freckles. "But it's not film, is it? It's memories of a warthog."

I know I have met him before, "Wait, I have met you before right? You're Mr. Redshirt?"

He smiles. "Yes, Ms. Anahat. Call me Fred."

" OK, Fred, you can call me Muriel."

Thomas and Jace both sigh at me for engaging in social niceties at this moment.

I return to focus on the screen. The image on this screen has no frequency of aether lines. I look at Thomas and find him wearing the spectacles and just staring at me. I step forward and gently remove them from his face and he squeezes my hand tentatively. I give the glasses back to Madame Kay.

Fred snorts, "The memories in you, do they have it?"

I check, "Nope, they kind of clouded with the sow's own aether."

Jace rubs his forehead. "Is there a way to filter them down?"

I sigh, "Do you want them? I can transfer them to you. "I reach out my hand.

He looks apprehensive. But he walks closer. "Alright, just these few minutes, nothing more."

His face becomes red and he begins to sweat as he takes my hand. He closes his eyes. It took a count to ten, and I was done. I withdraw my hand. He stares at his hand puzzled. "I don't believe your brief included mind magic."

Janette Bach

I am confused, "Brief?"

"You know, employee files." He says with a shrug.

I look away a bit confused, "How did you guys think I prevented being attacked by the vampires in the bar?"

Thomas frowns at me.

I know what they all know about me, "Come on, this is not news."

"Yeah, we knew you could do the blocking pathways thing, but the subtle control required to give a memory without intruding or allowing unwanted thought is news!"

I cock my head, "What is my nickname again?"

Jace looks away, "You're just called Muriel."

I sigh, "When no one thinks I hear?"

Fred nods and blurts out, "Mind-worm Muriel!"

"Do I need to do a diagnostic to make sure nothing unwanted entered my memory?" Jace asks.

I frown, "Can I have this conversation removed from my memory?"

Thomas smirks, he is quite aware of my ethics and how insulting this conversation is to me.

I shrug, "Check. I added nothing superfluous. OK. But by all means give yourself piece of mind."

Jace's frown deepens and he looks at Fred, then the other man, in supplication. Their faces fill with a look of concentration, then everyone's faces go blank.

I cross my arms, "Can we focus on the footage now?"

Jace has obviously shared it with the others and they all are staring into space. Madame Kay pokes me. "What did you do?"

I nod, "Just what they asked. They are all analyzing the data independently."

Maribel looks at the screen. "That child pressed against the glass has a hand raised."

I walk closer and examined it. "Where did the mushrooms appear?" I look for the remote. It is sitting on the top of the screen. I stare at the child's hand blob position and start the video. The mushroom bloomed into view from the hand and the subsequent grasses radiated from there until the screen swims with disjointed images.

The six young men all came out of thought at the same time. Jace nods at me with an apologetic look and looks at the screen.

I look at them patiently, "Well? Anything?"

They all shake their heads no. Jace nods at me and the screen again. "Anything?"

I gesture to Maribel, "Perhaps. Maribel noticed one of the children blobs had their hand raised and, well, watch this."

The men's jaws dropped.

Thomas interjects, "Is it common for young children to.." He swallows. "manifest?"

This was dangerous information for a vampire to know. I give him a nervous look. In the past, child Heska were abducted and used as blood sources to fuel a hive. A vampire hive having that kind of power available with no commitments or safeguards is terrifying. "It's rare, but not unprecedented."

"I guess this fits your whole sense of humor and love of animals theory." Thomas examined his fingertips as he casually says this, bringing me back to our earlier conversation.

I nod, "It does. Doesn't it?"

Thomas declares, "Preschools need to be inspected."

Madame Kay disgrees, "But not all people put their children in preschool."

I expand, "True, probably all preschools, pediatric offices, a zoo net, the children's museum, all playgrounds you can find. Put some sentry spells in affect. Will you have to get a permit for that?"

The young men nod.

Thomas scratches his chin, "Any help from headquarters, yet?"

I chuckle and absently shake my head no. I knew the system is currently strapped, because the young men with us normally man the feeds. I nod toward the men, "You guys heading back in?"

Fred and Jace both nod.

I look at Madame Kay, who is talking quietly to her niece. "We will get out of your hair." I lift the magic circle off Maribel and headed for the door, "Thank you for the soup."

Jace calls out, "We will let you know when the child has been located."

I nod, "Hopefully, someone more experienced in these matters will be available."

Jace rolls his eyes. He looks away.

Chapter 51

Tikkum Olum

When we make it to the street Thomas offers his arm. "How about you get rid of that hardware and I take you to dinner."

Deadpan, I say, "We just had soup."

He shakes his head and grins, "I imagine that wasn't enough for you if you were just off world hours ago."

I nod. I'm trying not to focus on how long it had been since I ate.

"You haven't slept since the fairy incident?"

I thought a moment. "Nope."

"Why are you blurry when seen at with aether sight?" He is looking at the cars as he asks.

I push the button for the street light and watch some leaves trail a mini cyclone from the wind. I observe a woman in a macramé vest chat with a person at the door of the shop. I wasn't going to answer this question. "Where were you thinking of going for dinner?"

He stares at me, "Why don't you answer?"

I throw up my hands. "Why do you ask questions I shouldn't answer?"

He put his hands in his pockets and kicks at the leaves on the curb, "Those young men got really uncomfortable, really fast, around you."

I smirk, "You don't make them all feel warm and fuzzy either."

The wind blows cold and runs up my spine. Something feels off.

He grimaces, "So that fairy incident? How did you end up in the middle of that?"

He was fishing, I shrug, "Gideon is a friend of my mother's, and technically family. She and he asked for my help, so I helped."

"That seems to be a problem with you."

I roll my eyes, "How, how is helping a problem?"

He shakes his head, "Why don't you say no?"

I start massaging the joints in my hands. We were discussing some of my tightly held beliefs and I feel vulnerable. "What do you know of Judaism?"

A shocked expression passes across his face. "Huh? You never brought up your religion before. Hey, wait, I've seen you eat pork!"

I chuckle, "Have you now?"

We are heading to the streetcars.

I begin to explain, "There is this concept called Tikkun Olam. It means fix the world. One of our jobs as a people is to find what is wrong in the world and fix it. That is why we can't leave good enough alone. We have problems accepting the status quo. If there is injustice, we can't just accept mediocrity, we have to be part of the solution or nothing is going to change. If I can help, I'm going to try."

He licks his lips, "Even if it means walking into a lion's den?"

I raise an eyebrow, "Or a blood den?"

His cheeks color. We got off at a stop two blocks from my house and walked there. I stood at the gate for a moment and watch the activity about the oak tree.

Thomas shakes his head, "What is going on with the squirrels?"

I grimace, "A problem I really need to address. I just haven't had a moment."

He taps at the gate slat tops. "Is it like the shoemaker's children? They never have shoes and your household problems are never fixed?"

I giggle at the analogy, "Not entirely, this is new and not as important as other things happening. But a huge mistake on my part."

I open the gate and he follows me in. We walk to the front door. I stand in the foyer and the surveillance equipment is removed. I are taking a breath. I am about to contact my parents on my plans but get distracted. Thomas leans in and pulls me into a long sensuous kiss. I freeze a second then and melt into the embrace. I don't care that he is releasing all kinds of seductive hormones. I am filled with a sense of contentment and wellbeing. Between the being up for two weeks and only just eating that soup, the fatigue hits me, I slump onto his shoulder. He leads me out the door, through the yard and up the block to a park and ushers me into a limo.

Circe Syndrome

He begins kissing me more. I pass out.

Chapter 52

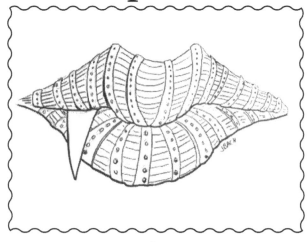

Steel Kiss

I wake with the tang of metal in my mouth. My skin burns and I feel as if my eyes are blood shot. I shudder, then vomit. I am on an extremely flat, hard, unforgiving surface. Before I open my eyes, my fingers trace the surface and I find some grooves carved into it. I open my eyes to the dull fluorescent light and stare at what I am laying on. I wince as I look about. Steel everywhere. All the walls, the beams in the ceiling and the surface I'm lying on. There are open gashes where ever my skin has contact with the metal. My blood is being collected in the groove and I realize I'm actually on an incline. Because it is moving away from me. There is a bowl collecting it. I note all I have on is cotton shift that had once been white stained in blood.

I reach for the aether. I tear. There is none. Fear flows through me and I vomit. I hear another voice, harsh and frustrated. "Get in there and clean that up Jim, or it will contaminate the blood!"

I have been on my side and I wince since every part of

me burns from the steel. I turn to look up at the ceiling. It is a mesh of steel wires. I blur my vision and watch a young man in a punk t-shirt and ripped jeans look at me in disgust as he stands over me. His hair is black and dyed with pinks and bright yellows. Tattoo's swarm his arms and his mouth is moving. The pain I am feeling is distracting me from his words. He motions for me to move. I tried but nothing happens; it seems that last movement took all I had. In disgust, he picks me up and moves me over. He reaches down to the end of the pallet and stopped the blood flow. He takes a bucket and scrub brush and begins cleaning up the vomit. He yells out, "She's conscious!"

Thomas appears and frowns down at me. "We have tried your blood in two different subjects and they have burned up! I have had blood directly from you before, why did that not happen to me?"

I play with my jaw trying to remember how to speak. How long had I been in this room unconscious and bleeding? My voice is a rasp when I do speak, "Why don't you give it a try now and show me?"

He begins to swear, "You know, don't you? You are not going to tell me, you stubborn bitch!"

I take a ragged breath and shift as my scalp burns and more blood leaks from my body. I wait for him to kick me in anger. When he doesn't I say. "I will die eventually."

There is venom in his voice, "I won't let you. You have been trapped here a month now and no one has found you!"

I always dampened the aether in my blood so the cells didn't catalyze it into more when a vampire drank from me or had it in a syringe. They has been no living spirit to keep the aether from exploding. I evaluated my position. This knowledge is why he is letting me be conscious. My burning skin is distracting, but my anger at myself for letting my guard down with this creature is palpable in me. I close my eyes to think through tactics.

Impatiently he calls out, "Samantha, get her some cardboard!"

The vampires saunters into the room with a garment box. With a long finger nail, she slices down the side creating a huge rectangle. Thomas leans down and picks me up.

I sigh, "Oh goodie, you going to kiss me again? Will I wake up at home this time?"

He glares at me, "I tried to do this the easy way. You wouldn't trust me!"

I feel the breeze as Samantha lays down the cardboard. He sets me back down on top of it. I hate myself, as an involuntary sigh of relief escapes my mouth. I think, "Yeah, I have no idea why I didn't trust you!"

He speaks gently, "How about an answer for why the subjects blow up in exchange for this comfort?"

I close my eyes, fighting a retort about comfort and cardboard boxes. In the end, this is heavenly at the moment. I think of the Art of War and the first rule is to let the enemy think they have won. It was time to lie, and I have to do it right. I look him in the eyes squarely and will myself not to blink, "Those syringes were spelled to dampen the power of the aether."

He put a hand to his chin, "By you?"

I look at him, "Can I have some water?"

He gives me a steely stare, "Is there aether in water?"

I breathe deep, give him something so he thinks I will cooperate, "Yeah, a bit."

"Enough to disable me?"

I shake my head, "I doubt it."

"Samantha hook up the IV." He calls over his shoulder. He cups my chin, "So Muriel, did you spell the syringes?"

Circe Syndrome

I give him a puzzled look; my mind is a bit frazzled still. I watch the IV pull roll into view. I note the aether in his veins. I pull in a little, he wouldn't notice.   As a slow plan fills my clouded brain, my body automatically starts a healing process burning through that bit of aether. I pass out, again

The End
For Now

Glossary

A

ASC: *American Science Collective or The Collective. The governing body of the United Citizens as it pertains to magic and supernatural*

Anahat: *Heart Chakra related to the Gevurah-Hesed on the tree of life. This involves the ability to escape preordained fate and determine one's own destiny in reality.*

B

Brah: *Pidgin English word endearment for brother used like dude in California*

C

Candyopolis: *Planet made entirely of candy Muriel made as a child.*

Chi: *Life force*

Circe: *Witch from Greek mythology (Odyssey) that turned men into pigs.*

Collective (The Collective): *Governing body of the United States citizens as it pertains to Magic and supernatural.*

Cyclops: *Strong humanoid creatures from Greek mythology with one eye. Some assist the god Hephaestus*

D

Dark Raven: *Observer of Odin and other gods.*

Dialyosefos: *Dissolve into light and travel the Aether.*

E

Eco Spa: *Planet Muriel created to visit like a spa*

F

Four Bam: *In Mahjong there are suits of tiles. One of the suits is bamboo when a person lays out the tile, they yell the number and suit. So, this is a 4-bamboo tile being laid in the playing area.*

G

Gazis: *Sapient Gazelle type creature that stands on two feet from Eco Spa*

Golem: *Anthropomorphic being created by non-organic matter. Usually clay or stone.*

Gremlin: *Royal Air Force creature that would eat up the engines of planes*

H

Heska: *A person who can manipulate the world with magic as an intuitive force.*

I

Ice Giant: *Chaotic beings who birthed the gods of Asgard*

K

Kowl: *Amphibian sapient species that destroyed their own eco system and made themselves extinct on Eco Spa.*

Kracious: *Cephalopod that looks like kelp. Huge with stinging poisonous barbs. Lives on Eco Spa and worshipped by the Sumans.*

L

Levi-toss: *Lacrosse using hovering skateboards*

Lockjaw: *Huge furry winged creature with massive muscular head and jagged teeth from Eco Spa*

M

Mahjong: *Tile-based game developed in China*

Malinini: *Pidgin English word means visitor, stranger, newcomer and/or foreigner*

Manna: *Pidgin English word means strength and power usually from divine origin*

Menehune: *Indigenous crafty small people who lived in Hawaii before it was settled by the Hawaiian people*

Moke: *Pidgin English word big and tough*

Mur Singers: *Swallow type song bird from Eco Spa with spiritual properties.*

N

Nymph: *Tree spirit usually looks like a pretty maiden*

O

Obyx: *Organization creating habitats that make magic possible across the universe*

Opake: *Pidgin English word for ghost*

S

Satyr: *Half man half goat from Greek mythology*

Selkie: *Seals that become humans on land*

Sneffel: *Trans dimensional being that likes to snack on powerful Heska convinced they are doing good for the universe*

Suman: *Aquatic sapient creature that lives underwater and is compatible with humans, They can breathe air and water.*

T

Talk Story: *Pidgin English word gossip, catch up, talking with friends and reminiscing*

Thrall: *A being chemically and emotionally dependent on a vampire*

Tesla-tronics: *Electronics company ran by Andrew Tesla main competitor to Muriel's father's business*

Tutu: *Pidgin English word grandmother, wise women, and or old woman*

U

Unawakened: *People unaware of the magical world or have not found the magic within themselves*

W

Wikiwiki: *Pidgin English word quick, fast, hurry and hasty*

Characters

A

Aiofe: *Morgan's domineering mother.*

Aaaar Nah Snort: *Selkie who swam with seals.*

Akamai: *Menehune of Oahu that shows Muriel around Hawaii.*

Andy Tesla: *Owner of competitive business to Muriel's father and brother.*

Anthony Phoenix: *Heska operative for The Collective. Little brother of Simon Phoenix who was engaged to Sarina and called it off.*

Arial: *Head medic in the fairy squad related to Morgan.*

Attilla: *Prince of the ruling family of trolls in Portland and childhood friend of Muriel's.*

C

Claudius: *Viper's Creator.*

Clay: *Golem of Mordecai and Shirley made of Red clay.*

Cleo: *Heska Socialite.*

Creok: *Heska animal Mystic of The Collective.*

D

Daedalus Anahat: *Muriel's Dad, took his wife's family name since he was an orphan.*

F

Fargus: *One of the three male Sumans Sarina had intimate moments with on Eco Spa and helps with the problem solving for the Suman community.*

Fin: *Friend of Muriel, Elf and her Masseur.*

G

Gideon McQweston: *Glinda's twin brother and a cousin of Morgan and Jasper.*

Gino: *Satyr that lives in Long Beach California.*

Glenprenode: *Tree Shaman with power issues on Eco Spa.*

Glinda McQweston: *Gideon's twin sister and a cousin of Morgan and Jasper.*

Gnasher: *Lawn gnome of the Anahat property.*

Gregor: *Suman, a being Muriel had a long romantic relationship with.*

Gris: *Grumpy leader of the Gazis on Eco Spa.*

H

Aunt Hannah Anahat: *Maxima's younger sister.*

Hestia: *Multi colored talking calico cat, sister of the order of Muriel on the planet Eco Spa.*

I

Isabella: *Latin Beauty, half Heska and half Siren in a long-term relationship with Jasper*

Irving: *Fledgling Heska*

J

Jack Oppenheimer: *Head director of the ASC office in Portland*

Jasper: *Distant Heska cousin of Morgan's.*

K

Madame K Laveau: *Witch from New Orleans and operative of The Collective*

M

Mazima Anahat: *Muriel's mother*

Merlin: *Morgan and Yacob's son*

Uncle Mordechai Anahat: *Muriel's mother's older brother.*

Morgan Anahat: *Yacob's wife*

Mothius: *Vampire Leader of Portland. Red curly hair suave*

Muriel Anahat: *The narrator.*

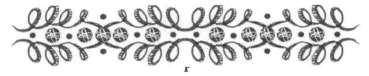

Ping: *Young man who helps save Anthony in space*

S

Sarina Anahat: *AKA: Sarah Anahat, Muriel's older sister.*
Samantha: *Mothius's vampire second in command.*
Aunt Shirley Anahat: *Uncle Mordechai's wife.*
Shamus: *Dwarf operative trainer for The Collective.*
Steven: *Fin's boyfriend.*
Mr. Stodge: *McQweston Barrister.*

T

Thomas: *Vampire and Collective Operative trying to get Muriel as a partner for The Collective and a partner in other ways.*
Trina: *Fairy Godmother that gives the birth blessing for Merlin.* **V**
Vic Opiate: *Professor and Elf*
Viper: *AKA: Frederick Thomas Grout, Vampire to be recruited into The Collective. Muscular, tattooed and has a Mohawk.*

Y

Yacob Anahat: *Muriel's older brother and the oldest of the siblings*

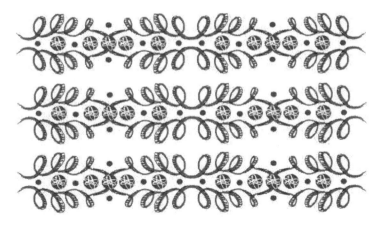

Janette Bach

Keep An Eye
Out For The Sequel:

Enthralled

Follow Janette Bach online:
www.springmore.net

52275258R00285

Made in the USA
Columbia, SC
01 March 2019